MA... ...ONS—

"With a tranquil heart, and trusting in the Living and Only God, omnipotent and all-powerful, all-seeing and all-knowing, I conjure you, Badad, daemon of darkness, and you, Lirion, daemon of darkness, to appear before me in the human forms by which I shall know you."

Shadows thickened around Evan's protected circle, and grew into a scream torn from hell. Wind howled its accompaniment of rage, and somewhere nearby glass exploded.

Pain. Unending waves of pain danced on his nerve endings. Evan knew that only the circle protected him from the full force of that agony, but he found himself drawn to the screaming faces twisting in the shadows. His determination wavered for a moment.

"I never wanted this," he whispered, but the knowledge that his enemies would have no such qualms hardened his resolve.

"Appear before me in the human shapes by which I have come to know you. Now!"

Camille Bacon-Smith

EYE OF THE DAEMON

DAW BOOKS, INC.
DONALD A. WOLLHEIM, FOUNDER
375 Hudson Street. New York, NY 10014

ELIZABETH R. WOLLHEIM
SHEILA E. GILBERT
PUBLISHERS

First Printing, January 1996

1   2   3   4   5   6   7   8   9

DAW TRADEMARK REGISTERED
U.S. PAT OFF. AND FOREIGN COUNTRIES
—MARCA REGISTRADA
HECHO EN U.S.A.

PRINTED IN THE U.S.A.

Chapter One

The universe comprises seven spheres, of which the outermost is the abode of the Archangels. There follow the seraphim, cherubim and thrones, the minor angels in which group are included those Guardian Angels, and the Princes, who reside in the second sphere, closest to man who holds dominion over the first sphere of creation, that of all matter in the universe. As there are seven spheres, so of Princes there be seven in number and their names are Azmod and Ariton, Paimon and Oriens, Astarot and Magot, and Amaimon.

Badad, lord of Ariton, slipped into his human persona as he put on the charcoal pinstripe suit coat. As Kevin Bradley he entered the office suite fronting a corner of Spruce Street. The sounds of the Porsches and BMWs seemed out of place passing in front of the brick sidewalks, hitching post, and boot scrapes of an earlier time, but the Society Hill offices of Bradley, Ryan, and Davis fulfilled the promise of Federal period Philadelphia just hinted at by the marble threshold. Darkly rich wainscoting met soft blue walls. French Aubusson carpets that mirrored the sculptured ceiling hushed Kevin Bradley's footsteps when he crossed the office furnished in the cool geometry of Hepplewhite, enough of it period authentic to soothe and impress the clients of Bradley, Ryan, and Davis, Private Investigators. George Washington would have felt right at home.

The woman in the reception area started nervously when he entered the room. She was about thirty-seven, angular and sharp-featured, with hair a nondescript brown that fell straight from a center part to her shoulders: the type that, under better circumstances, some would call handsome. Now tension pinched her features into a hard mask. She wore a pink suit that seemed out of place on her, as if the limits of her straight skirt caught her by surprise at each step. Badad led her into the tastefully austere office reserved for meeting clients and seated her in a spindle-backed chair at a comfortable angle to the windows. He noticed in passing the rich green of the side garden beyond the lace-paneled curtains. The azaleas would bloom soon; already the hyacinths and crocus had unfolded, the lilies of the valley that Lirion often wore in her hair just peeking out from the shadows. Lately the garden walls had begun to close in; the memory of why he stayed sometimes faded next to his restlessness to be away beyond the night and free.

A challenge might distract him, and Badad silently hoped the edgy woman in the new pink suit had more to offer than a wandering husband. He took his place at the cherrywood desk, slipped a pen from the inner breast pocket of his jacket, and opened the leather secretary in front of him.

"I'm Kevin Bradley. How can I help you?"

Badad—Kevin Bradley—smiled encouragement while the silence stretched between them. Finally, the woman reached into her handbag and pulled out a scrap of yellow paper. She twisted it nervously between her fingertips, but did not extend it immediately for Badad to see.

"My brother has been kidnapped."

"Have you called the police?" Kevin Bradley folded his hands and watched the woman across the antique desk.

The woman stared intently at the paper she threaded between thumb and forefinger. "They didn't believe me. Said it was a prank, but I know it isn't. The people who took Paul mean what they say. They'll torture him, or worse, if I don't find him in time."

"I think you'd better tell me all about it." He spoke softly, putting the woman at ease, but half ready to dismiss her as a crank. Badad stayed as far from the legal system as possible, but even he knew that the police took kidnapping seriously. With threats involved they could hardly dismiss it as a simple disappearance. She seemed to consider for a moment, then:

"Do you mean what you said in your ad?" She spread on the desk the yellow paper, a page torn from the phone book.

"Of course we do." He smiled, showing just enough of his straight white teeth to instill confidence, while he let a bit of puzzlement show in his eyes. "Which part do you mean in particular?" He understood perfectly now, but the case always went more smoothly when the client said it out loud at the beginning.

"This part." She pointed to a line in the ad. "Cases involving the occult handled with discretion."

The smile warmed his eyes now. The woman might indeed have the key to his growing discontent, but first she had to trust him.

"Complete discretion," he assured her in the tone he

would use with the bank at audit time, "but I'll need all the particulars if I'm to help you. And you should know, our rates are steep. Fifteen hundred dollars per day plus expenses, the first week payable in advance as a retainer, and the same due each week for as long as we are engaged on the case. We assign as many investigators as it takes, for as long as it takes, to resolve the situation. You may of course cancel our arrangement at any time, but there are no refunds. We guarantee results only on open-ended contracts, which means that you waive the right to terminate the contract for any reason."

The woman in the pink suit glared at him. "We are talking about my brother. I want to find him whatever the cost. But even you may find it difficult to make good on your claim."

"We are not charlatans, Miss—"

"My name is Simpson. Mrs. Marnie Simpson."

"Yes, Mrs. Simpson. Should our investigators determine that there is insufficient evidence for us to continue our investigation, we would of course unilaterally terminate the contract. While I cannot guarantee that you will like what we find, you may be reassured that all of our contracts have been fulfilled to the letter. We have never had to terminate a case from our end."

Marnie Simpson frowned down at the tattered advertisement. "I'll be honest with you, Mr. Bradley. I did not choose your agency. I found your ad lying on top of the ransom note in my dining room. For some reason the kidnapper wants you, a fact that gives me no confidence in you whatsoever. But I figure it this way: if you are working with the people who took my brother, you are my best chance of getting him back. If you are not working with these people, they seem willing to use you as a go-between, and you are still my best shot. Since the police have left me few choices, I agree to your terms. That does not mean I trust you, or put any faith in your claims."

Disgruntled, Badad silently gave his sympathies to the erstwhile Mr. Simpson. He considered sending her on her way, but hesitated. Someone dealing in kidnapping and the occult wanted Bradley, Ryan, and Davis on the case. How could he turn down the challenge, even delivered through an unwilling third party?

"I see." He cleared his throat, not quite sure what to say in the face of such enthusiasm. "I'm sure we'll change your mind about our services, Mrs. Simpson. In the meantime I'll need some background information on yourself and your family, your brother in particular. And I'll have to see the ransom note, of course."

Mrs. Simpson nodded her head. "My husband is Franklin Simpson, of Simpson Enterprises. I own and operate Carter Stables under my maiden name. My brother, Paul Carter, is nineteen—here's his picture."

She handed Brad a snapshot of a young man with blond hair falling nearly to his shoulders and eyes black as the pits of hell. Paul Carter wore some loose-fitting robe, white with arcane symbols embroidered at the neck and cuffs and with an upside-down pentagram stitched over the heart. A dark stone lay at the center of the pentagram.

"Actually, Paul is my half brother. After my father died, our mother had a brief affair with a sexual adventurer who disappeared before she even knew she was pregnant. That didn't seem to matter to Mother, though. She adored Paul, we all did, in spite of the struggle he made of his life.

"You have to understand," she urged him, "Paul was

searching for something. I never understood what it was, but for a while he thought he had found it with a group he met at a club in New York, a place called the Black Masque."

Brad sat up at that one. "I've dealt with the owner on an occasion or two." On a particularly memorable occasion he'd gambled with one of his own kind for the life of the half-human son he hadn't known he had. Evan, his son, had been searching, too, but he'd found only insanity at the Black Masque. Not a nice place at all. "What exactly is your brother into, Mrs. Simpson?"

"Everything. Paul had dreams; strange, frightening dreams. When we were children, he would wake up screaming from them. Therapy didn't help, drugs didn't help. Eventually he took to following every guru and fad that came along. I think he'd given up on stopping the dreams, he just wanted to understand why he had them. The Black Masque was his most recent answer, and for a while he seemed better. Then he seemed more frightened than ever. He told me he had to get away, to think, but they would never let him escape. Today I came in from the stables and found the house in shambles, Paul missing, and the message burned into the dining room table. I wrote it down for you."

Marnie Simpson pulled a slip of notepaper from her handbag and passed it to Brad. On it she had copied: "Return the Eye of Omage and death will be swift. Withhold the Eye and he will spend eternity longing for death that does not come."

"They are mad, Mr. Bradley. I don't know what this Eye of Omage is. I would give it to them if I had it, but I don't. And yet they may be torturing my brother right now because they think I am keeping it from them. I don't know what to do."

Brad stared at the message she had written, seeing not paper but his nemesis rising from flames into darkness. Omage. Not the first time the two of them would fight, nor did the focused enmity between Badad, lord of the host of Ariton, and Omage, lord of the host of Azmod, begin with the back room of a scruffy bar in the East Village. They both remembered the first time, when the lord of Azmod had battled as a god. Not his call, but saying no to the Prince of Ariton would be like this human hand saying no to his brain. A world of worshipers had died when Badad took the battle into the heart of that people's sun. Destabilized, the star sent planets scattering like the pieces from an overturned chessboard. Omage had not forgotten, would never forget Badad's interference in that little game. An old enemy. Brad wondered how Mrs. Simpson's young brother had become a pawn in a feud older than civilization on this backwater planet.

"You haven't gone to the police about this, have you, Mrs. Simpson?"

She looked at him and he held her gaze, just a flicker of what he was glinting in his eyes. She did flinch then.

"No, I couldn't. There would have been publicity, newspapers. They'd make Paul out to be some maniac looking for kicks and, ultimately, the police would shrug it off and forget it, another spoiled rich kid who got what he deserved."

"I see. And you don't believe it is some prank, or even a bizarre threat to keep your brother in line? It's been known to happen."

"Tell me that after you've seen my dining room table."

Brad nodded. "Agreed." He took the card she offered.

"I'll meet you at this address, at three tomorrow afternoon. I may have associates who will be working on the case with me. Until then, Mrs. Simpson, good day." He escorted her to the door.

Chapter Two

Of the second sphere, each Prince is not a being, but a mass comprised of a host of lords of daemonkind, of which each host must convoke in quorum, being 833 daemon lords, to call upon the powers of a Prince of daemons.

An almost imperceptible chill that stirred the air in the windowless study drew Evan's attention from the computer on the cluttered desk. He carefully scanned the room for the source of the disturbance. Two tapestried wingback chairs shared a standing lamp and a low table on his left, and an overstuffed leather couch faced him over a beaten brass coffee table from across the room.

All of the furniture, including the camel saddle dropped negligently in the corner behind the sofa and the dictionary stand next to the inner doorway, stood away from the walls to allow access to the bookshelves that lined the room. Evan noticed that the breeze from nowhere riffled loose papers stuffed atop a shelf of books on his right, but both the door at his left, leading to the agency's public offices and that set in the corner opposite him, leading farther into the living quarters, remained firmly shut.

A year as the junior member of the detective agency of

Bradley, Ryan, and Davis had taught him that doors meant little to his unorthodox partners, but the room still seemed empty except for himself. Evan waited, watching carefully, and caught the wavering in the air that signaled an incoming daemon. Lirion was in for a rough landing—right on top of a pile of books.

He grimaced as he dived for the corner, but wicked humor glinted in his eyes. The books skittered out of the path of the incoming daemon. Evan didn't.

"Shit, Evan. Are you trying to kill me, or just break my leg? Oh, that's what you're doing!"

The daemon had taken her usual human form—hair as dark as his nightmares and skin as pale as the hour before dawn, tall enough to stare Evan straight in the eye when they were standing up, and elegantly slim. Her eyes flamed a clear, piercing blue. Evan tried to forget that in her true form Lirion *became* the fire that, for now, burned only in her eyes.

At the moment, that fire lay hidden behind closed lids while the long fingers of one hand raked through his own chestnut hair. A single, manicured fingertip traced electric currents above his heart and lower, parting shirt buttons from their buttonholes in one languid motion. He felt the laughter in her kiss and expected the mocking challenge when they broke that first lingering contact.

She lifted one eyebrow, giving him a judicious appraisal while her fingertips skimmed over his hips, tantalizing through the supple fabric of his slacks.

"Want to make the Earth move?" Her fingers wandered across his thigh, but Evan mistrusted the look in her eyes.

"Are we talking about sex, or a small earthquake?"

She nipped an earlobe, hard. "With you? Think beachfront on the Arizona coast."

To Evan's consternation a familiar voice came between them. "If you two can spare a minute, we've got work to do."

Brad. Kevin Bradley to the world, Badad in the confines of this study. Evan struggled to a sitting position wedged between corner bookcases and weighted down with a still-intent Lirion on his lap. His rueful attempts to disentangle himself met with benign amusement. Here, in the private universe they created for themselves, the daemon partners played free of the constraints of human custom, often to the acute embarrassment of the mortal in their midst.

"Your timing lacks subtlety, cousin." Lirion glared at Badad, her features blurring as blue flame crackled in her hair. "I was about to broaden Evan's education."

Sparks snapped between them when she leaned to kiss Evan fleetingly on the tip of his nose. He rubbed his abused proboscis with the palm of one hand, glad the electric shock masked the dent in his dignity.

"Later, Lily." Evan returned the kiss absently, noticing the dark things that passed across his father's face when Badad thought he wasn't looking. They always underestimated him—it was the only advantage he had in the strange menage they were forging.

"How bad is it?" The last directed at the self-contained man who rested a hand casually on the back of the leather sofa. He could have been a banker or a stockbroker in that suit, Evan thought, except for the rare moments like now, when an unearthly wildness stormed across Brad's—Badad's—features.

"It can wait until we've dealt with St. George." Badad navigated the crowded study to his usual chair, a tapestried wingback. "How was Venice?"

If Lirion sensed the brooding storm around the other daemon, she gave no sign of it. She gathered her feet under her, reassembling most of her usual elegance.

"Damp, as always, but unlike some I could mention, Count Alfredo DaCosta knows how to treat a lady."

With a look that promised more retribution than he could handle, Lily quelled the retort rising behind Evan's sudden grin, but Badad took up the challenge. "Showed you his etchings, did he?"

She twitched an eyebrow. "Every last Master and Modern." A wholly spurious sigh, then: "Poor Alfredo. I'm afraid the dear Count's palazzo has a bit more empty wall space than it did yesterday."

"Does that mean you've been unfaithful again?"

Irony made a lie of Evan's indignation. Lirion tousled his hair with an air of innocence.

"Only once. Or twice. This week. But you'll always be my pet, little monster."

"Growl." Evan nipped at her wrist, brushed it with a fleeting kiss. He wondered briefly if Lirion tasted the afterbite of bitterness in his playful response. Feelings were human things; if Lily experienced them at all, she didn't show it. Evan had seen pride and a willful capriciousness in her, knew most humans fell beneath her notice while she saw him as a curiosity—a monster. In spite of it all, he felt himself tied to these two as to no others on his world. They were the source of his completion.

"Mr. St. George is paying by the hour." Badad called them back to business, the moment passing in the resettling of clothing and hair. "If the homecoming is over, can we see the merchandise?"

"Losing a bit of canvas and paint is the most exciting thing that has ever happened to Charles Devereaux St.

George. Waiting will just add to the suspense." Her smile had a predatory gleam and Evan pitied the art collector. Lirion picked her teeth with righteous citizens like St. George.

"Why do you treat poor Charlie like a slug, Lily? Is it his bald head and his paunch, or simply that he pays for what he gets instead of stealing it?"

Evan threw himself into the high-backed office chair. With equal parts exasperation and indignation he eyed the daemon perched on the edge of the desk. He would never ask the real question: If you despise humans so, why do you stay? The memory of the Black Masque, and the night that inextricably tied his life to these lords of the host of Ariton was like an angry red scar. They were all too polite to notice, but it still rankled that he owed his life to the whim of creatures he understood as little as they understood humans.

Lirion defended her displeasure with an indignant sniff. "Charlie *is* a slug, *caro mio*. He can't see two inches past his ledger books and he wouldn't know a good time if ten dancing girls set up camp on his front lawn."

"Alfredo DaCosta, on the other hand, would know just what to do with ten dancing girls." Evan drawled the words, dripping sarcasm.

"Evan can settle with St. George." Brad reentered the fray with a conciliatory smile. He went to a section of bookshelves that opened to reveal a fully stocked bar behind false book spines. He picked up a bottle with a bright red label.

"Coke, Evan?" A raised eyebrow met Evan's affirmative, but Brad filled the tumbler before gathering snifters and a bottle of the best Napoleon for himself and Lirion. Evan accepted the tumbler and set it aside, adding his own silent question to the one the daemon voiced aloud:

"You do have the painting, don't you?"

"Of course I have it." Lily pulled the canvas from the air and unrolled it atop the paperwork scattered on the desk.

"I don't know what they see in it." Lily took the snifter Badad held out to her. "Even the color is déclassé."

"It's his blue period." Evan examined the Picasso with a magnifying glass before pronouncing it genuine. Oblivious to his cousin's sneer and his father's smirk, he continued: "He couldn't afford much else, but still the talent was there. It shines out of the canvas. Ironic, isn't it? We'll get more for recovering it than he did for painting it."

Lirion shifted to the arm of Evan's chair, toying absently with the thick hair that fell stubbornly across his forehead. "You could always give your share to some poor starving artist," she suggested, more than willing to find the whole thing ironic.

"I am." Evan grinned back at her. "Should keep me in sable brushes until the year five thousand."

She rumpled Evan's hair. "You're impossible," she declared with a smile, "but I picked up this little trinket for you anyway, while I was looking for the Picasso." She drew a heavy pendant from a pocket in her slacks and draped the chain in Evan's hair, resting a smoky topaz the size of an egg on his forehead and balancing it on the bridge of his nose.

"Because it reminded me of your eyes. Am I forgiven for calling Charlie a slug?" She kissed the top of his head and laughed as he crossed the eyes in question to see the stone, then tilted his head forward to let gem and chain fall into his outstretched palm. She took the pendant from him and slipped it over his head, resting the stone over his heart. "There," she confirmed, "a perfect match."

"If Alfredo DaCosta had it, you can bet he didn't buy it," Brad reminded them. "Somebody will probably pay us for rescuing that little bauble."

Lily shrugged. "Meanwhile, they'll be looking for Alfredo, not us."

Evan wrapped his fingers around the stone where it lay. It felt warm there. Right. "I suppose Charlie St. George should thank his lucky stars you hate Picasso, Lily, or he would be out one blue period painting again."

"And he's already paid our bill," Brad reminded them. "You will get the thing back to him this afternoon, Evan?"

The human carefully rolled the canvas and slipped it into a waiting tube. "No problem. He's expecting someone from our office at four. That leaves you an hour to tell us why we are going to hate this new case."

He took a sip of his soda, while he stared consideringly at the man across the desk. Badad swirled the brandy in his glass, his eyes focused on the aromatic film that clung to the curves of the bowl. The daemon's attention seemed far away just then, and Evan guessed whatever memory played out behind those eyes brought more pain than pleasure. The idea that his father could feel pain came as a surprise; its connection with their new client started a slow curdle of dread in the pit of his stomach.

"If it's that bad, why didn't you turn it down?"

Badad really looked at him then, glanced away at Lily, but returned his attention to his son. "This time we don't have a choice. It's Omage. He's left his calling card, no question about it."

The name froze Evan where he sat. Omage. He couldn't,

not again. How could Brad even suggest ... try not to think, not to see, pretend everything is normal. ... He had a job, worked with strangers as human as he. Daemons were a fantasy, a bad dream, they didn't exist, not anywhere—especially not in this room. It was a bad dream and he could wake up if he tried hard enough. *Wake up. Wake up.*

The room never wavered. Agitated, Lily paced between the overstuffed chairs and the low brass coffee table piled with books—Kierkegaard, Walter Scott, Robert Ludlum— and Evan turned away from her, blocking the memory of her touch. Kevin Bradley sat forward in his chair. Evan felt the force of him but dared not meet Badad's eyes. Daemon fire lurked there: power beyond his comprehension, and a hunger for places that didn't exist except in Evan's nightmares.

"Not again." The pleading in his own voice disgusted him, but Evan couldn't stop it. This time, he would go insane.

"No." Kevin Bradley's voice, so soft, almost a whisper. He held Evan with the intensity of his look. "You're staying out of this one. Spend a month painting in the south of France, surfing off the coast of Australia, photographing penguins in Antarctica—anything that takes you as far as you can go as fast as you can get there."

"We can all go. Tell them we're overcommitted." When he looked at Kevin Bradley, Evan forced himself to see a father. He'd spent a lifetime looking for the man whose only legacy had been dreams filled with horror and the certainty that he was different—not mad—different. Ultimately, it had taken madness to find him, and Evan knew beyond logic or reason that he would lose his father if they took this case.

Chapter Three

And the lords of a host of one Prince may create alliances between them, but no lord treats with those of another Prince unless it be in Quorum, as one Prince to Another, to create the great alliances that may do war together, side against side. The lords of a host may hold a lord or lords of another Prince his enemy, or may choose not to recognize the existence of a lord of a neutral Prince, that he not draw his Prince into battle without his Prince wills it.

"We can't back down from this one." Brad threw the photograph on the desk and gave them a brief summary of his conversation with Marnie Simpson: "Paul Carter, age nineteen, brother to our client Mrs. Marnie Simpson and bastard son of the now deceased, then widowed, Ethel Carter: it looks like more than one cuckoo from the second sphere has been fouling nests on this little planet. Carter's missing from his home outside of Baltimore. Omage has him, he left our yellow pages listing on the Simpsons' dining room table—on top of the ransom note."

To the photograph he added the slip of paper with the words printed in Marnie Simpson's clear hand: "Return the Eye of Omage and death will be swift. Withhold the Eye and he will spend eternity longing for death that does not come."

Lirion winked in and out of the room as she paced her agitation between the spheres.

"Stand still, Lily!" Brad snapped. "I can't think when you do that."

Her temper, short-fused at the best of times, flared. "Why did you listen to that woman, cousin?" She said the word cousin as if it meant maniac, or masochist, or both. Blue sparks danced at her feet as she paced, her form wavered and solidified again.

"Evan's not the only one in this room with reason to stay clear of that place. Do you think Omage will cut cards with you for the life of every human who catches your sympathy? This time your battle could cost more than this planet is worth, and you can count me out. No doubt we will meet again in the second sphere once the dust settles, but don't look for me."

"We have no choice." Badad ground the words between clenched teeth. Almost as an afterthought he added for Evan: "There is more at stake here than our lives, or Paul Carter's life. Universes are at risk—yours, ours, maybe others. Lily and I are *bound* to this battle." He added the emphasis for Lirion. Words were traps for daemons, and this one—meaning the binding of a daemon to a task through its completion—carried more weight than the rest of the OED, unabridged, combined. Lirion grimaced, and he saw the memory of Ariton's binding flare in her eyes:

Madness, at first a gentle wave, jostled the delicate balance of the second celestial sphere. The ripple effect teetered through the spheres like so many tortured dominoes, each careening into the next until it passed beyond the awareness of the Princes of Darkness. That madness was human, and more. It tasted of Ariton and unwholesome alliances across the borders of reality, its presence among the spheres boding change in the nature of all universes.

For the first time in millennia the seven Princes brought together their hosts and took form. Azmod and Ariton, Paimon and Oriens, Astarot and Magot, Amaimon, each drew together out of the essence of the lords who served them, each host of 833 coalescing, becoming its Prince. Old enmities were forgotten as enemies throughout infinity put aside their rivalries to make war against the invading madness. In pillars of fire the Princes burned the message across the glittering darkness: Ariton had begun it, somewhere in that abyss where the forces of the universes froze and became matter. Ariton must end it before the fabric of realities of all the seven spheres crumbled. From the host of Ariton went Badad, daemon of solitude, and Lirion, the lily of heaven, to follow the trail of human torment to its source, the back room of an East Village bar on the planet Earth.

"This is your fault, Badad." Lirion snarled the accusation. "If we'd burnt that place to the ground and your bastard monster with it, we'd be home now and free."

Badad saw the shock on Evan's face, mortality reflected in eyes that measured a life span in the anger of Ariton's messenger. Defiant in the face of his own fear, the human threw death in the teeth of his daemon kin and dared them to take the next, irretrievable step.

"Should I blow my own brains out, or would you like the honor? Might be a kinky new thrill for you, Lily. Or maybe not that new. Is killing humans fun, Lily? Do you get off on people dying?"

Lirion raised her hand and Badad came out of his chair

in a single fluid motion. He caught her wrist and drew her gaze to the fire that blazed in his own eyes.

"Omage is the enemy, Evan. No one wants you dead." It was a lie. All the hosts of the second sphere wanted this one human dead. So did Lirion, once. He let go of her wrist and she resumed her pacing.

Lily was right in her way. One lightning bolt would have solved the problem, destroyed the nightclub called Black Masque and Omage's dirty little back room. How could he explain to either of them the impulse that had stayed his hand? Even remembering it now, Brad didn't understand.

He'd passed through the barrier between the spheres, fighting the waves of disorientation to their source. The human who set all the universes trembling drew him to the imprint of his own nature in the physical universe. Lily, passing through shadows only she could know, arrived a beat of his adopted heart later.

At first, he hadn't noticed the room. His own new flesh bombarded senses he did not understand with information he could not sort and he let that form dissolve in blue flame. As flame, he recognized the burning heart of Omage of the host of Azmod within the human body this enemy of his Prince wore. Omage knelt over the figure of a creature with no consciousness at all, just a barely animal pulsing of heart and lungs. Badad resolved again in corporeal form to confront his nemesis and, gradually, as he learned again the sensations a human body fed him, the room opened up to him in the flickering gold of a hundred candles. A small group of beings who held no trace of the Princes about them clustered around the unconscious one, their attention suddenly focused on the lords of Ariton. Omage, lord of the host of Azmod, held a bowl of stone beneath the unconscious creature's arm, collecting the warm blood dripping from the open wrist.

"You've come." Omage set the bowl down and stood, dusting off his hands. He stepped over a silver chain that bound the heavy collar around the unconscious creature's neck to the clawed foot of a high gilt chair. Smiling, he spread his hands wide. "Friends, our prayers are answered in unhoped for abundance. Welcome our guests, daemon lords of the high Prince Ariton. Ours not to command, but to worship." Omage bowed low, leading his followers in their obsequies. The humans ranged themselves behind his chair; none responded to Azmod's irony. "Is it not so, old friend? Not so grand a following as the first time we met, but a beginning. This time, of course, I had your help. I suppose I should thank you, but I see you haven't let your host-cousin in on the joke."

"You play a dangerous game, old enemy," Badad countered.

"Joke?" Lirion had interposed.

He had not answered, nearly didn't register the question at all. Suddenly it was there—Ariton—burning in his mind. The creature chained at Omage's feet had awakened; more accurately, perhaps, returned, and the fire of his own Prince glinted out at him through eyes hard with madness. So this was his son.

The creature smelled. Feces and vomit. Blood, and something else. Decay. Wounds festered on its arms, on its neck where the thick silver collar chafed.

Lirion twisted in angry flames around his head. "Kill it!" Her words crackled through his mind and he looked up. More of the surrounding room fell into place. Arcane designs in blood clung everywhere in the splintered light of the candles. Some of the symbols hurt to look at, others blurred his mind with strange hungers. One burned with daemonic fire, his son's blood painted on the wall. Omage sat in the high chair and pulled at the chain, dragging the ragged figure of Badad's insane get to its knees. "If you'd phoned ahead, I'd have held the show for your arrival."

Badad had seen enough. Home was a lightning strike away, until Omage brought his attention back to the human.

"Your father." The reptilian voice hissed the words. "I promised an end to your search." Omage kissed the forehead of the human with soft, wet lips curved in a smile of lazy pleasure and sighed, a sound like the scales of a serpent slithering across sand. "I never said it would be a happy ending."

Omage had leaned back in his high chair then, pulling the human's throat taut with the chain in his hand. "I suppose they've sent you to get rid of the creature."

Out. Out of there. Badad wanted out of this place, this form, out of the presence of an enemy he could not fight as long as the truce among Princes held. As long as the creature Omage called Badad's son lived.

"Now!" Lirion's voice snapped, sharp next to his ear.

The room blurred and thunder rumbled off the walls. He raised his hand to strike, and daemon-fire had glinted in his son's eyes. Badad knew nothing of the meaning of fatherhood, but he read in those mad eyes the expectation of death at his father's hand and found beauty in the need that reached beyond fear or despair.

"Father." The boy's voice was a choked whisper, a voice more accustomed to screaming in the dark than speaking. But anger seemed, for the moment, to hold back the madness. With blood-streaked hands the boy lifted his chain and held it before his eyes. "If you've come to finish what you started, do it. Do it! Bastard."

Betrayal burned in that wild glare. The boy seemed barely aware of his physical injuries, his accusations touching on something that Badad could not imagine, except that Ariton shone within him, and he had grown more than twenty years in this place of frozen time with no touch of host-cousins, no knowledge of his Prince. The hand fell, and Badad watched a drop of blood seep from the wounded wrist, mix with the suppurating oozes, and slide, gracefully, across the boy's clenched fist to gild the chain.

Suddenly, the thought of this human's death left a taste of ashes in the mouth of the body he wore in Earth's reality. Badad smiled, cold and hard in the flickering light; something trembled not quite seen in the shadows. Omage's followers fell back, hiding from his view.

"You know why I am here, lord of Azmod. We've played out your whims before, at your cost, and this time even Azmod is ranged against you. But you pique my interest. Give me the boy, and you can keep your worshipers."

Omage smiled in his turn and lifted his hands, palms upturned, to express defeat. "Kill him, then. As you say, I cannot stop you. Or do you have games of your own in mind? A deal, then. One cut of the cards. I win, he dies. You win, well, whatever."

The lord of Azmod reached, and an acolyte pressed a pack of cards into his hands. He lifted a small stack from the deck, showed a ten of spades. Badad followed his lead, showed a king of hearts.

"The boy is yours. Take him. If you want him."

"You're as mad as your human get!" Lirion prepared to strike, but Badad stayed her hand.

"No." Badad considered his prize. Well, a human life, after all, was a fleeting thing. It might be worth the moment out of the long reach of his existence to explore. But not as father or son, with all the promise and pain that bled from the tortured body of the boy. If he survived, they could ride together on a different wind, as companions.

At the last, Lily had agreed, for reasons of her own that he would never fathom. Until this moment, confronting Evan across a cluttered desk in the place they now shared, she had shown no regret for the weakness that sealed their fates to the human's. Evan's death could no longer serve a purpose, but Badad recognized the danger in Lirion's undirected wrath. His son saw it, too. The human would push at their limits, it was a part of him, but no regret Lily might feel later could take back the unconsidered stroke unleashed against a mortal body.

"This is between Princes, Lirion. It was never Evan's fight."

His words brought her up short, her eyes wide with the realization that this was Evan. Once dead he would be gone forever. "Don't be stupid. It wouldn't do us a bit of good to kill him now—Omage has already found another one."

"Then in the name of the seven Princes, will you sit down? We've got work to do, and a client who expects a Picasso on his doorstep at four." Brad waved in the direction of the leather sofa, as far from Evan at the desk as the room allowed. He kept his tone casual, and hoped his son believed the danger had resided only in an overactive imagination. Maybe, if Lily would just sit down, he'd even believe it himself.

"All right." She threw herself on the sofa curled on her

side, one hand carded into her hair to prop her head against the leather bolster, grumbling. "I didn't know him then. It wouldn't have been the same thing at all. Any clue as to what Omage's up to this time?"

In the fifteen billion years he'd known her, that was the closest Lirion had ever come to an apology. Brad finally let go of the breath he'd been holding. In answer to her question he shook his head.

"Just the note. He seems to have lost something and thinks we can find it for him. Like all good megalomaniacs, he's named it after himself—the Eye of Omage—totally obscuring any useful information."

"So, no facts. Any guesses?"

"Maybe." Badad took the photograph of Paul Carter from the desk and studied it, looking up at last to consider his son. Evan was still pale, and Badad suspected that he held onto the arms of his chair to still the shaking in his hands. But the half-human was alert and watchful, only his silence testifying to the aftereffects of Lily's temper. An old human expression seemed peculiarly apt: with friends like these, Evan scarcely needed enemies. By some cruel twist of fate, those enemies proved equally powerful.

Evan seemed to relax under his scrutiny, sensing that if Brad could turn his back on Lily the crisis was truly over. Brad wished the assumption were justified, but he knew the danger had just begun, and its focus rested forgotten over his son's heart. Lily was right; the gem was a perfect match for Evan's eyes.

Brad had grown accustomed to the convention of this time that men wore little jewelry, and stones only in rings. On Evan the jeweled pendant simply made everything around him look out of step. The thought scared Brad, and he didn't frighten easily.

"Couldn't you have settled for a postcard?" He dropped the photograph on the sofa beside her on his way to refill his glass and brought the bottle back with him, pouring a second for Lily. Evan's soft drink remained nearly untouched.

"It's the same stone." He watched his son over brandy almost the color of the gem, his eyes wandering to the jewel and holding there almost against his will. "I would have spared you this—" a whispered plea for understanding, the answering nod almost lost in mesmerized fascination with the stone.

"I think we've got the Eye of Omage."

"Are you sure?" Lirion moved to the desk, looking from the photograph to the jewel at Evan's breast. "It looks darker in the picture." She reached out as if to touch it, then hesitated, dropping her hand to her side.

"As sure as a guess can be," Brad confirmed, "Which leads us to two questions: How did Omage know we would have it before you stole it, Lily? And what do we do about it?"

"Shit." With feeling, then, "I need some fresh air." She disappeared in a clap of thunder and a small whirlwind.

"Evan?" Brad slumped into his armchair and watched his son. Evan stared at the photograph, his jaw clenched as if holding back the very memory of his own screams. Brad knew what his son saw, but had no comfort to give him.

There was little physical similarity between his own half-human son and the face that stared out of the picture, but Brad remembered the dead look in Evan's eyes when he'd found his son at the Black Masque. Paul Carter's eyes held that same look. More than one daemon had been seeding this little planet, but it only took one Omage to destroy them. Evan had been strong enough to survive both the dreams and Omage once. Could he ask his son to enter that pit again? Badad knew before the question shaped itself that he would never ask it, and wondered what was happening to him that it should matter.

Evan lifted the jewel from his breast and stared at it. "I don't believe in coincidences," he said. "I'm not even sure I believe in Mrs. Marnie Simpson. But I do believe in him." He dropped the necklace on the photograph and looked straight into the eyes of his father.

"I'm not afraid of dying," he explained. "It's something all humans have to do eventually. I am afraid of the emptiness that goes on forever. The dreams were bad enough, but Mac—Omage—made it real. I couldn't take that again."

Not all the wisdom of the seven Princes in all the seven spheres of heaven could tell him how Evan had survived to adulthood, had overcome Omage's ungentle ministrations. Against all reason, Badad felt fiercely proud that his son still lived, but could find no way to tell him so.

"You've been there since," Brad reminded him. "Once with Lily, a few times with the two of us. You can find your way home now, he can't trap you there against your will. But I meant what I said at the start of this. Lily and I will handle Omage. Get away somewhere until we've dealt with him, sent him back where he belongs."

"Can you? What if *he* is stronger?"

Badad waved the possibility away, but Evan wasn't buying the bravado.

"What could he do to you?"

Don't ask, Badad wanted to say, don't think the unthinkable until we have to. Aloud he gave the only answer he had: "It doesn't matter. We have to try."

"And Paul Carter?"

"Omage has shown us a simple rescue will never be enough. We have to send him back where he belongs. If we can, we'll pull Carter out of there. A lot depends on how strong he is. And then again, a lot depends on how strong Omage is. None of us may get out; that's why I want you as far away from the Black Masque as possible."

Evan studied him minutely, weighing emotion betrayed in the flicker of an eyelash. Finally he nodded.

"Okay. I couldn't go back in there anyway." He gave a rueful, self-deprecating laugh. "When it's over . . ."

"We'll find you. And, Evan, don't blame yourself because you can't do twice what most humans wouldn't survive even once."

"Yeah, well, there's no reason I can't poke around a bit at Carter Stables. We can take the Mercedes—I'm not transporting. I can pack when we get back tomorrow, maybe visit Jack and Claudia Laurence in London. Is that far enough?"

"Should be." Brad reached for the pendant on the desk, but Evan was there first, sweeping the jewel into a clenched fist.

"Sorry. I don't know why I did that." Evan stared at his hand as if it had a life of its own. "Can't leave it on the desk—I'll lock it up."

"Fine."

Brad watched a section of books behind the desk slide out of the way. Evan swung open the door to the safe and laid the stone on top of the personal papers that made them all real: birth certificates, deed to the house and offices and one to the condominium in Nice, stocks and treasury certificates. When Evan turned to face him again, the embarrassment had faded, but traces of the confusion remained.

"We'll need that to get Carter back."

"I know." Evan reassured him with a wry grin. "And right now I have an appointment with a Picasso."

Brad pulled open the door to the living quarters beyond. He waited until Evan retrieved the rolled canvas and closed the door behind them with a last nervous glance at the hidden safe.

Chapter Four

Among the Princes of the second sphere fall great battles, for the might of Princes must ever be tested, and each strives to be greatest among the Princes. And the Princes send out their hosts to do battle, and the lightning is the sword of the daemon, and the thunder his chariot, and the bloom of a new star in the firmament signals his great victory.

Evan twitched nervously in his sleep, trying to escape the dreams. *This must be what dying feels like,* he thought as some inner part of himself tried to tear loose.

He clung to the integrity of self that was more than just a soul, but included a body he was just learning to appreciate, a humanness that found expression in eating and shitting and making love and running. Inner vision was fine, but he needed his hands to work the clay and hold the brushes. He needed his smile and his scowl and the explosion in his chest when a feeling took concrete form beneath his fingertips. So he hung on, until suddenly the pressure was gone, and he was ... someplace else.

The darkness behind his lids passed into a greater darkness. He tried to open his eyes, and knew that he had no eyes, no throat to scream, no lungs to fill. Around him stretched not black, nor any of the mind's conceptions for the absence of light, but an absence of sensory referent to translate into the human experience of not-seeing. He had no up or down, no forward or backward, nor any sense of what those words might mean in this place. He knew he wasn't alone, and didn't know how he knew. Those others weren't friendly, but his rational mind recognized that they couldn't hurt him. He wasn't really there. And "there" went on forever—no way back.

No way back. The thought echoed in his mind. He knew that somewhere a body was screaming, but he couldn't reach it. The scream went on forever, because time no longer existed. And the others were somewhere; his *nonrational* mind warned that maybe they could hurt him. Long ago Sunday School lessons hinted at hell. He thought of Jack Laurence and sins committed while a bartender named Mac watched and smiled. Not even his guilt could conjure the images of his shame to relieve the darkness in which he hung. This was hell, and he had died, and there was no way out—

Then, a voice he could not hear shivered through him.

"Evan, wake up."

He knew that hands he could not feel shook the body he'd left behind, then a presence occupied the not-space that he thought of as himself in this place.

"Get your body up here, Evan."

The not-voice thought jolted him into self-will; Evan called upon the self of taste and touch and sight. Awake now, his body responded: he felt it shudder through the skin of reality into a place it had no way to be, and he became aware of physical sensation again. Nausea. Waves of nausea hit him while his eyes denied the truth his stomach told him. He was falling, falling, and there was no end to the falling because he wasn't moving at all, in a darkness his brain still denied.

A blue flame burned with no heat beside him, and he felt a touch on his mind like a teasing kiss. Lirion's voice floated on gentle laughter inside of him.

"Do you need a little gravity?"

The flame, transformed to a pulsing cloud the color of a summer sky, surrounded him, and weight settled on Evan's shoulders. Unfortunately, the direction to which his inner ears reacted as "up" corresponded to what his eyes saw as sideways. Falling over cured that problem, and Evan almost felt human again. Or whatever he was. He slapped his sides, hard, to be certain he was really there, and discovered an awkward truth:

"I'm naked!"

Champagne laughter bubbled through him.

"That's how you left it." Lily's voice, archly innocent, licked at his imagination.

The flame that was the daemon Lirion bathed him in a blue glow that reminded him of stories from his childhood about pissing during lightning storms. He would have crossed his hands over his genitals, but refused to give her something else to laugh at.

"Let's go home."

He knew it was the wrong thing to say when the flame glinted orange around the edges, a color that signaled Lirion's displeasure in waves of energy that pricked at the hairs on his arms and pulled at the skin over his temples. The flame disappeared, the sense of Lily with it, and Evan waited until the itch at his back warned him to turn. She wrapped him in blue flame, and he let her infiltrate his mind, pass through his body, a sensation like being tickled from the inside. When she had re-formed in flame beside him, he tried to pass it off lightly:

"I meant *my* home. I'm not exactly dressed for traveling." Keep it casual, and maybe she'd pretend his screaming hadn't wakened her in the middle of the night. "Let's go back to bed."

"Fool."

The flame snapped sparks off his nose, warning him that Lily didn't buy the breezy tone one bit. She waited, and Evan felt the challenge: she was leaving it to him.

He tried to calm the racing of his heart, but he couldn't hide the fear from her. He hated this place, and would have struck out blindly for any escape. Lirion was watching from the inside of his head, though—a feat she could accomplish only in her true form in the second sphere.

Slowly he focused his common sense on this most illogical of situations. He'd been here before in his body, with Brad and with Lily herself. Evan knew how to get home now, he just had to shape in his mind the picture of the bedroom as they had left it, sheets tumbled, outlines of bed and bureau and dressing table barely discernible in the night-shadowed room. He allowed the details to slide out to the periphery, all but Lily's big four-poster swathed in Alençon lace bed curtains. He firmed the image with the tactile memory of silk covers on fat down pillows, almost inseparable from the feel of Lily's body pressed along his side.

And they were back. The filtered light of a streetlamp slipping between the curtains left lacy shadows on the breasts of the woman beside him. Evan raised himself on one elbow to look down at her face and brushed a kiss softly over her lips.

"Thank you," he said, as her arms wrapped around his neck.

"You haven't sleepwalked in the second sphere in a long time," she commented.

They both knew what had brought the old dream back and sent the daemon part of him floating in his father's reality. Omage. But Lily had brought him home.

"You did it yourself, you know," she said.

He started, wondering if she could read his mind in this universe as well as in the second sphere. He wasn't ready to argue with her now, though—the memory of where he had been was still too strong.

"I can find my way back when I'm awake for the cross-over now." He accepted her praise conditionally: "The spontaneous shifts are something else. I've never had them when I was awake—I thought it was just a place I'd invented in my nightmares until Omage sent me through at the Black Masque—but I lose control when I'm sleeping."

He kissed her. Couldn't have got it up to save his soul, but he craved the physical reality of lips and teeth and clouds of black hair drifting over soft white skin.

"Why does my universe scare you so badly?"

Soft question, between nibbles, but Lily sure knew how to kill the mood. And just when—hell, it was a lost cause anyway. Evan sat up, ran the fingers of both hands through hair grown lank with sweat.

"There's nothing there," he tried to explain, failing miserably at conveying the absolute lack he felt in the second sphere. "Or, sometimes I sense something, off somewhere in a place that has no where, and it hates me."

A half laugh: "Other kids worried about monsters under the bed. My monsters dragged me into an emptiness so complete that I didn't exist there, a place where even the monsters would have been company, but they didn't exist there either, except for a touch at what consciousness they left me. I knew with that touch they would destroy everything I'd ever known to keep me there."

He saw the expressions pass across Lily's face, recognized the knowledge they both shared. Those others whose presence he almost felt in the second sphere were not the monsters. Evan was. Half of this reality, half of the other, he had no place in either. And he knew that once, all the Princes of that other place had united with one purpose: to seek his death. He touched her, running a finger lightly between her breasts, knowing that those Princes had sent her to kill him. Lucky for him that monsters turned her on.

"It isn't like that." She took his hand in hers, entwined their fingers, and nestled the basket of their palms over her right breast. Her eyes grew distant, a tiny smile compounded of memory and touch lingering in her face.

A worm twisted in the back of Evan's mind. How did she know what he was thinking? Lirion's next words reassured, her thoughts traveling a different path entirely.

"To us, the second sphere is not empty, but filled with stars and planets that *we* know as knots in the weave of energy that makes up the Universe. What your physicists are only now beginning to learn—that space is not empty, but filled with energy—we have experienced as creation itself, and all of it seethes with sensations. Not like these—" She lifted their meshed hands, kissed Evan's knuckles for an example, and snugged the hands comfortably around her breast again, "—but more like knowing, or appreciating.

"You see a painting, and feel a set of emotions you

translate as appreciation. We don't pass through the process of translation, or the separation between what we are and what we experience. If you could become the painting, love your own beauty, and then pass on, become the sunset, and love your own grandeur, you'd be getting close.

"You can observe the stars through a telescope, but you can't look at your own sun directly without burning out your sense of sight. We can enter into the very heart of that star, change its nature, and pass out again unscathed."

"It sounds beautiful when you describe it," Evan admitted.

Lily paused, her head cocked thoughtfully. "Yes. It is." She smiled. "Sometimes, after fifteen billion years, one forgets." She released his hand and leaned over him, arms crossed on his chest, and kissed the frown lines between his eyes.

"But?" she coaxed.

"I'm part daemon."

"Those are some of my favorite parts," she agreed.

Evan continued in spite of the distraction of teeth gently nibbling at his chin.

"I can travel to the second sphere, sometimes I can't *stop* myself, but I've never seen anything like you describe. I've never seen anything at all."

"That's because you are trying to see." Her hand dipped beneath silk sheets, teased him with manicured nails, and gentled the touch with fingertips. "Can you see what I'm doing?"

"No."

Long stroking touches, then: "Does that mean my hand isn't real?"

Evan wrapped his arms around her, rolled her on her back, and kissed her with feeling this time, more feeling than he'd felt safe to show her before.

"You're real," he agreed, moving slowly to the rhythm she set while he planted small kisses on her breasts.

Lily's hands drifted over his body, molded her fingers to his clenched buttocks. "Maybe we've been going at this all wrong."

Evan knew she meant the second sphere, but he needed to hear her say it. "Not everything," he coaxed.

"Oh, no." She smiled, and her arms reached round his waist, rolled him over. He saw the heat in her eyes, and the laughter in the face that hovered above him. "Some things we get just right."

Chapter Five

Of the Princes and their daemon hosts many tales are told, but of these most are falsehoods spread by the daemon lords themselves to mock humankind. For the true nature of the Princes one must look to their names, which are the fonts of their power in their own sphere, and the means by which man can bind them in the first. And of the nature of their Prince do the host of daemon lords share, as well as the characteristics of their own names make up their natures. If a man were to bind a daemon to his bidding, therefore, he must first know the nature of the daemon he binds.

Badad tried to submerge his impatience in the view outside the car window, but found little there to relieve the monotony.

"Why don't you pull over and let me drive? I know a shortcut."

Evan cast him a baleful look. "No, thanks. Your shortcuts don't usually include the car. Watch the scenery—people come from all over the world for this scenery."

His window offered a view of rolling hills covered in a spring-misted green, and split rail fences weathered a soft gray. Bare, spiky vines clung to the rails. In another month the vines would green, and bloom roses in June; now they looked like dead things frozen in the act of strangling their equally moribund host. The mud cast a thick brown pall over everything, including the fenders of the silver Mercedes.

"They're crazy," he decided, "and you are lost. Route 30 doesn't go to Baltimore."

"Well, Brad, it's like this. You can't breed thoroughbreds in a townhouse. It upsets the neighbors when the horses get out and eat the petunias. Carter Stables is northwest of Baltimore, but who except the natives and other horse trainers ever heard of Deep Run?"

Badad let his head fall against the padded leather seat back and closed his eyes. Counting to ten didn't help. Maybe a thousand and ten. Three hours in an internal combustion vehicle, even one as lovingly crafted as the Mercedes, tested the limits of his attachment to the man at the wheel. It would be different, he supposed, if Evan Davis couldn't pass through the interface between the spheres, but his son shared in more than a human heritage. The daemon in him called to the second sphere. Lily kept a feeler out for him at night, when that part slipped past self-control and human form to drift alone in the second sphere of his father's reality.

But forced, fully awake, into the reality of Badad and his kind until he had grown quite mad, Evan's horror had once destabilized universes. Over time Badad had shown him that with someone he trusted as an anchor, he could pass through the universe of the Princes with no harm to himself or the realities he touched in his passage. Now, however, the memory of Omage and his cursed back room paralyzed his bastard son in the physical sphere, stuck in a metal box passing through miles of northern landscape, still recovering from the shock of winter in real space.

To pass the time he considered the memories that had risen up to bind Evan to the material plane. Did those memories change the essence of humanness, like the human summons changed the essence of his own kind? Twenty-five years ago a human summons had drawn Badad into the material sphere and bound him against his will to this reality out of idle mischief he now recognized as jealousy. He'd won free of the human who thought he would master a lord of Ariton, but not before he'd seduced the girl, destroyed her coming marriage, and left behind more of himself than he had bargained for.

"How is your mother? You never talk about her." He'd never thought to ask before, and Evan looked at him strangely now.

"Didn't think you'd be interested. Didn't think you'd even remembered her."

"I don't, not much at any rate." Badad shrugged in answer to the sharp glance. "Just making conversation." Trying to untangle the web that bound him here, if he were honest with himself.

Evan wasn't buying it, but he didn't push for an explanation Badad didn't have. "You didn't ruin her life, if that's what you're asking. I saw her at Christmas—you were in Madrid, and Lily was wherever she goes when the weather turns cold. She still lives on Rosemont Street and teaches Chemistry at Edgemont High. One of these days she may even marry Harvey Barnes, the principal.

"She never blamed you for what happened. I think she's glad we've gotten to know each other; I haven't told her what you are."

"Would she believe you if you did tell her?"

"She'd probably try to have me committed. Wouldn't be the first time."

Tangled webs. They both fell silent; to go farther would be to admit they had already revealed too much. Evan's bitterness demanded an apology Badad did not have to give. The sacrifice of his own freedom demanded gratitude that Evan did not owe.

He'd never asked Lirion how she had been drawn out of the second sphere by the binding spell of a human or what task that human had set her. As the human summons had changed Badad, so that long-ago summons had changed Lily forever. His kind, like the humans, could not pass the barrier between the spheres alone. Once summoned to the material sphere with a formula of sound and symbol, however, the pattern of the passage imprinted itself upon the essence of what they were. Ariton had had few choices when he sent his warriors to stop an insane human's intrusion into the seven spheres; the part of Evan that was Badad had called to him as powerfully as the summons that created him. But Lily had shaken free of her Earth-binding long ago, and her anger at Ariton's command had shaken the heavens as she passed. That she agreed to this mad charade at all had surprised him. Little given to introspection, she had dismissed it as a whim, but Badad wondered. More tangled webs.

"We're there." Past the mailbox set on a post, and before the swinging sign with the horse's head and the words "Carter Stables" in black letters, Evan made a right between the open gates that crossed a narrow lane.

From the road they could see only a cluster of oaks and evergreens beyond the low rolling fields, but as they drew closer, Badad could make out black shutters on a white frame farmhouse. Once a straightforward double-pile

Georgian, the house now sprawled over two wings added by previous owners.

Evan pulled the car around to the side of the house and killed the engine. Lily Ryan waited for them in the doorway.

"What took you so long? The boy's not still afraid of flying, is he?"

Nothing of the night before showed in her expression—she quirked a smile only slightly malicious in Evan's direction and went on: "Mrs. Simpson said to tell you she'd be down before we left, but she needed a rest. In the meantime, I can give you the three dollar tour."

They rounded the back of the house, where someone had piled the broken furniture in a heap next to a cinder block fire pit. Kevin Bradley, Badad of the second sphere, gave it only a cursory glance.

"The big square building over there is the barn, and the longer lower one with the windows is the stable. Paddock and practice track are fenced off just beyond—you can see the track from here; it looks like an old dirt road going nowhere."

Badad followed the direction she pointed and found the structures, both white with black trim, about the length of a football field from the main house. At the fifty yard line an equally well tended bungalow wallowed in a sea of daffodils. "And that?"

"Used to be the foreman's house. Paul Carter has been living there off and on for a couple of years. She gave me the key. I was waiting for you to get here before I checked it out."

Brad nodded thoughtfully. He'd never seen the place where Evan Davis lived before Omage got his hands on the boy, and he wondered how alike these bastard children of two universes really were. Evan seemed to be thinking along the same line, tension tightening the corners of eyes locked on the low frame house.

"Why don't you check out the stable, see if anyone noticed anything suspicious yesterday. We'll meet at the big house when we are done."

Evan shook his head, but his eyes never left the bungalow. "I have to go in there. I have to know what it was like for him."

"He's a fool, you know." Lily addressed herself to Badad as if Evan were not there, but her follow-up remark was intended for them both: "Like father, like son. Let's get this over with."

The door opened into a roomy kitchen with little evidence of occupancy. Paul Carter had left no half-read mail on the maple chopping block table, no salt and pepper shakers on the formica countertops or cereal boxes in the cabinets. The living room showed little more of the man's presence; its rag rug and country casual furniture looked fresh from the pages of *House and Garden*.

"He doesn't live here." Evan voiced the conclusion they had all reached in their examination of the impersonal dwelling.

Lily ran a finger over an oak end table and glared at the dust she had accumulated there. "According to Marnie Simpson, Paul comes in every few months and stays a week or two. Seems to use the place as a detox center; cleans the booze and the drugs out of his system when the waking nightmares get worse than the ones he has at night, then drops out of sight again."

"Not in here he doesn't." Evan headed for the bedroom and stopped with his hand still on the knob. "Oh, my Lord."

Figuring one lord would do as well as another under the circumstances, Badad answered the summons. "What did you find?"

He stopped with a hand on Evan's shoulder and tightened his grip when the meaning of what he saw penetrated the shock. On the white bedspread Paul Carter had outlined a crude pentagram in black paint. Carter had made of the dresser a shrine to death. Pills—black ones, yellow, red, orange, and white ones—lay scattered like confetti among the weapons. The pistol was loaded, hunting knife unsheathed, razor blades scattered with the pills. On the bedside table a Jack Daniels bottle stood empty but for an amber inch evaporating at the bottom.

Badad moved past Evan into the room and stared at the shotgun tied to the high back of the room's only chair.

He barely comprehended mortality as an idea, the reality of the state of nonbeing as alien to him as were the humans whose physical form he now shared. That one of these mortal creatures would willingly contemplate his own nonbeing, would be the agent of his own nonexistence, disturbed him as nothing else he had seen in the physical sphere. Blindly he looked to his own half-human son to reason away the unthinkable, and found only memories there.

"Why?"

"Control."

Evan followed him into the room, reached to touch the pistol with his fingertips, then thought better of it and curled his hand into a fist. "Evidence." He delivered the aside with a self-deprecating smile. The reminder was for himself.

"When the dreams become more than you can bear, you always know that, ultimately, you have the power to stop them. From the time I was old enough to find some-one to sell it to me, I slept with a pistol under my pillow. Sometimes knowing that I could end it was all that kept me alive."

The thought of Evan with the side of his head blown off by his own hand revolted Brad. For this he had given up his freedom, bound to a scruffy crust of dirt on the backside of the universe to preserve the life of a human who would have ended that very life with the flick of a finger. But Evan still lived, he hadn't put a bullet in his brain. Something *had* kept him alive.

"Where is it now?"

"The safe. I don't need it any more." Evan smiled.

He hadn't quite worked out the nuances of human feel-ing, but Badad recognized that Evan didn't find the ques-tion funny. Gratitude came to mind, and the thought embarrassed him. Probably embarrassed Evan, too. "Any-thing else we need to see in here?"

Evan shook his head and led the way out of the bunga-low. Brad followed with Lily at his side.

"They are all mad," she grumbled.

"Maybe," he agreed, then smiled with real humor. "Or maybe we just attract the weird ones."

With one delicately raised eyebrow Lily questioned his sanity. He answered with a shrug and followed Evan into the main house.

Chapter Six

Each Prince of the second sphere holds within itself
both the male and female aspect, but in greater or
lesser proportion, so that the Prince may be seen to be
characterized more as one sex than another, as can be
determined by the Prince's name. Astarot, also called
Astarte and worshiped as a goddess by that name,
gathers her flocks with the scythe. Azmod is the temp-
ter, patron of all impurity. His heart is stone, harder
than diamond.

The woman waiting for them on the wide front porch wore well tailored but comfortably worn corduroy slacks and an Aran sweater in the same natural color over a pale blue oxford cloth shirt. Her boots looked expensive but had seen hard use. Otherwise she fit Brad's description, and her first words confirmed Evan's preliminary identification.

"I'm Marnie Simpson." She offered a callused hand in a firm handshake that belied the nervous smile.

Evan returned the smile with a reassuring one of his own and shook hands as briefly as possible. They seldom met at their best the clients who needed the special skills of Bradley, Ryan, and Davis, but to call Marnie Simpson unprepossessing would have been a charity. A bit too thin, the woman's abrupt, sharp movement reminded him of a puppet whose strings had somehow gotten tangled, as if she herself were not quite sure which limb would follow the command for any gesture. So why did he feel like she was sizing him up for lunch? The impression passed quickly, and he chalked it up to concern for her brother and his own misgivings about the case.

When Lily and Brad joined them, Marnie Simpson led the detectives through several rooms still in shambles.

"Please excuse the mess. The housekeeper was here when it happened. I found her on her knees in the pantry, a crucifix in one hand and her beads in the other. She quit on the spot with no notice, said the house was cursed and she wouldn't spend another minute in it. The stable hand hasn't quit yet, but he won't set foot in the house. Temporary help from the agency should arrive in the morning. In the meantime I'm on my own here."

Brad muttered comforting sounds that stopped when they entered the dining room in the right wing of the house. French windows overlooked a small garden, filling the room with late afternoon sunshine and, since yesterday, a chill April breeze. The glass windowpanes lay in shards amid the rhododendrons.

Lily was the first to state the obvious: "Omage's been here all right, and he didn't come in through the windows. Probably didn't break them to get out either."

"Pressure wave, no doubt about it," Brad agreed. "He was in a hurry."

Evan fingered the letters burned into the polished walnut table while memories turned to knots in his stomach. How had Paul Carter weathered the rending tear out of the here and now of sight and touch, through that other place where senses had no meaning? What was he going through this very minute? Defensively he backed away from the thought, concentrating instead on Mrs. Simpson's discovery of the ransom note.

"Paul had been staying here for a week or two. He was scared, upset, but you have to realize that he's spent most of his life that way. I had no idea he was in real danger.

"Frank and I had tickets for a charity concert and reception. It ended late, and we decided to stay in town overnight. We had a late brunch the next afternoon, then I dropped Frank off at Baltimore-Washington Airport—he had business in Dallas—and drove home.

"When I arrived, the table was as you see it, and as I said, your ad from the telephone book lay on top, like this." She centered a blank sheet of paper on the table.

"Whoever did this wanted your firm as go-between, and I'll do whatever it takes, including deal with the devil if that's what I have to do."

Brad countered her accusation smoothly, but Evan saw the anger flashing just beneath the surface. "I assume you mean that figuratively, Mrs. Simpson. We don't know much about you either, except that you have a lot of money and your brother keeps unsavory company."

Marnie Simpson reached into a pocket and pulled out a half-empty pack of Virginia Slims, tapped a cigarette out, and replaced the pack. "Point, Mr. Bradley. Insulting each other won't bring my brother home. . . ."

A shriek from the direction of the stable interrupted whatever Mrs. Simpson would have added.

"Summer Dancer!" The woman dropped the unlit cigarette and ran back through the house. "If that bastard has hurt my horse—" She slammed her way through the kitchen door, with the detectives right behind her.

"Omage?" Lily threw a calculating glance on the run, and Evan shrugged, finding himself wasting the gesture on empty air. Brad was taking the overland route past the terrified girl running toward them, so Evan matched his pace to Mrs. Simpson's.

Private school, Evan noticed absently. Plaid skirt and gray blazer with matching kneesocks and sensible shoes: someone had worked hard to make an unattractive girl even homelier.

"What was she doing in the stable?"

"She's Mary Palmer, my walker. Local tradition, the girls earn some spending money and get to work with the horses. Mary is the only walker Summer Dancer doesn't kick."

They caught up with Mary Palmer twenty yards from the kitchen door. Marnie Simpson wrapped her arms around the girl, brushing fine mouse-colored hair out of a tear-streaked face.

"What's happened, Mary? Is Summer Dancer all right?"

For a moment Mary stared at Mrs. Simpson as if she were a stranger. When the identity of the woman penetrated the shock, Mary shook her head.

"Binky. Oh, God, why would anyone do that to Binky?"

Evan saw the girl's eyes roll back and scooped her up from a grateful Marnie Simpson's slipping grasp.

"I'll get a damp cloth and a blanket," Simpson told him. They parted company at the kitchen. Evan carried the unconscious girl into the living room and arranged her as comfortably as possible on the sofa.

"Is the girl all right?" Lily materialized at his shoulder, her expression one of indifference marred only by a mild distaste.

"Seems to be. Don't see any marks on her, and her pulse has settled down. What did she see out there?"

"Something has killed something else. I'm not sure what it was, but it wasn't human. Whoever did it left no messages. Brad is looking for clues, wants you to join him if you're not needed here." The girl stirred, distracting them, then Lily dismissed him: "You're not needed here."

Marnie Simpson returned with the damp cloth, but she had forgotten the blanket. "Has Summer Dancer been hurt?"

"A man who called himself Lopi said to tell you that Summer Dancer is panicked, but otherwise uninjured," Lily told her. "He's taken the horse out to the paddock until he calms down and he'll clean out the stall when we've finished looking for clues. After that you're on your own. He's quit, says there's devil's business here and he won't come back until someone named Father Dave exercises the stable."

"Exorcise," Simpson corrected. "Cast out the demons who've possessed it."

"Why would a daemon want to live in your stable?"

Lily sounded so amazed that Evan almost laughed. Assuming they lived to have a later, he'd enjoy teasing her about bunking down in the straw. Now, however, Brad was waiting. He heard Marnie Simpson's non-answer—"You'd have to ask Lopi"—as he left the room.

The stable was cool and dim in the late afternoon. Evan followed the long whitewashed wall past several wide stalls, empty now. The horses would be brought in soon for the night, but not until the stable hand cleared away the mess in stall number four: the smell of blood would madden the other animals. Smart. He felt the rising panic himself. *Get out, get out.* Memories painted a room with

human blood, his own blood. Omage's victims, his aco-
lytes.

He slipped on something the color of old burgundy—
liver? spleen?—hacked into bits too small to identify without a microscope. Warm shit-smell mingled with the
ordure of stable and death. Evan gagged, rested a hand on
the stall to steady himself, and felt wet paste. Threads of
red and clots of dull green glistened in the bridge of con-
gealing fluids that followed his hasty withdrawal.

His lunch never had a chance. Evan made it to the next
stall, where he christened the fresh straw. Moving deeper
into the shadows he fell to his knees, wiping his hand
over and over on the clean straw piled there.

"Indigestion?" Kevin Bradley rested a hand on his
shoulder.

It stayed there while Evan rose to his feet, gathering
himself. He checked his hand, clean although nerve
memory retained the feel of gut-slime. Gingerly he curled
his fingers over the offending palm and stuffed the fist
into his pocket, following his father into Summer Dancer's
stall.

"Just a touch. I need a drink."

"There's a bottle in Paul Carter's room."

Evan met his father's gaze and held it, remembering the
days he'd once spent trying to forget. He swallowed with
an effort. "Coke'll do just fine, but it can wait until we're
done here." With an effort he turned his mind back to the
mess in stall four. "What was it?"

Whoever had killed the animal had done a thorough
job—gutted the thing and left the husk for the horse to
trample into an unrecognizable mass of hair and flesh and
splintered bone.

Kevin Bradley squatted beside the body of what was

once a small, hairy animal. "A goat, I think. A stable hand heard the girl scream. He found the horse stomping it to pieces in the stall."

"How did a goat get in the stable?" he asked. Under control now, he dropped down to examine the carcass more closely. "Was it alive or dead when it was put here?"

"The goat lived here."

Marnie Simpson answered the question. Evan hadn't heard her arrive, but he was prepared with his most professionally bland expression in place when he turned to face her. Only the tightness around her eyes hinted at her revulsion at the viscera-smeared stall.

"Binky was Summer Dancer's pet," Simpson continued her explanation, "Most of the stables provide them for their horses. They stay together in the stall—for some reason, the horses like goats, even the most nervous of them settle right down around their own pets."

"No horse could have done this," Brad pointed out, "The animal was gutted by an expert, and thrown back in the stall."

Evan agreed, examining the gut-smeared walls. "Given the redecorating, you were never intended to think otherwise, Mrs. Simpson."

"It's another warning. They could do this to my brother."

She gave Kevin Bradley a hard stare, and Evan saw something calculated flicker in her eyes.

"When I said I would deal with the devil, if that's what it took to get my brother back, I didn't realize how literally my word might be taken. Know, however, that I did and still do mean it. Do what you must to bring my brother home alive, and I will pay any price. Am I understood?"

She turned her back on them, cutting off any reply.

"Mary is shaken but otherwise unharmed. Her mother is picking her up. If that is all, I have a horse to calm before he does any major damage."

She swept out of the long stable, each step punctuated with the decisive snap of boot heels on rough-hewn boards. Looking at the pulverized remains of Binky the goat, Evan wondered what she considered major damage.

"What did she mean by that?" Brad asked when she was well out of hearing range.

"I suppose a panicky horse could hurt himself and not even know it until it's too late," he ventured absently. "Let's get out of here."

Outside, Evan filled his lungs with the clean spring air. "I don't think I'll ever get that smell out of my head."

"What smell?" Lily joined them halfway to the car.

"The smell of a stable, well kept except for the dead goat beaten halfway through the floorboards," Evan elaborated.

Lily shrugged elegant shoulders, dismissing the affair as just another aberration. "Humans have some strange customs."

Evan glared at her, but Brad distracted him from an angry retort.

"I don't care about the damn horse or the goat, Evan. What was all that devil gibberish about?"

"Oh, that." Evan laughed at the bitter irony. "She must think Omage killed the goat. Your kind have had some bad press over the years, you know. You're supposed to get off on tearing living animals to pieces. Humans are supposedly top of the charts. Goats come in a close second. You are also known to take the shape of a goat and dance in the moonlight, screwing witches."

Lily wrinkled her patrician nose in distaste. "Why goats?"

"Don't know," Evan admitted, "But it's been goats and devils for thousands of years."

"By all the Princes, these people are more barbaric than even I believed. What a stupid idea!" Lily stopped, and Evan could almost see the wheels turning in her head. "Our Mrs. Simpson doesn't strike me as a stupid woman, though."

"No, she doesn't," Brad agreed. "And she wasn't talking just about Omage. She meant us as well."

"Could she know about you?" The idea made Evan nervous. He reminded himself that she'd come to them for help. Her abrasive personality had little to do with the case and nothing at all to do with the threat Omage posed to them all.

"She obviously thinks we are in this thing with Omage," Brad said, "so it's reasonable to assume she puts us in the same category. The real question is, who or what does she think has her brother?"

Lily dismissed the problem with a wave of her hand. "If she thinks Omage gets off on trashing goats, then she doesn't really know anything about him *or* us."

They had reached the parked car, and the nagging itch at the back of his mind tumbled full grown off Evan's tongue. "If it wasn't Omage, who killed the goat? Why did they kill it?"

Chapter Seven

Oriens is the evil king of the eastern quarter; he rules the winds, and is called the devourer by flame. Paimon rules the western quarter, and is known by the sound of bells ringing out of time. He is the whisperer, carrier of evil tidings and deceit. Amaimon rules the southern quarter with violence and death. Beware the poison of his breath.

Evan reached around the computer for his coffee mug and found it empty again. A half-full coffeepot steamed on the bar set into the wall of books, but the short walk across the study seemed more effort than it was worth. Instead he picked up the Eye of Omage, absently stroking the smooth face of the topaz while he gave in to the mesmerizing flash of the cursor on the computer screen. Waiting for the computer to finish his search program, Evan let his focus drift, reaching for the connection that seemed to hover just out of his grasp.

He didn't consciously decide to put it there, but the pendant found its way around his neck. It felt comfortable, secure, and he closed his left hand around the solid warmth of it, considering his next step.

"You should leave your senses on guard when you do

that. If I'd been Omage, you'd be dead." Brad entered the room by the human method—through the doorway from the living quarters. He crossed the room and picked up the empty coffee mug from the desk. "Refill?"

"Do what? Yeah, thanks."

Badad filled the mug, and another cup for himself. "Go away when you think."

"Oh, that." Evan let his hand drift away from the gem and dragged his attention back to the here and now with an effort.

"It's called concentration; humans learn to ignore the things they expect to happen, and react only to the unexpected. Omage in the study I'd have noticed. You, on the other hand, have to exert some effort to ruin my morning's work."

"Anything interesting?" Brad held out the mug and he reached for it, but his father did not let it go. "When did you develop a taste for gaudy jewelry?"

Evan craned his neck to view the pendant at rest over his heart. "Wouldn't go with a Brooks Brothers suit, but the color's not bad with the black sweatshirt."

Brad still held onto the mug, and a glare reminded Evan that his daemon kin had little sense of humor and less patience.

"I took it out of the safe for inspiration, something to focus on." He let go of the mug to slip the chain over his head. "Funny, really: I usually feel uncomfortable with anything more ostentatious than a pair of cuff links."

Evan set the gem on the desk and coiled the heavy gold chain around it. "I wore a plain silver chain for a while, but I never bothered to have it repaired when the clasp broke." Claudia had given him the chain, and he'd broken the clasp trying to escape from the Black Masque a year later. Omage's chains were not so easily broken. He hadn't worn metal near his skin since he'd gotten out of there. Until now.

"This piece is different: I like to touch it, like the weight of it around my neck. I can't stand the idea that Omage might get his hands on it."

His eyes darkened with the fury that boiled over at the thought. Primitive consciousness fed him visions of his own hands strangling the daemon with the gold chain while his more rational self whispered truth—Omage might kill him, but the daemon could not be killed.

"That's what worries me." Badad's voice intruded on the dreamlike image, drew Evan home.

"Huh? Yeah, it worries me, too."

He let Badad pick up the stone, trying to mask the shudder that passed through him. Fingertips stroked his heart, setting that muscle to beat in strange, arrhythmic patterns.

The daemon sighed. "I'm starting to think that Omage never lost this little trinket at all."

"So what's he up to?"

Badad shrugged. "Setting serpents in our garden? I really wish I knew." He put down the mug and walked away with the stone. "Drink your coffee, it's getting cold."

Subject closed. Evan copied the daemon's shrug and drank. "Where's Lily?"

"New Orleans. She wanted fresh pastries for breakfast."

Evan didn't need reminders of their strangeness today. "We have bakeries in Philadelphia," he pointed out.

"But they don't make beignet like this." Lily materialized on the sofa, and set the box of sugary pastries on the brass coffee table. "Is there any more of that coffee, or has Evan drunk it all?"

If she noticed the tension in the room, Lily didn't show it. Evan saw his father relax and relented himself. Maybe the Rolling Stones were right. As family they might not be what he wanted, but right now they needed each other. It would have to be enough.

"Help yourself." Names and dates flickered into green life as the results of the morning's search marched across the computer monitor. Evan turned gratefully to the part of the investigation over which he had some control.

"We've lost him. He's been possessed by the electronic monster."

Brad's sardonic comment slid like a dart through his concentration. He was vaguely aware of the man trading a china cup of black sludge for a beignet, knocking the sugar off before biting the doughnut.

"Oh, Evan, really. What could be more interesting than breakfast at this hour?" Lily, and impossible to ignore, especially stretched out on the wine-colored leather of the sofa. Fortunately, he had his answer.

"Two things, really. Marnie Simpson, for one. I can't find any record of her or Carter Stables before her marriage to Simpson. Not surprising, necessarily. I was lucky to find a marriage certificate—records weren't as computerized eighteen years ago—but I'd expected a bit more, a birth record for Paul Carter maybe, or a death certificate for the mother, information on the horses they've worked with, something. I've set the ferret to look for newspaper photos and cross reference against the society pages in a hundred mile radius of Baltimore, but I don't expect to find anything. With an illegitimate kid in the family they probably kept a low profile. Can't hurt, though."

"Eat." Lily handed him a beignet. "You said two things. What's the other one?"

Typical of Lily to ask him a question as soon as he had a mouthful of the pastry. He swallowed it down with a swig of coffee and hit print.

"Franklin Simpson. He must have known his wife would be upset when Omage snatched her brother, but he went on with business as usual."

"So?" Lily countered. "He married the sister. Why should he care what happens to the other one?"

Looking from his father to his cousin, Evan found no comprehension. He frowned, wondering how they could have overlooked the obvious, then stopped himself. They were different, not superior. For Lily, fast food meant interdimensional travel to her favorite restaurant, but neither she nor Brad really understood about humans and families. Sometimes he let himself forget how different they were, but he couldn't afford to make that mistake on this case.

"How do we know Omage will stop with Paul Carter?" he asked. "Marnie Simpson may be next, but the loving husband hasn't come back to safeguard his wife *or* to give her the moral support humans need when their families are in trouble. No, Franklin Simpson didn't have to care about Paul Carter—he should have come home for his wife."

"Perhaps the happy couple are not all that happy," Brad suggested. He dusted powdered sugar from his fingers and wrinkled his nose. "Damn beignet." He glared at Lily, who met the unspoken accusation with amusement.

"Tasted better than an apple, didn't it?"

"Says Eve or the serpent?"

Evan waited until Brad had washed the grease from his hands at the bar.

"If you two are finished trading Biblical references, can

we get back to Franklin Simpson?" The sharp note in his voice brought his father to the printer.

"So what did you find?"

"It wasn't easy—he's got it hidden behind seven dummy corporations, but Bruce finally cracked it." Evan patted the Batman decal on the side of the monitor. "Among his many holdings, our Mr. Simpson owns an obscure little Greenwich Village nightspot. The Black Masque."

Lily did sit up at that revelation. Brad stopped at the safe and replaced the Eye of Omage—for some reason, it still made him uneasy—before going to the printer. The names of corporations marched down one side of the paper, with the dates Franklin Simpson, or one of his subsidiaries, acquired them on the other.

Evan followed the same information on the screen. A twisting trail led to the Black Masque, but it became clear with a little study that Simpson had picked up the club four years ago. Evan had been twenty then, half mad with dreams of darkness and looking for answers. Omage had been waiting for him, like a fat spider at the center of a web. But had the daemon strung that web, or had the human, Franklin Simpson, laid the trap?

Tearing off the printout, Brad handed it to Lily, who interrupted the brooding train of his thought with another disturbing question:

"Does Marnie Simpson know about her husband's connection with Omage?"

"Not from his financial statement." Evan studied the screen, typed rapidly for a moment, and frowned at the result. "He's hidden the Masque as part of his Viva Mexico chain of Mexican-motif nightclubs. I found it by cross-indexing known addresses against his records."

He pushed his chair away from the desk and pinned

Brad with a measuring stare. "Omage isn't working on his own."

"No." Softly.

Evan knew his next questions would strike at the heart of his tenuous relationship with this—creature—and he felt the threat brooding in the hooded blue eyes. Out of the corner of his eye he saw Lily snap to watchful attention, but he pressed the point.

"But who is working for whom?"

"That's no concern of yours, human," Lirion snapped. She rose from the couch and paced the length of the coffee table and back. A corona of blue flame surrounded her and flared into the room. "Get on your jumbo jet and leave the fighting to your betters."

"Not yet."

Anger sparked his response, and Evan saw it, let it go. Static crawled up his legs, across his arms as Lily's temper flared, but he would not back down. Too much of his past was tied up in his next questions. They *owed* him for that, and he had no intention of forgetting the debt. First they had to understand why it mattered so much to him.

"I never told you what those years with the Black Masque were like. . . ."

"If it bothers you, see a therapist. They get paid to listen. Leave Omage to us." Lirion turned away from him, confronting Badad. "I agreed to this charade for the novelty. Don't make me regret that decision."

Brad nodded. "I know it's been hard for you, Evan, but we haven't time to indulge in soul-searching. After we've settled with Omage, if you still need to talk, we'll listen." He flashed an admonitory glare in Lily's direction. "We'll both listen."

"There may not be a later."

Without waiting for an objection, he plunged ahead and found himself lost in the past he suddenly inhabited again. "I left home when I was nineteen, looking for something. You, I guess."

He came back long enough to acknowledge Badad, who stood halfway between the desk and his cousin with one elbow propped on a bookshelf. Badad did not react to the confession. No surprise there—Evan had long ago given up looking for signs of regret on that countenance.

"At the time I just knew that the dreams were getting worse. I couldn't go on that way. I mean, sometimes it took all I had not to put the gun to my head and pull the trigger. Other times I woke up sure I was dead, and scared that I'd spend the rest of eternity trying to get back from wherever the dreams sent me. I think that was the only thing that stopped me from ending it—the idea that the dreams were what you were left with when you died.

"I must have been on my own for about six months when I met Claudia. We got really close. I loved her, or I would have if I'd been able to love anyone then. At any rate, she loved me and I needed that. We lived together for about a year in a two-room walk-up in the Village. Claudia and I had the bedroom, her brother Jack slept on a cot we used as a sofa in the corner of the kitchen. Jack found out about the Black Masque first, and before long we were regulars."

"Is that the Jack and Claudia you are seeing in London?"

Evan nodded. Caught between the past and the present, he missed the significance his father placed on the names until Brad's next remark: "I thought you were staying away from the Black Masque end of the case."

"They're not involved," Evan assured him. "They were

experimenting with the underground, but Omage was exactly what I was looking for. I'd convinced myself that the dreams were my own evil side coming out when I lost control, and the Masque seemed like the perfect place to explore that part of me. That's how I knew about the goat, by the way. There was a goat's skull, with the horns intact, mounted over the bar, and I asked Claudia about it. She'd read up on it in a history course at Columbia.

"Mac was the bartender—Omage, that is—he told us to call him Mac. He said that anything we did was right as long as we wanted it badly enough. For the others it started out as drink and talk, and a little kinky sex: a dive into wickedness to wash the squeaky clean suburbs off their healthy white skin. For me it was more. I knew what I wanted, all right—an end to the dreams, or at least some validation that the experience was real—I just didn't know how to get it."

The memory mocked him. How he had looked down on the others, thrill seekers of the moment who knew little of the horror that he'd hidden behind a brittle smile. Hell itself had possessed his sleep, and he cursed the cowards who walked away, judging them too weak to face the waking reflection of his nights.

"Pretty soon Mac began to single me out. He said he could tell I wasn't like the others—something about my aura. I almost cut out when he started with the New Age babble. But he told me he knew about the dreams, described them as a place I went in my sleep. He made falling into the dreams sound more desirable than life. I *knew* better, but his eyes—he wanted it, I could feel his jealousy past the smile and the whiskey he slipped me for free."

"He would have hated you for that," Lily broke into the

stream of his thoughts, and he was surprised to find that she had walked over to lean against the desk. "Imagine someone cutting up those precious Picassos you value so highly and using them for toilet paper. You won't even be close, but you get the idea."

"I know that now," Evan conceded. "At first, though, I only cared that he believed me. Then things started getting a little crazy. By then I was drinking most of the time, and Jack wasn't far behind me. Mac started telling the others about the dreams, that I was some freak with a weird power, a gateway into another universe. I thought it was all hype, fast talk to fool the locals, but even Jack started to believe him.

"One night when Claudia stayed home, Jack got carried away with it all. He stood on the bar and slashed his wrist with a butcher knife, balled his hand into a fist and held it bleeding over the goat skull until he fainted. When he fell off the bar, somebody tied a pressure bandage around his wrist and threw him in the alley.

"I tried to stop him, but Jack was too far gone to listen and my own head wasn't that clear either. I couldn't reach the bar, and when I looked over to find Omage, Mac was laughing."

Evan shuddered. "That night I started to believe the dreams actually were a place, and that Mac belonged there. Somehow he'd been trapped here, and he hated us all because of it.

"The police must have found Jack, because Claudia called the next day to tell me they were leaving town. They never came back. I would have gone home myself, but Omage had the one argument that could convince me to stay: he said my father was from the place my dreams sent me, the same place he came from. He promised he would find you."

"More like *I* would find *him*," Brad corrected. "But what has this to do with Franklin Simpson?"

Evan could see that his father knew the answer, felt the air between himself and Lily twist into nervous eddies. She walked away, putting distance between them.

"What if Simpson doesn't just own the Black Masque? What if he owns Omage as well?"

"Only a fool would remain bound this long by a human summons!" Power crackled in Lirion's response; books caught in the pressure wave of her reaction tumbled from their shelves. She raised a hand and the wind died as quickly as it had risen, barely ruffling Evan's hair when it reached the desk. "And Omage is no fool."

"He hates it here—you said so yourself. So why does he stay?" Evan persisted. "Something, or someone, keeps him here. Whether it is Simpson himself, or someone who controls them both, the man who binds Omage is a threat to you, and through you, to me."

Brad picked up one of the fallen books—Frances Yate's *The Art of Memory.*

"You have a solution?" He challenged his son through slitted eyes and Evan's fingers trembled on the computer keyboard.

"If you are already bound, he cannot trap you."

"But we are free."

Evan wondered how his father could pack such menace into four words spoken softly, as a sigh.

"Then why are you here?" He knew the risk he took challenging the daemon, but his own life, and his father's existence in the material sphere, depended on the answers that Evan needed.

Anger flared in the daemon's eyes. Almost, Evan drew back, but he managed to hold his ground while the book in his father's hand curled and blackened. Brad looked down at the volume as it burst into flame, then set it carefully on the brass coffee table. It burned with a hot blue flame and crumbled into ash.

"Host loyalty is a different matter. We exist to do battle for our Prince, here or at home." His voice betrayed no threat, only the arrogance that Evan recognized as part of him. "No human can truly understand. We are the essence of our Prince, he speaks with the voice of the host. When we guard the gateway to the second sphere, we act out of communal need, according to our nature, not out of coercion. A human binding spell twists that nature against us. No human can possibly imagine a bondage so profound."

"Can't I?" He saw doubt pass across Badad's face. They shared a memory of Evan's captivity, but he knew that no altruistic motive would convince his father. Instead, he pleaded the self-interest the daemon would believe.

"If he binds you, he will kill me."

"So he might," Badad conceded.

Not human. The not-like-us realization raised the hackles at the back of Evan's neck. The look on the daemon's face told Evan to weight each word with care, lest it be his last.

"I could bind you, for the duration of this case. Just as a technicality, to protect us all."

Lirion interrupted then, laughing at him. "You are a fool, to risk your life for a bad joke."

The temperature in the room rose sharply. Lirion's expression told him that she found no humor in either the suggestion or the barely veiled threat. Badad never looked at his cousin, but shifted slightly to stand between the human and his daemon kin.

"Have you been listening?" he asked, "Do you have any idea what you are asking?"

"Probably not," Evan admitted. "I'm talking about a binding that lasts days, weeks at the most. How can that matter so much against a life span so long I can't even grasp it as a concept?"

"How long did it take Omage to rape you in that back room? How long to cut your wrists and send you crashing through the second sphere?"

Evan looked away, trying to escape the fire that burned in his father's eyes, the memories that turned his gut to stone. The words he never wanted to hear pursued him. Badad went on, inexorably: "Were you driven any less insane then, because it did not last forever?"

"No." He shaped the word, but could force no sound from a throat closed tight around remembered pain. Then, more clearly, "It wouldn't be like that."

"Yes. It would. Worse, in some ways. Time doesn't exist for us, Evan. It's always 'now.' Don't expect us to put what amounts to torture in perspective; that's a human trait."

Badad's steady gaze never wavered, and the human met it with his own truth. "I don't see that we have a choice. I'm asking you to trust me."

"Does he call up old debts or host loyalty? Not our Evan." Cold menace rode on Lirion's laughter. "Only a human could ask for trust, let alone expect to get it. He's more a fool than Omage ever was."

"You're undoubtedly correct, Lily." Badad finally faced his cousin. "But you overlook one important fact. He's right. We have no choice."

"You've been here too long," she countered, but without

the heat of her earlier argument. "You've grown as mad as
your half-human bastard."

Evan crossed to where she leaned on the wine-dark
back of the sofa, her arms planted like flying buttresses
supporting her on either side. He stopped to look up at
her, his right hand over her left.

"I want to protect you, Lily, not control you. Think of
what he's done to Mac. I can't stand by and let that happen to you."

"Even protection is a form of control," she countered.
"And you will hurt us more than Franklin Simpson ever
could. At least Simpson knows what he does for the enslavement it is. Only you would blindly ask for trust even
while you betray all that is Ariton within you."

Her anger crackled in the air between them. "I can't
stop you from trying, but listen well, monster—" Her fingers twisted under his, nails biting into the soft skin between the tendons that ridged the back of his hand. "Be
careful that you never lose control. If you do, I will surely
kill you, in ways that will make your time with Omage
seem like a wet dream."

Evan gave her a twisted grin. "I never expected anything else from you, cousin. I've compiled the sources I
could find," he picked up a sheaf of computer paper, "and
I think it's all here. Shall we begin?"

Chapter Eight

Magot, the magician, holds sway over hidden treasure, especially precious metals, but is known for trickery and for his evil countenance. Ariton, in other times called Egyn, is the ruler of the northern quarter who lays bare the secret, hidden things. He is known for the vehement force of his temper.

"Not here."

Neither Badad's son nor his cousin had needed the reminder that the study, a room they all considered a sanctuary from the outside world, was a poor choice for the afternoon's work. If Evan were successful, they would never again recapture the sense of invulnerability stamped into every book and chair of the crowded room. If Evan were not successful, of course, little of the study, or Evan, would remain to remind them of anything.

The living room was a marked contrast to the cluttered study. A short hallway led from the street-front offices, the only part of what had originally been two townhouses that retained the Federalist ambience, past the study to the right and the kitchen on the left. Beyond the hall, the walls seemed to fall away. The cathedral-ceilinged room opened up the width of both original houses, and sliding glass doors gave way to the courtyard garden beyond. A staircase seemed to arch unsupported to the second floor gallery and bedrooms, continuing out of sight to Evan's studio on the third floor.

Brad settled himself in the corner of the living room sofa with a copy of Evan's research. Usually he liked the room, not least because it bore the unmistakable presence of Lirion in one of her brighter moods: in the furniture coverings sparsely scattered with oversized daylilies, bright orange against a cream background; in the high polish of the hardwood floors, bare but for a few bright dashes of colorful throw rugs; in the cream walls punctuated by the spare images of the abstract expressionists. Today the bright bars of afternoon light spilling across the floor mocked his yearning for the dark reaches of home, more distant with each tie to Earth. Prisoner of the light, he mused, soon to be bound to the light-dweller, his son.

Evan had opened the wall of sliding glass that led into the private garden. The breeze was too cool, too damp, but no one moved to close the doors again. Brad pretended not to notice when the boy took the nearest chair, at right angles to the sofa, and shuffled through the papers he had gathered in his hand.

Lirion stood with her back to the cream-colored wall, one hand pressed against the invisible barrier of glass. She stared into a distance where Badad had no wish to follow, her face closed and tight around the things that haunted her there. She'd never said how she had been bound the first time, nor how she had escaped. Now that it might prove to be too late, Badad wondered what memories called to the daemon who stood unmoving at the threshold to the garden.

Badad still wondered if he could let go of his own self-will and place himself into the hands of the human. He knew beyond question that Lily would fight, and wondered if Franklin Simpson would prove to be the ultimate winner in the conflict. Weakened by a struggle against Evan, they would never stand against the will that had controlled Omage for four years.

"If Franklin Simpson wanted you, why did he go to all this trouble to attract your attention? Why didn't he just bind you like he did Omage?"

Evan's question struck uncomfortably close to his own misgivings.

"We don't know yet what he wants, but we've probably been lucky so far," he conceded. "Simpson, or whoever is using his corporation to hide the Black Masque, is greedy. He needs our true names to summon us. Omage knows who we are, but he won't give Simpson the information for free. He'd trade us in a minute for his own freedom, but so far Simpson hasn't considered the expedient that would lose him one daemon and gain him two."

Shadows filled his mind. Bound to the will of the enemy, the conflicting commands of Ariton and the human would soon have him as mad as Omage. He filled his eyes with the sight of the earnest young man curled into an armchair of exploding daylilies, a memory to hold through the lifetime of creation. Brad knew that he would kill his son before he would use him as a battering ram between universes.

"Luck seldom holds forever. Omage could have given us to Simpson at any time. Even if this case hadn't come up, we should have taken the precaution."

Evan nodded once, sharply. "It may not be that easy," he admitted. "First I have to figure out how to do it, and half of this stuff contradicts the other half. I can't see the point of most of it. Couldn't you just promise to do as I say and be done with it?"

"It doesn't work that way." Badad reminded himself to be patient, but old patterns of resistance, of battle, gripped him. His human form wavered in dark flame and settled again with an effort. "A binding creates changes at the very core of what our people are."

"Think of surgery." Her voice reached them from the place where Lirion relived nightmares only she could see. "Performed without anesthesia, for the purpose of joining you to a wild dog." Her smile was bleak. "Or, maybe, to a cockroach."

"That's not what you called me last night."

"It's not quite that bad, Evan." Brad interrupted the brewing argument before his own raw nerves pushed him into action without thought, too easy in a body that felt its emotions with the skin and the muscles as well as with the mind. "But the process has never been voluntary. You have to command, to bend the forces of the second sphere to your will. In a way you are at a disadvantage. Because you are half daemon yourself, you know those forces firsthand. They have invaded your sleep since you were a child. And you care about us. Neither of us wants to hurt you now, but we'll fight you—we can't help it— using everything we've got against you, and that includes your feelings about us."

"I didn't know."

"It doesn't matter," Badad pointed out, "because you're right. Simpson would destroy us as surely as he tried using Omage to destroy you."

Lirion let out a held breath and leaned against the wall, staring out into the garden. "Better the devil you know, eh?" she admitted. "Or maybe that should be your line."

This time when she smiled, the resemblance to a piranha was gone. Brad kicked off his shoes and stretched out on the sofa, shifting a pillow under his head. "So what do you need to know?"

"Well, for starters, if this part about four months of chastity is true, we're in trouble."

"What? Let me see that?" Brad skimmed through the list of conditions and stipulations Evan had compiled and snickered in spite of the tension. Sometimes human notions were too strange to take seriously.

"I'm not sure Lily could wait four months for your body, even if we had the time. We can dispense with the child clairvoyant as well."

"That's a relief. Snatching urchins off the streets is frowned on in this century."

Brad heard the lighter tone in Evan's voice with relief. The human would need all the confidence he could muster to pull this one off. Better not to tell the boy what complete shits the most successful practitioners of this particular skill were. Sensitivity just gets in the way when you are trying for raw power, and Brad had his doubts that Evan could be ruthless enough to wield that kind of control. He continued to peruse the list for the ritual detritus that had built up over the centuries: "I suppose we could go out in the woods somewhere, but it isn't necessary."

"In the ninth century, their time, a magician in a fair-sized Ukrainian town summoned a daemon but could not hold her."

Neither man moved while Lily's voice painted word-pictures on the glass. "There's a crater where the town used to be. The townsfolk all died horribly in the fire."

Brad closed his eyes, seeing the moment, the terror and rage she would have felt, forced into corporeal form in this world more alien to their true natures than the second sphere seemed to Evan. Freedom would have been her only thought then, the cries of the dying as meaningless as the tortured screaming of the flames or the crack of the dense forests of fir trees exploding in the heat of her passing.

She turned then, and Badad regretted the knowledge without understanding that drained the color from his son's face. In Lirion's remorseless eyes Evan had found a truth, that she had destroyed the town and all the lives in it, but not all the truth her story had to tell. As well blame the tornado or the hurricane for the damage it does. The fault lay with the hubris of a magician who thought he could tame the forces of the universe to his will. Soon, the fault would lie with Evan.

"I suppose the memory may linger in the warnings you've read," she explained, and only Badad heard the terror and loathing that gripped her still.

"Is that likely to happen again?"

Lily did not answer Evan's question directly. "It was an ugly town anyway."

"And?" Evan prompted.

"And I've gotten used to this house."

She threw Badad a fleeting look that held a promise Evan didn't see. The boy would die without the death of his city on his conscience; she'd contain the damage, if she could.

"That's good." Evan let out an explosive sigh. "Short of the mountains or the Pine Barrens there's no safe place to do this without killing people. And I'm *not* using the Ariton express until Paul Carter is free and Omage is back where he belongs."

"A sensible precaution this time," Brad agreed conditionally. "But you will need a safe place to work. As an alternative to a consecrated room or a clearing in the woods, you can use the pentagram in a circle."

"Is that really necessary?" Evan asked.

"I convinced that old Russian sorcerer that it wasn't necessary." Lirion's bitter laugh rattled staccato irony. "He died, and his whole grubby little town with him, for believing me."

Brad sat up, a hand on the arm of Evan's chair. His son had to understand if he were to survive. "You are bending the forces of two universes to your will. You must believe that you can do it, and you must believe that you are safe while you do. If you lose control for even a second, and you do not have absolute faith in the barrier that you build around yourself, you will be torn to pieces by the forces you are binding."

Lily joined them. Leaning over the back of Evan's chair, she kissed him idly on the top of his head. "Once you have begun, you must not leave the circle until the binding is complete," she admonished him. "Humans die quickly."

She snapped her fingers, and Brad shuddered, knowing in the sound the feel of a neck broken with the bare hands of his human body.

"Life ends messily for the unwary who try to bind a daemon, and if you were Franklin Simpson, I would take great pleasure in your death. But you, Evan—" she carded manicured fingers through his hair, "—you are part of Ariton, of us. We will carry the memory of your terror and pain, and your ending, through all eternity. But understand me—you *will* die."

Evan turned to face her, and she stroked a familiar finger from his temple along the curve of his jaw to his chin and touched the fingertip to his lips. If he read the ambiguous message in Lily's warning—circle or not, she expected to kill him—Brad couldn't see it.

"There are other, more pleasing memories of you I'd rather carry through eternity, little monster, so be careful."

He kissed her fingertip, took her hand in his and kissed her palm. "I'll stay in the circle."

Evan let her go then, and turned to his father. "So far we've got a pentagram in a circle. What do I do from there?"

Badad looked through the various formulas until one made the blood run cold in his human body. He felt the shape waver for a moment, and firmed it up again. "This one should do the trick." He pointed.

Evan looked at the passage. "I didn't know you believed in God."

"It's not a matter of belief. We don't have any stories about a supreme ruler in the sense of your Bible or Koran, if that's what you mean."

"Then there really isn't a God?" The disappointment in Evan's tone surprised him.

"I thought you didn't believe in that sort of thing."

Brad hadn't seen that look on Evan's face since he'd caught his son watching *Peter Pan* alone in the dark. Evan shrugged. "I guess I wanted to be wrong."

"Oh." That seemed to make sense to Evan, though only a human would understand why. But then, "A human might think of the Princes as deities," Badad offered. "Since the Princes are the combined presence of the lords in their host, we would be our own gods. Of course, not even the Princes know what goes on beyond the second sphere. We know there are five more—as many spheres as there are Princess—maybe your God does exist, and we just can't reach it."

"So why this particular spell?"

Badad relaxed a bit. This, finally, was a question he could answer without picking his way through a minefield of human association and irrational emotions.

"Could be any one of a thousand or more combinations, with or without religion," he said. "Could be a grocery list if you could work up an inner resonance to it. The summons works through a sequence of sound-feelings, and the binding through the working of sound and symbol first, and meaning last of all."

"What does that mean?"

"It means," Lily cut in with a fine disregard for Evan's always tricky sensibilities, "that certain sounds, if recited forcefully and supported by a certainty in the summoner, can twist the universes, and draw through the weak spot created there a daemon called by its true name, a sound-feeling that corresponds to one creature in all the known universes. The name has to be exact, but there are almost infinite combinations of commands that can twist the universe.

"This one—" she touched the paper, "—carries the correct sound variables, but it doesn't call on images that might remind you of Omage's back room. It doesn't matter to us, but you couldn't do it if you thought you were as bad as Simpson. This God stuff is supposed to make you feel safe about performing a morally repellent act of coercion against superior beings."

"Give us a choice and I'll be the first one to grab it, and the hell with morals," Evan countered. "I don't want to know how different you are."

"Just promise me one thing," she bargained. "Let me have Simpson."

"If he is at the root of all this, he won't get away. That much I promise." Evan accepted the kiss and turned his attention back to the maze of contradictory instructions.

"It says I need a wand of ash wood."

Badad found the directions on the paper, glad to move into less volatile territory. "Any symbol of the physical body will do," he explained. "The lords you bind must touch the symbol of materiality in your hand when they swear to obey you, but if you reach beyond the circle, you become vulnerable to attack. Besides being your symbol of sexual power, the wand has the advantage that every part of you, including your hands, stay on your side of the circle."

Evan frowned. "Lily's riding crop is about the length of the wand in most of the pictures."

The suggestion kicked the breath out of the daemon. For a moment Badad remained silent, stunned by the slow pain the words started beneath his heart.

"This afternoon will change who we are to each other for all times," he reminded his son. "Do you want the riding crop to be the symbol of what we will become?"

"NO!" Evan's horrified denial lay between them until a sly smile crept across the human's face. "My fishing pole, then."

Brad laughed, relieved to hear Lily's high clear laughter as well. She mussed Evan's hair as she might a terribly clever puppy. "You've never caught a thing with that fishing pole."

"Must have," Evan countered, "because the bait always disappears. Never had the heart to use real hooks, though.

Besides, if I'd actually hooked a fish, I'd have to do something with it, and that would spoil my nap."

"You're an idiot," she pointed out, "but I like it."

"It will do," Brad conceded. With the boy thinking through his symbols, they just might have a chance. "Do you need time to rest?"

Evan shook his head. "Better to finish it now. Give me half an hour to pull something together here."

Brad considered using the half hour to drift in the second sphere, but reconsidered. No point in tempting fate or Franklin Simpson. Lily met his eyes and shook her head, the warning understood and accepted. She preceded him up the stairs and stopped in front of her bedroom door.

"Can he do it?" she asked.

"Maybe," Badad answered. "If not, he'll be dead and Simpson won't need us anymore."

"That's not what I want."

"I know."

"Now that it's a question of who instead of when, I keep getting this urge to look over my shoulder, in case Simpson is breathing down my neck." She turned away, her head hung between drawn shoulders. "I don't like any of this."

Her bedroom door closed on the last words. Brad sighed and followed her example. Nothing to do now but wait.

Chapter Nine

The names of the seven great Princes are known to man, but the names of the daemon lords who make up their hosts are held close-guarded. But if a man can learn the name of a daemon lord, he may summon him, and bid him do his pleasure. But if his pleasure is to do evil, he will soon find his will overborne by the seduction of the daemon, who is terrible in countenance but who may take on a seemly appearance to cajole his master.

Evan waited until he heard the second door close, then he went up to his third floor studio. He ignored the easel that faced the north window and rummaged through the bottles on a shelf over the drawing table. The white seemed right: fill his circle with brightness rather than the black and brooding pentagram that weighed down Paul Carter's bed. He grabbed the tempera paint and the wide brush he used to gesso canvases, and headed for the garden.

A high brick wall protected him from being seen. Evan cleared the lawn furniture from the center of the courtyard and opened the glass doors to the living room as far as they would go. Then he began to paint a five-pointed star on the bricks. The background hum of traffic on Spruce Street and water splashing over rough, mica-flecked stones into a shallow pool hidden behind the tulips and the daffodils wove themselves into the gritty press of brick against his knee, and he filled the star with the sound and touch and smell of spring and home. When he finished the star, he knelt at its center and stretched outward to paint a circle around it.

The final stroke closed the pattern like a gate locking, more solid than the glass behind which the daemon would appear, and Evan wondered for a fleeting moment if he had the power to leave the circle at all. He dismissed the feeling as a trick of the imagination, tightened the lid on the paint, and stepped over the white lines to clear away his supplies.

He found the fishing rod in the attic and considered making a detour to the office for the topaz hidden in the safe. He resisted the urge. His attraction to the Eye of Omage unnerved him; the sense of security it gave him felt false at its core. He turned instead to the corner of the attic where he'd stashed the few things he'd brought from his mother's house and dug through the big square box that represented the first nineteen years of his life. It was still there, and he closed his fingers around his first drawing pen, drew it from the box.

When he was ten, and the dreams were so strong he sometimes forgot where the waking world ended and the dreams began, he would draw himself real again, endlessly. Those strange, twisted images of torture and despair had frightened his mother and disturbed priests and doctors alike: they read the plea for help, but could not find him in the wild place that trapped him. Finally, it was the images themselves that saved him. If he could draw the feelings, they must be real. In the images of his pain in pen and ink he found proof that he existed.

Until he found his father at the edge of madness, his grimy rapidograph had been Evan's personal symbol of his own humanity. Now, the images meant more to him, because they represented in pictures what he had not known in words: two universes struggled for possession of his soul. Time and again in his drawings, Evan had thrown his allegiance with the material sphere. He carried the pen to remind him of his choice, made at ten and at every moment since, to be human.

He knocked first on Brad's door, then on Lirion's to alert them that he was ready to begin, and returned to the tempera-painted circle in the garden. Grabbing a cushion from a lawn chair, he sat himself cross-legged at the center of the pentagram with his fishing rod across his knees and called upon his father and his cousin to submit to his command.

"With a tranquil heart, and trusting in the Living and Only God, omnipotent and all-powerful, all-seeing and all-knowing, I conjure you, Badad, daemon of darkness, and you, Lirion, daemon of darkness, to appear before me in the human forms by which I shall know you."

Shadows thickened around his protected circle, and grew into a scream torn from hell. Wind howled its accompaniment of rage, and somewhere nearby glass exploded. Pain. Unending waves of pain danced on his nerve endings. Evan knew that only the circle protected him from the full force of that agony, but found himself drawn to the screaming faces twisting in the shadows. His determination wavered for a moment.

"I never wanted this," he whispered, but the knowledge

that Franklin Simpson would have no such qualms hardened his resolve.

"Appear before me in the human shapes by which I have come to know you. Now!"

At the sharp command the shadows coalesced. Sunlight glinted off the splinters of glass that still hung in the door frame, jagged halos around his father and his lover who started toward him through the glittering shards scattered on the threshold. He recognized their forms and faces, but Evan's mind refused to accept as the same beings these creatures who paced just beyond the limits of his tempera fortress. Blood flowed from a cut on Badad's arm, left a smear on the jagged glass, and soaked its way unnoticed down his shirtsleeve, while the daemon spat threats at the human who dared summon him.

Lirion lured him with open arms, her hips thrust forward in a way that would have been enticing, except that he saw no recognition in her eyes, just the promise of death if he looked deeply enough.

"Come on, Evan. You know you want it." She unbuttoned her blouse, shed it, slipped out of her trousers, stood with her hands on hips clad in a scrap of lace as blue as her eyes, considering him.

"I can be anyone—" She smiled, and suddenly the reflection of his father stood nude before him, arms out. "Evan—" His father's voice, offering himself in counterpoint to the threats and curses of the bleeding original.

"Don't do this, Lily." Too many feelings tumbled out of locked places in his head to sort them out, but shame and sorrow lay like a wash over them all. He didn't want this knowledge, this bone-deep comprehension that they were different—not human, not bound by the feelings of a human—and that a part of him might be like them. He backed away, would have run but the circle stopped him.

"God, please don't—"

"No?" Lirion, in the form of his father, shrugged naked shoulders. "I can be anything for you."

With Badad's voice she laughed, but hatred burned out of the daemon eyes. "Risk is everything."

Lirion shifted again. Crouching before him, she became a panther—sleek and dark, with eyes that promised hell and dared him to love her. She growled, a deep animal sound that raised the hairs on the back of his neck, and he wanted to touch her, to run a hand over her back. He wanted to roll and tumble with her like they were two cubs tussling among the flowers, wrap his arms around her neck and bury his face in the thick, sleek fur that collared her. He lifted his hand and let it drop again, confused and frightened by the feelings that drove him and sickened him at the same time.

She transformed again: Lily Ryan, naked and flushed, wanting him. Evan bowed his head, buried both hands deep in his own hair, and tried to hold back his grief. What was the point of it all, if they had nothing left when he was done? Memories supplied the answer. Omage, with his father's face, driven mad until only the pain and terror of his victims made him feel whole. Lily, cold as frost, telling of a centuries-past captivity, a town dead for her freedom.

"I have to do this," he told her softly, and stood to demand the oath that would bind them to his command.

At that moment, Lily's face contorted, her lids fluttered, and she fell with a low moan into Badad's arms.

"We can finish this later," his father snapped. "Right now she needs help."

Evan took a hesitant step, and Lirion gasped, barely able to breathe, and curled in around her pain.

"Lily!" He dropped the fishing rod and went to her, dropped to one knee at her side.

Lirion looked up at him, and her smile curdled his blood. No time to retreat, they were on him. Hands reached for his throat, contorted into monstrous shapes before his eyes. In that moment he knew he was dead.

The pen in his pocket jabbed at his leg then, and he found himself suddenly unafraid. He remembered the night, dream-walking in the emptiness, and knew that the red-eyed beast that slavered over him, jagged fangs reaching for his throat, had led him home and loved away the sick dread. Whatever became of them now, she would always be the flame that had steadied him on the road home from places he once traveled in solitary madness. And Badad, whatever he might be, had once defied a universe to save Evan's life.

The shield of his certainty drove them back. Screaming foul curses in languages no human mouth could form, they hurled their own dread and pain at him, and Evan reached out, said the words to end the agony, to bring them home:

"You are summoned by the Honor and Glory of God, by my Honor that I shall cause you to do no harm or injury to others, and for the greater glory of all creation both in the physical sphere and in the second sphere. By this I demand your oath: that whenever and every time you shall be summoned, by whatever word or sign or deed, in whatever time or place, and for whatever occasion or service, you will appear immediately and without delay. You will obey the commands set for you in whatever form they shall be conveyed."

Then he realized the fishing rod still lay in the pentagram. Standing there, he felt the trap close around him.
He'd left the circle. Should be dead; would be if he
backed down now. But he needed the symbol of the physical body to tie them to the material realm. A wand. A
pen. He drew the rapidograph from his pocket, clutched
it tightly in his fist for a moment, then opened his fingers,
held his palm out like an offering, and met the eyes of the
creature he called father.

"Swear."

The image wavered, drew in upon itself, and strength-
ened again. Kevin Bradley, disheveled and shaking with
rage, the blood from the wound in his arm falling, drop by
drop, onto the bricks, stood before him and the daemon's
words fell like stones in Evan's heart:

"I curse the seed that spawned you. I curse the world
that shelters you. I curse the form and substance of your
existence. You are nothing, bastard monster of two universes, wanted by neither. In other times and places your
back would have been broken at birth, your twisted life
sucked back into the void before your first cry. I can still
correct the oversight."

"You could have, once," Evan agreed. His fear was a
slinking thing gnawing at the bars of his concentration,
but his hand held steady, the grimy white pen lying like a
scar across his palm. "But not now. You will swear your
oath to me, because we need each other."

Chaos churned in the blue eyes of the daemon, as
Badad searched within himself for the lie in his son's
words and found a truth he never wanted to hear. Evan
read the struggle in the trembling hand that reached toward him. When Badad touched him, he closed his fin-

gers around those of the daemon, the pen clasped tightly between their two palms.

"Swear," he repeated, calm now, and Badad nodded.

"I swear."

His father was changing subtly before his eyes, the lines of his face shifting out of old, familiar patterns into new maps of tension, but Evan had no time to ponder the transformation. A second daemon was poised to strike, growing darker and more terrible as she fought the familiar shape he had forced upon her.

"Swear," he commanded, and he projected all of his own frustration, his fear that even now Franklin Simpson might steal what was Evan's by right. Evan Davis was human, and could command if he had the strength. He was also of Ariton, and he had the right to demand loyalty of the lords of that Prince. He had the *right*.

"Swear. By Ariton."

She stood before him in the form he knew by touch in the dark and he held her gaze, waiting for the stroke that told him host loyalty held no power for half-breed monsters.

"By Ariton," Lirion answered, "I swear." Her hand bypassed the rapidograph extended on his outstretched palm, and instead rubbed familiarly between his legs. "Symbols are fine for strangers," she explained, "I prefer the real thing."

Evan sighed, his head tilted back, unsteady now that it was over and he found himself still breathing. "You can stop now," he hinted.

"Is that an order?"

She nibbled on his ear, but even her warm breath down his neck could not distract Evan from the mindless exhaustion that suddenly possessed him: "I need a nap."

She removed hand and teeth from his person with ill grace. "So that's the way it's going to be—"

Real distress crossed her face. Her grand exit ruined, Evan thought. Then he realized what that meant. He owned them. He commanded their movements now, and he hated it.

"I'm sorry. Let's get this over with right away." He stuffed the pen back into his pocket and took Lily's hand. "By my command, and until I next summon either or both of you, you will come and go as you please, and make decisions as you choose, except you may not answer the summons of any other, and you must answer my summons as you have sworn. Until and unless I formally summon and command you, you will treat me as you would do before the oath was sworn.

"In plain English," he finished, exasperation leaking out of every word, "unless we're in trouble and I have to use it, let's pretend this whole thing never happened."

He answered Brad's cocked eyebrow with a shrug and threw an arm around Lily's waist. She was working on his ear again.

"Aw, Lily, give it a break." Evan's head dropped to her shoulder.

"Is that an order?" she repeated.

Lily turned snide into a high art, but his father came to Evan's rescue. The daemon threw one arm around the shoulder of his cousin, and the other around the shoulder of his son.

"I think," he explained to his cousin, "that Evan has a headache."

This time, Lily accomplished her exit with panache. Evan's ears rang with the thunder of imploding air where she had stood. He gave his father a doleful look, and when hearing returned, informed him, "You're bleeding all over my shirt. Come into the kitchen and I'll see what I can do."

"Is that . . ."

Evan glared his father into silence. "Don't be an ass about this. I meant what I said at the start. It's just a technicality, so that Simpson can't get his hands on you."

He led the way into the kitchen and pulled the scissors and first aid kit from a drawer. "How are you going to explain this to your tailor?" Rhetorical question. Evan held up the sodden shirtsleeve, fine swiss cotton worked by Carlo Pimi from his little shop in Milan, and tossed it in the trash. "You need stitches."

Kevin Bradley shook his head. "Just bandage it, I'll take care of it later."

Evan did what he was told, almost afraid to disturb the uneasy peace with the questions he needed to ask.

"Have we lost everything?" he asked, his eyes firmly fixed on the scraps of gauze and tape that littered the counter. He didn't want to know, didn't want it put in words that would make it so.

"What do you think we had?"

"Don't know," Evan admitted.

"Maybe it is lost," Brad said, and his tone made Evan wonder what the last year had meant to his father.

"But if you mean, will Lily come back on her own, without your summons, probably. First she needs to find out for herself that it's not just a trick, that she really is free. The question is, what will you do when she does come back?"

Evan shrugged, staring into the sink as if the garbage disposal held some answer if he could only fathom it in the fall of the blades. "That wasn't Lily."

"Yes, it was."

Evan felt hands on his shoulders, turning him. He faced the man he'd found after a lifetime of searching, the father who was not a man, not human. Sorrow filled the eyes that glinted with the color by which Evan knew him in the second sphere.

"You can't keep pretending we're just folks who happen to disappear now and then. I meant everything I said to you, I still do. You make me feel things I don't understand. I believe you when you say you want to protect me because I have protected you and felt pleasure doing it. But even the pleasure of watching you struggle and succeed passes through the anger and pain of your creation. If I'd had a choice, you wouldn't exist, but I didn't, you do, it matters, and in all of creation I have no idea why that should be.

"For Lily it's different. Her rage runs deeper, and I think even she doesn't know why she agreed to stay in this sphere. But what you have to know is, to win free of you this afternoon, Lily would have offered anything she thought would pull you out of that circle. It worked the last time, because the man who summoned her wanted to use her, and more than a thousand people died for his mistake."

"But I *did* leave the circle," Evan objected.

Brad smiled. "Not to take anything from her, but to help her. In a way, your own stupid certainty saved you. Think of it as a test, and you passed. She'll come back, in her own time, if you let her."

Evan searched the calm eyes, warm now, settling back into familiar patterns.

"I hope so. In the meantime, I've got two hours before I have to leave for the airport and I'm going to spend it in bed. If the world comes to an end while I'm asleep, just leave a note."

He left Badad standing in the ruins of what had once been the living room, and ambled up the stairs without a backward look. Sleep caught him facedown on the bed, one shoe still dangling off his foot. He didn't quite waken when a soft body snuggled against his back, but his dreams grew more peaceful.

Chapter Ten

An' a man bind a daemon he must take care that his commands be clearly spoken and in such words as the daemon may not construe the command to do harm to his master. For the daemon looks always to be free, and the unconsidered word can be used against him who binds the forces of the spheres, even to his death.

In the dim light of early evening, Badad came to rest in the frigidly clean kitchen. None of them cared much for cooking, so the room saw little use. The service came in once a week, collected the coffee mugs and Coke bottles, and dusted the appliances. No memories here.

The old ceremony hadn't seemed so final with Evan in the house. Patching up the cut that ached a little if Brad let it, or sleeping in the studio-bedroom overhead, Evan demanded nothing. The boy acted as if he hadn't changed all the rules between them in a single afternoon. Then Evan was gone, and the truth hit him. Bound in blood and bone and the essence of his being in the second sphere, Brad had wandered through the house, absorbing the shock.

On automatic, he headed for the study. Evan's computer still blinked on the desk. Electric tentacles reached into data banks, lifting a bit here, a bit there that would fit together the jigsaw puzzle of Franklin Simpson's life. Evan was a real artist, and the modem-linked PC the boy called Bruce Wayne was his finest medium. If he hadn't had such rigid scruples, Evan could have been a better thief than Lily. *Was* a better thief—had stolen the freedom of two daemons who knew enough to keep from falling into any human traps. He'd suckered them both, and realizing that the human didn't really understand what he had done didn't help much.

Too many memories, learning to accept each other, feel safe. He'd burn the house to the ground just to forget the ragged thing he'd brought here a year ago to hide, to heal. Drifting between some dreadful longing and insanity, his arms carved up like a Thanksgiving turkey, Evan had thrashed out the nightmare of his captivity in this room. Brad remembered how Lily'd sworn at him for a fool while they filled the study with foam rubber—the clutter had come later, it was just an empty room with no windows then.

For two weeks they'd taken it in turns, following the daemon essence of the hybrid human into the second sphere and bringing him home again. Later, when he trusted Badad because the daemon was his father, Evan had let them teach him something of his nature in the second sphere. He'd learned that he could survive there, could find his way back, would be safe in either universe. So much for safety.

Out of there. Avoid the living room. Shattered glass and broken furniture beat jagged memory against raw wounds of binding—bowline knotted around his spine, tethered him right through the gut to the human. Evan was flying over water; Badad felt the pull of the tide and knew the bastard didn't even notice it. There was no justice, and somehow it gave Badad no pleasure to realize he'd been right about that all along.

Coffee. Might help the head at least. That's what brought him back to the kitchen, a set piece out of someone else's house. Only the coffeemaker worked overtime here. He cleaned out the old filter and put in a new one, put too many scoops in and didn't care, watched the water drip through it in a daze, and then poured coffee— mud thick enough to pass the spoon test—a mixing spoon would stand upright in the stuff, until the bowl disintegrated. Alone in the semidarkness he sat, trying to forget.

"Any more of that in the pot?" Lily slid onto a stool at the breakfast bar and bleared at him through sleep-puffed eyes. She took the cup he passed her, drank, and grimaced. "Now I know what humans mean by suicide."

"You came back."

She quirked an eyebrow at him. "Clever of you to notice, cousin."

"Evan thought you might not forgive him."

Lily pursed her lips, considering. "I haven't decided. He hasn't asked for anything yet; that was a surprise. It's what brought me back, actually. I thought if I confronted him, he'd do something, and then I'd know."

"And?" He'd expected a shrieking virago to descend upon him with a roil of storm clouds, had looked forward to blowing off some of his own steam in the explosion. An introspective cousin just tightened the screws pressing at each temple. Her answer didn't help.

"He was asleep. It seemed like a good idea, so I took a nap. I felt him kiss me once, on the cheek. When I woke up, he was gone."

The thoughtful frown lingered for a moment, then

Lirion's face smoothed into elegant neutrality that hid none of her confusion from Badad.

"I'm still trying to understand what happened. Men are pretty predictable about sex. If you can make the offer before they make the command, they're past their own defenses like their pricks are on fire. Evan was a sure thing—or so I thought. He's never turned me down before. And you were no help at all, standing there cursing him like a fishwife. When you saw I was getting nowhere with him, why didn't you try to seduce him?"

"The thought crossed my mind," Brad admitted. It really was funny, if his head didn't hurt so badly, and if the rope through his gut didn't twist when he thought about Evan. "But I knew it wouldn't work."

"You mean you don't have sex with him?"

"Never."

"You've missed a treat there." A smile tried to break through, fond memories rising through the morass of a wretched day. Then curiosity— "But if he doesn't like sex with men, you could have taken another form—"

"The form didn't matter," Brad explained as patiently as he could. It hadn't made sense to him at first either. "Would you merge with a lord of Azmod?"

Her horrified stare was enough; he knew her answer, the same as his own. Merging with one or two lords of your own host was pleasurable, but the merge created a force. When enough lords entered a merge together, a Prince rose of and out of that force. They *were* Ariton. When they merged as a Quorum, they became their Prince, the group mind shaping the will that directed wars and alliances across all of the second sphere. A lord who merged outside of his host risked entrapment in the group mind of a potential enemy. No daemon would even consider it.

Badad stated the obvious and followed with the obscure: "We don't merge with lords outside our own host, humans don't have sex inside their own kinship group. Omage in the shape of a bag lady could seduce Evan faster than I could if I created my form out of his own fantasies."

"What?" Lily's surprise took her voice into a register audible only to bats.

Brad shrugged. "I couldn't get a very clear story out of him at the time. I was trying to convince him it was an innocent suggestion, while he packed a suitcase to leave. He kept talking about idiots and two-headed babies and having me arrested."

"And which one of you was going to be mother?" Acid sarcasm, Lily's specialty, dished up with a fine supercilious curl to the lip.

Brad laughed. With Lily to goad him, thinking about Evan almost didn't hurt. "I don't think it's rational, cousin. It's just human: they're not supposed to sleep with relatives."

"So what does that make me?"

"When the discussion arose, he hadn't decided. And according to Evan-logic, if you can't figure out what the relationship is, then it must be distant enough not to count."

"Oh." Lily thought about that for a moment. "How do they do it?" she asked, then clarified the question. "For us, being human is like a game. Sex is a fun part of that, but I've never felt anything like host loyalty with anyone but Evan. The ones like Evan, though, born human with one body, one lifetime—how can they trust that to a stranger?"

"You taunted him with the answer to that one," Brad reminded her, a little proud in spite of himself. Evan was turning out to be one tough bastard, and some of that toughness was Ariton. "They risk everything."

"Like he did this afternoon." Lirion didn't mean sex.

Brad nodded, Evan's treachery, never forgotten for long, twisting the knot around his spine. "I didn't think he could do it, sure wouldn't have cooperated if I suspected he'd actually go through with it." He rubbed his head because he couldn't reach the pain in his gut. "I thought we'd taught him something about loyalty. . . ."

Lily took his hands, pulled them gently to the counter between them, and curled her fingers around his clenched fists. "You are looking at him through two sets of eyes, cousin. The body you wear believed he cared about you, and it feels this afternoon as betrayal. The lord of Ariton can only see what Evan did as unnatural—no lord can bind another to a personal will. The one set of eyes you haven't looked through is Evan's."

"And you do?"

Lily snorted, a very unladylike sound, one she usually reserved for Evan at his most obtuse. Brad wasn't sure he liked it aimed at himself.

"Let's just say I see the boy a little more clearly. He's a good lay, and affable as humans go. But he's only a human. Ariton is in there somewhere, I'll grant you that. Life burns brighter, quicker in him than in any other human I've ever seen. Sometimes I think I'll singe my fingertips just to touch him.

"But he's tried to bury that part of himself for all the

short years of his life. You can't expect him to act like a lord, because he isn't one."

"Even humans don't hold slaves, and that's what he's made us. How could he do that?" His son. He'd risked so much for this human, and now the binding tore at his gut like rope tore the hands clutching for dear life and slipping, wave-dashed, into the sea. He'd trusted Evan, alone of all humans, and his payment was a harsh lesson in reality.

"It hurt him, cousin." Lily gripped his hands more tightly, urgently, as if she had to share a newly discovered truth. "He took nothing I offered but left himself defenseless when he thought I was in pain. He held us because he believed it was necessary, and he's asked for nothing."

Brad searched her face for anger like his own, and saw an uneasy peace there. Intellectually, they both understood the need that drove Evan to bind them, but:

"It hurts." Not like any physical injury this body had ever known, it was the meaning of the pain he could not bear. Hurt worse the last time, but it hadn't mattered as much. That human was just a jerk, in over his head and with a case of the nasties for a woman who'd had the good sense to reject him. Not Badad's son.

"You killed Nicodemus Minor for doing this to you. How can you defend it in your lover?"

His cousin smiled a secret smile. "What does it feel like?" she asked.

"Rope." He rubbed the place just below his heart.

"Who holds the rope?"

Brad's mood darkened, but his glare didn't seem to bother Lirion one bit. "Evan, of course."

She shook her head, slowly. "You do." Her eyes dropped to their locked hands. "I thought the same thing," she said. "Then I left. When he didn't stop me, I just let go. That's when I knew he meant what he said. He is our shield, not our master. You can let go now."

Brad needed time to think, but already the room lay in darkness. He could just make out the mass of Lily's body, deeper shadow among shadows. Only the glow of her eyes seemed real to human vision. They had a job to do, and not much time to do it in.

"It sounds like you've forgiven him."

Surprise colored her answer: "I guess I have."

Slowly he let the fingers inside his gut unclench, let the rope slide free. He was alone in the darkness with Lily, and glad she couldn't see his face. Why did he suddenly feel abandoned?

"We have a little time," she said, and uncurled his fists, laid her palms against his open hands.

Badad thought of home.

Chapter Eleven

Beware the wrath of a daemon, for his memory is long, and his rage can bring mountains to their knees, or raise up mountains where mighty oceans ruled.

Home. Badad stretched, found joy in his own boundlessness. For a brief span of moments he could feel himself free again, unconstrained by a human body, a human master, or the edict of Ariton. He spread himself thin on the wind of creation, reached into the heart of stars to warm himself, felt each whorl and eddy of life that passed through him, unheeding or unknowing that he held them in the cold light of his consciousness. He longed for infinity, forever beyond the reach even of daemon lords, and reveled in that piece of the universe he filled like a lover.

A mind like his own, but brittle and sharp, full of laughter, touched him. He contracted, drew himself in on the sensation of Lirion's presence. He'd known they would merge from the moment she had taken his hands in human form and given him back his freedom. He still felt the binding, but as a tenuous link that neither let him go nor restrained him. He thought of labyrinths and balls of thread, human myths. As far as he could imagine that string would unwind. Should he find himself trapped, lost in some tangle of deception or captivity, he need only follow the thread back to its source. He'd never thought of Evan that way before—as guide, as defender.

Lily picked up the thought and teased him with it, a mind picture of Evan as a small boy, dirty-faced and ragged-kneed, stubborn and bellowing. Was that how he treated Evan? She replaced the image with one of her own—a man, mysteries begging to be discovered in smoky topaz eyes half hidden behind the chestnut hair that defied every effort short of a razor to control it. Lily would never permit that; the hair was a warning, like the muscular arms, the narrow hips, the strong, slim legs. This Evan exuded power freely, like sweat. Evan?

Laughter answered, and the two images merged. Which was true? Neither and both, but a chrysalis struggling to become what none of them could imagine. What would it mean to be of two universes, and survive the tidal pull between them? If Evan survived, he'd be the first. If they succeeded tonight, Paul Carter would be the second. Badad wondered if either sphere was ready for two of them.

The acrid thought fell between them, colored their merging with bittersweet tensions. They shared memories beyond time, relived the great beginning when the material sphere pressed relentless patterns into the flow of infinity, savored battles between Princes, quarrels and merging and separation again, a past untouched by humans.

Deliberately they avoided thoughts of the night to come, and of all the nights that had led them here. Now they would recapture what it meant to be Daemon Lords of Ariton. The essence that was Badad mingled with the essence of his cousin, and they felt the rush of purpose.

They were Ariton, and the power of Princes was their being. Their minds became one mind, with room only for sensation. Dense as a point, they reached toward that unattainable infinity, and knew the sweetness of each other. The bitterness of the battle to come only brightened the pleasure of the here and now: nothing existed except the single creature they had become, and they would hold that feeling like a weapon, defying the Princes and all the universes to tear them apart.

Badad felt the thinning, lessening of what they were, held on and sensed Lirion resist the separation. He knew her sorrow for his own, alone with only the memory of her presence. Himself again, he longed for that other thing that was not self but unity, that was Ariton.

Reality tilted, shuddered with alien presence, and Badad tasted fear and madness. Paul Carter, he guessed. Omage once again storming the bastions of the universe with half-human flesh. The distortion wave rocked them, passed on.

"We have to go now." His thought flickered in the darkness, and an answering flicker told him she knew.

They entered the material sphere through a dark alley that clung to disreputability on the not-yet-rehabbed fringes of the East Village. Drizzle glistened on the discarded plastic trash bags and brought a dull sheen to the broken macadam path between two buildings of Baltimore brick that sagged in on each other overhead. Across the street, deep gutters lined with flattened beer cans, crack vials, used condoms, the death's-head still leered from the swinging board sign above the door to the Black Masque. Black door, white bones glinting on the rain-washed black sign, smoked brick walls with no windows—the bar faded into the night. The door opened and closed again, spilled sound into the street but no light. The music throbbed like a fever, died with the closing of the door.

"This place is still a pit," Lily snarled softly next to Kevin Bradley's left ear. As they usually preferred when taking human form, they both wore black, Lirion a tailored jumpsuit in soft leather, white lily stitched on her left shoulder, Brad in slacks and sweater, a loose jacket pushed up at the cuffs. A bit upscale for this part of town, the clothes gave them freedom of movement without compromising on the aesthetics. Omage would hate that.

Lily rested one hand on his shoulder for balance and pulled unidentifiable trash from a black boot heel with the other, her nostrils pinched against the smell of urine and garbage in the alley. Spent hypos crunched underfoot when she shifted in the darkness beside him.

"You do have his trinket, don't you?" she asked.

Brad wore the smoky topaz beneath the sweater, suspended from its chain around his neck. It still felt cold where it touched his skin. He reassured her with a silent nod, then: "Let's get this over with."

He checked for witnesses to their unconventional arrival, but the street was empty. They crossed and entered the bar.

It hadn't changed much since the last time. Black candles flickered in the myriad holders, shadows closing and separating in the breeze of someone passing close to the flames. Bikers in leather and drifters in whatever scrambled for a place at the long bar, their faces gaunt and twisted in the candlelight, gleaming phosphorescent in the glow of the blacklight strobe.

Brad elbowed his way to the bar and threw down a twenty. "Where's Mac?"

The bartender pocketed the twenty and went on wiping glasses beneath the skull of a goat that still hung like a trophy over the bar. Dark stains fell between the upswept horns, splashed the skull, and washed over one empty orbit. The bones looked broken in the light of the strobe, the pieces suspended in the emptiness. The back room was worse, and the memory sank its teeth in and shook Brad hard. The bartender looked him over, took in Lirion at his side, and pursed his lips in a silent whistle.

"You friends of his?"

Brad gave his coldest smile, wild blue flame lighting his eyes. *Enemy,* that look said, and, *stand clear.*

"Let's just say we come from the same old neighborhood. Wanted to look him up before we went back."

The bartender considered for a moment. His glance shifted to Lily and found the same danger curled at the corner of her smile. He shrugged.

"If you know Mac, you know where to find him."

Brad nodded and let the press of the crowd carry him away from the bar. The music, too loud, pulsed through him while around him bodies moved to its rhythm, dancing, undressing each other in the corners, in the dark, white skin of breast and buttock glowing lavender in the strobe. Lily was with him. He felt her at his side, reaching out a hand to stroke a passing crotch as they cut through the tangle of grasping fingers and heaving flesh.

At the end of the room a woman crawled up the leg of a man standing over her with his jeans dropped to his thighs. A second man, on his knees on the floor, pushed into her in time to the music. Brad stepped over the kneeling man's legs, and met the glazed eyes watching him over the woman's hips—confused, child's eyes, seventeen at the most. Trapped in the rhythm of the music, the

THE EYE OF THE DAEMON

boy seemed to sense the deadening of his own soul, accepted it. The older man reached for him over the body of the woman, and the boy moved into the touch. Brad looked away, the connection tearing like a vein.

The door to Omage's back room was in front of him. Brad turned the handle and went in.

Nothing had changed. Ranks of candles cast golden light on the symbols crusted on the walls. Blood filled his nostrils, the smell, fresh with the fear and sweat still tangy at the back of the throat, mingled with the rust and corrosion of past offerings. Sometimes taken when not offered; Omage never wasted time on the niceties. The tumbled swastika that had poured from Evan's slashed wrists caught and held him. His son hadn't offered.

Omage had seen the power in Badad's son, had twisted that glittering flame to control the drifters and thrill seekers, to turn them into followers. Within the Black Masque Evan Davis had been a god, until the god wanted out. Then Omage's promise to give him reasons, to find his father, had ended in this room, shackled to the chair on which the daemon lord now sat. Here the dreams became reality. Cast alone into the silent darkness of the second sphere, Evan Davis had gone insane.

The memory of his son's torture in this place filled him with silent rage. Badad regretted only that he had not leveled the place to the ground when he'd found Evan.

"Omage, lord of Azmod." He acknowledged his adversary with a cool nod, never relaxing his guard.

"Badad, Lirion, lords of Ariton. Welcome."

Omage sat enthroned on his raised chair. Candlelight sparked the gold threads in the robes he wore, flashed off the rings that circled each soft finger. He gestured expansively with his free hand while the other trailed fingers lazily through the lank blond hair of the man chained at his feet.

"Humble as it is, I call it home."

Brad felt Lirion tense beside him and shifted onto the balls of his feet.

"Up to your old tricks again," Brad observed.

Paul Carter slumped against one pedestaled chair leg, his eyes turned inward on his horror. His steady whimper rose to a shriek, once, and he beat his head on the leg of the chair until the blood ran into his eyes. Semiconscious, he subsided into aching whimpers again.

The sight revolted him. Badad wanted no part of this broken creature, shared Omage's rage against the humans who subjugated lords to torment each other. But he remembered another boy in this room, taut at the limits of his chains and daring his father to strike him dead. Lirion shivered next to him, and Badad knew she remembered Evan in this place as well.

Her voice broke through his memories.

"Why are you doing this, Mac?"

Omage smiled and stroked Paul Carter's hair. "Because it pleases me." His eyes mocked the lords of Ariton, settled on Badad. "They are nothing, cousin. Nothing."

"They are our children." For Evan, not for Paul Carter.

Omage pursed his lips, shook his head, a charade of concern that the lord of Ariton should bother himself over a few bastards with a glimmer of the second sphere about them. "Not *my* children, surely," the lord of Azmod pointed out with calm reason. "Nor yours, nor Pathet's. Did you enter that woman of your own free will and leave a child there? No, a human trapped you in his circle and commanded you to ruin a life here, whisper a secret there. If that one hadn't been as stupid as most of mewling humanity, you'd still be bound to his call, just like I am to my master."

Impotent fury edged Omage's voice as he finished his explanation: "I destroy them because it pleases me, and it is the only pleasure he has left me."

Omage turned to the boy chained at his feet, drawing Badad's attention to the hand stroking Paul Carter's hair.

"Speaking of pleasure, cousin, how is Evan? Well last you saw him?"

He'd been expecting it, but still the question, drifting casually out of the middle distance, tied knots in Brad's gut.

Omage looked up then and smiled. "He was special, you know—not like this vomitous wreck that Pathet produced. Evan actually tried to kill me."

He laughed. "Of course, he didn't know how it is with us, but it did give me an uncomfortable moment. Human flesh is so vulnerable to injury, you understand. Feeling it die is disconcerting. Not an experience I would like again, but something new, done once, nevertheless.

"I stranded Evan in the second sphere for a week after that little trick; it took that much to break him."

Lirion grabbed his arm before he could raise power against Omage, and Badad let the reminder guide him. A conflict of force at the level simmering just under the surface would level a square mile of crowded city real estate. As a rule, Badad left that kind of urban renewal to the humans. And they had contracted to get Paul Carter out of there alive.

"Don't you think it's time you told us what you really want?"

"Want?" Omage paused, as if considering a new concept. "I want Evan back. For now, however, I'll settle for the return of my trinket. You do have it?"

Badad spread his hands wide. "The Eye of Omage?" He mimed incredulity. "It's melodramatic enough, I'll grant you consistency on that score, but it scarcely gives us much information to go on. Why don't you let the boy go, and we can work this as a straight contract. Cut out the middleman, so to speak—he doesn't seem to want the job anyway."

"You always did act the fool, Badad. I even know the moment it passed into our dear Lily's hands. Now, would you like to return my property, or would you prefer to see Mr. Carter perform for us?"

Omage pulled on the boy's chains until Paul Carter's head rested on his knee, his neck contorted, his breath coming in labored gasps. "Fly now, boy," the lord of Azmod whispered, and flicked a knife deftly across a distended vein. Omage had used that knife to open the veins in Evan's arms, and the blood that had dripped onto his son's clenched fist seemed to mingle with Paul Carter's blood dripping slowly onto the hand that held him. Wide-eyed, Carter screamed, his entire body rigid. Badad felt the shock rip through the boundaries between the spheres and echo in the place where Evan's binding chafed at his being. Omage winked out for a moment, appeared again as life returned to the corpselike man at his feet.

"When you are free of this, you will have to answer to the Princes," Badad warned, but he took the necklace from around his neck and held it up to the flickering candlelight. He eyed the topaz with contempt, and cast the same glance wide to include its namesake. "You can have it when you let the boy go."

Carter reacted to the glint of the gem. The dull-eyed

gaze drifted over Brad, past him, focused hungrily on the jewel in his hand. The boy reached out for it, but Omage shook his head, face set in mock sympathy.

"My dear, dear Badad, you still don't understand. The stone is only half the prize. Still," he brightened with artificial cheer that revealed the sneer lurking behind it, "Pathet has doubtless procured the other half by now, so we can call the bargain concluded.

"As I recall, I promised to release this young man from his misery in exchange for the Eye."

The knife flashed in midair and clattered to the floor between them. "You will take care to honor the letter of the exchange? His death should cause as little pain as possible. I'd suggest a quick thrust upward starting just below the sternum, entering the heart thus—" The knife flew into the air and hung suspended just pricking the skin of the chained man.

Too late Brad saw the light flicker in Paul Carter's eyes. The boy reached out, touched the blade with hesitant fingertips, then grasped the hilt in his right hand. He wrapped his left around the leg of the chair, fingers drifting over the intricate carvings, and steadied the hilt against the chains knotted there. With the knife caught between the chair and his body Paul Carter tightened his left arm, pushed against the knife. The blade plunged deeply. Blood spurted over the carvings on the chair, ran down the silver chains.

"Aahh." Carter smiled, released from his prison of nightmares at last. His eyes fluttered, opened with a hopeless sanity that offered Badad gratitude for long-sought peace. Finally he lay still.

"How many?" Badad asked softly, the gold chain of the Eye digging grooves in the hand clenched around it. The question was for Omage, but he never took his eyes from the body on the floor. Once, it might have been Evan's body. Could still be, if Omage had his way. "How many children who carried the fire of the Princes in their blood have you killed?"

The answer fell coldly between them. "One less than I wished. Evan still lives, until my master finishes with him."

"You are a stain upon the face of creation, Omage, and I will tolerate no more." Badad spoke softly, but the rumbling began at the sound of his voice. He gathered power and focused it deep in the bedrock on which the city rested, split stone and tore it just under the Black Masque. The floor buckled under them, tumbling candles from their sconces and heaving jagged teeth of paving stones back upon themselves.

Omage stood before them but made no move to stop the destruction. He raised his arms above his head and spun away in smoke, his laughter riding on the night while the wrath of Badad cast the Black Masque into smoldering dust.

Chapter Twelve

To the nature of a Prince of the second sphere each daemon lord brings both his nature and his talent, the first of which is his name, the second of which makes itself manifest in the employment of the secret arts. And of the daemon lords, Omage is named the Magus, magician and tempter, and in his name and the name of the Prince the summoner may demand both knowledge of the secret arts and all manner of treasure not yet known to man.

"Need a taxi, meester?"

The voice was familiar, the accent atrocious. Evan Davis glanced around for its source, and found him easily; tall and rangy, with the long loose stride of a Midwesterner, Jack Laurence towered over the English and European travelers like a corn-fed Paul Bunyan. Evan relinquished his suitcase, grateful for a friendly face after the ordeal of Heathrow Customs.

Matching the man's pace with an effort, he cast a nervous glance at his old friend. Jack wore his blond hair short now, his features thrown into harsh relief with no gold fringe to soften them. He caught Jack looking back and laughed, embarrassed. So, they were both worried.

"Need to sleep for a week, but I'll settle for a ride into town," Evan agreed. "How's Claudia?"

He kept his tone casual, but they both knew the question carried more than polite interest behind it. Claudia, whom they once called the sensible one because she drank less and kept them fed, had loved him. She'd never liked Mac—Omage—but she'd put up with the barkeep for Evan and her brother, until the Black Masque had almost killed Jack. Evan hadn't seen her since the phone call almost two years ago, when she'd said it should have been him in that alley, and that she was taking Jack away. They were running, as far and as fast as they could, and from him, knowing Jack wouldn't have done it for Mac. Somehow, around Evan, things just got crazy.

Jack shrugged, following the train of thought with an ease he didn't hide now that Evan had brought it into the open.

"She's stopped hating you for what happened that night, but she still cries a lot when she thinks about you."

"I'm sorry."

"Yeah, well, I'm supposed to find out how sorry you really are before I bring you home."

He should have expected this. Jack had sounded pleased to hear from him on the phone, but then, Jack had never blamed him for that night. Looking at the man walking next to him, matching him stride for stride across the burgundy-and-gray mosaic carpet, he realized that Jack did accept him with no questions about the past, or his present. But he still had to convince Claudia.

"Let's drop my stuff at the hotel," he suggested. "Then we can talk over a couple of those huge English breakfasts and a cup of bad coffee."

"Not on your life," Jack grumbled. "Most of the stuff

they serve here tastes like yesterday's dishwasher. I know a place on the way where the coffee may take the enamel off your teeth, but you can recognize what you are drinking. They even serve their eggs without beans if you're forceful enough. Then we'll decide where you'll be staying."

"I have reservations—"

The glare that bought him stopped Evan's objection. "Lead on, MacDuff," he agreed with only a twinge of foreboding at the poor choice of phrases. The last time he'd said those words, they'd just found a new little bar in the East Village. Maybe it was hindsight, but he'd felt his life turn on its axis that time, too. The feeling didn't get any better the second time around. Jack frowned, remembering, but he said nothing as he tossed Evan's case into the back of the battered yellow Volkswagen and ground the reluctant transmission into gear.

The eggs were greasy and the coffee—well, it wasn't tea, Evan had figured out that much. The place didn't even aspire to a decor, but they found a quiet table in the front window of the café, as far from the kitchen and the other patrons as possible.

"So," Jack began over his steaming mug, "you called from Philadelphia. Do you see much of the old New York crowd these days?"

"I left the Black Masque over a year ago."

Evan set his own mug down carefully, hiding the feelings the name conjured behind half-closed lids. "I would have gone sooner, but I couldn't." He rubbed a thumb back and forth across the scars on his wrists, hidden by his shirtsleeve, knew the gesture for nervousness and suppressed it.

"I know that feeling," Jack misinterpreted, speaking of a time when they hadn't wanted to leave. "Took waking up in Bellevue with a cop and a shrink hanging over the bed to pull me out. And Claudia, of course. Don't know what I would have done if she hadn't stuck by me. She's happy here."

Evan heard the warning—don't hurt her again—and regretted his decision to come to London. Too many memories lay between them, and too little understanding. Jack had gotten out before Mac turned nasty, before chains took the place of persuasion. Any explanation of that last year would only open doors on the horror Evan had come here to escape.

"I don't want a rerun of the bad old days, or to mess up anybody's life." he answered, knowing it was only partly true. He didn't want to hurt anybody, but if their friendship were to survive, some old wounds might need a painful cleansing.

"I'm still trying to make sense of my own life, and you and Claudia are a part of that. If there's nothing left, okay, I'll let it go. But we meant something to each other, damn it, and I have to find out if there's any of that left."

"Hey, buddy, we're still the dynamic duo," Jack assured him with a thumb upturned in the flier's salute. "I've missed your weird sense of humor—haven't met anybody else stupid enough to go along with my harebrained schemes either. Catwoman speaks for herself, though, and she's been nervous as a long-tail in a room full of rocking chairs since you called. Afraid you'll lead me astray."

Evan shook his head. "Not me, Jack. I meant it when I said I'd left all that behind. I knew I had to get away from Mac the night you carved up your arm and we watched you nearly bleed to death.

"Great show. Yeah," he murmured bitterly to himself, then remembered his audience: "I wanted to stop you, to help somehow, but I couldn't move. It was like we all became part of one ugly, snarling animal—circling dinner."

The words snapped off leaving jagged edges. Evan was afraid to go on, to confess a part of that night he had never told, not even to Brad. For Jack, because he owed him the truth—sure. Would have said so once. He knew better than to lie to himself now. He needed to say it all, to be forgiven. But not here, over greasy dishes surrounded by strangers.

The café seemed smaller with the subject of the Black Masque on the table. Evan glanced nervously at the counter where the short-order cook lounged in conversation with the room's only waitress. Logic told him no one could hear, no mark announced to a disinterested world that the men reminiscing at the window table had once danced on a daemon's string. But logic had nothing to do with his sudden craving for breathing space.

"Let's get out of here."

Jack Laurence must have felt the walls leaning in to catch each whisper as well; he called for the check and paid it. Evan followed him into the gray London morning. They turned away from the car parked in a lot—car park, Jack had called it—and walked toward the river. Rush hour traffic clogged the street. Soon tourists would find their way to the water's edge, but they'd still be in bed now, or waking up over hotel breakfasts. He wondered where Brad and Lily were, and a part of his mind felt numb when he thought of them. Paul Carter was safe now, or dead. Either way he could do precious little about it—he'd run. Though it was the sensible thing to do, he still felt guilty. Maybe that's why he'd decided to come to London in the first place. He felt guilty about Jack, too, but he could do something about that.

They were alone together on the footpath along the Thames, and Jack was waiting for him to finish what he'd begun. Time to clear the slate; Evan took a deep breath.

"We—I—watched you bleed," he said. His voice faltered, then grew stronger: "Each drop fell like a caress." He could feel it still if he closed his eyes, like fingertips stroking his throat, choking him while his skin crawled with wanting. Death-drug—death. He shook his head, denied the feeling its power, felt the wind, nothing but a cold damp mist blowing off the river, and spoke of the Evan then and now:

"Part of me hated it. I felt like I, Evan Davis, had somehow gotten locked in a tiny room in my own head. I was beating on that door, frantic to get out, while my body responded to the sight of your blood like your death was my lover. Something in me reached out to you, I wanted to feel your blood on my fingers and stroke my own body, anoint myself with the sensation of your dying. Sexual, but something more—" *Like the river.* The thought wrapped itself around his tongue, another mist like the one rolling off the Thames, tiptoeing up his arms, wrapping cold fingers around his heart and squeezing—

"Death was a sacrament we all shared. Then we were touching each other—didn't matter who, or who touched us. I don't think I even saw you fall."

"Yeah. That's how it went down, all right."

Jack Laurence nodded his head, expression grown distant, and Evan realized his own self-absorption that night had blinded him to the truth.

"You felt it, too?"

"Of course I did." Jack softened the retort with a slow smile that faded almost before it began. "I'd never tell the docs this—they'd lock me up again—but, God, nothing before or since has ever turned me on like that."

Laurence paused. The Thames flowed an arm's length from where they stood, but Evan doubted the man saw it; his eyes focused somewhere beyond the river. If he gave them half a chance, the same images would be leering at Evan from behind his own eyes, but he stayed in the present, kept the Thames at his feet. The past was dead.

Without turning, Jack picked up the conversation again with an apparent non sequitur: "Remember when Claudia was taking classes at Columbia?"

Evan nodded, then realized Jack hadn't seen the silent agreement.

"She told us how the Aztecs used to sacrifice their own people, cut out their hearts, by the tens of thousands." Laurence continued without prompting, but he did flick a quick glance at Evan. A sharp nod acknowledged the memory shared, then Laurence went on:

"We thought they were crazy. How could a sane human being willingly accept his own death like that? Well, now I know.

"My blood was a gift, my life a sacrifice for the pleasure of my God. Dying, I loved him. You. I felt my energy fill the crowd and their hands were my hands, their bodies my body. I was all of them—men, women, I felt what they felt, my energy fueled their frenzy."

"I'm no god, Jack. Not even close." Evan kept his tone low, but he couldn't entirely soften the implacable edge to it. Whatever he'd come here for, it wasn't to fulfill the fan-

tasy Omage had spun around him. Jack accepted the re-
buff with a sigh.

"I know," Jack admitted, "But you're not one of us
either. Behind your back we used to wonder what you
were—an alien stranded here or sent to judge us, the next
step in evolution, an angel."

"That was all nonsense," Evan lied. "I was somebody
Mac could use, and he made up the rest."

Jack answered with a bitter laugh. "Just because I act
like a fool doesn't mean I am one. Claudia was the only
one you ever convinced of that line, and you had hor-
mones working for you there.

"No, I made my mistake when I let myself believe I
knew what you were, and that we were important to it.
Don't ask for an encore—"

"I didn't ask the first time," Evan reminded him sharply.

"I know that, too, Evan; hear me out. I wouldn't do it
again, but I've never regretted that night. If I had it to do
over, I probably wouldn't change a thing."

"That's where we differ." A little of the terror that had
sent him to London leached the color from his face. "If I
could do it over, I'd stay on Rosemont Street and go to
Temple University like the rest of the kids in my neighborhood."

Jack shook his head. "And the nightmares?" he asked,
and Evan looked away, ambushed by the shared memories.

"Does Temple give courses in night terrors and astral
projection now? Health 101—how to cope with life as a
displaced deity? You needed Mac more than any of us. Be
that honest with yourself if not with me."

Honest. Evan felt the weight of chains again, saw the
face of the creature sent to kill him—his father.

"Before you left, Mac called me a god. Afterward, when I wanted to leave, he made me his prisoner. Yes, I found what I was looking for, but the price was too high. I'm not the only one still paying it; you and Claudia were my first victims, but not my last."

He remembered his father, snarling and wishing him dead, and Lily, who had tried her hardest to kill him just hours ago. The rewards of godlike power, he realized, were not eternal worship, but the bitter anger of the captive for his jailer. If Omage hadn't called them, using Evan's own terror to destroy the barriers between the spheres, the human would still be living half a life, lost between two universes, maybe locked in a state mental hospital by now. But Lily would be free in that place she loved. Brad, his father, would never have had to stand between the child of his captivity and the destruction of his home. The price for his own peace of mind had been the freedom, almost the lives, of those he had come to love.

"Honest," he said. "Knowing what I do now, I couldn't go through it again.

"This was a mistake," Evan concluded. They stood side by side, watching the river. Like the Thames, their apparent calm concealed rapid currents pulling them farther and farther apart. "We can't change the past, but here I am trying to do just that. Could still use a ride to the hotel, then I'll be out of your life." The south of France was lovely in April. Peaceful. He could be in Nice by evening.

He turned away, putting the river behind him. "I could take a cab, but you've got my stuff in your trunk."

"Boot," Jack corrected absently. "Claudia will want to see you. It will hurt her if you leave without saying good-bye."

Evan turned his head, met the question in Jack

Laurence's eyes, and smiled. "You're a bastard, Jack, and you play dirty. I'll see Claudia, but I won't stay."

"We'll cross that bridge when we come to it." Jack's confidence did nothing to reassure Evan. He suffered the hearty clap on the back with patience born of experience and followed Jack back to the car.

Chapter Thirteen

Lirion is the name of the one also called Lilith, the Lily of Heaven, lover of beauty, and lover of men. If anything be stolen, command her, for she knows all things of thieving, but be cautious. Lirion returns only part of what she regains, and she has been known to steal the heart of her master, crushing it in her grasp.

"This is Layton," Laurence announced as the yellow Beetle wheezed its way up a small hill lined with shops and turned onto a quiet residential street.

"Reminds me of Brooklyn," Evan commented.

The Volkswagen bucked to a halt in front of a narrow white house with a well-tended postage stamp of a lawn surrounded by a freshly painted white picket fence. Claudia probably had roses growing in the back garden. Evan got out of the car and stared hard at the upstairs windows, trying to see past the sheer curtains to the heart of the house beyond. The fifth floor walk-up they had once shared in the Village seemed very far away now. He remembered Lily and Brad trading Biblical badinage just days ago, and wondered if he were not himself some messenger of downfall or, less flattering still, just the apple an unsuspecting Jack Laurence carried into his sister's new-found Garden of Eden.

Jack opened the door and ushered him into the front hall next to a steep flight of stairs. "Claudia!" he called. "I've got a weary traveler here, looking for a little comfort."

"Evan!"

The squeal preceded the flying bundle of Claudia, launched from the staircase with a fine disregard for the laws of gravity or momentum. The force of her landing drove Evan backward, sandwiched between soft full breasts and a hard plaster wall covered in a faded pattern of palm fronds and bamboo lattice.

"I can't breathe," he gasped, quailing at the determined glint in her eye.

"You need mouth-to-mouth resuscitation," Claudia announced. She moved her hands to the sides of his face, traced the shape of his skull with a sculptor's attention, and pulled his head down to meet her upturned mouth.

The Red Cross might not have approved Claudia's version of first aid, but it had a certain appeal. Evan surfaced from the kiss with a grin, the dark memories of the morning burned away in the warmth of her greeting.

"Of course, I've always thought breathing was over-rated," he approved with a squeeze and a nibble.

She nuzzled at his mouth, drifting lips from corner to corner, and pulled away with a smile. "I've missed you, too."

"I can tell. How are you?"

"Late for work, I'm afraid." She glared at her brother, but affection softened the exasperation. "I wanted to see you before I left, but I have to run."

Evan finally took time to look at her, and noticed the

spring coat she already wore. In many ways, Claudia and Jack were opposites. Where Jack was tall and angular, Claudia only hit five feet with her shoes on, and she fought a never-ending battle with her bathroom scale. At that moment she seemed to be winning, but Evan knew from past experience she was closing in on her stalemate point. Her hair had once been as blonde as Jack's, but had turned a soft brown when Claudia was a teenager. For a while in New York she had colored it; Evan was glad to see she'd let it return to its natural color. Somehow, this Claudia belonged in a house with a picket fence and roses in the back. Sanctuary. The word rose unbidden in his mind, and labeled the feeling that grew in the light of her warmth. The past could not touch them here.

"I've made up the back room for you." Her words cut through the fog of his wandering attention. "It's barely more than a closet, but I've moved the boxes of books into the attic, and borrowed a foldaway cot from Nancy-next-door. Got to run. Jack, feed him some tea and get him settled. I took the afternoon off. Meet me at the shop at lunchtime, and we can show Evan the sights."

She gave him a quick hug. "Missed you," she repeated, and left on the run, the door slamming behind her.

"London suits her," Evan commented, pulling his eyes away from the door that still seemed to rattle on its hinges. "The question is, can London cope?"

Jack snorted. "They're used to the type," he returned, "Napoleon wasn't much bigger."

"But Napoleon didn't have Claudia's smile. I guess I'm staying."

"Too right, old chum. If you try to back out now, she'll have my head on a plate and then come looking for yours." Jack swept up his suitcase by its shoulder strap and took the stairs two at a time.

As promised, the room was the size of a moderately luxurious closet, and the foldaway cot dripped loose springs when Evan thought about lying down. But he dismissed the room waiting for him at the Savoy without a thought. Claudia's house enfolded him in her warmth; he felt her presence in the bright throws that covered the shabby sitting room furniture, in the rug loom that relegated the Victorian dining room furniture to a pile of chairs stacked on the table in a corner. Her rugs—exotic strips of velvet and lamé and glitter woven into abstract bursts of light and dark—hung on every wall. He didn't quite believe the one in the kitchen.

"Is that what I think it is?"

Jack looked up from the jar of instant coffee and rolled his eyes. "Yup. Bread wrappers. Every couple of weeks she takes it out back, sprays it with the dishwashing liquid, and hoses it down. Half the neighbors have them now. Only uses the English ones for Christmas—"

"Why Christmas?"

"The colors," Jack explained. "English supermarket bread comes in red and green packages, mostly, but Mom's bridge club in Dayton saves Wonder and Sunbeam wrappers for her and sends them over. Sort of a latter-day 'bundles for Britain.'

"The first few shipments arrived opened, then we had a visit from our local postal inspector. I don't know whether he thought we were making napalm out of hot dog bun wrappers or we were part of a colonial plot to flood the Island with Yankee refuse. Claudia sent him home with a Sunbeam yellow sunburst for his wife, and that was the last we heard of him."

Evan took the steaming mug Jack offered. "Leave it to Claudia," he laughed. "Maybe the State Department could use her in the Middle East."

"Bread wrappers for peace? Don't even think it," Jack warned. "We'll be hip-deep in plastic before the words are out of your mouth."

"She won't hear it from me." Evan raised the mug in a mock toast, bringing him face-to-face with the wide-eyed kitten painted on its side.

Jack lounged against the side of the sink. The mug in his hand had a picture of dogs playing billiards painted on its side.

"She still loves you, you know," he said too casually.

Evan stared into his coffee. He'd hoped to avoid this conversation, at least until the past day or two had faded a bit around the edges, but Jack wouldn't let it go.

"If you mean it about being done with Mac, you could pick up right where you left off. Remember how we used to plan it: you married to Claudia, us, brothers. The old trio—we'd be unstoppable."

Claudia in the bedroom, the loom in the dining room, and roses on the white picket fence. If they argued, Claudia might char the pot roast, but she wasn't likely to turn Evan into a pile of ashes on the carpet. He shook his head at the kitten on his coffee mug. Then he met Jack's eyes, defenses down and all the turmoil of the past week stamped on his features for a brief moment.

"Too much unfinished business," he explained, thinking of his father and Lily. They were tied by the command of Ariton and by his own binding for Evan's lifetime, a commitment he had made in return. Out of the corner of his eye he saw Jack Laurence rub the scar on his wrist, and he wondered again if coming here was a mistake. It seemed like he dragged shadows of the past with him wherever he went.

"I'm still trying to figure out what I am, and Claudia deserves more than that."

Laurence shrugged. "You've still got time to change your mind." Jack rinsed his mug and set it down on the drainboard. "In the meantime, we'd better get moving. When it comes to lunch, time and Claudia Laurence wait for no man."

Time. He checked his watch, still set on Philadelphia's Eastern Standard: 7:00 a.m.. If the night had gone as planned, neither Brad nor Lily would be pleased to hear from him at this hour, and Claudia was waiting for him.

"The door is this way, man." Laurence grabbed a handful of Evan's shoulder and turned him toward the back door with a solid nudge. "The tube will get us there in no time." Evan slapped his own mug on a counter and preceded his friend from the house.

They left Tottenham Court Road Station with a crowd of tourists and shoppers but after only a few short blocks Jack directed him off congested Charing Cross onto Denmark Street, a narrow, doglegged side street with more bookstores and pubs but a few less tourists. Jack led him to a shop with a swinging sign from another century that said "Thomas James, Bookseller" in Gothic script. A little bell above the door tinkled to announce them when they entered the shop, but no obsequious Uriah Heep of a clerk scurried from behind the old oak bookshelves to curl over wringing hands and beg to be of service. Instead, Claudia's cheerful but disembodied voice greeted them:

"I'll be right there. If you don't see what you want, I can check in the back for you in just a minute."

"Don't rush," Jack announced them. "It's just us chickens." He headed for the back of the shop and folded himself into the swivel chair in front of the ancient secretary desk while Evan prowled the stacks. Dickens—he'd been right about that—the shop was crammed with the novels in a variety of languages and all sorts of editions. Other shelves held the Brontës, Thackeray, and Eliot. He passed by the Browning, considered a Coleridge, and finally decided upon a copy of Walter Scott's *Ossian*. Brad would enjoy the irony of the Scots novelist and poet creating an epic with which to establish the Romantic antecedents of his dour nation. *Vanity Fair* tempted for Lily, but he decided that she wouldn't appreciate the joke.

"Excuse me, please, but you sound American."

Evan turned, found the source of the tentative comment walking toward Claudia from an aisle labeled "Travel."

"That's right," she agreed, hanging a dusty smock on a hook next to the desk.

The stranger was well dressed, tall, with sharp, dark eyes that cut to the bone and a faint hint of Europe in his Queen's English.

"Perhaps you could advise me on a matter of national etiquette," the stranger suggested. "But I haven't introduced myself. I am Count Alfredo DaCosta, and I recently made the acquaintance of a lady of American extraction."

Evan stopped, just out of DaCosta's line of sight, feeling like he was fooling no one but himself. The thief had to know he was there, somehow had linked Claudia and Jack to him through God knew what contacts the man had in the underworld. But DaCosta ignored him, playing out his game.

"I wanted to send her a gift to remind her of our visit together. I thought this might be appropriate, but—this is so embarrassing—I don't want to presume on our short acquaintanceship."

"Let me see, Mr., uh, Count—" Claudia didn't fluster easily, but DaCosta was smiling. Yep; this one would know what to do with ten dancing girls on his front lawn all right. Claudia pulled herself together with a little shake of her shoulders that reminded Evan of other days. She took the book bound in gilt and leather that DaCosta held out to her. "Ruskin's *The Stones of Venice*."

"We met in Venice, you see," DaCosta explained, "and the lady expressed a fondness for the stonework of that city."

Claudia nodded her head, reassuring the Italian count. "The Ruskin will be a nice memento, then. Shall I wrap it for you?"

"Please."

She took the volume to the cash register and rang it up. "What brings you to London?"

Polite small talk, but Evan could have kissed her. Just the question he would have asked, if he'd had a mind to add his own presence to the meeting he had given up as coincidence in its first minutes. DaCosta was as smooth as ever.

"There's an auction at Sotheby's tomorrow. They have a Matisse I'm interested in, though, Lord knows, between the Japanese and the Americans I'm not likely to get it. Sorry, I don't mean that as a slur," DaCosta hastened to add. It's just that old family fortunes don't go as far as they once did. Still, I thought I'd take a look myself. Have you lived in London long?"

"Just two years." She handed him the book. "I'm sure

the lady will enjoy it." A subtle reminder, there, that flirting with one woman while buying a gift for another might not be quite appropriate, even for an American. DaCosta accepted the hint with good grace, taking his book in exchange for a traveler's check, and turned to leave the store. Evan stood his ground and DaCosta gave him a brief nod suitable for strangers passing within a foot of each other in a place both might consider their own private find, but Evan saw recognition and something else—challenge or warning—in his eyes.

Taking it as a challenge, he spoke up: "Good luck with the auction. The Ruskin should be a winner."

"I'm sure you must be right . . . as an American." DaCosta nodded again, and left the store.

Claudia looked from Evan to the closing door and back again. "What was that about?"

"Nothing." He'd leave, tonight if he could get a flight. Or maybe he'd take the ferry, rent a car in Calais, and motor up the coast, maybe stop to do some sketching along the way. He could use the warmth of Nice. Right now, he didn't think he'd ever be warm enough again.

"Right, Batman." Jack added his opinion from his chair at the back of the little store. "Tell us another one."

Evan sighed. "He may be a friend of a friend. Or he might not." May be a friend, most likely an enemy. He knew Lily had taken the Eye of Omage, but how the daemon had lost it to DaCosta in the first place remained an uncomfortable mystery. "I never met him before, if that's what you mean, and he never mentioned her name." Half-truths, but his friends seemed willing to accept them for now.

"Oho, a she. That explains it, then." Jack unfolded out of his chair and sauntered over to the cash register.

"Couldn't expect you to spend the past two years as a monk, now could we?" He waggled his eyebrows suggestively.

"That's enough, Jack." Claudia took Evan's book, the Walter Scott. "Let me see that. You know Scott faked it, don't you? If you're really interested in folklore, you'd do better down the street; we can stop there after we eat."

"We can stop anywhere you want after lunch, but I know the story. Instant history—thought my father would get a kick out of it." He kept his face cheerfully neutral for her sharp scrutiny.

"You found him, then?" She hesitated for a moment, then finished wrapping the book in brown paper. Wary, her voice seemed to tiptoe around the fences Evan put between his feelings and the outside world, giving him the space he needed while she seemed to concentrate on tying off the twine. With Claudia he didn't want the fences, but he couldn't imagine just blurting out the truth either: *He's a daemon. Wasn't really happy to discover he'd left half-human get behind him, even less enthused when his boss from outer space told him he couldn't come home until I was dead. So far I've kept him intrigued enough not to off me and split. And by the way, I'm sleeping with his cousin, who is also a daemon. She gets kinky thrills having sex with human men—must think I'm okay in that department, because she hasn't offed me yet either.* No, that part of the truth was definitely out.

"Actually, he found me. He has his own detective agency: found me, got me straight, took me into the company. I work for him now, have for over a year."

"I'm so glad."

She rewarded him with a hug, enveloping him in the radiance of her goodwill. He took his package, putting aside the sudden uneasiness that he'd just been praised like a puppy who hasn't peed on the parlor carpet when he's been locked in the bathroom all day. Usually only Lily could make him feel like that—maybe it was just a guilty conscience.

Jack rescued him from drowning in introspection. The man draped one arm over Claudia's shoulder and the other over Evan's. "It's been a long time since breakfast. Can't we chew the fat over meat pasties?"

"Bad joke, brother-mine." Claudia rolled her eyes, patted Evan's hand. "You'll understand soon enough, no reason to scare you ahead of time." She called through the door to the back room, and waited until the porch-swing-in-need-of-oiling voice of her employer acknowledged her good-bye. "We're off," she announced.

Her brother dutifully picked up the straight line: "But not so crazy that we'd miss lunch." He shepherded them out of the shop.

A leisurely walk brought them to Covent Gardens—the place, Evan decided, where flea markets must go when they die. Vendors of luggage and cheap imported clothes jostled for floor space with record sellers and purveyors of china mugs with pictures of Big Ben on them. Jugglers and painted mimes and a trio of brass musicians playing marches vied for tips in the courtyard. Claudia led them past tables of questionable antiquities and the white elephant from Aunt Mary's attic to a food stall where she ordered three pasties and the same number of teas, "Because it's authentic."

"Purists," Evan accused with mock disdain as he brushed pasty crumbs from his fingertips. Not even the strong milky tea could wash away the savory and suet taste of the meat pie. "London has McDonald's now, you know." He crumpled the cardboard teacup and took aim at the cracked plastic wastebasket.

Jack Laurence blocked the shot, and the game was on then off again when Claudia took the cup from his hands and placed it meticulously in the center of the receptacle.

"Behave yourselves," she warned sternly, "or Mummy won't buy you a sweet."

"She's been here too long, Jack."

The rangy Midwesterner sighed and shook his head. "I'd have her deprogrammed," he explained, "but then I'd miss out on my sweet."

"You're both insane." Evan led the way to a flower stall and picked out a bunch of violets which he presented to Claudia with a grand flourish and a bow. "For the loveliest lady in London."

"Is that Evan Davis? Davis, it is you."

The familiar voice cut across Claudia's response, jarring Evan out of his playful mood. He turned and found the source of the voice coming around the flower stall with his hand extended. The man wasn't as bad as Lily made out—balding a bit, and the thick tortoiseshell frames of his glasses weighed heavily on his otherwise nondescript features—but what the hell was Charles Devereaux St. George doing in London?

"Mr. St. George."

Evan took the outstretched hand, surprised as always at the firmness of the grip. Lily's influence, he supposed; it wasn't Charlie's fault he had the shape and complexion of a beached flounder. He remembered a comment Lily had once made, that a man with as much money as St. George ought to own better fitting suits. This one looked like it might have fit ten pounds ago. He smothered an incipient grin and refocused on the man in front of him.

"No need for formality—strangers in a strange land together and all that. It's Charles." The newcomer addressed the correction to Claudia, bending his head in the merest hint of a bow. "And the lady is?"

"Claudia Laurence, Jack Laurence, her brother—old friends from college. And this is Charles Devereaux St. George, a client of our agency."

Evan completed the introduction, and held his breath. Since his arrival he'd been deliberately vague about the agency. The feeling that he'd abandoned his post—somehow failed that part of himself that was not human—lay too close to the surface for dispassionate discussion, and DaCosta already had ghosts walking on his grave. There were no coincidences in this business, and nothing would convince him synchronicity had brought the thief and his mark thousands of miles from their usual haunts to the same few square blocks on the same day. Knowing his client, Evan would bet that whatever was going on, Charlie would get the worst of it. But St. George beat him to the question of the day.

"So what brings you to London, Davis? An elusive Rembrandt? A disappearing Degas?"

"Just vacation, Charles. Visiting old friends, sightseeing, like any other tourist."

"I know—" St. George winked broadly and raised both hands, palms out in surrender. "You can't say."

"Not this time, Charles. Just vacation."

"They really are the best," St. George said in an aside to his avid audience of two, ignoring Evan's protestations. "But then, you must know that better than I."

He returned his attention to Evan. "And how is the charming Lily? I did so want to thank her personally for her efforts on my behalf. Having the Mont Parnass back in its place fills my soul with peace."

"Our fee was ample expression of your gratitude, Charles. But I'll pass along your appreciation when I go home."

"Thank you, my boy, but perhaps I'll call on Miss Ryan myself when I return."

"I'm sure she'd like that." Evan almost choked on the words, but he managed to keep his expression attentively neutral. Only someone who knew him very well could have seen the devil clicking his heels behind the placid smile. Jack Laurence knew him very well: The man followed the conversation as if it were match point at Wimbledon, his eyebrows arching higher at the obvious falsehood.

"In the meantime," St. George went on, apparently oblivious to the undercurrents of the conversation, "I have another matter I'd like to speak to you about. Had planned to call the agency when I returned, but you can save me a trip if you're amenable. It's not exactly your usual line of work, but I'm in a bit of a bind, time-wise, and I'd consider it a personal favor. Can we talk over dinner, perhaps? I'm at the Claridge, your friends are welcome, of course—we can discuss the confidential details later, if you decide to take the case."

He intended to beg off, planned to be gone by then, but caught the murder in Claudia's eyes. Her expression said "adventure"—a glimpse into a world of money and privilege she had only read about in books—and Evan admitted to himself there could be no harm in dinner. Charlie St. George might be as dull as Philadelphia in November, but he wasn't dangerous unless he tripped over his own feet and fell on someone. And whatever the man had on his mind could give him a graceful way to cut short his visit.

"All right, I'll listen."

St. George beamed at him, one hand on Evan's arm, the other shaking Evan's hand. "Eight thirty. I'll be looking forward to it." He shook hands with Jack Laurence, and then turned his full attention on Claudia.

"Not violets," he said, taking her hand and brushing lips just above her fingertips, "the lady should always have roses." With a final nod to Evan, he walked off briskly in the direction of the Strand.

Evan forestalled the torrent of questions poised to descend on him from his friends. "I'll tell you all about it later," he bargained, "but for now, let's pretend Charles St. George never happened. I seem to remember you promised me dessert."

Chapter Fourteen

*Of the great mysteries of the spheres, eternity is the
greatest, for each sphere is contained within its boundaries, yet each is boundless. Each was created, and yet
each existed before time, for all time.*

The part of Badad that belonged here, in the second
sphere, careened in the void, propelled by the memory
of pain that shrieked through him, through the universe of
Princes. Sense told him he was home, that flesh had no
meaning here, but the shock of meat-death held him still.
The moment when mind winked out caught him in its terrifying grasp, and he reached for something solid in the
void, finding only memory—

Fire. Flesh burned. Torn, flung in clods that quivered
with the cell-memory of life, the body that had been
Kevin Bradley hit the broken concrete of the Black
Masque's foundation. So this was death, a small voice that
clung to the identity of Badad the daemon whispered into
the maelstrom. He sought a distance from which to observe the experience, but found his daemon self drawn
into the very heart of his body-terror. Here or now twisted
out of true; just the moments before the explosion in

Omage's back room remained to him, watching the blood flow out of Paul Carter's body.

Then bedrock shifted, cracked. He pulled the motion into himself, collected it in the lens of his mind, and turned it on the building around him. He might have escaped then, transported out and let the damned humans shift for themselves on a world that rocked on its axis, but a face shaped itself in his mind. He owed host loyalty to that which he recognized as Ariton in his son, while the binding spell worked by his human bastard twisted his gut like an angry fist. Evan needed a place to stand, so Badad focused down, holding the damage within the burning walls of the Black Masque.

Screams reached him from beyond the door—humans dying, buried in the rubble of the falling building and burning with the bright blue flame that reminded him of Ariton, fed by the gas line snapped in the quake. He thought of human literature—the history they made for themselves—and added a touch of sulfur to the mix, even as he felt himself losing control of the backflash.

The fire reached the back room and blew. Surprised, Badad realized that he would not escape the physical shell of this body in time. He had not imagined one body, one blinding moment could hold so much pain, and he tried to break free. The sensations, more intense, more all-consuming than any he had experienced in material form, confused him. His sense of separation from the physical realm slipped away, and he became, fully and for the first time as it died, the body that he wore. Thought scattered and flew; only the demands of heart and lungs and the reptile brain at the base of his human spinal cord reached him, the imperative of the body to continue.

Then the darkness of nonbeing seeped into the body

that had been Kevin Bradley, through the ghosts of missing fingertips and toes, working inward to his heart, dimming his eyes. The roaring in his ears grew louder—the sound of flame, of flowing blood, of his own heart pumping the stuff of life onto the shattered floor. Finally, when sound, too, had ceased to reach him, Badad felt the last spark of motion leave his body. Dead, trapped in flesh that began to rot as the last breath stilled.

Top of the food chain to the bottom in the space of a heartbeat, his last sane thought before the darkness closed mocked him for the scorn in which he had held the humans. He could never have been one of them, could never have lived at all with the knowledge that this lay at the end of it.

Badad felt the tremors of his own damaged consciousness shudder through his universe. There were others of his kind nearby, minds flung aside in his careening race through the not-space that made up the second sphere. A familiar touch flicked a tentative merge through him and fled again.

"Immortal!" His blindness raged. "Death has no hold on me!" But the words had no meaning for him as he died again and again. A mind touched his, and he remembered a human sense—smell, of lilies of the valley massed in the shadows of a garden wall. For a moment the scent cooled the fire burning his mind away, then it was gone with a shiver of separation. He was alone again, curled against the horror of dying for all eternity.

Chapter Fifteen

*And of the creatures of the spheres, lords and Princes
and Archangels and Thrones, only those of the first
sphere, the dominion of man, know the limits of time
and space. Death is the one great mystery that con-
founds the rest.*

"Evan!" Claudia called up the narrow staircase, "Did you
fall asleep up there? We're going to be late!"

Evan shrugged his shoulders more comfortably into his
dinner jacket and adjusted his shirt cuffs to show a quarter inch below the jacket sleeves, wishing he had fallen
asleep. Jet lag had never left him this shaky before—not
since he had done his flying for Omage, and the similarity
of the feelings made him decidedly queasy. He was in no
condition to negotiate for the agency with St. George, in
no mood to make small talk when he just wanted to get
away from there as fast as the Dover train could take him,
or home, if things had gone really wrong with Paul Carter.

But he was stuck here, at least through dinner. There
were limits to the amount of hurt he could inflict on
Claudia, and he'd passed that limit long ago. But, dammit,
if he didn't have to get away for her own protection, he'd
have invited her out for a fancy dinner himself! Too late

for that now. He checked the mirror one more time—hoped Claudia wouldn't notice the tension that darkened the circles under his eyes—and headed down the stairs.

"I didn't fall asleep, and we're not late. And if we were, Charlie's got enough money to hold the table all night."

He stopped at the landing and whistled under his breath.

"You are beautiful." Claudia wore black velvet iced with silver lamé; Evan remembered seeing the tag ends of the fabric in one of the rugs that hung on the walls. He kissed her on the cheek, eased the hurt she tried to hide with a smile. "I don't want to seem too eager. After all, if St. George has his way, my vacation is over. Have I overstayed my welcome already?"

"Not in a million years." She gave him a hug, then moved away to get a better look at him. "Turn around, let me see you."

He complied with a full circle and took her hands when they were face-to-face again. "Do I pass muster?"

"And then some. You didn't pick that suit up at J.C. Penney." Not quite a question, her comment invited explanation.

"No." Nor would Carlo Pimi have appreciated the comparison. The thought of the Milan tailor in one of his outrageous displays of temper made Evan laugh, but Claudia was still waiting for an answer to all the unstated "whys?" that had lain between them through the afternoon.

"My father's agency specializes in recovery—art, mostly, sometimes jewelry. We have to be discreet, and that means blending into our clients' surroundings. Don't worry—I turn back into a pumpkin at midnight.

"Which reminds me—mind if I call the office?" he asked, "My dime—corporate calling card."

"Of course, call," she agreed, "but don't take too long, will you? Jack is warming up the car." She stopped him with a hand on his arm. "Just one question first. Are you really on vacation?"

Evan considered his options, from outright lies to the truth, and compromised, offering little information, but an answer to the question she couldn't voice. "I'm not here on a case, if that's what you mean, and no, I didn't plan to bump into Charlie St. George, though we did seem to be wading knee-deep in coincidental meetings this afternoon.

"I needed to get away for a little while, and I thought of you and Jack. We were friends once, good friends. It's taken me a while to get over that time, but I finally decided I couldn't throw out the good with the bad, not if there was anything left to salvage. That's really all there is to it."

"Thank you." She kissed him, gently, and let him go. "Phone's in the sitting room, E.T. Call home."

He found the ancient telephone set on a small table in the entryway between the sitting room with its faded palm frond paper and the hall. Rotary dial, heavy black base and receiver—the house must have been wired in the fifties, and no one had thought to upgrade since. Evan dialed the overseas operator and placed his call, waited impatiently as she made the connections. Finally, the sound of a ringing phone echoed satellite-tinny over the line. No one answered. He checked his watch: seven o'clock. It would be two in the afternoon back home. Brad or Lily should have answered, or the machine should have transferred his call. Unless something had gone very wrong. An operator broke into the line and he asked her to verify the number and place the call again.

He counted the palm fronds printed on the ancient wallpaper: one frond for each ring. Still no answer. An operator intruded again, insisted that he place his call later. For a moment Evan stood there, adding up palm fronds while a dial tone shrilled at him from the receiver heavy in his hand. Slowly he returned the relic to its cradle, his mind a blank.

"Nothing?" Claudia asked softly. He hadn't noticed her come into the room, couldn't shift his expression fast enough to pretend he wasn't worried. So he shook his head, giving himself time to pull his mind away from all the ugly possibilities an unanswered phone might mean. "I'll try again later. Right now we have a date."

A maître d' in full tails and a starched white stand-up collar and bowtie led Evan Davis and his companions to a table tucked into a discreet corner of the Claridge dining room. Charles St. George smiled and half-rose to greet them as they took their seats—Claudia at St. George's right, Evan at his left, and Jack Laurence across from St. George. "Evan, Mr. Laurence, and the best for last. Claudia—may I call you Claudia?" he took her hand, held it a fraction too long.

The attention rankled in the part of Evan's brain that whispered of caves and firelight and the music of hearts beating in rhythm with each other. His rational mind said "ancient history," rights ceded. Imagination supplied a picture from an earlier conversation—Claudia picking through the wreckage of a Midwestern town in the aftermath of a tornado—wholly at odds with the muted luxury of the Claridge dining room. Covering his confusion, he returned Charlie's smile with a bland rictus of his own.

The maître d' appeared again, this time carrying two

dozen roses in a crystal vase. Behind him followed a waiter with a flower stand. The roses matched the deep pink of the tablecloths and the delicate blossoms woven into the gold ivy that bordered the service. Claudia touched the petals of a bloom and smiled, first at the maître d' who set the vase in the stand next to her chair, and then at Charles St. George.

"I was right," he declared. "You should always have roses."

She smoothed his lapel where it curled over at his neck. "No one has ever given me roses before." She slid a glance sideways at Evan, and he read the accusation there. "They're beautiful. Thank you."

St. George accepted her thanks with a little bounce on the balls of his feet, and nodded toward a bottle resting label up in an ice bucket at his side. "I have champagne chilling for later—dom Perignon. And I took the liberty of ordering something special for dinner. I hope you like it."

"I'm sure I will," she reassured him with a pat on his hand. Lily would have laughed in poor Charlie's overeager face, but Evan found himself envying St. George for the gentle kindnesses Claudia showed him, and for the excitement that shone in her smile. Charlie had given her that, and Evan wondered why it mattered so much to him while the cave-brain whispered, "Mine."

"I've passed by here lots of times, but I've never been inside before," Claudia said, her eyes wide as she studied the room. She caught Evan's glance and tilted her nose ceilingward.

He got the unspoken message: This is how a lady should be treated. Back in their Village days they couldn't have paid the tip in a place like the Claridge, but he knew that look meant more than fancy restaurants. She'd always been there—a lover in bed, a mother when the nightmares came too close. Obsessed with his own search, Evan had never wooed her, had never made Claudia feel beautiful or important, or loved. With two out of three before the soup course, Charles Devereaux St. George was already ahead on points.

"All the most famous people stay here." She smiled pointedly at Charlie. "We could be sitting next to royalty this very minute and not even know it."

St. George returned her smile. "Or a rock star," he agreed. "The valet told me in confidence that Mike Jagger always stays at the Claridge when he's in town."

Jack choked into his napkin, reached for his water glass, but Claudia seemed not to notice the gaffe. Maybe she didn't listen to the Stones anymore.

"You don't say," Evan offered blandly. He took a breath to add that Lily avoided *Mick* Jagger when he showed up at the Savoy, but Claudia's glare silenced him.

When Claudia returned her attention to Charles St. George, her brother nudged Evan in the shoulder. Jack leaned over and whispered in his ear: "Watch your back, Batman. The Penguin is making off with your girl."

In the old days he would have brushed off the suggestion with a retort of his own: *Catwoman can take care of herself.* But he hadn't played in a long time, and it had always been Jack's game. *Past,* he said to himself, calling to mind Lily's cold perfection. He shivered, afraid to let go of the warmth of Claudia even as he reached for something he could touch with outstretched fingers, but could never hold. Jack brought him back to the here and now with a thud.

"This guy doesn't make his money on a press in his basement, does he?" Laurence whispered, persistent.

Evan glared at him. "He doesn't have time," he whispered back. "Too busy spending what his father left him." He turned away, hoping St. George hadn't noticed the exchange, and found the man staring at him with a little smile.

"Not quite true, Evan," St. George admonished. "Although I leave the day-to-day running of Papa's companies to others, I still take an interest in new acquisitions. But I never discuss business before dinner—"

The waiter arrived, set a slice of terrine de trois pâté in front of each of them, and Evan picked up a fruit knife and crust of French bread. Faced with a sea of cutlery, Claudia hesitated, then followed Evan's lead.

St. George took a bottle from the wine steward. "Spanish sherry, wonderful with pâté." He filled Claudia's glass and handed the bottle back to the steward to serve the remaining guests.

Jack took his gladly, but Evan shook his head. "None for me, thank you." He turned the glass upside down on the table.

"Very well, sir." The steward bowed and took a step back, but St. George stopped him with an imperious wave of his hand. "Come, come, Evan. Don't be a spoilsport. It's like drinking bottled sunshine, you'll love it."

"I don't drink anymore, Charles. I'm an alcoholic."

St. George reached for the wineglass. "The young are so dramatic," he said. "So you overindulged a bit in college. Everybody does—that doesn't make you an alcoholic, anymore than a fine wine over dinner with friends constitutes a binge."

"I'm sure you mean well, Charles, but I really don't want any wine." Evan gritted his teeth, wondering suddenly why he had ever felt sympathy for the bumbling little man.

Jack Laurence took a sip and smacked his lips appreciatively. "That leaves more for us." He lifted his glass and looked at the wine steward with a greedily hopeful expression.

No one spoke for a moment. The wine steward filled Jack's glass and drifted smoothly around the table, depositing the bottle at St. George's right. He left the tableau to the busboy removing pâté and the waiter standing ready with the asparagus bisque.

"I suppose you don't want any sherry for your soup either," Charles dismissed the unpleasantness with a grumbled attempt at humor.

Claudia smiled. She rested her hand on Charles' arm, but her eyes were on Evan, and they warmed him with the comfort and support she had always given him. "He wasn't there, Evan. He doesn't know what it was like for us in New York."

"Is that where you three met? In New York?" Charlie asked.

Evan felt the tension ease a notch between his shoulder blades, and caught Jack lifting his eyes in a silent gesture of relief.

"Yes," Evan said. "I was putting in an abortive semester at the Carnegie Institute, and Claudia was doing a little better at Columbia. Jack had his degree in accounting from Indiana University—"

"I was taking a year off to 'find myself' in the Village," Jack added. "As the oldest and wisest among us, I took it as my sacred trust to lead my companions astray."

"Evan!" St. George eyed him speculatively, rolling the

stem of his wineglass between his thumb and forefinger. "You naughty boy—you never told me."

Claudia's face had grown increasingly drawn as the conversation continued, and Evan realized that she was watching him for some signal. He gave the barest hint of a shrug, but his jaw tightened. Jack wouldn't bring up the Black Masque; the man had better sense than to regale Evan's client with the sordid details of that little adventure. The thought of Omage's name bandied about the dinner table curdled the soup in Evan's stomach.

"It wasn't a very successful experiment," Claudia interrupted. "Evan and I both dropped out of school without finishing our degrees. Jack got a job in the London branch of the Bank of America, I came with him to England, and now I work in a shop."

"And I went home to work in my father's business," Evan finished. "We just weren't cut out for the unusual."

"I don't know about that." St. George refilled Jack's glass and sat back while the busboy took away the soup bowls. "Unusual may be a bit strong, but the beautiful Lily is uncommon by any standards—not that she outshines the warmth of your own glow for a moment, Claudia, my dear." He patted her hand, a beatific smile plumping his cheeks. Evan ignored the speculative curiosity that narrowed her eyes, his own attention on the soft round hand that covered hers. He almost missed Charlie's next words:

"But I can't tell you how surprised I was to see you this afternoon, my boy." St. George turned a quizzical frown on Evan. "When we last met, I had the impression things were full speed ahead at the agency. Or am I blowing your cover—that is the expression, isn't it? Is Lily lurking in the draperies? Kevin poised to apprehend some nefarious second-story man?"

"Who's Lily?" Claudia turned bland interest on Evan, but he didn't buy the politesse for a moment. She had that intent set to her eyes she used to get doing Anthro assignments, and he felt distinctly uneasily knowing how well she could read him in that mode.

"She's my cousin. And before you ask, Kevin is Kevin Bradley, my father. They work together—we work together."

St. George perked up on that. "Ah! That explains it."

Claudia again, still on the scent: "Explains what?"

"Well, how close they seem. I would have guessed a more—physical?—relationship. Family, now—that *is* refreshing. But here is the main course. I don't suppose I could tempt you with a small glass of the Bordeaux, Evan? It's a 1963, lovely year."

Evan frowned. "Charles—"

St. George raised his hands in surrender. "Just wanted to be sure, dear boy. You could have hated the sherry and didn't want to offend."

The maître d', with a waiter following a step behind, positioned a cart bearing a large flaming platter at the side of the table. Evan ignored the display, dismissed the brief exchange with St. George as Charlie's own bumbling effort at conciliation. Lily. Her name lingered like the last strains of fading laughter, and memory carried him home. Yesterday she had tried to kill him, but he could imagine no life without her, only the pit of degradation that had been the Black Masque. Claudia was all the warmth that Lily lacked, but past experience told him she could not hold against the cold, bright will of his father's kind. Unconsciously he drew on the binding spell that tied the daemon Lirion to his bidding. He owned her, didn't have to worry that she'd grow tired of life in human form, strike him dead, and go home. She was *his*.

The thought made Evan sick. "No!"

He didn't realize he had spoken aloud until the voices at the table dropped away and he found three expectant faces watching him. Charlie was the first to speak, at once flustered and apologetic:

"I'm sorry, Evan, it was presumptuous of me to order the dinner in advance. If you don't like the crown of lamb, I'll have the waiter bring a menu."

"No, Charles. I'm the one to apologize." Evan gave a self-deprecating smile, but kept his eyes expressionless—as he expected, only Claudia noticed. "The dinner is fine, lamb is a particular favorite of mine. My mind was somewhere else completely."

"I knew it," St. George fretted. "You *are* on a case. Is it the auction at Sotheby's tomorrow? I'd planned to bid on the Matisse—don't tell me I need your services already!"

"Don't worry, Charles," Evan reassured him, while Alfredo DaCosta's presence in the city clicked smoothly into place. Poor Charlie. The thief seemed to have taken a particular interest in his collection.

"As far as I know, they're expecting no trouble, but you might want to pick up a little extra security. I can recommend a good firm we've had success with here in the past, but I'm not working this trip. Lily and my father are busy on a case closer to home. I did the preliminary workup for them, and then I was free for some much-needed vacation time."

"That reminds me," Jack pushed a cut of the meat onto the back of the fork and held it poised, "did you get in touch with your office this evening?" He popped the bite into his mouth, and chewed with more attention on Evan than on his meal.

"No one was in," Evan answered abruptly.

St. George leaned forward, curiosity furrowing his brows, and Evan cut short the question he was about to utter with a noncommittal explanation. "I expected them to be out. Unfortunately, Lily must have forgotten to turn on the machine, or to alert the service—she forgets pretty regularly when I'm not there to take care of it. I should have more luck when we get back tonight."

Claudia pinned him with the stare that saw right through him. Her frown said she knew his light tone was a lie. Later, his own small nod answered. He was relieved when she let him concentrate on his plate.

Jack gave him a knowing smirk, sliding a glance in his sister's direction and raising his eyebrows mockingly. Claudia glared at them both. "I don't know what you two are cooking up between you, but I have a feeling it means trouble."

"Us?" Jack lied blandly.

Evan shook his head, exasperated. "Not *us*, Claudia. I can't help it if your brother won't behave himself in public.

"By the way, Charles, the lamb is delicious," He steered the conversation to safer ground before Jack could open his mouth and put them both in Claudia's doghouse: "Why don't you tell me why we are here while my defenses are down?"

"It's a simple project, really." St. George waved his knife dismissively. "I'm considering the purchase of a small business in Italy. The prospectus looks good, but one can never be too careful in these matters. I'd like your agency to do a little checking for me—background checks on key personnel, current investors, that sort of thing. We could fly down to Venice after the auction tomorrow, spend a couple of days looking the place over, and I could photocopy the files you will need while we are there."

Venice. Evan looked at his plate, considering. "As you know, Charles, it's not exactly our line." But he dearly wanted to know what connection Charlie's new company might have with Alfredo DaCosta. He met the man's anxious gaze, and St. George pressed his case, leaning over his elbows on the rose-colored tablecloth.

"Of course. I'm certainly not offering something as glamorous or exciting as finding the Hope Diamond, but frankly, I don't have time to find another agency I trust the way I do Bradley, Ryan, and Davis.

"Evan, I need results quickly—the board meets next week to consider my proposal, and I have to know what I am buying by then."

"I'm on vacation," Evan reminded him, but St. George persisted.

"Time is of the essence. I'm willing to pay anything within reason for the inconvenience. In fact, why don't you bring your friends along? The job shouldn't take long, and I'd love the opportunity to introduce la bella Claudia to the jewel of the Mediterranean. Can't you persuade him, my dear? You belong to Venice."

Claudia stared at St. George. "Jack and I have to work tomorrow." She stressed the word "work," a gentle reminder that a kitchen-garden life awaited her return from the glitter and light of her Cinderella evening.

"And I can't accept a case until I discuss it with Lily and my father," Evan added.

Jack just mumbled "La bella Claudia?" under his breath, but Evan could feel the irritation mounting in the man. He cut off any comment from that corner with a promise—

"When I check in later tonight, I'll present your case. If they can free up some time, I'll let you know. Then, just fax them the information you have, and they can run the search. Lily will follow up with you when we get the preliminaries." She wouldn't like it when he told her, but he thought maybe the prospect of seeing Lily again might get Charlie off his back.

"I really need this vacation, Charles."

"I can see you do, my boy. We can talk about it tomorrow—let's not spoil dessert." A look passed across St. George's face so fleetingly that, in the muted distraction of waiters clearing away the main course, Evan wasn't sure he actually saw it. Possessive beyond hunger, that look said Evan's will was nothing.

Chapter Sixteen

Badad of the host of Ariton is called the solitary one, keeper of secrets. Slow to wrath or to make alliances, his passions once aroused run deeper than the secrets he holds. Summon Badad to reveal things hidden, but beware. Badad is Ragnarok, the end of all things in fire and cold.

"**D**amn."

Evan ran the fingers of his right hand through his hair while the left clung to the phone receiver. Jet lag was setting in with a vengeance; he'd been up for thirty-five hours, at least one of them in a battle for his life. Maybe more than one—he still hadn't figured out dinner. His body craved sleep, but his mind had him by its metaphoric teeth. No answer. Still no answer.

He looked at his watch again—eleven o'clock—and figured out the time difference: it was six in the evening on the East Coast. If Brad and Lily had come home since morning, they'd have found the machine switched off when they checked for messages. Assuming all had gone well, they'd have set the machine and left him to get on with his vacation. No answer this morning could have meant anything. He rubbed at the scars on his wrists—

three thin white lines—knowing what no answer this evening could mean.

Memory hit him like a wall. Omage, in that godforsaken back room, stroking his face, his chains, crooning softly over the knife. The daemon's followers—friends, until then—held him down, arms outstretched over an alabaster bowl dulled to bloody rust, while Omage opened the veins with his silver knife, the shock flinging Evan into the second sphere.

He understood now that when his body lost consciousness he lost his anchor to the physical universe. Then, he had drifted alone in the void, reaching for a handhold on reality with no fingers to grasp with and nothing to hold, his screams backed up somewhere behind a throat gone lax from blood loss.

Three times they had opened his wrists, and each time he believed was the end—he would die, this time. He'd spend eternity alone and insane in the second sphere while his body wasted slowly in its prison. Or he'd come back mad, curled gibbering against the throne of his master until Omage got bored enough with him to finish it.

A tumbled swastika crusted on a barroom wall in the Village was little enough to show for a life. He stared back from the other side of that void, and he knew he wasn't the same person now, wasn't quite where he was going either. Tempering did that to a man, like the working of a blade. Between the stages he was vulnerable, less so with each change. Not ready yet, he knew, but maybe close enough. Had to be: he was going back.

Transporting was out. Evan knew that under normal circumstances he could handle the transfer, but he had no way of knowing where Brad and Lily had run into trouble. Maybe it was safe—or maybe the fighting had spilled over into the second sphere. British Airways might be slower, but he figured he had better odds on surviving the trip. In the morning, he decided. The shape he was in he'd be useless any sooner. Worse than useless, he'd be something else for Brad to worry about.

"Did you reach anyone at home?" Claudia had moved quietly into the room. The words gentled their way past his abstraction, no sudden jolt of adrenaline shocked his return to awareness to find her in the room.

"No," he answered, the phone still resting in his lap, and then, because he owned her some explanation for what he was going to do: "They may have run into trouble on a case. We didn't expect it, but it happens sometimes. I'll try them again in the morning. If there's still no answer, I'll be leaving on the first flight out tomorrow."

"And what happens to us?"

Evan stared at her blankly for a moment, wondering what dinner had been about if Claudia still wanted to put things back together again. "I'll be back."

"When? In two weeks? Two years? Am I supposed to spend my life waiting for you to drop into it, never knowing when you are going to walk out again?"

"You left the last time," he reminded her.

He stood up, returned the phone to its stand, and grabbed his jacket, mind still refusing to let his body rest.

"Where are you going?" Claudia's voice, trying to understand, terrified to watch him go, held him at the door.

"Nowhere." He didn't want company for the dark thoughts that preyed on him tonight, needed least of all her reminder of a life he could have had, if his father had been a traveling salesman or a con artist—anything but the creature he was, with what that made Evan.

"Just for a walk." And then, because it was the one thing he could give her, "Want to come?"

"I'll get my coat."

He watched her walk away, knowing Lily would have plucked his jacket from his fingers and laughed at him when he shivered in the dark. Yesterday Lily had tried to kill him. He should be running fast and far in the other direction, not heading back into the fire. But she was Ariton, like his father. Family, and not a damned thing he could do until tomorrow. He followed Claudia out the door.

"Did you have a good time tonight?" Evan winced at his own question—asinine thing to say, like commenting on the quality of the mattress during sex. Too many ghosts followed them past the iron fences and the ones of metal links, of chains. The ease of the afternoon had gone, leaving them stranded—not strangers but pretending to be.

"One for the memory book," she answered.

So she still had the old *Webster's Unabridged,* bulkier now with a rose from the restaurant pressed between its pages—the C's, for Charles, he guessed. She always filed the memories away like that. He wondered if she still had the cocktail napkin from Black Masque filed under B, and what, if anything she had preserved in the E's.

"Right under C," she added, as if reading his mind, "for Claridge."

"You and Charlie seemed to hit it off." Right. Follow stupid with cliché. Why couldn't they just talk?

"He's *your* client, Evan," she reminded him. "Did you expect me to be rude to your business contact?"

A pause, while they both considered how far the truth of that covered the evening. "He was sweet." Her grin followed the admission. "And he *did* try so hard. Mike Jagger."

She laughed then, the sound bright and clear against the night. "Do you suppose he has any idea who the Rolling Stones are?"

"I'm not always sure Charlie knows what day it is," Evan commented, "but he pays our bill on time and he has a collection of impressionist and modern art that puts most museums to shame." He stopped. "I thought you liked Charlie."

"Fool."

Claudia reached an arm around his neck and he bent down, knowing but allowing himself not to register her purpose. She kissed him slowly, deeply, and he clung to her, remembering the feel of her in his arms and waking up in her bed in the apartment the three of them had shared in the Village. Her fingers traced the fragile line of bone at his temples, carded into his hair and held him while he returned the kiss, his arms around her waist now, holding on to Claudia and all that was normal and right between a man and a woman.

"So tell me about this Lily—" Claudia's mouth still so close to his that the words caressed, lip upon lip, and slid through his defenses like the tip of her tongue flicked across his senses when she said, "this Lily."

Evan stepped back and remembered how to breathe. "She's my father's cousin, like I said," pulling back from the question. Lily had tried to kill him yesterday—so had his father. He hadn't felt this alone since he'd tried to leave the Black Masque and discovered exactly how much Omage hated him.

Claudia stood, warm and solid, a step away and he reached out, fingertips tracing the curve of her shoulder, the line of her arm, the bend of her elbow. Wanting caught him like Mike Tyson's fist in the gut. Below the belt. He wanted to crawl up inside her and hide there in the warm, moist darkness of her body. Evan closed the space between them, knowing he had no right to do it, no right to screw up her life because he couldn't face his own life alone anymore.

"I need you," he said because it was true. If he tried hard enough, he could forget that he had to leave in the morning. He rested his forehead against the top of her head, rubbed at the silk of her hair, and wished they were home, safe behind her picket fence and her rosebushes. The longing to drop to his knees right there under the streetlight and bury his face in her belly burned up the inside of his legs, sent electric shock waves through his arms.

"Tell me why." She took his hand, started to walk again, and he followed. "It's been two years, Evan—why now?"

"Why did you leave?" He couldn't help it, the hurt at being abandoned yet again leaked into his voice. None of it had ever been his fault.

"I was afraid."

Claudia walked with her head down so that her hair fell forward and hid her face from him. Evan kept pace with her, steered her around a corner with a hand at her elbow, and slowly she explained:

"I know Jack told you about our dad dying. Heart attack on the golf course—nothing anyone could do. At the funeral, everybody kept saying how lucky he was going that way. No pain, doing what he loved, we had to be grateful for that. Grateful. God, I was furious. He never even said good-bye!

"Jack seemed to buy into the whole spiel. He went back

to school after the funeral, finished his degree. When he decided to go to New York, I was angry all over again. How dare he leave us, just like Dad did!"

"I don't understand." Evan stopped her. "He was away at school, but that was okay. What made New York so different?"

"You're not from the Midwest," Claudia reminded him ruefully. "When you grow up in St. Louis, New York isn't real, it's something they make up for the movies. I had to *make* it real, so I applied to Columbia. That way I could go, too; Jack wouldn't be leaving me behind.

"That first year, I was convinced we were right in St. Louis all along—New York wasn't real. Somehow, we'd fallen into the Twilight Zone—I kept expecting to see things in black and white, figured Rod Serling's ghost was going to show up any day and tell me to click my heels three times and recite 'there's no place like home.' You weren't Rod Serling, but you made a close second. I think my anger reached out to yours: if I could make it go away in you, my own would disappear, like sympathetic magic.

"I hadn't counted on Jack. You didn't have a father. I didn't realize at the time, but Jack really envied you for that. After all, a father you don't know can't hurt you when he dies."

"You'd be surprised," Evan objected, remembering the terror when he believed he was insane. "At least you knew who you were. There were times I'd have given my life just to know what my father looked like."

"I know." Claudia raised her head, shook her hair back into place. "I recognized your anger, remember? It was a lot like mine; figures that the reasons would be a lot alike, too. Jack saw you differently, though. He couldn't be you, so he manufactured stories about you to explain why—

you weren't human, you were a god. Mac fed the fantasy. Jack started believing it because he wanted it to be true.

"When the police called, I thought it was you in the hospital. I knew about your dreams—you'd woken me up with them enough—and I saw you falling for Mac's line like it was made for you. *I* wanted to be the one who helped you break free of your nightmares. Maybe it was jealousy, but I hated Mac. Bellevue just made the hatred less irrational.

"When I got to the hospital that night, I found Jack alone with the police and the doctors and the I.V. of whole blood running as fast as they could let it. You hadn't even brought him in. The doctor told me he almost died in the alley behind the Black Masque. All I could think of was 'how dare Jack do this to me.' Just like our father. I could have killed him myself, but down deep I *wanted* it to be you."

She raised her hand, forestalling Evan's objection. "I know it wasn't your fault. Mac was using you, just like he was using Jack and the others who hung out at the Black Masque. But *you* were the fantasy, not Mac. If you hadn't been a part of it, I wouldn't have come that close—" she pinched her thumb and forefinger together, almost touching, "—to losing my brother."

"I'm sorry. I should never have come here." He'd known it from the beginning, just as he'd known he couldn't let it rest with all the unspoken feelings festering in his soul.

Claudia laughed at him, at herself maybe; there was more regret than humor in the sound. "You're wrong," she said. "I got over blaming you for what happened to Jack pretty quickly, once he was on his feet again. Then I got mad because it hadn't mattered enough to you to find us again."

They had come full circle; the picket fence that girded 42 St. Mary's Road appeared out of the night mist just ahead. Claudia looked into his eyes, waiting for answers to the questions she had asked at the beginning of their walk, and it was Evan's turn to stare into the middle distance. The warmth of her hand in his anchored him to the suburban London street while he called up the memories he was never quite successful at banishing.

"At first," he explained, "I didn't have a choice. After you and Jack left, I went to Mac, told him I was leaving, too. He didn't like the idea, so he locked me up." The memory prickled at his skin, cold sweat chilling him in the evening breeze—chains at neck and wrists and feet, Omage touching him, the delicate trace of his silver knife flicking playful cuts at his throat, his groin. Sometimes the knife drew blood—pain seared his memory—sometimes Mac just teased, knifetip raising a red welt that promised more and burned anticipation into his brain. Sometimes the daemon used the human body he wore like a knife—*Don't ask for the details*, a thing whimpered in his mind—while flashback turned his stomach, set the tremors running through him again. His hands shook. He knew Claudia felt it, but she seemed to find something in his face that she didn't want to know. She turned away, but her hand squeezed his more firmly.

"But you got away," she prompted.

Evan heard the reassurance behind the questions. He had gotten away. He was safe, at least until tomorrow.

"Not on my own," he conceded. "My father found me there, tricked Mac into letting me go. Lord, I don't know why he even bothered; I was a mess. Some days I didn't even know who I was. For the first few weeks, I was sure I had died and hell was just another practical joke the

universe was playing on me. With Brad's help, and with
Lily's, I started to pull myself together again. Gave up the
booze, even the cigarettes. I thought I was over it until
this case came up. It should have been safe enough for
them both, but something's gone wrong—"

"And you feel guilty because you weren't there to return
the favor when they needed you," Claudia finished for
him.

It sounded too pat, too trite when she put it that way.
"I owe them my life," he said. "And my sanity."

"Do you love her?"

The question made him smile. "We've been lovers," he
admitted. And because he owed her the truth, "We probably will be again. But actually *love* Lily?" He shook his
head, at a loss for words to describe the daemon Lirion to
the woman before him.

"It's not like that between us," he tried to explain, but
the words wouldn't come. "She's beautiful," and he knew
that was the wrong thing to say the moment the words
were gone.

"I don't know what I feel for her," he finally admitted.
"I suspect it's a game with Lily. Sometimes I think maybe
she does feel something for me, other times just being in
the same room with her is like jousting with high-tension
wires." Evan stopped, backed up, and tried again.

"It's just sex for her, I know that. She has other men.
She'd never think to hide it from me—I don't mean that
much to her. It scares me, because she's part of what I
am, what I spent my whole life looking for, and we don't
even like each other a lot of the time."

He couldn't tell Claudia about the other part of their
relationship, the challenge in Lily's smile, the dare that
pushed him to test his body and his skill against her hun-

ger. He wanted her to need him. In his fantasies she would come to him, beg to please him, and he would take her in his arms—a regular Rhett Butler. He settled for the fact that she let him live.

"But you wouldn't leave her."

Not a question, Evan had to answer it anyway. "Not until she loses interest. So what does that make me?"

In the Village he'd met men who sold their bodies for money; Evan figured he was going cheap, whoring for a place to call home. He knew he was being unfair as soon as he thought it. He *wanted* Lily, and hated himself for wanting her while his hand locked with Claudia's hand, while Claudia's kisses, the feel of her arms were still warm on his skin.

"Unhappy."

Evan had to back up a minute, remember the question she was answering. There didn't seem to be anything else to say. "I'm getting cold." He headed back to the house.

Claudia left him at the stairway to the second floor. "Good night," she said, and kissed him lightly on the cheek.

He watched her for a moment. She took the stairs slowly this time, not running up them like she usually did. When she disappeared around the corner, he sighed and walked back to the kitchen, looking for something to warm him, and knowing that he wouldn't find it in this lifetime. *Settle for coffee and the illusion of comfort.* Jack Laurence was waiting.

"Hey, meester, wanna sleep with my seester?" Mocking, Jack offered his own mug, steam rising from the coffee paled with too much milk.

Evan stared at him for a minute, then shook his head.

"Go to hell, Jack. I'm not in the mood." He turned to leave, but Jack stopped him.

"I'm sorry, Evan. Sit down, I'll make you a cup."

Evan sat, reconsidering the coffee. "Nothing for me, I need to sleep sometime tonight. What do you want?"

"Just some company," Laurence explained. "I thought that's why you looked us up in the first place. Or did you?"

That one hit home and twisted. Evan wanted his motives kept well out of this.

"I'm leaving tomorrow," he blurted. "There's trouble at home. I already told Claudia."

"I'll bet that went over real well. Charlie have anything to do with your decision?" Cool blue eyes, with none of the fire of the lords of Ariton but a dangerous perceptiveness of their own, took his measure. "What are you running away from this time?"

"Not a thing." Evan slumped in his kitchen chair and stared at the floor between his feet planted a yard apart on the stained linoleum.

"I don't feel special, Jack, but I can't help what I am. For a long time after Brad pulled me out of the Black Masque I thought of calling, but I couldn't face you. It's my fault you almost died." He met Jack's eyes, let the man see the honesty, soul to soul. "I wanted your friendship, not your worship; finally decided it was time to look you in the face and tell you so."

"Lucky for all of us I figured that one out on my own—decided even E.T. needed a friend and elected myself to the position." Jack punched him lightly on the shoulder, then grew serious again. "But that doesn't explain why you've been jumpy as a flea on a hot skillet since you arrived."

"Mac found another one like me; it's what got me seriously thinking about that time again, and how I'd let the Black Masque destroy our friendship. His name is Paul Carter, and his sister hired us to get him back. Brad and Lily were going after him the night I came here. Brad got me out, I figured he could do it again, but something's happened. They never got home."

He sat forward on the kitchen chair, as if he could communicate his determination with his outstretched hands, but those hands kept shaking, giving away his fear: "I owe him my life, Jack. I have to go back, help if I can, or die trying."

Jack had to know he hadn't come here to hide, but to stop hiding from his friends. "I promise," Evan said. "If I make it out of there, I'll be back. Maybe we can start over then, okay?" He offered a tentative smile, realized it was wasted.

Somewhere along the line Jack Laurence had stopped tracking the conversation. He sat with his head tilted over his mug, a frown creasing his forehead.

"I didn't think you *could* die. Figured you for immortal or something. Maybe even hundreds of years old and pretending so people wouldn't get suspicious."

Evan laughed bitterly. "No such luck. My mother is as human as yours. This body is the only one I've got; I last as long as it does. My father's from somewhere else—not quite outer space. It really is a lot like Mac described it, because he's one of them." He paused, remembering.

"Anyway, I don't know if they're immortal, but I do know we can't kill them. I tried. I felt Mac stop breathing under my hands. Then his eyes opened, he grinned at me, and thanked me for an interesting experience. He threw me bodily into the second sphere—that's where they come from. By the time he brought me back, I was pretty much insane. I don't remember a hell of a lot after that."

"Is Charlie one of them?"

"St. George?" Evan started to laugh, realized he was nudging hysteria that had nothing to do with the question and everything to do with no answer at home on the phone. He grabbed Jack's mug, choked on a swallow of cold coffee before he brought the laughter under control.

"Sorry, Jack. It's not you, just, well, if you knew Lily's opinion of Charlie, you wouldn't even ask. No, he's as human as we are. I met him on a different case entirely, and he was as inept then as he was tonight."

"Not so inept, old chum." Jack took his mug back. "He was making time with your girl, after all."

Evan stood up and stretched. "She was just making sure I was paying attention," he countered with a smug grin. "Anything else can wait until I get back from Philly. Now I need some sleep."

"Sure thing, old buddy. Just don't wait two years this time."

Evan heard the sincerity, answered it. "As soon as I take care of business at home. Promise." He put out his hand, and Jack took it in a firm handshake.

"Deal," Laurence agreed. "And figure out how you really feel about Claudia while you're at it. If you love her, fine. If you don't, get that straight, too. Like I said, I don't want her hurt."

"Deal."

Evan left the kitchen with thoughts of Claudia, the evening at the Claridge, and his fears for Brad and Lily back home warring for his attention. As much as his body craved rest, sleep seemed far away.

Chapter Seventeen

Of the alliances of Princes, Oriens most often allies with Paimon, Ariton and Amaimon, and likewise Astarot most often allies with Magot and Azmod. But in battle alliances may change, except that Ariton never makes alliance with Azmod, nor Paimon with Magot.

Badad stared at human hands bleached pale in the light of morning: his hands, he realized. Motionless as stone, they rested on the table in front of him.

"Drink this, you need it."

Lirion slid a cup of thick espresso between the hands and he grasped it. Holding onto the warmth and solidity of the cup, he tried to focus on the night before and how he'd gotten there, while the images slipped away like ghosts almost caught at the corner of the eye. He drank, and only when the cup was empty did he recognize it for his own service. So they had made it home.

"How did we get here?"

Lily pinned him with her own sardonic sneer. "I pulled you out of the rubble that used to be the Black Masque and transported one step ahead of the local constabulary."

The memory surfaced in splinters. Omage. Paul Carter, dead. "I could have used some help a little sooner."

Lirion shrugged. "Not my fight," she pointed out. "Your paternal aberration has already cost me my freedom. Don't expect me to take on your enemies for the miserable life of every half-human bastard our kind has ever produced on this inconsequential rock."

Marnie Simpson would have to be told, but later, when he could think. "We had a contract."

"*You* had a contract," Lily corrected him. "It was a trap, you know."

"A trap, yeah, but what was the bait? Paul Carter, or the Eye?" His hand went to his breast where the jewel had lain, cold as the whisper of death. Gone now. Where?

"I put it in the safe." Lily anticipated the question. "You weren't thinking straight at that point, but I wasn't letting Omage get his hands on it. Not if he wanted it that badly."

"You don't feel it, do you?" he asked her instead.

She shook her head. "I picked it up as a joke. I expected Evan to lecture me on taking more than the contract called for, like he usually does. The boy has no sense of humor; it usually takes him a while to realize I'm doing it just to get him going. This time he never did figure it out."

"And you've never asked yourself why you chose that in particular, which put us back in the middle of Omage's machinations again? Or why you didn't just leave it in the rubble after the explosion?"

"That bastard! But how? What is the damned thing?" Lily glinted blue flame in her rage, which was as much chagrin, he supposed. But Omage hadn't gotten what he wanted. Evan was safe, thousands of miles away from the twisted evil that Omage had become, and the stone could wait until he was thinking more clearly. He turned his attention to the more immediate problem: "How much damage did we do?"

"Not much." Lily settled into dark sarcasm. "You didn't sink Manhattan if that's what you're wondering—only half the block is in ruins. The news is calling it a gas main accident. Doesn't help the crowd in the bar, of course, but I admire your subtlety."

"I don't remember," Badad admitted.

"I'm not surprised." Lily refilled his cup and sat down with one for herself. "You lost your temper. A very impressive sight, but not smart in a human body. I think you suffered a backflash from trying to contain the damage, though I don't know why you bothered."

He answered her challenge with a look that needed no explanation. She knew the answer to that one.

"Evan. Well, you succeeded there. No one is reporting earthquakes or firestorms, and the planetary orbit remains stable, for which the locals, including your ungrateful offspring, will never show their gratitude."

Brad shrugged. "As long as I don't have to pay damages, I don't really care." As long as Evan still had a home to come back to, and he wasn't sure whether that was his choice or the effect of the binding, but it mattered.

"That's not quite all of it."

Lily stared at her cup, then caught him with a look he didn't quite recognize. Envy, fear, desire: for a moment she reminded him of the faces moving in the half-light of the Black Masque.

"Omage transformed before the walls came down, and so did I. You didn't. Your body died."

A flash of animal-memory—blind, unreasoning terror of

the meat-mind dragging him into panic-paralysis—then it was gone again.

"What was it like?" Lirion, on the trail of a new sensation. Her eyes glittered with a hard blue light. "How did it feel?"

"I don't remember."

He shuddered, suddenly cold. Day-to-day, they had no trouble separating their own true natures from the instinctive drives of the bodies they wore. Pushed to extremes, the animal mind gained ascendancy—time to bail out, to transform before identity submerged in the wave of uncontrolled feeling. Death was more, a stillness past fear where identity ceased to exist at all. The memory hovered just out of reach, but the change it had wrought in him lay very near the surface. He understood now why Evan feared the dark.

"How long have we been gone?"

"Since midnight yesterday. The day before yesterday, technically. The backflash really fried you; you've spent the last thirty hours discharging all over the second sphere. The humans will be picking up a new supernova in Orion, and you involved Ariton in a host-debt to Kaitar of the host of Paimon, but I managed to keep it below the level of a battle between Princes."

Brad nodded. The last thing they needed was to push Paimon into an alliance with Azmod over this fiasco. Too tired to dwell on the politics of the second sphere, he turned to the subject closer at hand.

"Has Evan called in?" He pushed his way unsteadily to his feet and made for the study, stopped at the safe and checked that Omage's jewel was really there. A weight settled on his shoulders when he took it in his hand, and his vision grayed around the edges, cleared again when the door to the safe swung closed with the stone inside.

Lily followed, and stopped to check the answering machine. "Forgot to turn the damn thing on."

Unbidden, Omage's words returned to him: "I want Evan back . . . the stone is only half the prize."

"It isn't over yet," Brad reminded her. He grabbed the printed bits of data from Evan's search program and sank into his favorite chair.

"Your brat is more trouble than he's worth, Badad." Lirion dismissed the boy with a flutter of the fingers of one hand, returned his patient stare with sour acceptance. "All right, it couldn't hurt to warn him. He left a number here somewhere. Then sleep—you need it more than I do. Death seems to take a lot out of you."

"Yeah."

Evan dead, forever. He shivered, suddenly cold in the windowless room. "Where's that number?"

"Right here." Lily dialed, then: "Hello, Evan Davis, please. He checked in yesterday. Did he leave a forwarding number? Thank you."

She hung up. "He never checked in. Canceled the room yesterday, left no forwarding number, just a message that he was staying with friends."

Brad let his head fall back against the tapestried upholstery of his wingback chair and probed for feeling through his son's binding spell.

"I'm too tired to think," he admitted. "He's safe for the time being. Upset about something, but I don't sense any adrenaline surge. Probably jet lag."

Lily lifted one sardonically elegant eyebrow. "I thought you let go of that—what did you call it?—rope."

"So did I." Brad thought for a moment. "It's only there

when I look for it. I think I'll know if he gets into trouble, but beyond that the sensation is too vague to be of much use. Don't you feel anything?"

"Not really." She shrugged. "When you talk about him, there's something. I don't give him much thought the rest of the time. And right now, all I can think about is sleep."

"You're right." Brad agreed. "We'll need to be in better shape than this when we tell Mrs. Simpson her brother is dead. I don't think she's going to take it well." He dragged himself out of his chair and dropped the printout, still unread, on the desk as he passed. "Four hours should do it. I'll meet you back here at one."

The white farmhouse had changed since their first visit. The French windows had been repaired, and the broken furniture and debris piled next to the fire pit were gone. Daffodils still bloomed in the garden, however, and the run from which the town took its name struck silver sparks in the distance as it had before. Past the foreman's house, where Paul Carter had constructed his shrine to death, horses frisked in the sunshine of a meadow. "Summer Dancer seems none the worse for the loss of his dearly beloved goat," Lily noted.

"He's a beauty." Brad ignored the sarcasm in her voice. Strong and free, the animal drew him. "Powerful. Look at him run, and he's just playing." Someday, when this case was over, when Evan set them free again—

Lily gave him a sly, sideways glance. "You'd make a fine stallion with the right handler to break you in." She laughed. "I wouldn't mind taking that ride myself."

He watched the horses play for a moment more, but they both knew the peace was deceptive. "Let's get this over with."

Marnie Simpson opened the door after only a short delay.

"I didn't hear your car pull up." She led them into the airy living room and sat at the edge of an Empire-style armchair facing the front windows over a Louis Quatorze sofa. An end table with a lamp and an ashtray stood beside her chair.

"We left the car in the lane and walked the rest of the way," Brad lied smoothly. He looked around the room: Persian carpet, chair set next to the side window, sofa, coffee table. Lots of woods polished to a warm glow, lots of brocade in muted tones, but most of it was expensive reproductions from periods that only clashed if you'd been there when. "Do you mind if we sit down?"

Marnie Simpson gestured to the Louis Quatorze sofa, and Brad settled himself awkwardly, sacrificing comfort to Twentieth Century American posture.

"I'm fine," Lily demurred. She wandered over to the side window that gave a clear view of the foreman's cottage. *Ball's in your court, cousin,* her silence told him. She would be there as backup, but it was his case, his obsession.

"Do you have news about my brother?"

Brad turned his attention to the human woman, but found no welcome in the closed set of her face. The agency seldom had bad news to report. Sitting across from Marnie Simpson, he vowed to keep it that way—he didn't like this part of the job one bit. "Yes," he said, "I'm afraid we do. Would you like to call your husband?"

Marnie Simpson dismissed the suggestion with a cutting gesture, using the side of her hand like a blade. "Paul and Frank, my husband, never liked each other. Whatever you have to say, I doubt that Frank will be particularly sympathetic."

"Very well." He leaned forward, his clasped hands resting between his knees. "We made contact with your brother's kidnappers at a place called the Black Masque."

Simpson reached into the pocket of her tailored slacks and brought out a crumpled pack of Virginia Slims. "Paul had mentioned the place, I told you that." She hooked the last cigarette with a crooked finger and brought it to her lips, returned the pack to her pocket, and withdrew a lighter. "He knew he was in danger there; that's why he came home. Did you see him?"

"I'm afraid so." Brad paused while she lit the cigarette and set the lighter down on the end table next to her chair. "You have to understand, Omage's methods are quite vicious. Your brother was barely alive when we found him. Omage made it clear he had no intention of freeing Paul; he only agreed to see us so that he could flaunt what he perceived as our ineffectiveness against him. We goaded him, and he made the mistake we were waiting for. But Paul was too far gone. He saw that chance for the only kind of freedom he could imagine, and he took it."

"What are you trying to say, Mr. Bradley?" Mrs. Simpson's brittle voice chilled to ice.

"Your brother is dead, Mrs. Simpson. In his condition he could hardly imagine escape and, frankly, I don't think he saw rescue as freedom."

"This Omage wasn't wrong, then, was he? Ineffective just about sums it up." Simpson flicked the cigarette ash into the china ashtray with a single sharp tap of her index finger, returning the cigarette to her lips in the same motion. "What did you do—gamble my brother's life that you could get him out of there without giving up the ransom?" Agitated, Marnie Simpson stood and paced toward the window, stopped short at the cold light in Lily's eyes. "Was this Eye of Omage worth the life of my brother?"

"He means your brother took the only way out he's ever known." Lily turned deliberately to the window. "Take a walk through Paul's bedroom, Mrs. Simpson. Sit in his chair and feel the press of his rifle against the back of your head. Touch his razor blades, swallow his pills, drink his whiskey, then tell us whose fault it is Paul died."

"I tried to help him." Still as stone, Marnie Simpson whispered the words.

"You couldn't have stopped him, any more than we could." Brad leaned forward, his head caught between his hands. He was so weary. "Paul felt he had no choice. In a way, neither did Omage."

"You may be right about Paul—" she turned sharply, pinned Brad with a glare that had wheels turning wheels behind it. "I'd be a fool to live next to that house and deny it—but don't expect sympathy for his murderer. What was he looking for—what was the Eye of Omage?"

"A stone," Brad raised his head to meet her anger. "A topaz; Paul was wearing it in the picture you left us. We don't know how Omage lost it, or why he wanted it back so badly."

The intensity of Marnie Simpson's concentration on Brad's upturned face never wavered, but the anger vanished like a door closing behind her eyes. "A stone of that size must have considerable value," she suggested. "Did you find it?"

Brad met her gaze levelly. Foolish, he reminded himself, to suspect every human reaction that didn't match the ones he'd seen in Evan. Marnie Simpson had watched her brother's struggle from the outside, far from the dark and dangerous places that haunted Paul Carter's dreams. She'd been left to cope with the chaos left in the wake of his struggle. Why did that flare of anger, so quickly suppressed, make him uneasy?

"We found it," he said, "and we offered the stone for your brother's return. Omage, however, had other plans. The ransom note promised a swift end to Paul's suffering, murder instead of torture, but not his release. We had a good chance of pulling your brother out of there anyway, but Paul had given up. As it was, we barely escaped with our own lives; there was nothing more we could do."

"I'm sorry you were in danger." Brad heard no regret in her voice; the word sounded perfunctory, like good morning to a stranger on a rainy day. "But I'm not really surprised you couldn't help my brother. Paul was never strong."

The bitterness in Marnie Simpson's last words surprised Brad. Lily stood by the window; with the woman's back to her, the daemon hadn't bothered to school her expression, and Brad saw the familiar cool disinterest sharpen to attention. She met his glance with a quirk of the brow, then frowned as Marnie Simpson roused from her brief reverie to ask:

"Do you have it with you? May I at least see this stone my brother died for?"

Brad spread his hands wide. "I'm sorry, but it's locked in the safe." We don't usually walk around with evidence of capital crimes in our pockets. Brad rephrased the thought with more tact for the bereaved sister. "The police will have to be called, and of course we will hand over the jewel as evidence. Until then, it seemed most appropriate to keep it in a safe place."

"Must we call the police?" The woman twisted her hands together, distress clear on her face for the first time during the conversation. "Paul is dead, by his own hand, and you are correct. For my brother, suicide was a matter of time. But the scandal, his name in the papers—"

Brad coughed delicately, unnecessarily, but it bought him a pause in the flow of words, and Marnie Simpson's attention. "There is the matter of the body."

"My God. Of course." The woman paled. She stubbed out her cigarette and reached a trembling hand into her pocket. "Damn." The pack was empty; she crushed it, threw it into the fireplace. "I need a cigarette. I'm sorry, I'll be back in a moment."

Alone together in the formal living room, the detectives relaxed almost imperceptibly. Lily leaned against the window frame, arms wrapped in front of her, legs crossed at the ankle. "She's a cool one," she commented, her eyes pinned on the doorway through which Marnie Simpson had exited.

Brad rubbed his forehead, considering. "Until I mentioned her brother's body. It was like he hadn't really existed until then."

"Didn't like the idea of the police being involved, did she?" Lily added.

Before he could reply, Mrs. Simpson returned, a lit cigarette in one hand. "I'm sorry. I'm not accustomed to losing control, it's a weakness someone in my business can ill afford.

"Go on, please. You were talking about Paul's—" she hesitated, then finished, "—body. Where is he? I'll have to make arrangements to have him brought home. I should have the address of the place that took care of everything for us when Mother died." She fell into her chair. "The police. My God, the scandal."

Brad crossed to her side, awkward in the role of comforter. "Let me call your husband. He can deal with the police, identify the body."

"Frank is out of the country, on business." She drew on the cigarette and put it out half smoked, stared vaguely at the stub, then drew out another and lit it. "His office has the number." She clutched at Brad's arm with her free hand. "Where do they have Paul's body now?"

"That's a little difficult to explain," Brad began. Fortunately, Lily took up the story.

"There was an accident, a gas main explosion just minutes after Paul died. We escaped in the confusion, but Paul's body was buried under the rubble, along with several dozen patrons of the club Omage used as a front for his activities."

"Were there other survivors?" Simpson asked abruptly.

LIly handed off the explanation with a glance, and Brad continued. "We suspect Omage made it out in time, if that is what you are asking. As far as we could tell, the rest were dead."

"Then I can only be thankful you came to no harm. I'm sorry." Mrs. Simpson put out her third cigarette and pushed the hair away from her eyes with the back of her hand.

"This has been a shock, you understand. You are right, of course. I have to contact my husband, and then I really must rest. I'll have Frank's office contact you about your fee."

"We'll be making our report to the police, but you have the agency number, should the police start asking questions. If we can be of any help, please call on us."

"I'll keep that in mind."

Marnie Simpson led them to the door and closed it behind them. They walked until an old elm tree obscured the view of the lane, then transported home, falling unceremoniously into their accustomed places—Brad in his wingback chair, and Lily sprawled full length on the leather couch.

Lily relaxed with a gusting sigh. "I'd rather face an audit by the IRS," she declared, "than spend ten seconds in the same room with that woman."

"She's a little cool."

Brad considered the interview while he dragged himself out of his chair and collected the brandy and a pair of snifters. "I can remember thinking, 'Evan would never do that' from time to time, but I've never found humans terribly predictable. Especially Evan."

"I was watching her pretty closely when you were talking." Lily took the snifter, swirled the brandy, and sipped it. "Whatever she says, Marnie Simpson is glad her brother is dead."

Brad considered the middle distance for a moment. "You're probably right."

Chapter Eighteen

Kaitar means the high place, from where the daemon sees from a distance, but his Prince is Paimon, the whisperer of deceit. Pathet is fear, and fruitfulness. His Prince is Azmod. Fear abounds where Pathet passes.

Evan woke in a pool of sunlight angled too high. Muzzy with sleep, he identified the nagging urgency slowly. Late. Trouble. A phone ringing, no answer, echoed in his mind. He'd planned to be on a plane by now, on his way home. The memory burned away the last of his morning fog.

He rolled out of bed and headed for the bathroom, showered and shaved while his head made lists. Didn't have to pack much, because he hadn't bothered to unpack when he arrived. He needed a ticket on the first flight out, but first call home again, hope for a message.

Coffee at the top of the list, Evan came down the stairs two at a time and stopped in front of the telephone, conscious of the sweat clammy on his palms and prickling at his temples. He picked up the receiver, impatient with the slow return of the rotary dial, and waited for the overseas operator to come on the line:

"Hello. May I have the number you are calling?"

He gave the private number and his message code; finally, the tinny ring echoed through space. Once, twice, then the answering machine connected, passed him through to his messages.

Lily's voice grated flat and mechanical in his ear: "Evan, we're home, more or less in one piece. If you're calling before evening, your time, we're asleep. After, we'll be out again, but you can reach us through the service if you have an emergency."

Evan felt the tension leave his neck and shoulders. It may have been touch and go for a while—he could tell that from the weariness he'd never heard in her voice before—but they were safe. He still had a home, a family. Even the rest of her message couldn't dampen his relief on that score:

"Unfortunately, the package was damaged beyond repair," she continued. "It wasn't built for hard use. We'll be speaking to the original owner this afternoon, but our friend in New York is already looking for a replacement, so keep your eyes open. Leave us a number where we can reach you if anything else turns up."

Evan waited for the signal beep and read off the Laurence's telephone number while he processed Lily's cryptic message. So Paul Carter hadn't made it. Anger boiled behind his eyes, and outside the wind picked up, whistled through the windows. A week ago he hadn't known another hybrid like himself existed—he remembered his shock when he first learned about Paul Carter, and how he'd shared Lily's revulsion in Carter's bedroom even while he was remembering a gun under his own pillow. None of it was Carter's fault, not his life, certainly not his death.

Evan knew that only a part of his anger was for the boy,

dead in the Black Masque's back room. As long as Paul Carter lived, Evan was only half the freak he had been before. He knew that the survival of his kind was possible. Omage had taken that fragile security away from him. He clenched his fist around the telephone receiver, fighting the storm that tightened in his chest, while outside thunderheads churned and lightning flashed.

Omage was a son of a bitch; that was hardly news. For some reason that only the daemon knew, Omage wanted him back. Evan figured that staying alive and free would be his best revenge, and Charlie St. George's offer suddenly seemed a lot more attractive, something simple, clean, and as far from New York as he could manage on short notice. Not that distance made a difference to Omage; it just made Evan feel safer. He might even have time to do a little checking on Alfredo DaCosta while he was in Venice. He added a short message about St. George's request for a corporate background check in Venice with his recommendation that they take the case, and rang off with a promise to call back with details later.

The storm slowly died away while Evan tapped the telephone receiver thoughtfully with his fingertips. He'd call Charlie, take the case. But first, coffee.

He expected to have the kitchen to himself, but Jack was waiting with a cup of coffee and yesterday's newspaper.

"What time is it? I thought you were going to work today."

Jack stared at him, not quite frightened, Evan realized, but uneasy. "It's ten thirty. Did I hear you on the phone just now?"

"Yes." Evan frowned. "I paid for the call on my credit card, if that's what has you worried."

"Don't treat me like an idiot, old chum."

Evan stopped on his way to the kettle, surprised, but Laurence hadn't finished:

"Did you reach your relatives from outer space?"

"Inner space, to be accurate, but yes," Evan answered, "There was a message from Lily; she and my father are fine."

The anger, so quickly suppressed a moment before, surfaced again. Omage was out of reach, but as a substitute target, Jack Laurence gone cryptic and suspicious on him did a good job of planting a bull's eye across his own chest.

"What's the matter, Jack?" he snapped. "Suddenly bored playing with the freak? Decided the game's no fun anymore?"

"Not a game, Evan," Laurence answered. "It's never been that. Let's call it trust. Since when did Batman hold out on the Boy Wonder?"

"I don't know what you're talking about." Evan filled the kettle, banged it down on the stove, and grabbed a mug— turtledoves cooing in a tree, for God's sake.

"I went to the office this morning; this was waiting on my desk." Jack nudged the tabloid with his coffee mug. "I don't read these rags myself, but someone on the staff usually leaves a copy on my desk when there's a story about the States. I thought maybe you would have an explanation for this one."

The headline read: "Sodom and Gomorrah, American Style" and below the headline was a picture of a New York neighborhood well known to Evan Davis and his host, one particular landmark lying in ruin.

Evan fell heavily onto a chair, the promise of coffee forgotten. He buried his face in his hands and ran his fingers through his hair, dragging it back off his forehead. They both knew the place, but Jack seemed to want him to say it. "The Black Masque. Has Claudia seen this?"

"Not from me, but someone may mention it to her at the shop. We'd better come up with a good story before she gets home." Laurence took the paper back and began to read aloud:

"In the United States, the New York skyline was lit by more than neon last night. A freak accident filled the darkness with a column of flame visible for miles in all directions. According to authorities, a gas main ruptured beneath a building in the city's Greenwich Village section. It was midnight—the proverbial witching hour—when blood rained down with falling brick at the location of a private drinking club notorious for its sin and corruption even in the city that never sleeps. Witnesses drawn from their beds by the shattering blast described the scene as horrible, terrifying. 'I felt the earth move,' reported one observer, 'I fell to my knees, sure that the end of the world had come.'

"Rescuers reported hearing victims, buried in the destruction, screaming for help, while the terrible heat and the instability of the fallen building turned back all efforts to save the dying. According to police, no survivors escaped the holocaust. At least fifty people died in the explosion. More accurate figures will be available after forensic specialists assure themselves that they have accounted for all limbs and body parts."

Jack's voice faded, the voices of the dying heavy in the silence. Fifty people. God! Was that what Lily meant by "hard use"? The kettle shrieked; Evan didn't notice until Jack got up and filled his mug, then added coffee crystals.

Jack set the mug in front of him and waited. "What kind of trouble are you in, Evan?"

"Do you actually think I had something to do with this?" It would have sounded more convincing if he could keep his hands from shaking. Omage could have brought his own foul nest down, out of spite, but somehow he knew his father had done this, or his cousin.

Not human. The words screamed in his mind. They didn't think like humans, didn't value life like humans. They called themselves lords, and knew his world as a flicker in their endless night. Fear that had become too familiar tightened his gut, turning it over. Fifty people dead. Did he share that part of them, the part that killed without thought, the way he shared their passage into the second sphere?

"I was on a plane, two hours out of Heathrow if they got the time right." *Should have been there, should have stopped them.* The past just wasn't worth fifty lives. "If they got any of it right."

Somewhere at the bottom of his soul a knot that had been there so long he'd forgotten what it felt like not to have the pain loosened. He knew inside himself that it was true, like a prisoner in the dark knows when his shackles are undone. Omage's chamber, caked with Evan Davis' blood, had fallen. The sacrifice was over. But at what price, what price? "I swear, I had nothing to do with this."

"Drink your coffee."

Jack folded Evan's hands around the mug. Jack didn't blame him. Evan stared at the tall blond man, saw something in eyes the color of a Kansas sunrise that shook him.

I don't want to know, his mind screamed, while his words betrayed him. "I don't understand."

"No, you never did," Laurence agreed with a rueful smile. "Your father did it, you said he was going in to rescue another, uh, what do I call you? Your kind, I mean?"

Evan shrugged. "Paul Carter didn't make it. As far as I know, that means I don't have a kind; I'm the only one."

Jack Laurence grunted. "That pretty much clinches it, then. You're mortal all right. Do you still need help? You've got it—just say the word."

"Why?" He didn't expect this, wasn't sure he wanted easy acceptance. His father had just murdered fifty people and he wasn't taking it that well himself.

"I told you." Jack shook his head, then spoke slowly, as one does to small children or shock victims after an accident: "Once I would have died for you in that place. I'm not surprised that someone would kill for you, and I can't see them going back there for a stranger. I just need to know what comes next."

"Stay out of it, Jack." How could he tell the man that it had never been for Evan, that Brad and Lily had their own reasons for doing things that mortals didn't understand—otherwise, fifty people dead were his fault, and he couldn't deal with that.

"I didn't know anything about this, certainly wasn't expecting it, but it fits with Lily's message." Evan drank, put down the mug. "Whatever took out the Black Masque isn't finished yet, because there was at least one survivor. Mac got away, and if I understood Lily's message, he wants me back. I didn't lie to you, Jack." But he realized suddenly that he had brought danger into this house, and he had promised he'd left that part of his life behind him.

"I haven't done anything. I don't know why he wants me—"

"Mac doesn't care about what you've done, Evan; he never did. It's what you are."

Not human. Evan shuddered, afraid of the knowledge of his dual heritage. Did it make him a killer like his father, like Lily? What did Omage want of him?

"But why?" he said aloud. "There's nothing I can do that he can't do better, in our world or in his."

"Maybe," Jack conceded. "But how much do you know about what you can do? I mean, did you know your father could knock down buildings? Do you know you can't?"

Evan didn't like the direction that thought took him. He shrugged off the creeping sensation that pieces of his life were fitting themselves together around Jack's questions. Some things about himself he didn't want to know.

"Whatever his reason for wanting to get his hands on me, he has to find me first. I'm packed, I'll be gone as soon as a taxi can get here. Tell Claudia I'm sorry. If things had been different . . . just say I'm sorry. And you haven't seen me since New York, if anybody asks." He got up and turned toward the hall, but Laurence grabbed his arm.

"Where are you going? What are you going to do?"

"Yes, Mr. Davis, where *are* you going?"

The stranger's voice froze them in place.

"Who are you?" Evan turned to face the man who stood with his arms crossed in front of him, leaning against the refrigerator. The stranger was as tall as Jack, but thinner, pale-skinned, with light brown hair hanging almost to his shoulders.

"How did you get in here?"

"I am called Pathet, I can tell you that because you

won't live long enough to use it. I'm a distant relation of your father's, and I entered in the usual way—for our kind." The man unfolded his arms, held out his empty hands, palms up. He smiled, thin lips stretched over straight white teeth, but something vicious glinted in green eyes. A predator: Omage had eyes like that.

Evan remembered another time, blue flames licking with no heat against his skin, Lily and Brad in the second sphere teaching him that he could take his body into the place his nightmares traveled and return at his own command. In their eyes he found the mark of what they were, and in these eyes he knew the stranger.

"Omage sent you. You're one of his."

"Clever boy." The stranger moved away from the refrigerator, his arms loose at his sides. "But not too clever. We are Azmod, cousins, if you will, but I do not answer to Omage. He's quite mad, you know. But then, of course you do; he's played his games with you before, hasn't he, boy?" That slow, almost sweet smile reminded Evan of chains and a silver knife, of Omage stroking his skin and flinging him into the second sphere. Did his father feel that pleasure when he killed?

Jack Laurence squeezed his arm, offering support, and turned to face the daemon in the kitchen. "Who are you? What do you want? Evan?"

The first two questions were aimed at the stranger, but the last looked to Evan for answers. The stranger, Pathet, frowned. "Control your human, half-breed, or I'll do it for you."

Evan nodded his head, once, sharply. What hope he had of keeping his friend alive depended on keeping the stranger's attention focused on himself. He answered

Jack's questions, but his eyes never left Pathet's face. *This is for you,* that look said. *I know what sent you.*

"He's one of them, like Mac—his real name's Omage, by the way—and like my father. And you were right, Mac still wants me. The question is, why? What is it about us—Paul Carter, me—that Omage needs? Like I said, I keep coming up with just one answer. Nothing. But a human, now, a human might want to know what we half-breeds can do.

"Omage isn't working on his own, is he?" Evan snapped the question, and the stranger narrowed his eyes. *So.* "Whoever is running Mac has you on a string, too."

"Come with me and find out, clever boy." The smile had more than ambient malice in it now. Hatred had a name: Evan Davis.

"Evan isn't going anywhere." Jack Laurence stepped between the two creatures in human form.

"Jack." Evan grabbed his arm, spun the man around to face him. "You're out of your depth. If you understand anything I've said, you've got to know that. Let it go; I'll be all right."

Jack laughed, a short, bitter sound. "If you believed that, you wouldn't be here. Remember when I said I wouldn't do it again?"

Evan nodded, their conversation by the Thames fresh in his mind. *My blood was a gift, my life a sacrifice for the pleasure of my god. Dying I loved him. You.*

"I can't let you—"

Jack Laurence smiled. "You can't stop me." He turned to the stranger, who stood taller, green flames lighting his features. "I won't let you take him."

"No!"

The daemon Pathet smiled and raised his right hand.

Green flame shot from the palm, snapped like lightning, and hit the floor where Jack Laurence had been standing. With no time for anything more elegant, Evan hit him with an awkward tackle, heard Jack's head crack on the table going down.

"Are you hurt?" Evan stood and offered his friend a hand. Jack's eyes took a moment to focus, but he took the hand and dragged himself to his feet.

"Let it go, Jack." Evan pushed the man gently back into his chair, leaning over to hold the mortal's attention on himself, not on the daemon lounging against his refrigerator. "You can't stop him. Killing you won't even slow him down. Think of Claudia."

"And what about you?"

Evan shook his head. "They want me alive for something. And you're forgetting, I have powerful allies now. It isn't like it was at the Black Masque. My father will find them; you don't want to be in the middle of this when the fighting starts."

With a reassuring squeeze to Jack's shoulder, Evan straightened and faced the daemon. "All right," he said. "Leave him alone, I'll go with you. I can transport, but I need a guide."

"No problem," Pathet agreed. "Just give me a minute— I want to leave a message for Ariton."

The daemon contemplated Jack's down-bent head. "I don't often miss," he admitted apologetically, then, "and I don't like it when I do."

He struck suddenly, with the sound of the sky tearing open, and a pile of cinders smoldered in a blackened circle of linoleum where Jack Laurence had been sitting. The kitchen chair was gone as well. "That's better," he said, dusting off his hands. "Much tidier all around."

Evan retched as the smell of burning flesh hit him. Too fast for him to intercept the strike, it was over. Evan bent on one knee, reached a hand to the charred circle and pulled back, afraid that touching the greasy ash would make it real. *Not even time to scream,* Evan realized, and the thought turned his stomach again.

"You promised to leave him alone." He should have known better, should have expected trickery and betrayal, but he'd gambled his own worth to Pathet's master against the life of his friend.

"Yes, I did," Pathet concurred seriously, then he smiled. "I lied."

"You will pay for this," Evan swore in the face of the daemon, and Pathet laughed at him.

"What can you do to me that my master hasn't already done, clever boy?"

"I can send you back to him a failure," Evan answered. Trembling, he almost doubted that he could move. But his memory fed him Lirion's voice, soothing and mocking as she led him into the second sphere. He had learned to move through that realm with his body and his senses intact, and he did so now, snapped out of reality with a clap of thunder and pushed thoughts of nausea and nothingness away. Loss swept him like the insanity he had known at Omage's hands. He screamed—endlessly, soundlessly— and the void trembled in his passing.

Something pulled him toward home and he rejected it, not ready yet to cope with his father's murders, or his own by inaction in Jack Laurence's kitchen. He shaped an image in his mind of a safe place—Covent Gardens. The stranger might be following, but Evan took an extra minute to ease into the physical universe; appearing in public in a flash of lightning would draw more attention than he could afford right now. For a moment he stood next to the stall where yesterday he had bought violets for Claudia. Then he dusted himself off and walked away.

Chapter Nineteen

A daemon, hound, remains so until the master of the daemon releases him, which requires not intention but the speaking of the words that set the daemon free. So a man who would hold a daemon will refrain from converse with that daemon which will, by answer of a seeming innocent question, pronounce the words that free that spirit.

"There, mate, watch where you're going." A man in a soccer jacket with Arsenal on the back elbowed Evan in the ribs. Dazed and confused, he stepped back, stumbling against a man behind him. A crowd surrounded him, pressing him forward, but Evan had no memory of where he was, or how he had gotten there.

Smoke caught at the back of his throat and reality kaleidoscoped, time and place recombining in dizzy patterns. The crush of people around him was real. Other people's clothing scraped roughly against his shirtsleeved arms. Evan heard the murmurs of the curious and the voices of the uniformed policemen at the center of the crowd urging them to move on. But the image of Jack Laurence, dying, swamped his senses. He saw green flame and smelled burning flesh again, gagged on the lump in his throat and wiped cold sweat from his face. Pathet's mocking smile lingered in the air like Alice's hallucinatory Cheshire cat, fading slowly.

"What happened?" Evan said, because asking the more urgent question—where am I?— would attract too much attention.

"IRA." the man in the Arsenal jacket stated with certainty. "Planted a bomb in this 'ere bookshop. Owner's dead. They took him out just a minute ago—you must have passed the ambulance leaving when you come up."

An explosion in a bookstore. Evan nodded absently, a cold weight settling in his gut. "Was anyone else hurt?" he asked, more scared to hear the answer than he had ever been of anything in his life. "I have a friend, I think she may work around here."

"Don't know yet, coppers are still looking. You're a foreigner, aren't you? You look a might peaky—'oy, over here—" The man raised his arm above his head, pointing down at Evan. "Got a Yank here says he knew someone in the shop."

"I'm not sure," Evan began, but a man in a crisp tan raincoat had him by the elbow, drew him a bit apart from the crowd.

"I'm Inspector James." The man in the raincoat flashed his identification, returned it to his inside breast pocket and drew out a small notebook. He opened it and examined the writing there for a moment before he looked up at Evan again. "I'm sure this is a bit of a shock, sir, but I need to ask a few questions."

Evan shook his head, trying without success to clear the fog that seemed to shroud all conscious thought but one. "A woman—was a woman hurt in the explosion?" he asked.

"Now should there have been, Mr.—?" Inspector James waited with bland attention.

"Davis, Evan Davis, and I don't know." Evan paused, trying to remember. "She worked in a shop like this, but I'm not sure—" He looked around him. The street seemed vaguely familiar, but he'd been to the bookstore only once. It had looked different then—no crowds, no fire brigade or policemen, no smoldering wreckage—but yes, the same place. The imperative that had driven him here asserted itself. "I have to warn her—"

"It's a bit late for a warning, sir. There was a young lady who worked in this shop; were you and she having a spot of trouble, then?"

Ponderously, like the world was passing in slow motion, Evan worked through the expressionless voice to the meaning of the words.

Too late. *Was* a young lady.

"She's dead." He twisted his way through the policemen holding back the crowd, heading for the smoking ruin of the bookstore. "Oh, God, what have I done? Claudia!"

Hands grabbed at his arms, pulled him back, away from the heat that wavered in the air around the smoldering building.

"I didn't say she was dead, Mr. Davis." The inspector took his arm, led him to a patrol car, and pushed him onto the back seat. "Now why don't you tell me exactly what you have done."

"Nothing. Everything." Evan shivered, realized he was still in his shirtsleeves.

"You seem to have lost your jacket."

Evan looked blankly at the inspector—James, he'd said, Inspector James—saw distaste tighten the lines around the man's eyes. They both wanted the same thing, but

Evan put his chances of convincing Inspector James of that at nil. And given the way they'd started, he couldn't say he blamed the man. He shrugged his shoulders, not thinking fast enough and knowing he wasn't up to a game of cat and mouse with Scotland Yard.

"I didn't realize I'd need it when I came out this morning."

Only half the truth, it explained only half the cold he felt. At the first hint of Omage's involvement in the Carter case he should have run as fast and as far as his gold card would take him in the opposite direction. Jack would still be alive. Or later, if he'd gone with Pathet, the daemon wouldn't have come after Claudia. Bad choices all down the line: starting with the gun he hadn't used on himself when he was Paul Carter's age, he'd been buying his life with other people's blood for years. Evan wondered if he would ever feel warm again.

"I see." The inspector flipped through the pages of his notebook, lips pursed. "You called out a name a moment ago—Claudia, I believe—is that the young lady's name?"

"Yes—Claudia Laurence. She's twenty-four years old, about five feet tall, shoulder-length brown hair, brown eyes—" Warm, dark eyes with soft lashes that brushed his cheek like a breath when he held her. "Light green coat, I don't know what else she was wearing today."

She was wearing that coat when he saw her yesterday, he remembered; the weight of her tingled up the inside of his arms, the press of her kiss warmed his lips for a moment and left only the cold. The memory of her touch ripped away the numbness that had held feeling at bay. Guilt brought a cold sweat to his temples. Over and over in his head the single thought taunted him: he never should have come here. The inspector's voice brought him back to the present he would have to live with.

"Yes, sir, that fits the description of the young lady who worked in this shop. Did you know her well?"

Evan stared at the inspector, fought back the pain squeezing the breath out of his chest. "She was a friend, a good friend."

"Was you say. You know for a fact, then, that she was in the shop when the explosive device went off?"

"You were telling me, Inspector." Evan glared at the man. "I arrived after the explosion." Claudia had to be alive, or none of this made sense.

"So you say, sir." Inspector James looked back in his notebook, then glanced at Evan with an air of professional indifference. "About that statement you made a moment ago, Mr. Davis—'What have I done—' What, exactly, have you done to the young lady?"

Evan tried to pull his thoughts in line, matching the policeman's anger. "Nothing, Inspector. In my business, you make enemies. I'm a private investigator with Bradley, Ryan, and Davis in the States." And past time he started acting like it, he reminded himself. He wasn't nineteen anymore, he wasn't helpless, and the police still hadn't found a second body in the mess any one of his enemies had made of the bookstore. As a corpse Claudia was useless, but as a hostage, she had trade value for one half-human who might have loved her once.

"Ah." Anger passed fleeting across the bland face of the policeman. "Have you given the details of your investigation up at the Yard, then, sir?"

"No, Inspector." A warning might have saved at least one life, maybe more, but there had been no warning. "I'm here on vacation, didn't actually have anything to report. The agency is working on a case closer to home; we specialize in recovery work, art mostly. Our clients prefer discretion to retribution, and the less scrupulous collectors we recover from usually play by the same rules. Sometimes they don't, but I can't think of anyone we've annoyed in the last year who might do something like this." But Pathet had been very annoyed. And Alfredo DaCosta had tried to tell him something yesterday. . . .

"Someone did it, Mr. Davis. A list of the most likely suspects might be helpful." The inspector jotted a line in his notebook. "In the meantime, if we should find an extra jacket in the shop, I'm sure you won't mind trying it on for us."

Here, at least, he was on safe ground. "You won't," he assured the officer. "I didn't wear a jacket this morning, and I had just arrived when that man in the crowd called you over."

"Mmhmm." The word could have meant anything. Inspector James glanced briefly at his notebook again. "But in the event we do find your jacket, where are you staying in London, sir?"

Evan rejected the truth without a backward glance. The inspector hadn't believed one word since the first, and bits of charred bone and blackened ash in the kitchen in Layton would clinch any doubts James might have. So he improvised, buying time. "Claridge's. I'm staying with a client, Charles Devereaux St. George. The room is in his name." They'd have to find Charlie to discredit the story. Then they'd have to find Evan.

Inspector James wrote down Evan's name, Charlie's, and that of the hotel, tore the sheet out of his notebook and motioned to a man in a plaid sports coat. The man was younger, and his anger was closer to the surface. He took the slip of paper, nodded at James' instructions, and gave Evan a poisonous look as he walked away. Until that moment his danger from the police had been a distant thing, an obstacle to circumvent. For a fleeting moment Evan wondered where the greater threat lay: in the open-eyed malice of his enemies, or in the blind justice of Her Majesty's judicial system.

"Just a few more questions, Mr. Davis."

"Of course, Inspector," Evan answered politely, almost grateful to have his attention drawn away from the younger policeman.

"I don't have in my notes why you were visiting the shop just now—"

"Lunch," Evan stammered, while his mind screamed at him to get moving. Two people were already dead because of him; if he didn't find her first, Claudia would make three.

"And what time were you supposed to meet Miss Laurence?"

"Noon." Evan buried his head in his hands, wishing the inspector would go away, knowing the man would stand there all day until he was satisfied that he'd wrung the last word out of his only suspect. Evan didn't fool himself. He looked as guilty as sin, and it didn't help that he felt guilty as well.

"Noon today, Mr. Davis? What time did you say you left your hotel?"

For an insane moment he considered telling the man the truth: *I left through the second celestial sphere just after a daemon of the host of Azmod burned her brother to a cinder over morning coffee in Claudia's kitchen. He would have killed me, too, but he had orders to bring me back alive. Unfortunately, my closest friends keep getting in his way.*

Instead, he gave Inspector James a curt nod, while he wondered if they had an insanity plea in England, and whether they still hung convicted murderers. "I don't know what time I left the hotel, Inspector." He held out his wrist, showed the man the watch still set for home.

"Lucky mistake for you, wasn't it?"

"I don't understand—" Evan frowned at the policeman, confused. The inspector showed him his watch.

"It's after one o'clock. You missed your lunch date by almost an hour. If you'd been on time, you might have been caught in the blast yourself."

He must have run from the house in Layton before eleven, but Evan remembered nothing from the moment he transported until the man in the soccer jacket jostled him in the crowd. Pathet already had more than an hour's lead on him.

Inspector James checked his notebook again. "We'll have to contact Miss Laurence's next of kin, let them know what's happened here. Would you happen to know who that might be, Mr. Davis?"

Evan roused himself to consider the question. Jack and Claudia had a mother still living in St. Louis; their father had died of a heart attack the year before they'd all met in New York. "In the States," he confirmed. "I don't have the address with me, but I can call home for it this afternoon."

"That would be fine." James closed his notebook with a snap and slid it into his back pocket. "You don't seem to have your passport with you—"

Evan shook his head. The passport was back in Layton,

side pocket of his carry-on, but he kept that information to himself.

"Then you won't mind if I take a look at it when I drop you off at your hotel."

"That isn't necessary, Inspector. I'll take a taxi, call home for that address, and stop by your office with the passport."

"I think I'd rather see it sooner, if you don't mind. One more question. We found this lying next to the dead man—" Inspector James reached into the front seat of the car, pulled out a bundle, and handed it to Evan. The plastic bag contained a small leather-bound volume, burned and curling up at the corners from water damage. The book was open to the flyleaf, on which someone had scrawled the words Evan D—, almost illegibly, in flaky char. "Could you tell me why the dead man's last thought should be of you?"

Until he saw his own name inscribed in the ruins, a part of Evan's mind could believe that the explosion had nothing to do with him, or with the Black Masque. Pointless to try and deny the words were there for him— Omage could reach out for him anywhere, drag him back into the darkness where nothing could save him from the terrors of his own endless night. But Inspector James would never understand the message. Suddenly a hand was at his shoulder, pushing him down.

"Don't faint, Mr. Davis. And don't vomit on my shoes, if you please. Seems we have jogged something loose in your memory. Care to tell me?"

Oh, yes, just tell the good inspector. Lily would enjoy the joke, if he lived to tell it to her.

"Not a memory, Inspector. I had nothing to do with this—" He rested the fingertips of one hand on the plastic

covering the blackened book, felt nothing of the daemon
who murdered to taunt him. "But somebody wants you to
believe I'm a cold-blooded killer. I didn't think anybody
hated me that much. I was wrong, and now people are
dying for that mistake. I guess that does make it my fault."

"A pretty speech, Mr. Davis." Pale blue eyes pinned
Evan with a measuring look. "We haven't found the deto-
nator or any traces of the explosive used, but it appears to
be something we haven't seen before."

"And you think I have?" Evan challenged. "Being a private detective isn't usually this eventful, Inspector. I don't
carry a gun, I don't chase bad guys in fast cars, and I've
never fought anything more resistant than a balky computer program. I've never even seen a bomb, and as for
constructing one, I flunked chemistry in high school. If it
takes more mechanical expertise than screwing in a light
bulb, I'm out of luck."

"But you say you have enemies who do command exactly that expertise."

"Like I said, Inspector, until today I didn't know that either. Unfortunately, whoever did this left my name, not
his own."

Nobody on the material sphere had technology like
that. For a slightly annoyed daemon trying to make a
point, though, it had been easy. He rubbed the scars on
his wrist, remembering.

"An accident with a bread knife, Mr. Davis?" Inspector
James stared at the thin white lines, drawing the wrong
conclusion most people did.

"Ancient history, Inspector." None of your business, Evan's tone implied.

"Perhaps." Eyes met eyes again; Evan saw uneasiness
there, wondered what the policeman saw.

"We're not making any accusations yet, Mr. Davis. When we get a line on the explosives, however, you will be the first to know."

"Evan—is that you?" Charles St. George shouldered his way through the policemen, stepping gingerly over fire hoses and bits of charred wreckage.

"Charlie—"

"Can I help you, sir?" Inspector James pulled the notebook out of his pocket again. "Are you an acquaintance of Mr. Davis?"

His expression still bland, James stepped between the two men. Evan wondered if that face ever gave anything away, or if the policeman had feelings to reveal at all.

"This is Charles Devereaux St. George, Inspector. I'm staying with him at Claridge's."

Charlie passed him a sharp glance that said, *Explanations later,* but picked up the cue. "Actually, Evan works for my company on contract. He's here to arrange secure transport for a painting I plan to purchase at auction this afternoon." St. George looked from one man to the other with growing concern. "You can't possibly suspect Evan had anything to do with this!" he gestured expansively to take in the police and fire brigade as well as the blackened hole in the row of shops. "His credentials are impeccable."

"That may be, sir. We have no firm suspects as yet, but we must consider all the possibilities," Inspector James answered politely. "You say you were to purchase a painting at auction today, sir? If you needed extra security, I assume we are discussing a work of some considerable value?"

"A Matisse. It goes to auction at Sotheby's this afternoon. My agent is authorized for the purchase, but I thought Claudia—Miss Laurence—might find the auction exciting. I was calling to see if she might like to take the afternoon off, sort of an impromptu adventure."

St. George stopped a moment, as if the import of the place and Evan here in the police car finally penetrated his flustered consciousness. "My God, Evan, was Claudia in there?"

The policeman made another note in his book. "That's not yet certain, Mr. St. George. But tell me more about your relationship with Miss Laurence. She seems to have been a very popular young lady."

"I came by to take Claudia to lunch," Evan explained.

"Of course, dear boy, how foolish of me not to realize. But you didn't say anything last night. I presumed too much on dinner, I see."

"Then you haven't known Miss Laurence long, Mr. St. George."

Evan could almost feel the policeman's ears prick up. They'd call it a lover's triangle, he guessed, and point to the innocent shop owner caught in the spurned lover's jealous retribution when they hanged him.

"Evan introduced us yesterday, we all had a lovely dinner together at the hotel, and I thought—"

Later, if they found her alive, Claudia could let him down gently. Evan could see no point in shattering the man's romantic illusions now: "I already told Inspector James that Claudia and I were just friends, Charles—"

"Yes," the inspector interrupted. "Did the young lady spend the night at your hotel?"

Charlie bristled like an indignant hedgehog. "Of course not! After dinner, Evan took Claudia *and* her brother home. It was all quite proper!"

"A brother. Hmmm. Wouldn't he be next of kin, Mr.

Davis?" James riffled through his notebook, apparently found the entry he was looking for. "I thought you said Miss Laurence's family lived in the United States."

"They do," Evan persisted while the knot in his gut twisted tighter. He had to reach Brad before the police found what was left of the Laurences' kitchen. "Jack left town this morning."

"I see. Then you would know Miss Laurence's local address."

"Of course." Evan gave the inspector the address of the house on St. Mary's Road. "I'm an American citizen," he reminded James. "If you plan to arrest me, I demand to speak to the American Embassy."

"Arrested?" Charlie demanded sharply, turning to the officer. "You said you had no firm suspects. I thought this was a simple case of the IRA trying to scare away the tourists and you were trying to keep it a secret."

"No, sir," James objected. "We've made no final determination on the cause of the explosion. Until we do, however, I suggest that neither of you leave London."

"Then I assume I may take Mr. Davis back to the hotel?" St. George put a hand on Evan's shoulder, bent over, and peered into Evan's face. "You look like death, old boy. Do you need a doctor?"

Evan shook his head. "I need a phone. Have to call home."

"Of course. Wait just a moment, I'll get a cab."

"You won't get a cab down here, Mr. Devereaux; my men have cordoned off the street at the corner." Inspector James motioned a uniformed policeman over. "I'll have Sergeant Breckenridge take you back to the hotel."

Charles straightened to his full height. "Unless this is an arrest, Inspector, we'd prefer to take that taxi."

Inspector James slipped his notebook back into his pocket. "As you wish, Mr. St. George. Claridge's, you said? I'll stop by for that address and a look at your passports as soon as I've finished up here."

"And you will let us know if you hear anything about Miss Laurence?" St. George asked. "You must understand, we are most concerned."

"Of course." The policeman nodded once. "I'll see about getting a taxi down here for you."

He gave Evan a measuring look—for a noose, Evan decided—and walked away, his raincoat flaring out behind him in the late April breeze.

A suite. Charlie never did anything halfway, it seemed. The salon breathed a quiet elegance from the sculptured ceiling to the graceful chairs scattered about the room.

"Sit down before you fall down, dear boy." St. George motioned to a brocaded Queen Anne chair next to the telephone and headed for the bar.

Evan sat and looked around him. Several closed doors punctuated the ribbon-printed wallpaper, but Evan was too exhausted to wonder where they led. In one corner of the room an elaborately carved walking stick rested against the wall. Evan shivered when he looked at it, realized the shapes trailing from the rounded knob at the top were grotesque faces, mouths wide open as if frozen in mid-scream.

"Here, drink this, it will steady your nerves."

St. George pressed a glass into his hand—the smell of whiskey kicked the craving into high gear even while it brought back memories that turned Evan's stomach. The booze would take it all away for a time, but when he came down, Claudia would be dead.

"Not now, Charles." He set the glass on the desk and pushed it away, buried his face in his hands, and rubbed at his forehead with his fingertips.

"I'm sorry, Evan, I forgot." The glass disappeared, Evan heard the splash of liquid hitting the sink, the sound of running water. "Just let me call down to room service for some coffee, then I'll get out of your way. You can lie down a bit after you call home."

"Coffee would be a godsend, Charlie, but I don't need to lie down. I've got to find Claudia."

"Find?" St. George paused with his hand on the dial. "I thought, I mean from the way that policeman was speaking—"

"She's not dead, Charlie, I'm sure of it. I have to find her before the people who snatched her get tired of waiting and do something stupid."

Charlie dialed the number, waited for an answer. "Who are they—never mind, confidential, right? Did her brother really leave town, or is he missing, too? —Oh, hello? Room service? Yes, I'd like a large pot of coffee sent up, service for two, and a selection of cold sandwiches." He gave the room number and hung up.

"You seem to be taking this pretty calmly, Charles." Evan watched the man pour himself a brandy and lift it to his lips, savoring the bouquet. "Aren't you a little bit afraid that policeman might be right about me?"

"Nonsense, my boy." St. George set down his glass, and walked over to stand in front of Evan's chair. "What do these foreigners know anyway? We Americans have to stick together."

They both turned at a knock on the door, but St. George waved at the phone. "Must be the coffee. You go ahead and make your call."

Evan dialed up the switchboard and gave the operator his number. While he waited for the connection, a hand slid a china cup and saucer steaming with strong black coffee onto the desk. He looked up, a distracted "Thank you" half formed, and clenched his fist around the telephone receiver.

"You."

Pathet smiled his predator's smug confidence and Charlie gave a nod, the good host. "You two have met. Then I don't have to make introductions."

The daemon picked up the cup of coffee and took a sip, set it down again. "Finish your call, human."

Evan ignored the command. "What have you done with Claudia?"

St. George slipped up behind him and wrapped a comradely arm around his shoulder. "All in good time, my boy. Our dear Lily took something that belongs to me. I want it back. Later, when my property has been restored, we can talk about your lady friend."

Evan glared at the man, his own temper reflected in the mirror-hard eyes that mocked him over St. George's false smile. Slowly, deliberately, he set the receiver back on its cradle.

"Tsk." Charlie shook his head in a travesty of regret. "You really should pick your friends more carefully, old boy."

Evan felt the prick of the needle, and then nothing.

Chapter Twenty

A man who would bind a daemon to his will must always remember that the daemon does his bidding in anger and always means his master ill. Accordingly, great care should be taken in the binding and ordering of the daemon, or the daemon will twist the words of the command to the greatest harm of the master, even to the master's death.

Once, twice, the phone rang. Kevin Bradley reached for the receiver, never made it. For the second time that day the rope sensation tightened around his spine, wrenched his gut, and died on a wave of suffocating nausea. Human form wavered, steadied, then the shattered glass and broken furniture around him came back into focus.

"What's the matter with Evan?"

Lily shrugged. "I don't know that it was Evan. The operator said the call originated in England, but whoever it was hung up before I could answer. Want to take a hop over there and check?"

Badad focused his daemon sense inward. A moment ago the link with his son had surged with an adrenaline rush that screamed "danger"; now there was nothing.

Alive, surely: The rope, as he had taken to calling Evan's spell, still bound him, but he caught nothing of his son through it. The emergency, whatever it was, seemed to be over. "Maybe later."

He returned his attention to the chaos that surrounded them. The glazers had repaired the glass doors, and a cleanup crew outside scrubbed at the pentagram on the bricks, removed broken glass and twisted lawn chairs from the garden before it started to rain. When the afternoon shower began, the men would move inside. Soon, only the uneasy feeling in his gut would remain as evidence that a human had bound Badad of Ariton in this place.

"I was hoping it would all go away while we were gone," he said with a rueful frown.

"Gravity," Lirion reminded him. "Broken or not, material objects have a tendency to lie where they fall until you move them." She kicked at a splinter from an end table on her way to the kitchen, and Badad watched the chip of wood skitter across the floor.

"I didn't do it, you know." She took in the destruction with a gesture. "All this, I mean." She only confirmed what he already suspected.

"Neither did I."

Lily stopped at the kitchen door. "That leaves Evan. Not the first time either. I'm not the only one throwing sparks when we argue. Do you suppose he knows?"

Brad shook his head. "I don't think so."

"Interesting." Lily gave the matter some thought and came to the conclusion, "Very interesting," before passing out of view in the doorway.

"Yeah." Badad wondered how much damage his son would do before he admitted he needed some help controlling his daemon side. Nothing he could do about it now, but they'd have to talk about it when Evan came home.

Home. The word came too easily when he thought of Evan. He picked up a shard of glass, turned it over in his hand. Blood streaked the edge—Badad remembered the cut on his arm from the other side of body-death. The new form he wore looked like the old one, reconstructed exactly, except for the damage. He'd gotten used to the face in the mirror, identified it like a map. *If I look like this, I am on the material plane. It is the late twentieth century Western Earth time, as counted from the last bloody murder that seemed to matter to these creatures.* With an abrupt gesture he set the blood-streaked shard on an end table and turned away, leaving thoughts of dying flesh amid the broken fragments of a pottery lamp.

"Coffee?" Lily returned with a cup in each hand. She gave him one and drank from the one she kept. With her free hand she shifted a thin sheaf of computer paper from under her arm and lifted it so that she could read the print. "The results of Evan's search program. Want to take a look?"

Brad took the sheaf of paper. "Not here." Memory of what had happened in this room and the garden beyond crawled like rats over his skin, from his fingertips to the base of his skull. He ignored the sensation, angry suddenly at all humans and at himself for the decisions that had put him here, and headed for the study, away from the eyes of the cleanup crew.

"Anything from Evan on the machine?" Brad settled into his chair, the printout supported on the crook of his right knee, ankle propped on his left. He sipped at the coffee and set down the cup.

"He called this morning." Lily settled behind the desk,

Evan's place, ankles crossed on the desktop. "I checked the messages while you were explaining the damages to the workmen— Punk vandals on skateboards on their way to South Street?"

Brad shrugged. "It worked. For a few minutes there I didn't think the young guy on the cleanup crew would come into the garden at all."

"Smart kid," Lily agreed, "The place makes me nervous myself these days."

"Know what you mean." Evan's uneasy presence haunted the painted circle, but whether as a sense of present danger leaking through the spheres or the lingering terror of a human binding the forces of Ariton, Badad could not tell. "So what did Evan have to say?"

"He said he bumped into Charlie St. George in Covent Garden, was going to Venice tomorrow—make that today—to do a security check for one of Charlie's businesses. Seems there's trouble in paradise."

"Danger?" Brad looked up sharply, relaxed when he caught her predatory grin.

Lily waggled her eyebrows suggestively. "More like woman trouble, I suspect. Or boredom. Maybe he discovered that his old chums have settled into deserved obscurity. For all his protestations, our Evan needs the action—he is his father's son, after all." She saluted him with her coffee cup. "What did Evan's ferret program turn up this time?"

The answer lay on Brad's lap, in the printout from the computer that, for reasons too irrationally human for the lord of Ariton to understand, Evan called Bruce Wayne. Brad lifted the paper and worked his way slowly through the complex network of associations.

"This has possibilities. No record of a Marnie Carter,

but there's a picture of a Madeleine Carson that's a close fit for our bereaved Mrs. Simpson, barring the hairstyle and the date. Could be the mother."

"Society pages?"

"Mug shot. Seems our Mrs. Carson was also known as Sister Madeleine, camp show psychic. Appears there was a child clairvoyant in the act. Could be our Marnie Simpson. Let's see—" He turned the page and froze. "Shit."

"Problem?" Lily dropped her feet from the desk and leaned forward to take the printout.

"Did you say Evan made contact with Charlie St. George?"

"Uh-huh. According to Evan, old Charlie's buying a business of some sort in Venice, wants us to do the security check on the current Board and some key execs. Doesn't trust Italians, I guess. Evan decided to take the job. Like I said, the vacation didn't turn out quite as expected."

"No, it wouldn't." Brad unfolded himself from his wing-back chair and dropped the printout on the desk on his way to the safe. The stone was still there—he took it out, hefted the cold weight of it in his hand.

"What's Charlie's picture . . . oh. Shit." She shuffled through the pages.

"That's our perpetually-out-of-town Mr. Simpson," Brad explained unnecessarily. "Charles Devereaux St. George." Married, it appeared, to the child clairvoyant, and brother-in-law to her half-daemon brother. He didn't bother saying it, just waited, the stone a cold and mocking presence in his hand, while she followed Simpson's financial empire to its source in the printout.

"Mr. Simpson is not the self-made man he claims. In

fact, he owes his start in the business world to Francis St. George, deceased." Her glance, speculative, come to rest on the smoky topaz. He reached for her hand, turned it palm upward under the stone, and closed her fingers around it, shielding his own from its unnatural chill.

"Related to our Charlie?" He moved away and sank into his own chair, grateful for something solid under him.

"His father. It appears Mr. Simpson may have been planning Omage's little coup for longer than Ariton knew. Until nineteen sixty-seven Franklin Simpson was a minor hood, no significant connections, just a couple of convictions for petty theft. It seems reasonable to assume that he upped the ante. The real Charlie St. George probably ceased to exist about the same time."

Lily ran her fingers over the smooth plane of the stone's face, her eyes closing for a moment over cool meditation. "Dead?"

"Probably," Brad agreed. "Wouldn't have been that hard to do. Francis St. George died in a boating accident. The search only turned up one body, but that doesn't mean he died alone."

"Back at the Black Masque," Lily reminded him, her eyes wide open now, "Omage said he knew we had this thing," she held up the topaz by its chain, "the moment it fell into our hands. If Charlie St. George is Franklin Simpson—"

"It's been a setup from the start," Brad finished for her.

"So, the Picasso was bait, Paul Carter, too, if Simpson is running true to form. The trinket was the target all along."

"Not just the stone," Brad corrected her. "Omage said it—he wants Evan. It's the half-breeds; Simpson probably married Marnie Carter just to get close to her brother. Do you suppose she knows?"

Lily examined the printout more closely. "She probably knows some of it. Given the dates, they must have met when they were both still nickel-and-dime con artists. Can't imagine she knew Omage would kill her brother."

"I'll bet Mac knew, though. Probably Simpson as well. Evan would never go back to the Black Masque on his own. While Omage kept us busy stopping his latest attack on the second sphere, Simpson had a clear shot at Evan. Did he leave a number?"

"Simpson?"

Brad glared at her, and Lily sifted through the papers on the desk, came up with the London phone number Evan had left with his message. "He was staying with this Laurence woman and her brother."

A faint trace of scorn tinged her voice, and Brad crooked an eyebrow at her over the phone receiver.

"Jealous?" he suggested.

"Disappointed," she countered. "I thought he had better taste."

Brad reached for the telephone. "Maybe he does." He left the meaning ambiguous, knowing it would annoy her, and dialed the number.

"Laurence residence," a politely bureaucratic British voice answered, waited.

Jack Laurence was American. Brad said nothing.

The voice spoke again, "Who is this?"

"May I speak to Evan Davis," Brad asked, trading information in the hope of obtaining some. "This is his office calling."

"This is the police, Mr.—"

Brad wasn't giving that much away. "Is Mr. Davis there,

officer? Of course we will be happy to cooperate with the police—Interpol?"

"London, Inspector James speaking."

Brad heard a murmur of voices in the background, a muffled order to trace the call.

"If you put Mr. Davis on the telephone for a moment, I'm sure he will confirm your identification and we can get on with your questions."

Rigidly polite, the policeman's annoyance still made itself heard an ocean away. "We'd like to speak to Mr. Davis ourselves—Mr. Ryan?—but the gentleman seems to have disappeared."

"Can you hold a moment, Inspector?" Brad let four minutes sweep the face of his Rolex, the telephone receiver pressed to his shoulder. He gave Inspector James plenty of time to trace the call, information the overseas operator could have given him as quickly.

"As it happens, two of our operatives are on a case in London now," Brad lied smoothly. "We've made contact, and they'll meet you at the Laurence address in about ten minutes, Inspector. I trust their on-site judgment better than any help we can supply from here."

"We'll be here, Mr.—"

Brad hung up, met Lily's curious frown. "We're too late."

"He's not dead." Lily seemed to turn inward for a moment, sensing the same internal tie that Brad felt himself. "I'd know it if he were."

She rose from Evan's chair, paced around the desk. The cold light of home glinted in the blue flames of her eyes. "Not dead—yet."

"What does that mean?"

"Cousin, cousin." Lily sat on the arm of his chair and

ran long fingers, spiked with perfectly manicured nails, through his hair.

He caught her wrist, hard, and pulled her hand away. "I'm not one of your human playthings, Lirion. We may be stuck here together, but I'd still make an enemy you can't afford."

"Maybe," she agreed, her voice as hard as his own. "Or maybe you've been here too long. Maybe that half-breed monster of yours means more to you than Ariton.

"Think, cousin. If he summons us, we have no choice but to answer. If he doesn't, well, we know Franklin Simpson's not above a little murder. We'd be free, both of Evan and of Ariton's charge that holds us here."

She paced the room, from the chair to the bookcase and back again, gold chain clutched between the fingers of her clenched fist, the Eye of Omage held before her like a prize. Her voice dropped almost to a whisper, but it carried all the force of desperation as she repeated the one word: "Free."

Darkness closed over Badad's vision. Evan dead. He'd known since they'd faced each other across Omage's stone floor that he could not bear to watch the human die, could not be a part of his son's mortality. Someday, when decay had set in, when the life in the man had grown dim, he could accept death for his son. Not now, certainly not so soon after his own brief experience with life ending.

"Could you make that same choice if you had to face him with it, say, after Omage had run at him?" he asked.

"Probably not." She dropped the stone on the desk. "But I don't have to. Azmod has seen to that."

"It won't be that easy," he countered, and gave logic rather than face the accusation that came too near the mark: "Simpson didn't go to all this trouble just to kill Evan. A straight hit would have cost a lot less and he could have done it without all the globe-trotting. Paul Carter is dead. He needs Evan to break through into the second sphere."

That got through. Lily tensed. He could see host loyalty at war with self-interest in her eyes, knew she'd come to his own uncomfortable realization. She confirmed his fear: "We've made that a hell of a lot easier for him, too."

They'd spent a year training the boy to control his passage through the second sphere. His son didn't like it, but he could do it at will now. In Evan Davis, Ariton had handed the enemy a lethal weapon, trained, and pointed at the second sphere. But that weapon had a will of its own. "Evan won't do it."

Lily gave a short bark of humorless laughter. Sarcasm edged her words: "You don't know humans. He'll do it all right, he's got the same weakness they all have."

"Which is?"

"He doesn't want to die." She gave him another cold smile. "And that's your fault, too."

He had no answer to appease her. Knowing what death meant, he wouldn't blame his son for anything he did to hold mortality at bay. He did have a question: "Why? There's nothing in the second sphere for humans. Evan's made that clear enough."

Lily frowned, and Brad saw the old explanations tick over in her head, fall away. Omage, making another move in his long-standing feud with Badad, or simply gone mad, they could understand. But what stake could a human have in all of this?

"We'll have to ask Charlie, né Franklin Simpson, when

we see him, won't we?" Lirion smeared a polite smile over a hunting snarl.

Brad picked up the stone, hefted it thoughtfully in his hand for a moment, and locked it in the safe. "After you."

Broken crockery lay scattered in the ashes on the floor—turtledoves on a curve of ironstone and the fragments of dogs in green eyeshades, standing on their hind legs with cue sticks stuck somehow to their forepaws. Greasy black ash streaked two words across the white enamel of the refrigerator door: Evan's name, and the word "Venice."

How perfectly circular, Brad thought. He remembered Lily returning from Alfredo DaCosta's palazzo in Venice with a stone the color of Evan's eyes. Just a few days ago, but it seemed like an age of human time—was this what Einstein meant by relativity? Did Einstein have a son?— Brad made an effort to corral his scattered thoughts.

The games of Azmod had never been subtle: the message, not in human blood perhaps but in the blackened bits of charcoal that once had been flesh and bone, told him where he'd find Evan. The house in London was a warning. It could have been his son's body burned to ash. It still might be.

"How did you get in here?" A young man with a face a bit too pink, in a uniform a bit too tight, confronted them across the blackened circle on the floor.

Lily pulled out her license, smiled. "I'm Lily Ryan, this is Kevin Bradley. Our office called, said an Inspector James wanted to talk to us about our associate."

The constable puffed out his cheeks while he looked at the identification. Finally he let the air out with a plosive gust. "The inspector's this way—watch you don't step on the evidence—he'll want to know how you got in here."

"Yes, he will." The man in the tan raincoat took them in with one sweep of sharp, clear eyes. He was taller than the constable, older, and more solidly built. Experienced, Brad saw, but the mass on the floor that had recently been at least one human being and breakfast for two still made him flinch. He took Lily's I.D. and scrutinized it carefully before handing it back. "How did you get in here?"

Lily put her I.D. in her coat pocket. "Through the back door. We saw the police cars out front, came through the alley to avoid the reporters."

James inspected the daemon's face as carefully as he had her I.D. "And to get a look at the scene of the crime, no doubt." Not a question. "Your office said you would answer questions about an associate, Evan Davis."

Brad matched the inspector's understatement: "Of course. What exactly seems to be the problem?"

"Murder, Mr. Bradley. We believe your Mr. Davis murdered his friend Jack Laurence here this morning, and that in an attempt to murder Mr. Laurence's sister, he set off a bomb in the bookshop where she worked, killing the proprietor early this afternoon."

"That seems out of character," Brad objected mildly.

"On the contrary." Inspector James pulled out a battered notebook, his expression grim. "According to your Federal Bureau of Investigation's computerized crime-link, Mr. Davis appears to have been associated with Mr. Laurence through a Satanist cult in the States. Police records indicate that Mr. Laurence almost lost his life at the hands of cult members two years ago. According to the police report, accusations against Evan Davis were made at the time and later dropped." The inspector paused. "For someone who has just claimed that such behavior is out of character, you don't seem surprised, Mr. Bradley."

"I'm not," Brad agreed. "Evan's past with the group you mention is no secret at the agency. He had no idea what he was getting into when he joined them, and when he tried to leave, they made him their prisoner. Believe me, he was as much their victim as Jack Laurence."

"That is Evan Davis' story, no doubt."

"That is *my* story, Inspector," Brad interrupted. "I was in the rescue party that found Evan Davis, half dead and in chains, and brought him out of there two years ago. If you had seen what I did, you would know you should be looking not for Mr. Davis, but for his captor."

"There is no captor, Mr. Bradley; if there ever was one he is dead now, in a suspiciously timed gas main explosion in New York. No, we do not suspect Mr. Davis of that crime—we know he was in transit out of Philadelphia at the time. He may have had an accomplice, but that is not Her Majesty's problem. This is." He pointed to the blackened heap of ash, then to the door of the refrigerator. "And that."

Brad followed the direction the inspector pointed in, and then turned back, barely containing his scorn. "Does the FBI report also say that he's stupid enough to sign his name to murder?"

"Not stupid, no." Inspector James put his notebook away; Brad recognized the ploy but felt the tension mount in the small silence anyway. "Insane, probably. He's been in and out of psychiatric care since childhood."

A stroke would kill the man, or a bolt of Ariton lightning—one more puddle of ash to join the first one on the floor. Brad restrained himself. Killing Inspector James would give him temporary satisfaction, but it wouldn't help Evan.

Lily stepped between the two men. Brad felt her anger like heat against his human skin, but she turned a conciliatory smile on the inspector. "Evan is missing," she pointed out. "And, for our very different reasons, we all want to find him. Until we do, I'd suggest we cooperate."

Inspector James pursed his lips and rocked back on his heels, rubbing one hand through the back of his thinning hair. "You can start," he suggested, "with the suspect's known contacts in Venice."

Brad shook his head. "None," he lied. "He's never been there, as far as I know. I suspect the second part of the message has nothing to do with Evan. Maybe it's a list. You say the murderer blew up a bookstore in London, maybe another place in the States. My guess is, Venice is his next target, someplace small but public if he keeps to his m.o."

"I'll mention that in my report," James remarked with no great conviction. "Where can we reach you if we have any more questions?"

"The Savoy," Lily offered. "We keep rooms there whenever we're in town. May we go now?"

"Of course. Constable Dodds will see you out." The inspector turned on his heels, moving past them toward the front of the house, already deep in conversation with an aggressive young man in a loud plaid sport coat.

Lily took Brad's arm until they were out of sight of the small house on St. Mary's Road. "They've taken him to Alfredo DaCosta. Pity we didn't run Evan's ferret program on him." She sighed with spurious regret. "And we had so much in common. If I didn't know better, I might have guessed he was one of ours."

"You both like champagne, sex, and other people's property," Brad objected. "That hardly qualifies him as a lord of Ariton, or of any Prince.

"It does complicate the picture," he added more seriously. "Is Simpson running Omage, or is DaCosta running them both?"

"I don't think Omage did this." Lily stared through him for a moment, and he waited for her to put his own suspicion into words: "It's not his style. Besides, your fireworks at the Black Masque rattled his teeth a bit; he could have done this job or taken out the bookstore, but not both, not so soon."

"Rival factions?" Brad asked the rhetorical question.

"Only one way to find out," Lily returned the obvious with a hunter's grin. "Inspector James is not going to like this." She vanished. Badad followed.

Chapter Twenty-one

In the days of Egypt, there were three prophets, and Moses was one, and Atlas the Astronomer, brother to Prometheus, but the greatest was Hermes, called Trismegistus, the thrice great, known as Thot by the Egyptians. And all that was known of philosophy was the gift of Trismegistus.

"Evan! Wake up!"

The urgent whisper filtered through a blanket of fog. Gradually awareness returned with the feel of a soft bed under his stomach and a hand on his arm—Claudia, beside him, and home, in the womb she'd made for them in the tiny apartment. He relaxed with a sigh, wondering what Jack would make of the dreams this time. They'd been weirder than usual; better lay off the Vat 69 before he started seeing pink elephants on the street. Evan reached out to draw Claudia closer, bury himself in the haze of mother-sister-lover feeling she wrapped around him. The shackle on his wrist stopped him short.

Jackhammers slammed into both temples like the granddaddy of all hangovers when he lifted his head. Not dreams, then. Jack was really dead, and Claudia lost in the explosion—no, here beside him. Pathet had kidnapped her, something to do with Omage and Paul Carter in New York. Charlie St. George was involved as well, but he couldn't figure out how. Couldn't think past the jackhammer in his head.

"Evan, are you awake yet?" Claudia's voice. She shook his shoulder, fingers digging deep into the muscle.

"I think so." The shackle cut into raw skin, distracted him. Time to transport out of there—wherever there was—find Brad and Lily. He didn't like the idea, but it beat being chained to a strange bed, God knew where.

"What did they do to you? I've been trying to wake you for hours."

Claudia. She couldn't travel the only route open to him, wouldn't much appreciate it if he left her there. So much for bugging out. "Sorry." Evan rubbed his forehead against his shirtsleeve. "Drugged, I think. Doesn't feel like he hit me. Are you all right?"

"I'm cold and scared and mad, and I'm naked as a jaybird," Claudia explained with very little patience. "They took my clothes, then you took the blanket and lost it off your side of the bed. I can't reach it, because the bastards who brought me here chained my leg to this side of the bed. They'll be back soon, and I don't want to face them stark naked, so get the damned blanket back up here."

Evan rubbed his eyes blearily and squinted. She was naked, all right, and the huge bed looked like Catherine the Great might have entertained her horse in it. Oversized pedestaled feet gave way to carved bedposts that supported the heavy Doric-style canopy overhead. The bedcover, a deep burgundy velvet cut to reveal the gold threads beneath the nap, lay in a heap near the foot of the bed.

"Give me a minute, I can't reach—" He rolled over and

struggled to sit upright, his legs hanging off the side of the bed, his brain still muddy with the drug. "Here—" He stretched as far as the shackle would allow and snagged the cover with his foot, nudging it closer to the head of the bed until he could grasp it with his free hand.

"Where are we?" he asked when Claudia had settled in a steamy bundle wrapped in the heavy fabric.

She shrugged the cover off her shoulders and wrapped it around her breasts, freeing her arms to the cool breeze drifting through the windows open at either side of the bed. "It ain't Kansas," she finally answered. "More than that, I was hoping you could tell me."

Their elegant prison was a perfectly square room, walls and floor covered with delicately veined marble, pale rose on the walls, a chessboard pattern on the floor. Two brocaded armchairs sat grouped on opposite sides of a small table to the right of the door, and a low wooden chest with an elaborately carved base balanced the grouping on the left. The room held no other furniture, but a few barely noticeable marks on the floor showed that other pieces, probably chests like the one that remained, had been removed. The walls were free of decoration, but above the level of the elaborately carved lintel the ceiling rose in late Gothic splendor over carved arches limned in gilt. Between the arches, frescoes crowded the ceiling like an overheated carousel.

The paintings took his breath away. *Titian*, he thought, then backpedaled. He wouldn't bet his reputation that the master had ever set a brush to that ceiling—probably students, but good ones, well versed in their teacher's style. The colors were so rich, the images so vibrant he almost thought that if he could reach them, he'd find flesh beneath his fingers instead of paint.

Eight scenes around a central painting, each depicting a scene important to the arcane magical cult of Hermes Trismegistes, vaulted overheard: over the door, the traditional grouping of the twelve virtues and twelve temptations appeared, with the twelve sibyls and twelve prophets facing them from over the bed. At the far left from where Evan sat on the bed, the artist had painted the seven planets with their ruling deities, and on the far right, a figure grouping that Evan guessed represented Isis, a globe showing the celestial spheres above her head, with Moses at her left hand and Hermes at her right.

Between the key representations at the cardinal points, the artist had painted a series of scenes depicting the myth of Osiris: Osiris teaching the Egyptians how to plant wheat; the Egyptian god Seth striking down Osiris on the bank of the Nile; the trial of Seth; Thot, the father of Osiris, and Isis, sister and wife of the dead god, raising Osiris from the dead. To emphasize the metaphoric relationship, in this fresco Osiris carried not the symbols of Egyptian kingship, but a Christian cross in his hand.

An elaborate pentagram filled the central apex of the vaulting ceiling. In the spaces between the five points of the star, fierce warrior angels with bows and arrows at the ready stared grimly outward, defending an angel representing one of the arts in each angle. The center of the pentagram held Evan's attention. A figure in classic Greek attire with wings at his feet—Hermes again—sat with poetry on his left and music on his right. The artist had used the same model as he had for Thot, Evan realized, but the two characterizations showed very different aspects of the man. Where Thot wore the expression of the stern judge, Hermes had the thoughtful demeanor of a teacher. Like all the frescoes, this one had an elaborate nature background suffused with light and texture. But the figure of Hermes seemed to glow of its own light, rather than reflect the rays of the sun. Analyzing the light and shadow on the trees and rocks, Evan realized that all of the light in the picture seemed to originate with the figure at its center.

The magician looked down from his lofty position with warm brown eyes, the full mouth softened in a pensive smile beneath the hawklike nose. Hair in dark waves, cut short in the classic Greek style seemed out of place on that hauntingly familiar face. *He's looking right at me,* Evan thought, *and he knows what I am, what I have been.* Was Titian's student a bastard of two universes, a monster like himself? Had he lived to see his talent wither in the torment of his soul, or had he died like Paul Carter, mad and in despair? He turned away, shaken that a long dead artist could affect him so deeply, and concentrated on the problem at hand. Where were they?

Not Rome, he decided, dismissing his first guess. Even the Borgia Popes hadn't gone this far in depicting the magical philosophy. For that matter neither had Titian, though the paintings reflected his earlier style. Together with the sounds floating through the window, however, he had enough to hazard a guess:

"Probably Venice."

"Very good." Mac. Omage. "In fact, we're visiting an old friend of Lily's."

The breath caught in Evan's throat, strangled him with memories. Not again. He turned and faced the creature of his nightmares. Charles Devereaux St. George followed the daemon, balloon glass in his hand, a hard smile on his face. At his side St. George carried the walking stick Evan had seen in his hotel, its length elaborately carved in the twisted gargoyle features of the damned. Age had smoothed the carvings and darkened the wood, but nothing could dim the sense of evil that pulsed from the thing. The awkward, hesitant movements were gone. St. George sat in one of the armchairs and rested the cane against the table beside it.

"Meet our host," St. George gestured with his glass at a third figure, in a white linen suit, who followed the others into the room. "Alfredo DaCosta."

DaCosta seemed taller, but maybe that was the company he was keeping these days. He had the chiseled features of a hawk, and Evan remembered the eyes: predator's eyes that missed nothing over a prominent nose narrowed in distaste. So the whole thing was a setup. Except the meeting in the bookstore. St. George expected the introduction to surprise Evan, and the Italian count seemed to want it that way.

Another, more recent memory ticked at him. The expression was different, but a quick look at the ceiling, found the man staring down at him from the center of the pentagram. Evan met the glance of the model for Hermes. The man said nothing, but sadness touched the hard eyes. Evan wondered how long it had been since Alfredo DaCosta had allowed the world to see the open wisdom in the painting, but he made only oblique reference.

"Did Lily find this room interesting?"

"Miss Ryan never had the pleasure," DaCosta answered softly, "Our acquaintance was very short, and the room is seldom used."

He retreated to the low chest against the wall where he sat hunched forward slightly, arms linked around his knees, his heels dug into the old wood of the chest. With

a last measuring glance at Evan, he turned his brooding
study to the toes of his hand-stitched shoes.

So Lily didn't know DaCosta's secret. That meant he
wasn't one of theirs— Something else, then. He'd bet St.
George was in the dark, wondered if Omage knew, but
read only a lurking madness beneath the malevolent features of the daemon.

"What's going on, Evan?" Claudia's voice, sharpened
with panic, drew his attention back to the problem at
hand. She clutched the heavy bedcover tightly around her
with both hands, and moved to the middle of the bed, as
close to him as the shackle around her ankle would allow.
With a quick, nervous glance at Omage, she entrusted
modesty to the grip of one hand and reached out to him
with the other.

"Tell the lady, Evan." Omage taunted from his place behind St. George's chair. "She deserves to know why her
brother died."

"Dead?" Claudia looked at him, desperation in her eyes.
"He's lying. Tell me he's lying." She studied his face for
a sign to hold onto, but he could give her nothing, didn't
know what to say. "Oh, God, Evan, what have you done?"

He held his hands out to her, open, empty.

"I hate you!" She lunged for him across the bed and fell
facedown, trapped by the shackle at her ankle, tearing at
her hair and screaming into the overstuffed mattress.

"I tried to stop him." He knew it wasn't enough, had
known it in the kitchen facing Pathet across a sea of
ashes. He'd thought he could outrun the forces that had
shaped him, and instead he'd brought disaster after him,
right down on top of the only friends he'd ever had. She
didn't seem to hear him, didn't notice when he covered
her again with the heavy bedspread.

"God. God. God." Litany or mantra, the words fell softly into the mattress while one hand opened and closed spasmodically in her hair. She ground the knuckles of the other against her teeth, as if trying to hold back the choking sobs that punctuated the endless repetition.

"Let her go, St. George." Begging was easy with the sounds of shattered grief rising muffled from the bed. "She has nothing to do with this."

"Oh, Evan." St. George saluted him with the balloon glass. "How you have managed to survive this long with your naïveté intact is beyond me. Let her go? After all the trouble I took to bring her here?"

Evan knew better than to expect pity from Omage; the daemon was probably enjoying the whole thing. He turned instead to Alfredo DaCosta, perched solemnly on the wooden chest. An artist once had found something noble in that face, not kindness perhaps, but a strength of character for which Evan now searched in vain.

"I can't help you," the man explained. "I'm sort of a hostage here myself."

"I hadn't noticed." Evan stared pointedly at the shackle on his wrist, let his breath out in a long soft sigh, folding in on himself as he did. Senseless to argue with the thief. Whatever he was, DaCosta had made his decision to keep it well hidden. He could blow the man's cover easily enough. Even Charlie would make the connection if Evan pointed it out, but then what would he have? One more enemy, and he'd be no closer to escape than when he started. He slumped to the bed, rubbed his forehead in a vain attempt to placate the road crew blasting in his skull.

"Why?" he asked, looking for order in the chaos St. George had made of his life. "She's not like Paul Carter or me. She doesn't know anything about this."

St. George ignored the question while he sniffed at the brandy in his glass. "Delightful. Are you sure I can't offer—but we've already had this discussion.

"Of course she knows nothing, my dear boy." St. George returned to the question offhandedly over the brandy. "That is precisely her value. Against Omage, or even yourself, she's completely helpless. Fool that you are, that matters to you. So it's really quite simple. You can leave any time you want. I can't stop you, nor can my companions. Do your disappearing act, however, and she's dead before your feet hit ground again. Do what you're told and the lady lives."

"My father will find us."

St. George laughed. "I'm counting on it. He has something that belongs to me, stolen from this very house."

"The damned stone," Evan realized. "The Eye of Omage."

St. George tilted his head in confirmation. "Until he returns it, I can only control you through the girl. If Mr. Bradley cooperates, we can dispense with the young lady's services—let her go, if you will."

"Dead or alive?"

"That's entirely up to you, my boy."

From behind St. George, Omage gave a spurious sigh, followed by a deep chuckle. The daemon wandered to the window and looked out. "Give him what he wants," Omage's gaze shifted briefly in St. George's direction, returned to the scene outside the window, "and it's up to you whether she leaves through the street door or in a sack in the canal."

"Go to hell."

Mac chuckled again. "Now, son of Ariton, we both know hell's a fairy tale. You've been there, seen the beauty of it. You want it for yourself. Don't deny it, no one here will believe you." The daemon's smile told of secrets shared, of knowledge beyond the grasp of the merely human among them.

Tumblers clicked in Evan's head, pieces slotted into place. The drug-haze cleared, and suddenly, the headache didn't matter. "He doesn't know, does he?"

"Clever boy." Omage grinned. "A pretty game, and fitting, I think."

"It stopped being a game when the killing started." Evan turned to St. George. No, the name didn't fit: the softness, the timid awkwardness were gone. "Who are you?"

The man reached in his pocket for a pack of Camels, pinched off the filter, and tamped the load before putting it to his lips. He lit it with a monogrammed gold lighter. Inhaling deeply, he let the smoke curl out around a smile. "Franklin Simpson. Call me Frank, all my enemies do."

Another piece of the puzzle clicked into place. "Not real broken up about your brother-in-law, are you?"

Simpson frowned. "Oh, but I am, my boy. Think of the time and expense I've taken with Paul, and all for nothing. Still, we cut our losses and go on."

A setup from the start. Evan stared the man straight in the eyes, wouldn't give the bastard the satisfaction of even a moment's defeat. "I suppose the distraught sister will be joining us."

"Shortly," Simpson confirmed. "She hasn't the travel advantages of your sort."

"A pity." Evan winked out of real space, returned next to Simpson in the blink of an eye. Claudia lay on the bed with her face averted, exhausted in her grief, but the shackle that had bound Evan's wrist dangled empty from the bedpost. Evan gave his full attention to their captor.

"Well, Frank, I don't know what our friend has told you about the second sphere—his home—but there's nothing for humans there."

"Do make yourself comfortable." Simpson offered the pack of cigarettes, showing little surprise. Evan took one. He left the filter in place and accepted a light, staying between Franklin Simpson and the bed. He took a drag and let it out, the cigarette pinched between thumb and forefinger, cupped in the hollow of his palm.

"Nothing for me, you mean," Franklin Simpson continued. He smiled indulgently. "You want to keep it all for yourself. I can understand that, would do it myself if I could get my hands on it. But I can't, so I'm willing to cut a deal."

Claudia stirred on the bed behind him, and he turned to face her. She stared pointedly at the bracelet of raw flesh where the shackle had been. "Who did you sell out this time, Evan? God, how I hate you."

"At least let me free her leg," Evan bargained

Simpson shook his head. "Not yet. Later, perhaps, as a reward for good behavior."

Evan had no doubt whose behavior was in question. "I'm sorry," he repeated, at a loss to repair the damage he had done.

"Tell that to Jack." She pulled the bedcover more tightly around herself, drawing attention to her own nakedness while she stared accusingly at his shirt. He undid the buttons and slipped out of it, shifting the cigarette to free his arm; she took it without a thank you and glared at him while she worked her arms into the sleeves and pulled the shirt closed over her breasts.

"Did you tell any of the truth this week, Evan? You even lied about the damned cigarettes!"

"These?" Evan lifted the smoke, drew again and returned it to his side. "Some vices are harder to let go of than others." The ruddy end of the thing might be the only weapon he had in a fight. "And given the circumstances, I'm not real worried about cancer."

Simpson laughed at the exchange. "Imagine a lifetime of that, Evan," he taunted. "It's not too late. We can still sack her into the canal."

"Keep her out of this, Simpson." Evan jabbed the air with the cigarette. "If anything happens to her, you get nothing out of me. Nothing."

"Have it your way, my boy. Just trying to be helpful."

"I can do without your help. Let her go, then we'll talk."

"And have her miss the party? Patience, my boy. Soon the fun begins in earnest."

Chapter Twenty-two

And Hermes was called thrice great. As a king, he ruled with learning, as a philosopher he gave to the people writing and all manner of language, and as a priest he gave man the means to draw the influences of the heavens by means of words to the greater glory of his works, and described the influences of the decans and the zodiac.

Venice. Given his choice, Brad preferred his study, but he did sometimes wish that Evan had been born Venetian. The city breathed contradictions, felt old as no city its age should, felt wise like no city of merchants should. A city where old magic died slowly, like the old stone palaces, worn down by the fatalism of its people. A city of churches.

Badad wondered why of all places Lily had decided to transport via Basilica San Marco. She knew how he felt: churches of any kind made him nervous. They harbored mystics who stumbled upon recipes for piercing the spheres and drawing lords of the hosts of Princes into the material sphere against their will. He'd long ago decided that the only safe human was a secular humanist, the only safe public building a bank.

"Shall we go?" he asked. Lily nodded, and they made their way from a side chapel dedicated to a bejeweled Madonna, through the main basilica, and out into the square. The domes of San Marco glinted in the sunset, but Brad turned his back on the building with a frisson of foreboding.

"Ca' DaCosta, Alfredo's palazzo, is over there." Lily pointed to where the Grand Canal looped back on itself, out of sight behind the palaces and tenements that crowded the city. She linked one arm through his, cosmopolitan in black linen. Crossing the Piazza, her stiletto heels snapped gunshots on the paving stones; sharp red nails tilted the black-lacquered brim of a broad straw hat to protect her eyes from the lowering sun.

They passed an outdoor café—long impersonal rows of square tables with yellow-checked plastic tablecloths and folding metal chairs—and Lily grabbed his arm, pulling him over to sit down. "But first, we have to talk."

She gestured for a waiter, ordered a Campari and soda. Brad recognized the obdurate tilt of her chin. He ordered lemon juice in mineral water, and when the waiter had gone, he glared at her. "What are you doing?"

"Enjoying Piazza San Marco at sunset—" She smiled at the returning waiter and sipped her drink. "—Since I can't imagine why else we would be on this monster hunt."

"That should be obvious even to you, Lily." Brad moved his glass in small circles, leaving a trail of condensation on the plastic tablecloth. "Evan's missing. Azmod took him, and your friend Alfredo DaCosta is holding him, for Franklin Simpson or his own reasons, we don't know. We're here to get him back before they torture my son into punching a hole through the seven universes. That is why Ariton put us here. Remember?"

Lily set her glass down carefully and leaned forward, her elbow on the table, her chin resting on the back of her hand.

"I remember." She enunciated clearly, as if to a somewhat dimwitted child. "And if I'd known that keeping your bastard alive would bring me to this, I'd have killed him where he stood two years ago."

"You have to admit it's been interesting." The smile didn't work.

"The Chinese have a saying—"

He wasn't going to win this one. "I know."

She dismissed the argument with a flutter of blood-colored fingernails. "Think for a moment like Ariton, if you still remember how. Humans now command a lord of Azmod to force half-breeds into the second sphere where they invariably go mad, and for nothing, which, according to Evan, is what the second sphere holds for humans.

"Those humans have apparently taken prisoner your half-breed bastard, again, only now he has the training we gave him to do what he is told and stay sane while he does it. With that same training he can transport out of there any time he wants, but for reasons unknown he has not done so. And you want to rush to the rescue like the Canadian Mounties in an old movie, even though the boy can save himself if he wants, we would be free if they killed him trying, and we could kill him ourselves with the backlash if we have to fight Omage for him. And that's if Mac doesn't finish him off for spite."

"You're right," Brad agreed, "and it doesn't make sense. Evan is just a small part of the problem. I admit, I want to get him back alive."

He closed his eyes for a moment to steady himself, couldn't let Lily know how important that goal had become. When he opened them again, she was waiting. The daemon Lirion stared through him with a look that said she knew everything and cursed him for a fool.

"Maybe I have been playing human for too long," he defended himself. "I *like* the boy."

Lily returned the self-evident confidence with a wry smile. "When I think with the skin of this body, I do understand, cousin; like you, I could lose myself in this form, attach myself to places, and even your bastard monster. When I am Lily, he draws me. We share senses, human flesh and Ariton fire. But he's not Ariton, he will never understand what it means to be a lord of the second sphere and his ignorance may destroy all the known universes."

"Not just Evan," he reminded her, and sipped his mineral water with lemon, wishing irrelevantly that he'd asked for ice. Lily was right. He did attach himself too easily to the physical, to habits of flesh.

"There may be others, if not now, later. The death of my son won't stop DaCosta or Franklin Simpson, or whoever is behind this mess, from trying again. We have to find out *why* they torture the Evan Davises and Paul Carters of their world to drive them into the second sphere: what the half-humans can do that one of our own kind can't, and what their human masters stand to gain. Once we understand what they are doing and why, we'll take them down."

Lily looked at him thoughtfully for a moment, absently stirring her drink. "I suppose you've got a plan."

"The start of one. They've got Evan again, so they'll be moving their own plan ahead. We'll watch, listen, see what they do." Brad looked at the bill, drew three crisp

Italian notes out of his pocket, and dropped them on the table. He held out his hand. "Shall we?"

Lily took his hand, rose smoothly like a well oiled spring. "A stakeout," she agreed while they walked along the square. "We'll have to change form. If Simpson really is St. George, he'll recognize us."

"Not human." Brad considered the problem. "We couldn't get close enough. Birds, though, might work. Who'd notice a couple of pigeons peering in their second-story window?" He poked a toe at a particularly stubborn bird pecking grit from between the paving stones of the square.

"Put a lot of thought into that one, did you?" She glared at him out of the corner of her eye, stopping to kick at a complacent pigeon that stood in her path. "Move it or die, chump.

"I won't do it. A falcon, maybe—beautiful, sleek, dangerous—" She threw back her head and grinned, showing sharp, white teeth. "—Falcons eat the damned pigeons. I could identify with that."

Brad looked at her, seeing beyond the human form to the companion of his exile, the brittle taste of her tension sharp on his tongue—innocent murderer, as he who understood death could never be. "Suits you," he agreed.

Lily sniffed, a last show of indignation. "We're a little exposed for an inconspicuous shift."

"Perhaps." Brad took her elbow, led her toward the many-porticoed building that faced the piazza. "But it's the perfect time to view the archaeological treasures of Venice."

"They don't have any," Lily objected. "And you picked a strange time to go tourist. Your bastard's in trouble, remember?"

Brad didn't answer, but as he stepped under the cover of the portico, his shape wavered and dissipated into mist. A moment later, Lily dissolved in a scattering of dust. The bright beads of her eyes, set in the sleek head of the falcon, shot lethal bolts at him. She took flight and he followed, banking north over the canal.

A Renaissance masterpiece in its own right, Ca' Da-Costa turned a masked face to the canal. Arches of weathered Gothic filigree held aloft on shallow pilasters punctuated each of the three sets of two double windows on each of the three main stories. Crumbling stone balustrades underlined the window groupings to emphasize the mystic trinity. An attic turned its unadorned double windows on the canal and to each side. Most of the house lay shadowed by the growing darkness, but the attic windows were open, a soft light negotiating a compromise with the falling night.

Badad landed on the roof and settled on a windowsill that offered a view of the attic room beyond. Lirion made a pass at the lower stories before she followed, the ruff of feathers around her neck distended. Clearly, she hadn't expected to find anything in the attic but stacks of old furniture. Alfredo DaCosta was full of surprises.

The front window overlooked an elaborately carved bed. Badad saw a girl huddled at its center in a shirt he recognized as Evan's, her arms rigid bands wrapped tightly under her breasts. Evan stood with his back to the window, facing Charlie St. George—Franklin Simpson, according to Evan's ferret program. The night air carried a voice through the window, and the daemon cocked his head to listen.

"If anything happens to her, you get nothing out of me. Nothing."

Brad recognized Evan's voice, heard the strain in it, and Franklin Simpson's spurious concern:

"Have it your way, my boy. Just trying to be helpful."

"I can do without your help. Let her go, then we'll talk."

Evan again. Badad wondered for a moment who the girl was, guessed that Simpson, or DaCosta, knew they couldn't keep Evan against his will. A hostage to hold him, then; probably that girl Evan had gone to see in London. Didn't have to be—with the boy's capacity for guilt, a stranger would do just as well. Evan's captors didn't know that, though. Simpson was talking again.

"And have her miss the party? Patience, my boy. Soon the fun begins in earnest."

Brad saw the door open. Evan's back was to him, he couldn't see his son's face, but the tone of voice held no surprise, just a weary expectation. "Marnie Simpson. I can't say it's a pleasure."

A second figure followed the woman into the room. Tall, slim, with light brown hair falling straight to his shoulders, the newcomer's eyes sparked Azmod green, inhuman.

Evan identified him: "Pathet. I should have known you were the bitch-queen's lackey."

Marnie Simpson flashed a casually possessive look over her shoulder at the daemon lord behind her. "Come now, Evan. That's no way to talk about the father of my child."

A familiar voice followed with a gleeful chuckle. Omage moved out of Franklin Simpson's shadow. "Nothing like a father's love, right, Evan? Or, for that matter, a mother's."

Chapter Twenty-three

*And Hermes, known as Mercury to the Romans,
brought to man the knowledge of art and the mysteries
of the planets and their movement among the stars.
And Hermes told them that the sun was the center of
the universe, to which the Earth turned its face in
praise.*

"Paul Carter was your son?" Evan asked the question of
Marnie Simpson, but his glance darted beyond her,
caught the eye of the daemon, Pathet.

The daemon laughed. "Don't expect me to care, boy; I
don't share in the insanity of Ariton. Alive, Paul Carter
was a danger to my universe and yours. Dead, he's just
slime to fertilize the ragweed."

Pathet slouched languidly into the easy chair across the
table from Franklin Simpson. He lifted a glass and saluted
Evan with it, an expression of amused annoyance playing
across his features.

Indifference had murdered Paul, as ignorance had almost destroyed Evan. Bile crawled up his throat with the
memory of a shotgun taped to the back of a chair, ready
to blow Paul Carter's head off when the nightmare of his

own existence grew too horrible to bear. He forced it back
with a drag on the stub of cigarette in his hand.

Her walk all sharp angles, Marnie Simpson drew close
enough to touch him. "Nice to see you again, Evan.

"Paul was a tool," she explained. "Like Pathet, or Mac
here, or you. Yes, he was my son; unfortunately, Paul was
also defective."

Evan held his muscles still against the shudder of revulsion that fought his control. Rage for the man he had
never known, twisting alone in the same hell that had
haunted Evan's dreams, boiled over. He wanted to destroy
the woman who stood so cool and self-contained in front
of him, wanted to send her careening through the second
sphere and watch her body scream on the other side of
that barrier, watch the silence and the darkness beyond
imagining drive her mad as it had done to him, to Paul
Carter.

The thin curtains tangled in the wind that twisted
through the windows. It lifted his hair and pressed
Marnie Simpson's blouse against the sharp angles of her
body. He felt distant eyes intent on him then, darted a
glance around the room. From his place behind Frank
Simpson's chair, Omage licked his lips nervously. Calculated fear edged the daemon's hunger, and Evan clenched
his teeth around the urge to strike at the woman in front
of him, knowing the act would bring slow death at the
hands of her creatures. Gradually the wind died down
around them.

Evan took a deep breath, calmed the surging beat of his
heart. Whatever she did to him, he owed it to Paul Carter
to speak. "Why did you let it happen?" he asked, "Paul
didn't have to spend his life torn to pieces by what he

was. He didn't have to die. His father could have taught him control."

"Me?" The daemon shook his head slowly. "Not my style."

Marnie Simpson cast a quick glance at the father of her son, the doubt clear in her eyes. "You flatter me," she said.

She reached into her pocket and pulled out a pack of Virginia Slims, tapped out a cigarette. "A light?" The woman took the burning stub of Evan's cigarette, lit her own from the glowing ember at its tip, then dropped the butt, grinding it into the marble parquet.

"Thank you." Mocking.

She drew on the cigarette, let out the smoke again, taking a moment to collect her thoughts. "Think of Pathet as a rogue stallion, Paul a yearling with bad wind, and Mac, well you know Mac. I could only do so much with the material at hand."

Chains clinked on the bed behind him, broke the link with Marnie Simpson that held him transfixed in horror.

"Who is she? I don't understand any of this." Claudia stirred, her voice dazed as if she were trying to wake herself from a nightmare. "You're all insane."

"You're probably right," he agreed. "Mrs. Simpson," he gestured an introduction, "was a client. She said Mac had kidnapped her brother but would release him if a particular ransom were paid. According to her story, Mac left a note, instructing her to hire Brad and Lily to make the exchange, a jewel called the Eye of Omage, for Paul's life. Brad pulled me out of the Black Masque two years ago. We figured he could do it again for Paul Carter. Apparently, it was a lie from the beginning."

Claudia shifted, pulled Evan's shirt more tightly around herself, and addressed her plea to the other woman. "I'm sorry if something has happened to your son, I know how you feel. My brother is dead." She choked on the word brother. "But your fight is with Evan's father. Evan had nothing to do with it. He wasn't there, he can't possibly be responsible for what happened."

Good try, but Evan knew it wouldn't work on the woman who had given her own son to Omage as a plaything. Franklin Simpson knew it, too. From the depths of his armchair, the man chuckled.

"My dear, sweet Claudia. We did not invite Evan to join us for what he knows, child, but for what he is. As Evan's lover, you are here to persuade him to cooperate."

"I'm not—"

Simpson half-closed his eyes above a conspiratorial smile. "Don't confuse me with my dundering alter ego, sweet. Dinner last night was a wonderful performance for an audience of one. But we both know that every word, every glance for Charles St. George was an arrow pointed at Evan Davis' heart."

"Is he good?" Marnie Simpson stroked a speculative hand down Evan's arm, like checking the legs of a thoroughbred. "He should be, he's had a good teacher. Their kind understand about sex, don't they, Evan?" She tilted her head in salute to Pathet, who raised his glass in acknowledgment.

"That's none of your business," Claudia replied, more sharply than made sense if she really wanted to survive this mess. "You're wrong anyway. I don't mean anything to him. Just let me go."

"As soon as Evan gives us what we want, you'll be free," Marnie Simpson assured her.

Marnie Simpson's idea of freedom had more to do with feeding the fish than feeding the soul. Her hand ran up his arm, found the tension at the join between shoulder and neck. Evan tried to ignore the touch, but felt the adrenaline charge, fight or flight.

"I can't, you know that," he told her.

"You will." She took a drag on the cigarette, blew the smoke in his face.

"Evan!" Claudia pleaded. "Why are you doing this?"

"A lot of lives are at stake," he explained. "Yours, mine, whole worlds, maybe. I don't have a choice." He knew it wasn't enough, knew she wouldn't believe the truth, that all life, in all the spheres known and unknown, might depend on what they did in this room.

"I don't believe this is happening." She subsided into the folds of the velvet bedspread, let the shirt hang loosely while she dug the heels of both palms into her eyes. "I don't believe any of it."

He'd gotten her brother killed and Claudia kidnapped, and he wasn't sure he believed it himself. But they had one hope left—distract his captors into making a mistake, and take advantage of it when it happened—and he clung to it. In the meantime, maybe he could find out *why*. He picked the cigarette from between Marnie Simpson's fingers, took a long draw, held the smoke in his lungs while he reversed the cigarette between his thumb and forefinger. When she retrieved it, he let the smoke out in a slow, thin stream.

"I'd still like to know how you did it. We connected your husband to the Black Masque, but Paul's record was clean."

Marnie Simpson shrugged. "I'd been studying our friends for years. At first it was just part of the act. My mother contacted the spirits through the pure spirit of a child clairvoyant. I played the kid until I was sick of it, then I met Frank. I was fifteen and he was about thirty, and we set up a scam of our own. By then, I realized that some of the spells I'd been reading might really work."

"The grimoires all agreed," Frank Simpson added "that if you could control the right ones, daemons could make a man richer and more powerful than any mortal. They hinted at immortality itself. Rich was relatively simple. The spell worked, and my future wife bound a water daemon who killed St. George, along with his father, in a storm at sea. We picked the St. Georges because Charlie had been out of the country for years, and we shared similar builds; with Rachiar's unwilling assistance, I stepped into poor, ineffectual Charlie's identity. And his wealth in Philadelphia. Since Charlie had lived out of the country for years before the accident, no one considered my own long absences out of the ordinary. We used some of the St. George fortune to seed the business ventures of Frank Simpson, rising entrepreneur, elsewhere."

"So much for money." Evan looked around them: marble walls, marble floors, and Alfredo DaCosta as Hermes at the right hand of Isis on the ceiling. He focused on the man himself, bent over his knees on the wooden chest pushed up against the wall. Above DaCosta, the same face carried the heavy headdress of Thot, passing judgment on the murderous brother Seth, the Cain and Abel of the gods. Medea seemed more appropriate at the moment, but that didn't explain DaCosta. "What is his part in this little charade?"

The man looked up at him, a veneer of pained innocence covering bitter humor and something else that scared Evan to his socks. He looked again at the Judgment of Thot, saw open there the hidden message in

DaCosta's eyes. "I'm just an innocent bystander," the man explained.

Evan shook his head, rejecting the answer. "There are no innocent bystanders."

DaCosta accepted the correction. "Perhaps not so innocent. I stole the wrong Picasso, it seems, and landed in the middle of a quarrel about which I know nothing."

That was a lie, but Evan let it stand with just a glance at the painting over the man's head. He deliberately looked around him again, hoping his acting was up to the bored indifference he tried to convey to his captors.

"And this is your idea of power. Hiding in an attic—elegant," he apologized with exaggerated diplomacy in an aside to DaCosta, "—but still an attic, with two daemons who will fry your bones to cinders if you give them half a chance. Does intimidating a thief and a shop clerk really give you that much of a thrill?"

Claudia's voice cut in, wary but stronger. "Easy on the shop clerk, chum. I'm an anthropologist, temporarily out of work."

Her own warning, then, not to underestimate her. Maybe she had believed there were lives at stake, after all. Marnie Simpson ignored the interruption, but her husband snorted his contempt.

"Power over the spheres, Evan," he corrected, "over the wealth out there, where they come from and you visit, and the secret of their immortality. But you're right, we made a slight error in judgment with Rachiar."

"You made the mistake," Marnie Simpson corrected him with asperity. "The damned thing almost killed us."

"But he didn't," Frank pointed out. "We needed a better plan, something more controllable over the long haul."

"Pathet was my idea, one of my better ones, I think."

She summoned the daemon with a gesture, and he came to her, held her shoulders between his hands. Twisting slightly at the waist, she patted the daemon on the cheek, turned the proprietary gesture into a caress.

Frank watched them with avid attention. "We needed a hybrid, sharing the powers of daemons but controllable as a human."

"I decided to create one," Marnie Simpson explained. "I was still fifteen—"

"And beautiful." Franklin Simpson closed his eyes, a connoisseur's smile lighting his face. "The fragility of youth in carnal communion with the powers of Darkness. Magnificent." He hunched in his chair, quivering, a flush rising to meet slowly raised eyelids. He reached out, and Evan thought the man would go to his wife, reclaim her, but he let the hand fall again. The smile turned to ice.

Pathet covered the woman's hand where it rested on his cheek, pulled it free. Her fingers bent, clawed bloody streaks into his face in parting, and hung in his grasp between them, dripping blood.

"Someday," the daemon said, "you're going to make a mistake, and I will kill you." He smiled as he said the words, turning them into a lover's promise.

"Haven't yet," she pointed out, but she let his hand fall to his side.

Evan stared at the bloody streaks for a moment, caught in the memory of blood on his father's arm. Deadly hatred had twisted Badad's face, and betrayal had shadowed his father's eyes when he bound the daemon to his will. He wondered where Brad was now, if Lily was with him, but he resisted the urge to summon them with the binding spell. He wasn't like Marnie Simpson, didn't ever again want to see his father look at him with the hatred Pathet reserved for the woman who controlled him. More important to Evan, he knew that human life was short, but the memory of daemons went with them into eternity, an immortality of its own. He wanted the memory of his life to be one of honor, if nothing else.

Marnie Simpson ignored the daemon seething at her back. "My mother was out of jail by then, and she persuaded the doctor to falsify the birth records for a slight increase in his regular fee. We were rich by then, you see. And there would have been a scandal. I was underage, and I certainly didn't want Frank to go to jail for a crime he hadn't committed." With one bloody fingertip, she slowly traced the skin stretched over Evan's breastbone.

"Nice." She leaned forward, licked the sweat from the hollow of his throat. Evan's stomach muscles fluttered with involuntary tension as her hand followed the fine line of hair to his navel.

"Mother died soon after Paul was born."

"Accidental death, no doubt," Evan volunteered. No accident at all, he was sure.

"Unfortunate, of course. Frank and I married. We spent years training the boy."

The knowledge that Paul's tormenters had inflicted that suicidal madness deliberately, for some purpose of their own, turned Evan's stomach, but he still didn't understand.

"Why? What was he supposed to do?"

Pathet answered, sardonic pleasure hiding behind the words. They shared a secret, these lords and Evan. The fleeting twist of Pathet's smile said that he knew the half-breed would enjoy the joke.

"They were training the boy to invade the second sphere, to rule there as a proxy king. Little Paul would take their orders from here and put them into action in the second sphere. For his mother, he would strip the wealth out of the purview of the Princes, bringing the lord of the hosts under the sway of his human puppet masters. There he would learn the secret of eternal life."

"That's insane." Memory of that other place, the emptiness that no half-human could long survive, settled in a ball in Evan's churning stomach.

"The forces that move humans often seem so," Pathet agreed. "You, for example, had them worried."

"Me?"

Pathet nodded, pure malice in his grin that told Evan there was nothing personal in it; he was just passing along the misery.

"From the days before you were born, when the daemon part of you first traveled alone into the second sphere, your presence was noted, the special taste of your passage recorded in the memories of Princes. I passed along the information. Paul wasn't the only monster in the universe; they had competition."

"My brother was right about you." Claudia's voice accused him, but Evan looked into her eyes and found a shaky understanding there. Not happy about it, but after years of denial, she was finally convinced. And he found something else in her wary expression: contempt for their captors. Underestimating her might be the mistake they needed; Evan answered the voice, not the eyes.

"If you mean that my father's not human, yeah, he was right. Don't expect any miracles, though. Mostly it just drives us crazy."

"Not miracles, perhaps," Marnie Simpson agreed. "But you have your uses, and your dangers. We had to find you. Mac was bait— Not the only one, but the one you found.

Frank wanted you dead, but I persuaded him to keep you in reserve, in case we weren't successful with Paul. I was right, and that's why we are here."

"I'm not a bad person." Marnie Simpson held up her cigarette, stared at the burning tip before taking a slow drag. "I've kept you alive, after all, when Frank would have killed you out of hand. But you have to understand: your father murdered my son. I'm entitled to compensation. 'An eye for an eye,' you know. A son for a son."

"My father didn't kill Paul, and he won't let you kill me."

Evan hoped he sounded more sure of that than the last few days had left him. He remembered the newspaper article about the Black Masque. Fifty dead, including Paul Carter. Would his own death mean more than a ripple in the eternity his father inhabited?

Movement distracted Evan from the contemplation of his own imminent mortality. Alfredo DaCosta unfolded himself from his perch under the fresco of Thot. "If you don't mind, I'd rather not hear all of this. I'll be downstairs if you need anything."

All eyes turned to the stately thief, but Franklin Simpson spoke first. "No one leaves this room."

"Be reasonable. I'm hardly likely to go to the local police, now am I?" DaCosta countered with a gesture that took in their surroundings. "I didn't pick up my collection at Christy's; some of these works have been missing since the Nazis passed through Paris. I value them almost as much as I value my own freedom, and I have no intention of sacrificing either to a sudden attack of conscience. The less I know, however, the easier it will be to set that seldom-used organ to rest."

Simpson flicked a quick glance over the man. "Don't trust him."

"What could I tell the authorities?" DaCosta argued. "That Americans with daemon accomplices are planning to take over the universe from my attic? They are hardly likely to bring out the antiterrorist squads for that, are they? The mental institutions in this country are worse than the jails. Silence is my only option."

"Go." Marnie Simpson dismissed him, and answered her husband's objection. "You were wrong to let him hear this much."

DaCosta dipped his head in an abrupt sketch of a bow and left the room.

"Follow him." She touched Pathet on the shoulder, gestured at the door. "And kill him discreetly. We don't want any attention yet. Come back when you're done with him."

"Yes, master." The daemon bent low in a mocking travesty of DaCosta's bow.

Secrets again. Evan thought about the frescoes overhead, wondered what Pathet knew.

"I don't want to kill you, Evan." Marnie Simpson hooked an elbow around his arm, led Evan back to the bed. "I'd much rather make you a king, if only a puppet one, as Pathet so eloquently put it. But I hope you're right about your father, because he has something I need."

"The Eye of Omage," Evan supplied.

"Clever boy," Marnie Simpson approved. "The jewel works like a homing device, and your agency was more helpful than I could have hoped in tuning it. It's simple, really. I control Mac, Mac controls the jewel, and the jewel controls you. You will go where you are sent, or you will die, rather horribly, I'm afraid.

"Of course, only a fool would depend on the affection of your father's kind. You will tell us his true name, or your lady friend will die."

She pushed him down, leaned over him like a carrion bird, grinning over the bright ember of the cigarette she held in her hand.

"His name is Kevin Bradley, that's all I know," Evan objected.

Marnie Simpson laughed. "Don't treat me like a fool, boy. I haven't much patience. You'll tell me what I want to know, and you'll do what you're told." She snapped the shackle back on his wrist.

"I know you can escape this as easily as think it." She sat next to Evan on the bed and slipped the tip of her index finger between the shackle and his wrist, scratching the abrasion.

"I'll even let it go this time, because your little Houdini number told me everything I needed to know about you. But if you try it again, I'll give your girlfriend to our old friend Mac."

She turned her head, addressed the daemon seething in the corner. "You'd like that, wouldn't you?"

The daemon snarled. His eyes fixed on Claudia, a cat watching a mouse just out of reach, waiting for the wrong move that would make the girl his.

"I thought you would." Marnie Simpson turned her attention back to Evan; he shuddered as her fingertips drifted lazily over the line of his shoulder, the curve of his biceps. "Well, Evan? We know our Mac's . . . esoteric tastes, don't we, boy? I can't force you, but I think our interests run in the same direction."

"I can't tell you anything."

"You can, and you will."

Staring into the lit end of her cigarette, Marnie Simpson smiled. "Hold the girl," she ordered, "If Evan tries anything, kill her. Take your time about it, of course."

Everything she planned for him was in that smile, focused on the burning tip of the cigarette. Evan tried to separate himself from the pain he knew would follow, but instead grew hyper-aware of every sensation. Sweat bloomed in pinpricks, trickled hot trails down his temples, his armpits. With his arm chained above his head she would see the sweat beading in the hair under his arms. Illogically, the realization embarrassed him, and he tried to bring his arm down. The shackle cut into his wrist but did not let him move.

His jeans clung, too hot, too tight, around his thighs. *Don't think, don't think*—superstition crawled between his legs. She would know if he thought it. She wouldn't think of it if he kept his fear above the waist. The sheet, limp with sweat, itched at his back.

"The name, Evan."

Chapter Twenty-four

Trismegistus teaches that man once passed immortal through the spheres as rational mind, and seeking understanding, found in Nature great beauty, and flew to her breast, the mountains of the Earth, and mated with her and became flesh, joined in two natures, the mind and the body, mortal and immortal alone of all the spirits.

Alfredo DaCosta crouched out of sight of the open windows. "We have to talk."

Badad cast a baleful eye on the man. Humans seldom roamed their rooftops chatting with falcons uncharacteristically roosting in their rain gutters. But Alfredo DaCosta had secrets even Lily had not discovered—the attic room was a case in point.

The man stroked a finger down Lirion's breast. She snagged the offending digit in a beak designed for tearing flesh, but did not break the skin.

"Beautiful in any form," he asserted with a smile just for her, then grew more serious. "But you stole something from me, a smoky topaz about the size of a fist, and I really must have it back."

He teased his finger away from her. "They're going to

torture your son until he gives you up to them," he said to Brad. "They need the jewel to control him, and I can't let that happen—you are not the only guardians of the spheres.

"There's a cafe on the square. We can talk first, or I can go back inside and do what I was sent to do."

The man stood silently and picked his way around the attic projection overlooking the canal. When Badad rose into the air to follow, Alfredo DaCosta had disappeared, but the flickering candles on the tables of the café set his course. He spiraled lower, swooped under the columned portico of an unassuming church, and adjusted the cuffs of his shirt beneath his jacket. Lily followed a moment later, her hair a splash of the second sphere against the white gauze of her dress. Arms linked, they wandered among the scattered tables until they found DaCosta with his back to the rough stone wall, the fragile barricade of a cordial glass in front of him.

He stood when he saw them, held out a chair for Lily. "More beautiful than a night in Venice," he declared, "though once this city would have been a worthy rival." He smiled reminiscently at her, and Brad wondered at the affection he saw there, for the city, for Lily, and for something Brad thought he understood. Not human, then, but fond of the creatures as Brad was fond of Evan.

Lily was answering, her own smile warm with memories of Alfredo DaCosta and Venice that Brad did not share. "It still is."

"Not like it was," DaCosta insisted. "Even the stones are dying. The sea takes back its own, always."

A waiter appeared unobtrusively at DaCosta's side, with a smile and a bow for Lily.

"Three of the usual, Gianni."

Brad waited until the waiter moved away from the table, then commented, "You've been here a long time, then." He posed the statement as a question that brought another smile to DaCosta's lips.

"Since the beginning," he agreed.

"The founding of the city?" Brad asked.

Alfredo DaCosta laughed. "Of creation," he corrected. "It was a mistake." He gestured gracefully with a hand that seemed to embrace not only their small table, but land and sea and sky and more.

The waiter returned, set their drinks in front of them. When he had gone, DaCosta continued his explanation.

"Unlike the Princes, my own people suffer an inordinate curiosity about our neighbors. Like yourselves, however, we had no access to the other spheres, until in his enthusiasm, one of our searchers—humans would call them scientists—literally blew a hole between our two universes."

Alfredo DaCosta held up both hands. He spread the fingers of his right: "From what we have since learned, the searchers believe that the second sphere must consist of what, in material terms, would be considered space, but without time. You are immortal because time has no meaning in the second sphere."

He spread the fingers of his left. "We can call the third sphere the temporal sphere, since that is the aspect that concerns us most here. Time is our medium, we move in it much as fish move in the seas of Earth. Like the Princes, we are immortal according to human reckoning, though the term has no real meaning for us.

"Unfortunately, the two spheres proved incompatible. The material universe came into existence when they touched, when space and time converged." He demonstrated, intertwining his fingers. "Humans call the space-time where they met the 'big bang.'"

The moment remained vivid in Badad's memory, a marker in the eternity of home. More of the pieces fell into place. He mirrored DaCosta's earlier gesture, encompassing not only the city, but the universe that held it. "And all of this acts like a patch on a leaky boat."

"So to speak," DaCosta agreed. "The material sphere represents both barrier and access between your home and mine."

"Evan was wondering if there was a God." Lily lifted her glass in salute to DaCosta. "Now we know."

Brad added his own salute to Lily's with a sardonic tilt to the eyebrow. "I don't think he'll be pleased to find you've been sleeping with the Divinity, cousin."

"Not God, please," DaCosta corrected. "I've gone that route a time or two already."

The count lifted his glass, stared into the gold liqueur backlit by the flicker of the candle at the center of the table. Half-hidden behind the licorice-scented barricade, something implacable crossed his face, left behind only the bland insouciance of the Italian aristocrat. Brad saw judgment in that fleeting look. Not omnipotent, perhaps, but for his son, the distinction could prove moot.

Back from the place where he once walked as god, Alfredo offered a twisted smile. "Divinity is highly overrated. Too high-profile, makes it damned hard to get a date. I didn't create this universe anyway; I just watch it. A guardian angel, if you will. At most an Archangel."

"And the angel Alfredo appeared before them—do you have any parlor tricks up your sleeve?" Lily teased. A warning look told Brad she hadn't missed that fleeting glimpse behind the facade, but for now she would not see.

"A few," DaCosta admitted. "When this is all over, we can compare notes." He grew more pensive, suddenly. "I sometimes wonder, though—"

"What?" Brad asked, knowing the answer already. The same question bothered him.

"If we created the material universe, perhaps someone, something, created us as well."

"I wonder what their watchdogs think of what we're doing here today." Brad sympathized with the guardian. His own time on Earth was bounded by the life span of his human offspring. What would it be like to watch eternity tick by in the measure of the sea reclaiming the land?

"I hope they find their task more interesting than our own." DaCosta seemed firmly in control again. "Of our guardians, most travel through large expanses of this universe, maintaining a sporadic check for flaws in space-time through which the spheres might randomly touch. A very few of us keep watch over intelligent life wherever it arises.

"Until recently, the system was pretty self-regulating, dead boring when it wasn't disgusting. A handful of the persistent and unlucky would manage to bring lords of the hosts of Princes through—that's how we found out about you. Few of the human summoners lived to tell about it." Lily's eyes slitted, and DaCosta faltered, rested a hand over hers on the table. "Some crossbreeding happened from the start. Not often; your kind and theirs aren't all that compatible, and humans are obsessed with sex, not with procreation. Those rare exceptions were enough to keep me on my toes, even though they never lived long enough to cause much trouble. Most societies murdered any hybrid in childhood, as a monster, as soon as the child started behaving strangely—screaming, nightmaring, the sort of things Evan used to do. The locals didn't know what they were killing, you understand, just that it wasn't like them. Once in a while a hybrid would survive into adulthood as a social pariah, an outcast and completely mad by then. The hazards of the life usually finished the job their societies began."

"It's odd, really." DaCosta contemplated his drink. "Things have been slow for a couple hundred years. I might have been growing complacent—forgot the most important thing about this species, its talent for believing two or more mutually exclusive contradictions simultaneously, and for denying the evidence of its senses when they conflict with those beliefs. Once again, the mortals of this place began to fling daemons at their enemies."

Badad little needed the reminder. The face of a laughing woman rode the crest of a memory: Evan's mother. Flung at her indeed, a jealous suitor bringing ruin on a woman of no accomplishments and few aspirations. He'd known little of humans then; the touch of flesh, his own form, revolted him. With time and choice he'd grown accustomed to the latter. The memory of Evan, beating himself to death against the second sphere in a room with no windows still fueled his aversion to human touch. Never again. He renewed the vow he had made then: never again.

"Twice now in this age your kind have created hybrids," DaCosta continued, "who behaved as hybrids always have. Paul Carter was a failed experiment, with predictable results; he survived until he was old enough to remove himself from the horrors of his own mortal existence. In that, we've been lucky so far—they've always managed to kill themselves, or be killed, before they had the chance to procreate. Unfortunately, our friends the Simpsons are more cold-blooded about the whole thing than most. With Paul Carter gone, they've turned again to Evan Davis."

There had been nothing cold-blooded about the rage that had dragged Badad out of the second sphere, that had ruined a woman's life—except that Evan said he hadn't ruined it—that had blinded the man to the dangerous game he played when he antagonized a lord of the host of Ariton. Nothing at all like the chill purpose he heard in Marnie Simpson's voice. "But why?" he asked. "What do they hope to gain?"

"I'm afraid Pathet has been leading them a merry chase with promises of power and immortality," DaCosta said. "And Omage enjoys the joke too much to burst their bubble."

"Power over what?" Lily interrupted. "According to Evan, the second sphere holds nothing for humans."

Brad coughed a short laugh. "He means that literally. Evan says that the second sphere is empty to human senses; that's why the children go mad there."

"Interesting," DaCosta agreed. "The Simpsons seem convinced that the second sphere is like Earth, but richer and without defenses. Streets paved with gold, the whole Eldorado-New World bit straight out of the fifteenth century speculative travelogues. They came up with the notion on their own, but Pathet keeps the fiction going with casual references to wealthy merchants and a population of sheep."

"I've always found the Princes a bit more temperamental than that," Lily objected with a wry smile. "They won't like what Pathet has done at all."

DaCosta returned the smile. "I can't say; never met a

Prince, just the occasional, and most unsheeplike, emissary. I can tell you this," the guardian leaned over the table, "immortality is out of the question, even for the hybrids. Time is as much a part of them as space is. When both converge, the clock starts ticking. Sooner or later, it stops. Try to separate them again, and you've got ground meat on your hands. Ground meat that rots, and not even the Simpsons can stop it."

DaCosta paused for reflection. "In spite of their efforts, just as likely because of them, Paul Carter's clock stopped sooner, the way mature hybrids always have, insane, of suicide. And that should have ended the crisis.

"You, however, have complicated things quite a bit." DaCosta stared across his drink at Brad, the guardian's grim frustration meeting the daemon's implacable will. *Don't push it.* Brad's grim countenance shouted the unspoken words. Understanding flared in DaCosta's eyes; the guardian said the words anyway:

"Evan Davis should be dead as well, or harmlessly mad in a padded cell, disturbing the business of Princes but leaving the rest of the seven universes in peace. Never in the history of the material universe has a daemon sire wasted on its progeny more than the energy it took to destroy the misbegotten creature. I don't know why you decided to intervene—"

Nor could Brad explain the pull his son had exerted on him. If the boy had begged, he would have died. The wild challenge, not for release,but for proof that his father was no saner than the creature who enslaved him, sang Ariton in the place where human cell mingled with daemon essence in the body the daemon wore. Evan lived because Evan was Ariton, not because Brad grew too human.

"—but you truly have created a monster in this man.

With the training you have given him, your son is the wedge that can destroy us all."

Brad stood, turned his back on the man at the table. Ca' DaCosta pulled at him, a visceral need to be in that other place and stand between his son and the forces of three universes massed against him, but Lily answered the man with her own challenge. Brad hesitated, waiting for the answer.

"How?" she asked defensively. Brad knew she'd never understood why he'd let the boy live. But they were Ariton; host loyalty demanded a unified front. "Untrained and in Mac's hands, Evan was wreaking havoc with both our universes. With a little training, he's learned how to control his passage through the second sphere without raising a whisper."

"That's the problem." Alfredo DaCosta intertwined his fingers again, an echo of his earlier gesture. "Humans share equally in both our universes. Only the hybrids, with the balance tilted toward the second sphere, can move in that direction. We feel certain the hybrids have the potential to pass through the second sphere and breach the barrier to our own universe, with catastrophic results. Until now none has survived the second sphere with enough mind left to direct him farther. Evan is stronger than I imagined; I suspect he's more powerful than he knows."

"He is," Lily interrupted with a warning. "But he denies it. Won't transfer through the spheres unless he has to, and he's stirred up a few things, sparks, winds, that he attributes to me, or to coincidence. Nothing he can control yet, and he won't learn while he's pretending it doesn't happen, but he'll be harder to kill than you think.

Push him to the wall and he'll call on the part of himself he hides from without realizing that he's done it."

"I thought as much," DaCosta confirmed. "If he chooses to fight in the material sphere, you may be the only two creatures in the universe who can stop him."

Brad dismissed the prediction with an impatient gesture. "Evan's not the explorer type. He hates the second sphere, wouldn't go looking for more universes if his life depended on it."

"If Marnie Simpson gets her hand on the Eye of Omage, he won't have a choice."

"Why?" Brad sat down again, fighting the feeling that told him to find Evan now. He needed information, and DaCosta seemed to have it. The jewel in particular had troubled him since Lily lifted it from the man who watched him from across the table. "It's more than just a polished stone, but what? And what were you doing with it?"

DaCosta closed his eyes for a moment, opened them slowly on a sigh. The cloying perfume of the anisette hung over the table. "You haven't touched your drink," he noted, and took a sip of his own.

Brad ignored the glass in front of him, waiting.

"I can't tell you what it is—the knowledge is too dangerous. Somehow, Omage found out about it, and with his usual hubris he called it the Eye of Omage. I stole the jewel to keep Azmod from using it and covered my tracks with a few emeralds and the Picasso—so far I've convinced them I'm a harmless thief with an unfortunate attraction to gaudy jewelry. They must have realized that Paul Carter was a lost cause, too insanely suicidal for their plans. Evan had survived, but they needed both the boy and the jewel to successfully put their plan into action.

"The solution was simple. As Charles St. George, Franklin Simpson hired your agency to retrieve the stolen painting. Mac would have known Lily couldn't resist the gem. It calls to your kind, especially if you've been too close to Evan. I expect Evan did the rest. The Eye, as Mac called it, would have drawn him like a magnet draws iron shavings. It draws Omage as well. You led them to Venice, Lily. They threatened to go to the police about my collection unless I gave them the use of my chamber.

"The rest you must have discovered on your own, or you wouldn't be here. With the girl as leverage, Evan will give them your names. They need bind you only long enough to get the jewel back. For the safety of all our universes, you will have to destroy it first."

Brad contemplated the thick, sweet-smelling liquid in his glass. "The Simpsons won't like that. They've made a major investment in this project—Mac, Pathet, all of this—" He flicked a glance across the piazza, at the brooding shadow of Ca' DaCosta." They aren't likely to let Evan or his young lady go free after they have seen and heard so much."

His cousin surprised him with a possessive glare at the reference to the Laurence woman. "If Evan is connected to this jewel as you say, its destruction could kill him anyway," she guessed, then added, "I don't like it when my toys are broken."

"You are talking about a choice between the life of your monster or the continued existence of three universes." DaCosta drained his glass and set it down. "And the boy will die anyway in the destruction he causes."

Brad stared at the man in front of him, sick at the images he conjured. "What do you expect me to do?"

DaCosta sighed. "Give me the Eye of Omage. As for the rest, if you'd asked me two years ago, the answer would have been simple. Kill him, or let him die on his own. The spheres never mix well, and he was no exception, half mad at the best of times, pushed over the edge entirely by Mac's tender attention.

"You've got a weak spot I never thought I'd see in one of your kind. That doesn't change things, it only complicates them. Evan has to die; his life isn't worth the risk he poses even without the jewel. You can do it, make it as easy for him as you can, or you can go back to Philadelphia, read a good book, and I'll take care of it for you. I won't leave it to Marnie Simpson, I promise you that. Your job will be done, you can go back into the darkness until the next one."

Brad stared at the man, conscious of the binding that made the man's suggestion impossible, and of the thought that made it more so. Lily spoke the words ahead of him, and he smiled in spite of himself, to know what truth she finally accepted.

"Evan's too much fun to play with to give up so easily," she began, then added, "he's also Ariton. Host loyalty dictates we must protect him."

"He's also human," DaCosta countered. "A monster. If we don't destroy him now, he will bring down three universes, maybe more. And he won't stop to consider what his actions do to Ariton, because Marnie Simpson won't give him that luxury."

Brad agreed with that. "So we kill the damned Simpsons, destroy the stone, and send the lords of Azmod back where they belong."

"You think it will be that easy?" DaCosta asked.

"Easier than killing my son," Brad countered. "Much easier, since he's bound us to his will."

DaCosta stared at him blankly. "And you still defend him?"

Brad shrugged. "It isn't like the Simpsons, or any other binding. I thought it was, at first, but the feel of it is different."

"And how is that?"

Lily answered, her own bemused smile supporting her cousin. "Part of something," she realized aloud. "Like being part of Ariton."

"Not always pleasantly," Brad added. He didn't feel the pain, just Evan's shock, a gasp for breath that started at gut level and fought against a throat closed tight around a scream. He was on his feet and running before the words left his mouth: "It's begun."

Chapter Twenty-five

Hermes Trismegistus teaches that in Egypt at one time man grew weary of the great glory of the All, that which he encompassed in his person and his memory of the heavens, and made idols of clay and drew into them the spirits of the air, daemons commanded by the words that the Thrice Great had given them.

Holding the cigarette like a scalpel, Marnie Simpson traced a line from the throat to the base of Evan's sternum and crossed it over his heart. The pain that followed snapped the tension, replaced it with something infinitely worse. Evan heard a scream that seemed to come from somewhere above him. *The frescoes,* he thought, *the frescoes are screaming.* Only when he stopped, his throat too raw to shape the sound, did he realize the scream was his own. Caught between the urge to tear his own burned flesh from his body and the pain that seared his nerve endings with the slightest touch, he curled away from the heat, gasping.

Slowly he recognized the sobbing next to him. Claudia, held frozen with Omage's knife resting lightly above her breast. Jack Laurence was dead and his sister soon would be. Too late for both of them now, he knew, but he had to try.

"Let her go," he begged, his voice somewhere between a gasp and a cry.

"You know I can't do that." Chill humor laced the words. They both knew better: Marnie Simpson would never let Claudia go. Until she held the Eye of Omage, only Claudia kept Evan here. If he betrayed his father, gave Marnie Simpson the jewel, Claudia would die. She'd seen too much, heard too much to walk out of this room, alive—*his fault, his fault.* His touch was a sickness as deadly as the woman's above him, no less so because he wanted it to be different.

Evan stalled for time, willing himself to believe. Brad would come for him, pull them out of there like Rambo Meets King Kong. In the meantime, he had to keep Marnie Simpson's mind off Claudia.

"I don't know anything," he pleaded.

"You're lying."

Marnie Simpson's voice, seductive, barely a whisper in his ear, warned him. He braced himself for the pain that squeezed the air from his chest. The glowing coal at the cigarette's tip found the pulse point at his throat and traced the vein with slow deliberation. Her tongue followed, licking delicately at the burn, a gesture that his clouded mind read as comfort even though it gave no relief from the pain.

"Tell me what I want to know, my sweet," she whispered. "Give me the Eye of Omage and I'll set the woman free. We can rule the universe together."

"Rule what?" he gasped, too confused by the pain to say anything but the truth, "There's nothing out there but the dark."

"Lies." The cigarette followed, burn trailing burn, as delicate as the work of a surgeon.

The muscles in Evan's back locked, arched above the bed. He screamed again, surprised that he could make the sound, and then the universe centered on the slow tracery of the ember. All sense of time, place, even his body, went away. He was in Omage's back room again and he was going to die fighting the terror and the pain and the voices in his head, this time promising relief if he would just say the name.

"DaCosta's gone." Pathet stood framed in the doorway beneath the fresco of the twelve virtues and the twelve temptations. "He's not in the house," the daemon reported.

The cigarette lifted, still close enough that Evan felt the heat, far enough not to carve another burn into his skin. He fell back on the pillow, grateful for the distraction, and dragged air into his lungs. Silver trails wept fire across his chest, his abdomen, his neck, and arms. So far she'd stayed clear of his face and his groin—*don't think, don't think; she'll hear*—he willed his imagination under control, but the pain still cut short each breath.

Claudia sobbed beside him, held fast by the shackle on her leg and the knife in Omage's hand. Evan stretched his own hand toward her, and she took it, held on tight. She was crying for him, he realized, and took comfort from her warm grasp. Help would come, Brad would find him if he just held out long enough—he tried to communicate his hope through their clasped hands.

"That's impossible." Franklin Simpson slouched open-legged in his chair, drinking in the wounds on Evan's chest. Sweat stood out at his temples and above his upper lip. He ran his tongue over his lips and took a deep breath, countering the daemon's information without taking his eyes from the figure on the bed. "The doors are sealed to humans; he must be in the house somewhere."

Marnie Simpson nodded agreement. "Forget DaCosta for now. He's here somewhere. We can take care of him when we leave."

She examined her handiwork with a thoughtful pout. "Not exactly stoical, are you, boy?" A fingernail caked with the blood of her daemon lover traced the line of a burn, asked another rhetorical question and underscored it with light pressure on a weeping scab. "Have you been telling the truth all along?"

Evan gasped, his eyes locked with hers, the vow he'd made to Lily burning in his mind. *Family.* He would not surrender Ariton to the torment that had driven Omage mad, to the woman who had caused the death of her own son.

A fingernail found pain, traced it. "It makes sense. Your father would be a fool to reveal his true identity."

"The lord who calls himself Kevin Bradley is a fool." Pathet joined Marnie Simpson at the bed, leaned over to murmur intimately in her ear. "But even he would not trust his human offspring. Others of his kind, however, know things."

The daemon slid a hand beneath her blouse and squeezed her breast, but only Evan could see his expression. Laughter and hatred mingled on his face, and triumph. "Kevin Bradley is yours, for a bargain."

"I can command you to tell me," Marnie Simpson looked into the green eyes of Azmod; Evan saw a test of wills there. "I don't make bargains."

"You can command," Pathet agreed. "But there is information, and then there is useful information. It will take longer than you've got to obtain the latter by command, but I think we can arrange a simple trade—two for the price of one, shall we say?"

"You'll give me Lily Ryan as well?"

Pathet nodded.

"In exchange for?"

"My freedom, of course."

"And mine." Forgotten in the exchange, Omage leaned over the girl on the bed, his knife drawing blood in his eagerness, "I can give them to you. Free me and keep your sex toy."

"I still need you, Mac. Your time will come."

The daemon subsided, snarling, and Marnie Simpson turned her attention to Pathet. "You've been a stunning failure so far. Your son is dead, and I'm no closer to the Eye of Omage than I have been since it was stolen."

Taking the cigarette from her hand, Pathet dropped it, crushing it out with one foot. He sat next to her on the bed, his hip grazing the burns on Evan's hyperextended underarm.

"I can change that." The daemon spread his hand wide, cupped the woman's face, and reached fingers deep into her hair. He pulled her closer and kissed her, nuzzled at her neck. Evan noticed that the marks had disappeared from Pathet's cold face. Death eyes the color of poison, of rot, fixed on him, shared with Evan the contempt of a lord of the host of Azmod for the woman in his arms while they promised death for Badad's child and the world that held them all.

So Marnie Simpson would have the lords of Ariton in spite of what he had suffered to stop her; it had all been for nothing. Trapped in the vision of echoing darkness, hope faded in black pin dots that obscured Evan's vision.

The smell of blood and his own burned skin gagged him. Exhausted by fighting the madness of the creatures around him, a flash of betrayal colored his struggle. Where the hell was his father?

"Yes." The woman acquiesced with a sigh of pleasure. She pulled back far enough to read the threat in the daemon's face and smiled, aroused, Evan realized, by the danger as much as the caress. He shuddered, nauseated by the revulsion he felt for Marnie Simpson, and the waves of despair that crashed over him.

"I'll give you one more chance to redeem yourself. But I won't bargain for names. When I have them, Bradley and Ryan both bound to my will, I'll let you go. First, I need the names."

Pathet nipped at her ear. "His name is Badad, lord of the host of Ariton, and she is Lirion, also of the host of Ariton. You can command their presence, of course, but you run a greater risk of trickery that way. They are fools, but not stupid."

Marnie Simpson smiled at him, stretched her neck for him to nuzzle deeper. "What do you suggest?"

"Use the boy, he's Badad's weakness. Then, when you have them contained in the circle," his eyes flitted to the pentagram overhead, "you can bind them in safety."

The plan would fail, Evan realized. If his father cared at all, he would be here now. But caring was human. Once again the knowledge of the alienness of Ariton crawled like lice over his scalp. The binding he had done to protect them had sealed his own death. When he died, his father and his lover were free again, of him, and of Ariton's task in the material sphere. They could go home. The thought was all the more bitter with the taste of the death he had caused. The only friends he'd ever had, dead just for knowing him. His father was going to let him die.

"Your concern is touching," Marnie Simpson addressed the daemon at her side. "You will take a message for me?"

"Anything." The daemon ran a hand down Evan's leg. "Not much longer," he said. The macabre joke bubbling in his eyes turned Evan's stomach. Not much longer and he'd be dead.

Honor seemed stupid at the moment; he could command the lords of Ariton. Calling on his father for survival was not the same as the tyranny with which Marnie Simpson and her husband controlled the lords of Azmod, but that subtlety of motive would be lost on his daemon kin. The gesture seemed pointless anyway. Mind dulled with exhaustion and pain, he knew only that he could not spend a lifetime alone in his difference. Better to die now.

Marnie Simpson was looking past him, at Claudia, who listened wide-eyed while their captors decided their fate. Claudia. She had to live through this—one good thing out of the whole mess of his life had to survive. But the words that would command the lords of Ariton slipped through his mind like a breeze.

"Nice shirt," the Simpson woman said. "But not your size. How gallant of our Evan, to sacrifice fine Italian workmanship for a lady's modesty."

"Cut if off her," she ordered Omage. "I want the pocket."

Omage cut through the fabric, drawing a thin track of blood where he cut too deeply over her breast. Claudia keened between clenched teeth, her eyes locked on the knife in the daemon's hand. First, he cut out the pocket. Then, grinning, he cut each button free. Marnie Simpson took the knife and the ragged square of fabric.

"Poetic symmetry," she said, examining the knife. "Kevin Bradley will appreciate that." She stretched Evan's shackled hand palm upward, traced the threads of scar tissue on his wrist with the tip of Mac's knife, the same knife that in Omage's back room had cut the scars, an eternity ago it sometimes seemed. Sometimes, like now, it seemed like yesterday.

Too much. Evan felt himself cut adrift in a part of his mind where the pain filtered dimly and time had no meaning. In that too-familiar place he drew himself into an imaginary ball and pretended that he did not exist. Almost, he didn't feel it when Marnie Simpson cut a line parallel to the silver threads. Blood welled from the cut, and the woman—*Paul Carter's mother,* the thought flitted mockingly through his mind, she knew the tricks, had seen it all before—wiped it with the ragged pocket.

"Take this to his father." She handed the dripping cloth to Pathet. "Tell Mr. Bradley that I request his presence and the return of my property, the Eye of Omage. I'll be counting the minutes. On Evan's fine young body." She leaned over him, kissed Evan softly on the lips.

"Go," she commanded without looking back at the daemon.

Claudia's scream, tight with hysteria, pulled him out of the safe place in his mind. Evan squeezed her hand, felt the return grip strong and steady that belied her horror-filled eyes. Then she pulled her hand away, covering her mouth.

"I'm going to throw up," she moaned.

"Shut her up," Marnie Simpson ordered.

Omage leered. "Give me my knife," he pressed. "You won't hear another sound out of her."

Marnie Simpson glared at him. "Until I've got the jewel, we need her."

"It's up to you," the daemon conceded, "but I've seen it before. A lot of them think they can take anything. Then—" He shrugged. "A little excitement, and you've got piss and vomit all over the floor."

"I need the bathroom."

Claudia Laurence grabbed at her stomach, and Simpson dismissed the younger woman with a disgusted curl of her lip.

"Take her to the bathroom, but leave the shirt here. She won't be going anywhere like that. And don't let her out of your sight. We don't want her getting into mischief, do we?"

Omage nodded, a lascivious grin lighting his features with the putrescent glow of something dead overlong. He stripped off her shirt and dropped it in a heap next to the bed before he undid the shackle at Claudia's leg. "Bathroom's this way—" He lifted her roughly to her feet by her elbow.

Claudia bent to clutch her stomach again, and slipped out of the daemon's grip. Two steps and she was out of the window, diving headfirst off the roof and into the canal, her arms held stiffly above her head.

Omage followed dumbly to the window. "She's gone," he said with a shrug. "They do that sometimes, kill themselves. I don't know why."

Dead. He would have raged, would have followed, but he couldn't think past the pain to making the image real in his mind. More than grief, he felt abandoned. Why did she leave him behind, still living, when he would have died to save her?

Franklin Simpson came upright in his chair. "How did she get out? You said you sealed the house."

Omage grinned, pleased with himself, and shook his head. "Not exactly. You said to seal the doors against humans. You never mentioned the windows."

"You will be punished," Marnie Simpson informed the daemon, sharing a glance with her husband. Then she made the same promise to Evan, stroking his zipper with the tip of the silver knife. With Claudia dead, it didn't seem to matter.

From the painted ceiling above him the sad, dark eyes of Thot watched and judged. Marnie Simpson brought the knife down again, and Evan cried out, a single word like a death rattle torn from his throat:

"Father!"

Chapter Twenty-six

The pentagram, five-pointed star inscribed within a circle, is a symbol of protection. If a man were to call a daemon and he stands within the circle, the daemon cannot touch him. But beware not to cross outside of the circle until the daemon has been sent back to the place from whence it comes, or he will be torn limb from limb in the spirit's wrath.

"Evan."

Badad appeared in a ripple of troubled air and reined in an anger fueled by an emotion he had never felt before. Fear, new-learned at the meat-death of his own body, screamed from human nerve endings for the shaking man on the bed. Shock, Brad realized, but not entirely from the wounds. Clear fluids oozing from shallow burns that streaked Evan's body mingled with the sheen of cold sweat. Brad felt his heart beat in the rhythm of the blood dripping slowly from an opened wrist to the pillow; had to hurt like hell, but not actually dangerous unless infection set in. Something he couldn't see was killing his son.

Haunted eyes the color of the stone lying like a dead thing on his breast opened on him. "I knew you would come," his son acknowledged. But the relief was too sharp, too sudden.

Abandoned. The shadows in Evan's eyes still read abandoned, and yet he had not drawn on the binding that permitted no resistance—just the one inhuman cry, too full of pain, of Brad's own fear, to carry the weight of binding in it. That call had cut through Badad like the bloody knife Marnie Simpson held over his son's heart. Brad recognized the knife. Paul Carter had died on it, Evan had painted a room with his own blood drawn by it.

"Sorry I took so long." Brad paused. "Don't you think it's time we went home?"

"Can't. Can't think, can't shape it in my head." Evan seemed to stare right through his jacket, drawn to the jewel he carried next to his skin. "The Eye—let me see it." The chain at his wrist sounded hell-chimes when Evan reached out his hand.

"Yes, Mr. Bradley, let him see it." Marnie Simpson turned to greet him, the knife held casually between them and a proprietary hand resting on Evan's abdomen.

Brad ignored the woman, his plans for a swift and vengeful rescue shot to hell in the marble room. Evan wasn't going anywhere on his own, and Marnie Simpson didn't look like the 911 type. He drew the smoky topaz from beneath his shirt. Its cold weight fell on his breast where Evan and his captors could see it.

At the window, Omage clasped his hands together, a dissipated monk in unholy prayer. "You do good work," he admitted. "The boy is more thoroughly tuned to the jewel than I could have hoped. Your dash to the rescue has discommoded our young friend quite severely.

"It's his lifeline, you see. The stone anchors the human in him to the material sphere. While the Eye of Omage," he bent his head a moment, the maestro humbly accepting the accolades of his devoted fans, "remains safely here in his human reality, young Evan can pass into the second sphere without losing himself there. The holder of the jewel controls him, draws him back, you see. When the jewel passes into the second sphere—well, let's just call it uncomfortable. If Evan should find himself in the second sphere at the same time as the jewel . . ." The daemon shrugged. "We haven't had an opportunity to test this particular eventually yet, but neither were built for the consequences. It would probably tear the boy to pieces. At the least, it would destroy his mind. Would you kill him then, Ariton? If the boy survived that far, would you finally kill your mad human bastard?"

Evan reached for the stone, let his hand fall again, but Brad ignored the gesture with an effort. "You misinterpret my presence." He held out his empty hands with a conciliatory smile. "I'm here to protect Ariton's interests. If that means saving the boy, fine. If it doesn't, I'm reasonable. For my kind." He couldn't afford to look at Evan, didn't want to know if his son believed the lie. He gave Alfredo DaCosta's hidden room a cool overview: gaudier than his own taste ran, but the aging stone walls, the chessboard floor, suited the count. Portraits on the ceiling—Thot, Egyptian god of time and lordly justice, later Hermes— told a story of the guardian moving West.

DaCosta still sat in judgment, his words echoed in Badad's being: "Evan has to die . . . make it as easy for him as you can, or . . . I'll take care of it." How could he tell the guardian, who had watched millennia of death from a distance, but who had no more real understanding of what dying meant than Lily had, that Evan would never die easily, at any hand?

But DaCosta waited out there, beyond the marble walls and painted memories. Here, on the guardian's chessboard, the first moves of the battle would come. Brad assessed the forces ranged against him, found there mostly pawns.

Almost as sweaty as Evan, Franklin Simpson sprawled in an armchair at Brad's right. The human's expression mingling sour impatience with triumph: looked like he got his kicks watching. Probably interrupted at the big moment, old Frank looked like he already anticipated a bigger one. Simpson's lackey, Omage, stood next to the window with the keen joy of battle in his eyes, and Brad abandoned all hope of keeping this beneath the notice of Princes. For the first time he realized how closely Mac's human form resembled that of his master: evil little doppelganger of an evil little man. A cruel joke, and Mac never did have a sense of humor.

Marnie Simpson's smile, white queen to black knight, told him she anticipated the game. "The death of your son doesn't enter into my plans, Badad, lord of Ariton. But a bargain for his services? I think we can deal."

His true name stole the breath from Brad's human body, pulled at the very center of him where Ariton beat like a human heart. Betrayed. Quick as the thought, he knew Evan read the accusation in his face, saw hope bleeding into bleak endurance, and a challenge to believe in him or be damned. A martyr's look: why did Evan wear it now? Marnie Simpson stroked sweaty hair from the boy's brow with a gelid smile. Her eyes swept from son to father, testing, hard as old iron but pitted and brittle with it. Not far from the snapping point, Brad figured, but the thought didn't reassure him. White Queen. Of the three, she was still the most dangerous.

That didn't count Evan, who had given away his name. The game fell apart when he looked at Evan, who lay in chains at Marnie Simpson's nonexistent mercy. Evan held the lord of Ariton in his palm, and would hand that over, too, if it kept him breathing a few minutes longer. Brad remembered death. What would he give to hold that darkness at bay, if this life were all he had? Not Ariton. Were human loyalties that different? A week ago, he would have said not. Today he looked at his son and saw no shame, just soul-killing certainty that if Marnie Simpson's insane schemes didn't kill him, his father would.

Not yet, Badad promised silently, *not until I understand.*

"This place will never make Michelin's; I thought I taught you better taste." He pursed his lips in mock appraisal—never let them know it matters. "The accommodations aren't bad, but the service is atrocious. Minimal tip if I were you, son. And I'd have a word with housekeeping about the beds. I suppose all that blood is yours?"

"Our hostess had a bone to pick." Evan made the effort to answer in kind, but it cost him. Metal links chinged as he shifted his arm for a closer inspection. "Radius and ulna, to be exact."

He fell back, drained by a weariness that went beyond the wounds Badad could see.

"Jack and Claudia Laurence are dead." Unspoken, the words *My fault* fell heavy between them.

Brad shrugged, a veiled suggestion of hidden knowledge in his eyes. "Fire and water," he said. "How biblical. Of course, Noah had a boat."

He paused a moment, took the stone from around his neck, and held it by the chain in his outstretched hand.

"Miss Laurence said you needed this. She seemed to think it was important."

"Claudia."

Evan whispered the name, his eyes closing for a moment as he absorbed the truth of it. When he reached again to touch the stone, his arm held steady. Recovering from the effects of the stone's transfer through the second sphere, Brad guessed, and more. Claudia Laurence was alive, fished out of the Canal sputtering about kidnappers and daemons and a ransom in stolen jewelry.

"An unfortunate accident," Marnie Simpson demurred. "The girl's survival, I mean. But not critical. I have you now, Badad, and I have the stone. That should suffice to keep our young explorer in his place."

Pathet appeared at the woman's shoulder. "I found him for you—" The daemon nodded at the lord of Ariton. "As promised."

"He's here." Marnie Simpson seemed unwilling to award her own knight the point. "Where's the other one?"

Pathet shrugged. "Ask him."

"Well?" The woman rose from the bed, pulled a cigarette from the pack. "Got a light?"

Pathet snapped sparks between his thumb and middle finger, lit the cigarette.

Not Evan, then, but the fear Evan had brought into the open when they started this caper. "So Azmod cut a deal." He nodded, certain now, wanting Evan to know it, too. "But not Omage. He's tied up with the stone somehow; you may still need him. So Pathet's been whispering names in your bed."

"It could have been Evan," Marnie Simpson reminded him.

Brad shook his head. "He's my son." He smiled at

the man struggling to sit upright on the bed. "I trust him."

"How warm," Franklin Simpson rumbled from his chair. "How touching. Let's get on with this before I vomit. Where is Miss Ryan? Or should I ask, where is Lirion, lord of the host of Ariton?"

"Right here." Lily usurped Marnie Simpson's place on the bed. She stayed her hand inches above the puckered lines that crossed Evan's breast, then curled her fingers into a ball to keep from touching.

"We pulled your lady friend out of the Canal for you. She's going to have one hell of a case of conjunctivitis, and you are not one of her favorite people right now, but she's safe, with a friend."

Her glance, like Brad's own, searched as much as supported. What Brad saw in his son's eyes satisfied him: not the madness or the despair he'd found at the Black Masque, but anger. Something hard, unyielding as the stone, glinted from smoky depths. Evan lay back, undefeated and waiting. Brad turned his attention to Marnie Simpson. It was time to play out the game.

"What do you want?"

The woman gave Brad a proprietary smile. "You. And Lily, of course. You did answer my summons, however indirectly issued. That makes you both mine to command for as long as I can hold you."

"You know it doesn't work that way." Lirion stood and faced the woman; Badad joined her.

Lily continued: "We have agreed to no bargain, and with so unsubtle a statement of your intentions we are hardly likely to do so."

Brad nodded his agreement. "You can't hold us. We've come for Evan, and we'll be leaving with him. Now."

A snarl from the corner out of the room reminded Brad that they were not alone. Omage's face raged out of true, and he exploded in a whirlwind of dust that Franklin Simpson settled with an upraised hand.

"Our forces seem evenly matched," Simpson pointed out.

Pathet glanced from the human to a smoldering but subdued Omage and flashed Badad a sardonic twist of a smile. No love lost there for a half-human bastard, but a grudge running deep against the human who bound him.

"When you are bound, I'm free," Pathet explained. The smile he turned on his lover was not a pleasant thing. "I'll be just as free when you are dead. Hope I don't have a choice to make in battle."

Marnie Simpson laughed. "That's why I like you—always a challenge. Badad, however, has more predictable . . . desires?

"You said you wanted a bargain. Here are my terms." She faced Badad, all trace of humor gone. "Your allegiance, and that of Lirion, for the life of your son."

Evan would give him up to keep living, to stop the pain. *Accept it, understand it,* the part of his mind that remembered death said, and Badad realized that, yes, he could endure the twisted insanity of the Simpsons if his son still lived.

"He'll go free?"

"Give me the stone, and I'll release him right now. I'll have the occasional errand in the second sphere for him, but once he has that under control he'll be free to come and go as he pleases. We'll have no need of chains or shady little back rooms."

Brad watched his son, waiting for a word, a sign, but Evan shook his head.

Confident, Marnie Simpson watched the exchange. "Of course, your agreement is merely a formality—simpler, but not necessary.

"This room has an interesting decor, don't you agree? Particularly the ceiling art—a pentagram." She stepped out of the circle and her husband began the words of binding:

"By my will to command over the heavens and the earth, in the realms of the living and the dead and the eternally damned, I summon you Badad, lord of the host of Ariton, and you Lirion, lord of the host of Ariton. By this I conjure you: that you will appear immediately and without delay in any form I so command, whenever and every time you shall be summoned, by whatever word or sign or deed, in whatever time or place.

"You will obey the commands set for you in whatever form they shall be conveyed and for whatever purpose. If you should resist any command so issued, you will burn in the eternal fire of damnation now and until the end of time. So Swear it now by my rod, and bind it in the everlasting essence of your being."

Simpson rose from his chair and walked forward purposefully, a cane bound thick with age and the evil of the men who had carried it through time extended like a sword in his outstretched hand. The faces carved into the cane's surface screamed in Brad's ears, and he saw Lily wince, press her hands to the sides of her head.

"They can't make any bargain with you; they belong to me."

The level assertion fell like the cold darkness of home in the circle, washed away the oily taste of old torment that pulsed from the head of Franklin Simpson's cane. With the others, Brad turned to the source of the claim.

Evan sat at the edge of the bed, his legs swung over the side. He rubbed absently at the chained wrist with his free hand. A memory of horror hunched his shoulders, but he faced his enemy with calm certainty.

His half-human bastard reached for him, and Badad knelt, elbows resting on his son's knees. Evan fingered the jewel in his father's hand. Smoky topaz eyes met Ariton blue. He spoke to Badad alone.

"If you hadn't taken me out of the Black Masque, I'd have been dead the way Paul Carter died, or still Mac's prisoner and insane. Fight them, yes, but don't ask me to trade your agony for my life. I can't do it."

"You disappoint me." Marnie Simpson's voice cut into the sudden silence, reminding Brad that others awaited the outcome of the conversation. "Did you believe we offered any option but complete capitulation?"

The woman took a step toward Evan, and Lirion moved between them. "You've got your own pets. Keep your hands off mine."

Sparks crackled in the air; responding to the threat, Pathet moved in, eyes slitted, a wry smile bringing a true light to his face. The lords could understand this: battle was their natural state, and Azmod had never made alliance with Ariton.

Marnie Simpson continued her explanation to Evan, the words damping the energies of Ariton building between the natural enemies.

"You belong to me. Your life for the life of my son. Tell him to give me the jewel now and you will live. If your father tries to leave here with the stone, I will send my minions to hold him in the second sphere until you are useless to either of us. When the jewel moves into the second sphere, your human reality collapses, you see. You can hold onto that reality by strength of will for a short period, but the effort costs. Your soul is being torn in two, you understand.

"But of course you understand. How long was Badad in the second sphere to come here? The flicker of a moment, and you felt—how? Like the universe had torn in two around you? Imagine that, going on for the eternity of a battle between your forces and mine. If you should try to leave here with the stone, they won't have enough left to bury when you get home.

"So. What will it be, friend Evan?"

She ignored the forces of the second sphere now, intent on the man who would bind his own father to enslavement by his enemies, or who alone could set in motion her war to conquer universes. At first only Badad seemed to notice that the energy snapping in the room flowed from that same source. A concerned glance from Lily told him she felt it, too.

"I am human, like part of yourself," Marnie Simpson circled the bed, stalking her prey. She sat where Claudia had been, reached for Evan across a tangle of burgundy velvet.

"Our lifetime is short, gone in the blink of an eye to our immortal associates. They couldn't care less for you. Is a moment of discomfort for them so great a price to pay against the next sixty years of your life?"

Badad churned through their options while he listened to the seductive reasoning. Evan had survived the jewel's presence in the second sphere once since it had attuned to him, but he was pumping out energy like a reactor gone wild. Could he live through another transfer so soon after the last if Brad made for home? Would he believe his father had abandoned him to his enemies then, or would he know to transport after, following the beacon of the jewel home?

With a quick look around the room, he gave the question up as moot. Omage would try to stop him, and Pathet—they had no choice. Here or in the second sphere, the battle would take more time than Evan could afford. Lily caught his glance; the almost imperceptible shake of her head showed that she had been considering the same options, had drawn the same conclusions. Marnie Simpson was right about that. They couldn't get Evan out with the stone, they couldn't get him out without it.

"What do you want?" Evan's voice. Brad studied his son's face, but saw no change when Marnie Simpson's tongue followed the trace of her sharp red nails along the line of Evan's jaw.

"I already told you: the jewel. And your associates' contracts. Once we have conquered the second sphere, you are, for all intents and purposes, free. From time to time I may call on you for special tasks, when I need someone I—trust—who can pass into the second sphere. Other than the aforementioned well paid jobs, you won't even know the jewel exists."

"And if I change my mind?"

Franklin Simpson raised his cane like a scepter. "I wouldn't suggest that, dear boy. Omage has wanted his freedom for a long time. I might decide to give it to him— and the jewel, as a going away gift. I don't think there's much chance he'd bring it back in your lifetime. Fun way to die, no?"

Evan searched his father's face, but Brad had no comfort to offer. "I can't transport you out, not with the stone. And we're not alone in this. Other forces want you dead."

A quick glance at the frescoed ceiling told Badad his son knew about DaCosta. "One of yours?"

"No. Not one of yours either." Not the time to tell his son he was a threat to the survival of three universes. "I don't know how strong he is, or what he can do to you. I may not be able to stop him."

His son nodded, seeing his truth, and answered his captor. "You haven't left me a lot of choices."

"I'm glad you see it my way, dear boy." Simpson grinned, showing his worn, tobacco-stained teeth. "Do we have a bargain?"

Evan look away from him then, straight into the eyes of his tormentor, and Brad shuddered at what he saw there.

"A bargain? I always thought the devil was one of their kind. Didn't know he was human." He placed both hands on Brad's shoulders. The shackle around his wrist strained at its limit, digging the raw welt deeper into his wrist, but Evan seemed to have forgotten it. Again his fierce expression demanded Badad's complete attention, shut out the rest of the room.

"You've taught me more than you know."

Badad waited.

"Give me the jewel."

Irrational anger shook him, and Brad recognized both his resistance to any forced command and his fear for the one who commanded. Couldn't his stubborn human get see reason?

"I won't be able to protect you." He grabbed the chain that shackled the wrist to the bed and shook it until the pain on his son's face brought him back to sense. The damaged wrist began to bleed, but the battle to come would do much worse. Brad focused his rage on the cuff in his fist until the metal under his fingers glowed red and burst in a shower of sparks. Evan eased his arm to his side, but Brad shook the twisted metal in his face.

"If we lose, you could spend the rest of your life like this, torn to pieces by the damned stone."

Evan stopped him with a look. "Mac told us what happened at the club. I'm not Paul Carter, Father. I could have been, once, but thanks to you, and Lily, I *know* who I am. You have honored me with your contract; allow me the honor of my decision."

Lily objected with a sour laugh. "The backflash alone will kill you. A battle among our kind can destroy this little world of yours—not if we try to destroy it, but if we just don't try hard enough *not* to."

"Then take the battle to your own ground." Evan turned again to Brad. "Give me the jewel."

"You'll be trapped here, with them—"

"Choices? Looks to me like they all leave me dead or a prisoner at the end. I have the right to decide what the ending will be. Leave the stone with me and go. Fight for all of us."

Time itself seemed to hold its breath, then Badad bowed his head. He placed the gold chain around Evan's neck, touching the unruly hair lightly in passing, and placed the stone precisely over his son's heart. Evan winced—burns crossed there, a focus for Marnie Simpson's attentions—then he relaxed, as if the stone itself somehow eased the pain.

"You're a stubborn son of a bitch, Evan Davis." Brad's smile was shaky; he shared none of the confidence of the human's cocky answer:

"It runs on my father's side of the family."

Lirion shifted uneasily. "I hope you two know what you are doing."

The expressions of father and son said they were riding the wind of creation on this one, and Badad couldn't hide his conviction that it would be a stormy ride.

"That's what I thought." Taking Brad's place at Evan's side, Lily held her lover's face between her hands. "Remember what you are." While Brad stood guard over them, she kissed him deeply, searching his eyes for the knowledge he hid from himself. "You have more power than you know— Ariton is a part of you."

The moment hung between them, snapped when Omage moved toward the bed. In human form the daemons locked in battle, then together the lords of Ariton and Azmod moved into the second sphere.

Chapter Twenty-seven

When Princes do battle, house against house, the heavens thunder. New stars are born in their passing, and ancient stars die.

Free of human form, Badad shifted into the welcoming darkness, felt the tides of creation lift and carry him, touched the sudden there-ness of what the material sphere saw as star. He spread himself thin to sense the battle, Lirion a blue flame in his mind. Pathet moved surely in a lick of green flame across his senses. Omage shivered in a nexus of acid sparks, whiplashes of feeling snapping out as he tumbled in the void—like Badad's own uncontrolled spasms after body-death in the Black Masque. But Omage, canny in his twisted madness, guided his own path.

They were not alone. Lords of the host of Ariton approached, a whisper flickering sensation growing stronger, a sense of thickening presence. Not yet the 833 that made a Quorum, but the number grew: host-cousins Sibolas and Saris; Anader the cruel, so cold he sent a shiver through the gathering host; Caromos, who filled the senses of Ariton with a swift, fierce joy. In the part of himself that had learned to shape experience by time in

the material sphere, Badad remembered a past, before
Evan Davis, when he merged with Caromos for the pleasure of that lord's laughing touch. In passing, Badad
flicked recognition, respect. No warrior, Caromos came
closer to knowing infinity than any lord, and for a point in
the great continuum, Badad had almost shared that
knowledge. Now they would fight together, for the honor
of Ariton.

Badad sank tentacles of being into the heart of a star—
not Earth's son—where Omage lay in wait. The lords of
Azmod gathered in his wake, enemies of Ariton in the being and essence of the hosts. In the memory of all eternity
there had never been an alliance between these two, a
fact imprinted in the thoughts of Sclavak, giver of pain,
and warrior Sarra, Gilarion, bloated Holba, Hifarion. Loyalty of the most obligatory bound them to their tormented
host-cousin Omage, but a ceremonial hatred for Ariton
met its equal in the lords of blue flame.

Sclavak moved after Lily; Badad felt the bright flare of
her presence. Conjunctions of forces that were planets in
another reality tore from their orbits, unraveled like string
in her path. Laughing Caromos tickled fat Holba, darted
from the fray to itch at Gilarion in a lick of blue flame on
green. Loyal Caromos. Princes would decide the purpose
of the battle, but Caromos already knew the enemy.

Badad found Omage, forced a merge with the mad daemon, heard the voices screaming in his enemy's mind, felt
the tearing claws of binding wrapped throughout his being. This, he remembered, was to be bound with hatred,
forced to the will of planet-crawlers in the material
sphere. His own binding lay heavy in the darkness of his
being, reminded him that pain and death, and better

things, like brandy smooth on the tongue, were also real. Badad fought for his son's life.

Omage exploded outward. Energy driven in concentric bursts from the focus meant destruction on the material sphere, sent shock waves through the spheres beyond their own. A thousand years from now, a human standing on the Earth would look up and see the great outreaching rush of the explosion. If the Earth survived the battle. The lord of Ariton stilled in his pursuit. Conscious suddenly of fear, he waited for DaCosta's weaknesses in the fabric of the universes to bring an end to eternity.

Pathet whipped across his position, sent him tumbling with a sardonic pass. Images of Evan screaming his pain transferred in the partial merge—This is Ariton?—Pathet's scorn lingered, and Badad's memory of flesh in pain resonated in the battlefield.

Lords of Amaimon, Oriens—traditional allies of Ariton—and Paimon, sometimes friend, sometimes enemy, gathered to observe the battle. Magot, Astarot, allies to Azmod in many wars, came together, taking sides. Princes fought for honor, and the question went out: What honor is at stake? Where the advantage to settle hidden slights in the name of alliance?

Badad spread himself across the darkness to lick at the consciousness of friend and foe. Alfredo DaCosta's warning, with the images of death as he had felt it, moved like ripples through the second sphere. He became the memory even as it faded at the edges: fear, shock, pain, and felt the horror of his cousins, allies, enemies.

To Princes with no beginning, DaCosta's tale of creation and destruction meant nothing. Alien emotions, strange feelings, they were thrown back at him, some in denial, some in anger. Hifarion of the host of Azmod fed another memory into the weave of choices: ripples of insanity passing through the spheres, lords sent out to find the source and end it. Evan Davis. Ariton had failed, the monster stilled lived to threaten the stability of the spheres. Azmod would end it for the honor of all Princes.

Badad fought back with the image of Paul Carter, monster creation of Azmod, half-human and completely mad, dying. Like Evan, Paul Carter was only an instrument. Where two had grown, others might rise up.

Harumbrub of the host of Ariton gave his presence to the battle, and drew upon the host for a Quorum. Lords shuddered in the black expanse of existence, gathered swiftly, flame in darkness. Ariton gathered in the group mind of its Prince. Out of the many voices of its lords, one thought held sway: Earth would die. First, Azmod would pay for the threat Omage had set in motion. Princes gathered, sent out scouts, warriors, and stormed through the second sphere, loosing waves of destruction.

Chapter Twenty-eight

The God Thot, called Hermes Trismegistus by the Greeks and Mercurio Tertius by the Romans, gave to man the words by which he might travel, but only in his spirit form. For the mortal part of man is bound to the world of the flesh and does not take part in the power of the word.

Evan gathered his shirt from the floor and worked his arms into the sleeves. The cloth hurt like hell against his burns, but Evan felt safer covered. Just as well the buttons were gone, though: he couldn't have endured the rub of the cloth across his chest. Not like the Eye of Omage. The smoky topaz rested like a balm on blistered skin, as if it had always belonged there. According to Marnie Simpson, it was a part of him now.

Shaking off the physical shock of daemons shifting out of the material plane in battle status, the woman stirred on the bed. Her eyes promised retribution, and she still held the bloody knife in her hand. Evan considered a dash for home through the second sphere, dismissed the idea with a shudder. If the fighting between between Princes didn't grind him up just for being in the way, the Eye of Omage would rip him apart instead.

He'd been handed better choices in his day, but that didn't mean he was helpless. Lily's parting words still echoed in his ears: "You have more power than you know— Ariton is a part of you."

His father, a lord of Ariton, had created a small earth-quake, killed fifty people with no remorse. Did he want to be a part of that, share that kind of power? No. Did he have a choice? Not, it seemed, if he wanted to live.

Alone with her husband and their stunned captive, Marnie Simpson seized her opening. "Get him—get the stone!"

Her strident voice jerked Franklin Simpson out of his frozen inertia. The man lunged for him, cane raised over-head, and Evan blocked, wrapped his hand around the heavy carved wood. The force of the blow opened the wound on his wrist again, but the reality of his own blood scarcely penetrated the chaos that attacked his mind. The stick. Evan knew then that the faces in torment on its surface were not simply carvings, but the desperate souls of the men and women who had wielded the thing through time.

Loathing rose in him to batter at the chaos. His body shook with revulsion, vibrated with a fine-tuned tension. Vaguely, as if from a distance, he sensed Marnie Simpson moving up from behind with Omage's knife, an empty threat—he was useless to her dead. He kept his eyes locked with the man who wielded the souls of the damned like a bludgeon. The unhuman strike bolted through him like lightning, into the hand that blocked the cane. With the sound of thunder, Simpson's wand cracked. Split. Shattered. Fragments flew before the screams of freed souls fading, fading.

One scream remained: Marnie Simpson, bleeding from

a dozen lacerations. None of the cuts seemed lethal—Evan felt the knot in his stomach loosen—but she'd be picking splinters out of her teeth for a good long time to come.

"My God. My God." Franklin Simpson backed away, stuttering.

"I don't think He's listening." Evan stared at his hand, where the first layer of skin had burned away. "Shit."

"Bravo." Alfredo DaCosta stood in the doorway, an appreciative audience clapping his hands slowly while a knowing smile spread across his features. "Lily was right. You do take after your father."

"How did you get in here?" A pale Frank Simpson stared from DaCosta to Evan Davis.

"Seen a ghost, Frank?" Evan asked offhandedly, then turned his attention on the newcomer. "What do you want?"

"It *is* my house," DaCosta pointed out.

Evan ran his good hand through his hair. A quick scan of the room confirmed what he already knew. "Then you'll know where the telephone is. We have to call the police."

"And tell them what?" DaCosta asked, "What has gone on here today that any sane carabinieri would believe?"

"Kidnapping, for a start," Evan countered, but he saw the problem. The truth would give him the credibility of an asylum escapee.

"Unfortunately, Interpol is looking for *you*. A matter of two murders in London. Our mad friends would most likely receive a medal for detaining you."

"We can't just let them go!"

Evan's frustration exploded in sparks that lifted the hair on his body and DaCosta responded with an Italian shrug, not indifference but accommodation. "That remains to be seen. At the moment our guests are not my concern. You are."

Frank Simpson snickered in the background, but the sound faded on the instant. Alfredo DaCosta dropped the persona of the rich dilettante, became Thot, lord of Time, passing judgment here and now. He recognized that face: a god on DaCosta's painted ceiling, a god standing before him on the marble checkerboard floor.

"Why?" Evan asked. "What are you?"

"We haven't time for explanations. Call me a guardian, if you need a category.

"As for why, you present my species with a problem." DaCosta sighed, and Evan realized that whatever the count was, he didn't like what he had to do here.

"In a better universe, there would be a place for you. As it is, your very nature threatens the continued existence not only of your world, but of all the material sphere, and several other spheres as well."

The guardian smiled ruefully. "If you were as grasping and mean-spirited as our friends, the Simpsons, this would all be much easier. Unfortunately, your good intentions don't mean a thing. You will go where you are told, do what you are told by whoever holds that little bauble presently dangling from your neck, even if it means that your worlds, and mine, will cease to have ever existed."

"Even the Simpsons wouldn't do anything that stupid," Evan objected. "They'd die, too."

"They're human," DaCosta said as if it explained everything. "Have they believed what you've told them of the second sphere?"

Evan shook his head, seeing the problem. "Do you understand yet what you've done?" he asked the woman who had retreated to the armchair by the door, then answered his own question from the look in her eyes. "No, you're halfway convinced he's lying to trick you. The other half is trying to figure a way to use it to your advantage if the count is telling the truth."

DaCosta agreed, took the logic a step further. "Our friends here may not be the only ones on this planet who have read the wrong books. The key is the stone, and you, Evan. As long as you exist, you will be a weapon that malice or stupidity can use to unmake the spheres."

Evan frowned; he didn't like the direction the guardian's argument was taking. "Let me get this straight. You're not talking about Interpol now. You plan to kill me, so that no one else can force me to destroy the universe."

"Nobody ever said you were stupid," DaCosta replied.

"And you expect me to stand here and let you do it, for some nebulous future good that will be served just as well by locking these two up for the next few decades."

"It's not that simple. Our friends here are a small problem; humans die."

Marnie Simpson whimpered a "No," but DaCosta ignored her.

"The real problem is the next time. We can't predict what it will be, so we have to clear the board now, so to speak."

He cleared his throat. "I promised your father I'd try to make it as easy as possible."

Evan stared at the man. The floor seemed to fall from under him, leaving him stranded in pain so sharp it left him gasping for breath. "My father agreed to this?"

He was alone again, in a dark more complete than the second sphere, fighting flashback while the sticky blood on his arm drew memories from his nerve endings, lost and dying in Mac's back room for reasons he had never understood.

"He couldn't," DaCosta reasoned. "You've bound him; he can't do anything, including making an agreement, that would harm you." The guardian considered him for a moment, his mouth downturned. "But that's not what you're asking, is it? Given the freedom to choose, would he have agreed?

"No, never," he admitted, and the darkness lifted, Evan's lungs rose and fell, drawing in air again.

"I expect he'll fry this little mud ball right down to its basalt roots when he realizes you're dead," the guardian finished.

Evan turned away, denying the images that filled his mind. For a moment his eyes locked on Marnie Simpson, pale and still, against the faded brocade of the chair. The woman shook her head, dazed.

"I didn't know," she whispered. "I didn't know."

"Would it have mattered if you did?" He shook his head, answering his own question and rejecting DaCosta's prediction at the same time. "You're asking me to trade not only my life but my planet for your immortality," he reminded the guardian. "I'd be a fool to agree.

"It's the jewel you're afraid of anyway," he figured. "Without it, I'm too strong for them." He smiled at that, understanding Marnie Simpson's mistake and DaCosta's real fear. "I'll bet Brad's part in that really pissed you off."

DaCosta grimaced. "Do you understand what Badad has done? Never in the history of this planet has a lord of the Princes taken more interest in the get of his human binding than to kill it. Once your father had trained you to travel between your two universes, I had to step in. You are too great a danger to us all."

"I believe you." Evan lifted the Eye of Omage from around his neck and extended it to the guardian. "So take the damned stone. Destroy it. Your home will be safe, and so will mine."

DaCosta shook his head. "I tried, when I had it in my possession, but nothing I could do would touch it. Someone has to carry it to the second sphere, and drop it into the heart of a star there."

"There aren't any stars in the second sphere."

"You can't sense them with your human equipment," DaCosta explained, "but they are there. Unfortunately, I don't have that access. Given that your relatives are tied up elsewhere, you're the only one left who can do it, but you're tuned to the damned thing now. Like Mac says, being in the second sphere with the stone will probably kill you."

"Maybe not," Evan pointed out. "Omage was working with Paul Carter when he created it. He remembers me as his prisoner," the memory made him shudder even now, "but he couldn't guess what my father has taught me. I'm stronger than he knows."

"Not that much stronger. A star in the second sphere is still a star; you'll die destroying the stone unless it destroys you first in the transfer."

Evan nodded, his eyes on the floor. He felt the sweat break out on his upper lip. *Damn, damn.* "It'll be bad, won't it?" He darted a sharp glance at DaCosta, found recognition of his own horror carved in the grim face. They were talking about a plunge into the energy nexus of a star.

"I can't say," DaCosta answered with a fleeting smile. "As I said, I've never been there. But, yes, I expect it would be pretty bad."

"But if I die in the unmaking of that thing, it was my choice, my risk. One my father will not feel honor-bound to avenge with the destruction of my world." Ideas on that scale made no sense to him, so he thought of his mother, and the house he grew up in, and Claudia's roses. Not so small a consolation, in the larger scheme of things.

"If by some freak accident you should actually survive it, I would still have to kill you." DaCosta looked genuinely sad. "As you point out, you have become too strong to control; a mistake could end the existence of your spheres and mine. I can't take that risk, and I can't ask you to endure what it will take to destroy the jewel."

The guardian withdrew a small case from his pocket. "It will be painless," he said, "I promised that much."

Evan stared at the guardian for a long minute, remembering a time when he might have said yes. He tightened his fist around the gold chain in his hand and held it close to his heart.

"I have a job to do," Evan said. "But this isn't finished."

He gestured with a nod at the Simpsons. "Keep an eye on our guests; if they contact Omage, I'm in trouble." Ironic, that. He was out of the frying pan and into the inferno already. "And I still have confidence in Europe's finest."

He slipped the chain around his neck and sent the part of him that was Ariton into the second sphere, drew his body to follow into that nonplace. The afterimage of the guardian's judgment followed, burned into his retinas.

Chapter Twenty-nine

*Trismegistus teaches that a man who leaves his body to
the worms may pass through the spheres of heaven,
and at each sphere the things that cling to his mortality shall fall away, like sin, until he passes beyond the
reach of knowing with a pure soul. But the spheres are
inimical to mortal flesh, which shall not abide there.*

Evan felt himself turned inside out by the stone around
his neck. Up, down, sideways had no meaning. Words
from childhood circled like a mantra in his mind—God
help me. Please, God, make it stop. Make it go away—but
no help came. He vomited, it seemed forever, alone in the
void with his vomitus and the stone burning chaos into
his soul. He tried to form a shape in his mind the way his
father had taught him, a picture of a star cold and distant
in the night sky, but the stone bound him to the chaos.
Coherent images disintegrated before they could form,
running away from him in scattered shards of sanity.

The sense he'd felt before, of malevolent forces set on
his destruction, grew stronger, amplified in the stone. In
his mind it became a wall of blue flame burning without
heat in the distance. The wall of flame drew closer, and
stubborn pride firmed his resolve—he would not face his

father's kind like this, would not let the lords of Ariton know him for his weakness. Focused on the stone, Evan concentrated on the murky shadows at its heart, and slowly he felt the chaos fall into patterns of swirling energy pulsing, throbbing, within him. He waited, and the flame swept over him.

The host of Ariton. Evan felt the rush of personalities that were not lords but the sum of the host, not quite yet a Prince, but moving toward that group mind with thoughts that merged and flowed, no boundary where one began and another left off. Parts of the host, like the separate tongues of flame that leaped in a bonfire, crept through Evan's back brain where the reptile still lurked, tickled through the memories of running with sunshine on his face and watching the rain beat against the window, warm indoors with his pens and paper, paints and canvas. They found madness, and sex. Claudia was in his mind, and Lily—security and risk.

Out of the places he never shared with anyone, not even his father, they dragged the first time he'd night-traveled in the second sphere, a frightened child alone, the first time he'd stood next to his mother while strangers pawed at his drawings and asked him why he was so angry, so frightened. The strangers didn't like his answer, that something pulled him out of bed at night and how lost and terrified he was in the darkness where it left him. Disturbed, they called him, seriously disturbed, and shook their heads, sure they knew what ailed him better than the fatherless boy in front of them.

Ariton drew from him the memory of Omage, his despair, his pain and fear. Badad touched his mind then, one presence among the many picking through his memories, almost lost in the chorus of leaping tongues of Ariton-fire.

Powerless to detach himself from the host, his father still managed to find the door he thought he had locked forever on an empty room with no windows. His own weakness sickened him, the filth and the madness and the sudden, terrifying plunge into the darkness he now traveled.

Then he had feared the second sphere as if it were death itself. Now that he knew better, he feared it more for the destruction this battle might still bring to his home. DaCosta's images—Earth a blasted, lifeless rock, a billion billion creatures murdered to revenge one death— echoed in the darkness. He met the fear with anger. Always the anger had pulled him back from the edge where Omage pushed him, and he used that anger again. He wouldn't let Omage kill him, wouldn't let DaCosta do it either. And he sure wasn't going to die over some stupid stone. But if he failed, if he didn't make it this time, his world had to survive. Call it a legacy: his death had to mean something.

His anger built, pulsed from him in waves. *My choice.* He sent the message surging back through Ariton's massed flame with the power of the binding spell. The flames licking at his mind recoiled; he felt the blistering heat of their hatred, impotent against the shield of that binding. Then he was alone with his father's oath lingering in the dark. Ariton would have him dead, but his father would protect his home against the judgment of Princes.

If his father's Prince wanted to kill him, Evan reckoned Ariton would just have to stand in line. Right now the stone around his neck had first dibs. He recognized the tug at the jewel. DaCosta said a star would draw the Eye like a magnet, but the truth was more like longing. He

passed through space with the speed of thought, more
and more one with the nature of the second sphere as he
searched deeper into the stone for direction. The desire at
the heart of the stone became his desire. The forces that
gathered in his path, flames of green and indigo that
twined in battle at the periphery held together against him
at its center, but could not stop him. Evan felt the presence of Omage within the sickly green of Azmod's fire
and burned a true blue light that flared Ariton and more.
Space twisted his revulsion, and Azmod fell back, his
companion fled bleeding images that it did not understand except that the end of everything approached with
the swift charge of Ariton's monster.

Evan felt that fear and would have laughed, but as he
penetrated the outer reach of the nearest star the pull of
the stone grew stronger. Whirling eddies of energy caught
and tore at him, left no room for other thought. Evan felt
the energy burn him, shred him, but drawn inexorably by
the stone, he could not turn away. He became the thing
that drew him, stone and star and human and Ariton, all
one creature reaching toward completion with a yearning
that felt like home, and the horror caught him.

Earth. He was taking the stone home, to the center of
his own star. Dimly he remembered Badad talking about
other battles between Princes, and the deaths of stars. He
was going to die, and home would die with him, torn
apart in the destruction that would mark the passing of
the stone. Not Ariton or DaCosta, but he himself would
destroy the very thing he had come here to save.

No! His fury and rage compressed into the single sylla-
ble, he sent his denial out into the second sphere. A wall
of flame like Ariton but flickering with a yellow glow drew
closer with his death echoed in the minds of the lords

reaching toward that density of purpose that would be a Prince. He reached for it in his wrath and felt the nature of reality shudder around him while at his touch the host tore itself into shreds that struggled to re-form as it fled.

Still the jewel drew him down, into the well of energy that danced through him. He was dying, felt nothing but the surges of power around him, heard nothing but the roar of that energy, not a sound but itself a physical pain. With his last thought he denied his death, the death of home in a well of pain that pulled all of creation after him. Dying.

Darkness moved between him and the stone. Evan found a light shimmering at its depths. Drawn to that light, he felt able to move again. He followed until he was contained within a brightness as blank as the dark that had preceded it. The roar faded; he knew that only the light separated him from the screaming whirlpool of energy that was his sun in the material sphere. Through the light he felt the swirling battle between Princes like a distant storm, but he could not react to it, could do nothing but hide in the light and question his own sanity. *Father?*

"Ungrateful fool. Badad has his own problem right now." *Lily.* Not words, but he knew her by the touch of her mind in the second sphere.

Safe. Could have cried, laughed, and the confusion of his feelings washing out over the universe in giddy waves that distorted the battle around them.

"Not yet," Lirion warned tartly, drifting through his head like she belonged there. "Stop attracting attention. You shouldn't be here; if it weren't for the binding, Ariton would give you up in a minute, so don't expect any help."

"I met Ariton." Evan supplied her with the memory, and he felt surprise filter through her efforts to conceal it. She probed deeper and he let her see the images of Azmod, of the other, not proud but infinitely exhausted.

"You've been a busy boy," she finally said. "I'm surprised you're still alive."

"I was angry," Evan offered, an echo of the rage he felt at his own death in the explanation. Then he added wryly, "And I was dying anyway."

He felt her doubt, saw her memory of a universe twisted out of true before it steadied itself in familiar currents of energy filled with the presence of the forming Princes. Then she laced her mind around the connection between himself and the stone, saw his intention, and shuddered.

"Why?"

He answered with images of home, and she understood then.

"Give me the misbegotten thing," she ordered him, and Evan sensed the weight lift from his soul. "Go home."

Something in her softened. He felt a cool touch, like fingertips across his heart. "You won't die today at Ariton's hand. I'm not sure the Princes can kill you now." She paused, and he felt again the feather touch of sadness in her mind, the question that still lingered. Would anything be left of him after the stone was destroyed? "I can't promise more, little monster."

With that she was gone. He thought about home, his room with the sun shining on white walls, the study where he'd learned how to be both human and daemon and survive the pull of both universes on his soul. A longing almost as strong as the pull of the stone filled him. If the destruction of the Eye of Omage killed him, he wanted to die at home. But another image took its place, a face with planes sharp as the facets of the stone, with

eyes full of sorrow. The eyes of a judge. Alfredo DaCosta
had once held the stone, and bereft of its presence, the
part of himself that belonged to the stone followed its
trace to its source.

He felt eyelids closed over sight, wind whipping at his
clothes, his skin. He opened his eyes, black pawn on a
white square, and saw a figure waver in front of him.

"The jewel," a distant voice insisted. "Who has the Eye
of Omage?"

From a lifetime ago, before his plunge into the sun,
Evan resurrected a face to go with the voice: Alfredo
DaCosta, and the guardian wanted to kill him. The
thought drifted like cotton candy through his mind, then
vaporized in a flash of unbelievable loss. A cold hand
reached through the barrier between the spheres to rip his
heart out. The jewel was gone, destroyed. He collapsed in
a heap at DaCosta's feet, realizing that, somewhere beyond the molten lead that pulsed through him where his
blood should be, he was no longer falling.

Chapter Thirty

Hermes Trismegistus teaches that to understand the mysteries of the universe, man must become those mysteries and hold in his head the images of the sacred in the celestial spheres of the heavens. When a man attains the perfection of the art of memory that will hold the heavens in his grasp, then will he truly hold the power of the universe in his mind.

Something soft but solid lay beneath Evan. A bed. He was back, then. He remembered the pain, knew Lily had destroyed the jewel, felt its absence as a dull ache, a phantom pain lingering like a Kirlian shadow around the place in his mind where the gemstone had threaded itself into his being. Slowly he opened his eyes, found Alfredo DaCosta in the flesh looking down at him. Above the man his image as Thot, god of Time, bore the same stern expression.

"You're alive." DaCosta seemed surprised. The guardian sat on the bed beside him, a small black case in his hand, and Evan tried to move away, found his arm once again shackled to the bedpost. Figured.

"You've been unconscious for about an hour," DaCosta told him. "Can you understand me?"

Evan nodded slowly, taking in his surroundings, the gentler tones of the man at his side. "Water," he said, surprised at the croak his throat produced.

"Water, if you please," he said, and Evan realized they were not alone in the attic room. Franklin Simpson handed the count a glass and moved out of sight again. DaCosta lifted Evan's head, held the glass for him, but gave way when Evan pushed himself up on one elbow and reached with his other hand for the glass. He saw the Simpsons then, Marnie Simpson sitting pale and tense in one of the room's chairs, her husband standing behind her. Both watched him like carrion birds waiting for the kill.

He turned away, realizing that for all their petty evil they didn't matter anymore. The stone was dead, had left him feeling numb, incomplete, but already he was growing physically stronger. Simpson came forward again and took the glass away, and Evan struggled to sit up under DaCosta's unwavering scrutiny. He ran tired fingers through his knotted hair and rubbed his hands over the stubble on his face. He felt like shit, figured he must smell about as bad. DaCosta was pretending not to notice. The guardian slid a chair within arm's length of Evan on the bed, and sat facing him, elbows on his knees, chin resting on hands clasped around the black case. The dark hawk's eyes stared at Evan, making him squirm like a bug on a pin.

"You surprise me," Dacosta said. "I thought you were dead for a while, your mind, if not the rest of you. Can you talk?"

Evan nodded.

"The stone. I need to know about the Eye of Omage. Who has it?"

"Why?"

"I know it's been rough for you, Evan, but try to think. Whatever else was happened here, those two still bind Omage. If they get their hands on the stone, they can try again. I can't let that happen."

"We didn't know—" Franklin Simpson protested, but his wife cut him short.

"Shut up, fool. He wants it all for himself, can't you see that?" She tried to smile at DaCosta, but Evan saw the corners of her mouth twitch. "But I'm sure we can make a deal."

"See?" DaCosta ignored the Simpsons, his attention wholly on Evan, who let his head fall back in exhaustion.

"It doesn't matter—Lily got rid of it." Evan choked on the words. "I felt it die."

For him, the jewel had become a living thing, a part of him torn out and thrown into the raging energies of a star. But he was still alive, had been cast adrift in the chaos at the heart of the stone, had passed through the outer surface of a star, stood up to Ariton and its enemies, and survived the destruction of his anchor in two universes.

You're welcome. Sarcasm, Evan only thought it. Pointless to expect gratitude from the creature painted on that ceiling.

DaCosta stood up, paced to the windows, and looked out. "That should be impossible. There's no way you could have survived the destruction of the stone." He continued his nervous movement to the center of the room where he turned a penetrating stare on Evan. "But, of course, you have done so, haven't you? Which makes my duty here all the more pressing.

"I'm sorry, Evan. I would have taken care of it while you

were unconscious, but I had to know about the stone. I
never wanted to cause you more pain."

He watched DaCosta take a hypo from the black case.
The count held it up to the light and compressed the
plunger a fraction, tapped the needle to break the air bub-
bles. So the man—or whatever he was—intended to kill
him.

"You will go to sleep, and just not wake up. That easy.
You know you're tired, you know the lost feeling where the
Eye of Omage tied you to the Earth will never go away.
Let me make it easy for you."

"Right," Evan said, and this time sarcasm cut the word.
"And what would you do to keep from dying? Kill a man?
Two? A hundred? Destroy a world? What right have you
to make that judgment?"

"Not a right. An obligation. It's why I'm here. You are
the last remaining danger to the design."

"What design?" Evan had a sick feeling he didn't want
to know.

"This." DaCosta moved the hypo in a tight circle. "The
material sphere. Call it science, call it art, you are the last
rogue element that can destroy it all."

"We've had this conversation before." Evan let his out-
rage transmute into a blind, defensive fury. "I've had
enough of the games," he gritted between clenched teeth.
"Dying is not easy. Neither is living, but I made my choice
long before I met you."

He'd spent most of his life fighting to stay alive, and he
was good at it. That one talent set him apart from the
Paul Carters and the Jack Laurences who succumbed to
the lure of martyrdom. Outside the wind rose, blew the
gauzy curtains into a twisted tangle at the windows. Lily's

words, "You have more power than you know— Ariton is
a part of you," echoed in his mind.

Evan called upon the power of the elements that he
had seen his lover shape, that had killed fifty people in
the Black Masque. He stood, snapped the chain at his
wrist with a shower of smoking metal splinters, and
shaped the wind into a shield with his upraised hand,
forced it outward.

"Clever boy." DaCosta rocked on his feet, recovered,
and deflected time. They stood again, white king on black
square facing black tower on the white, while the ignorant
pawns who had brought them to this point cowered in the
corner.

Evan gathered the wind that battered him. "I won't let
you kill me," he told the guardian. He could feel the air
pressure rise in the room, and he compressed it, shaped
it like a charge, while he drew energy through the soles of
his feet from the house itself, from the land resting uneasily on the sea. The house rocked on the pillars of its foundation sunk deep into the mud flats of the lagoon, and
Alfredo DaCosta moved them again, minutes this time:
Ca' DaCosta had not shaken, air pressure was normal.
The effort raised a fine mist of sweat across the guardian's
brow, at his temples.

So DaCosta had limits, no more control over matter
than any human, more power over time. Evan drew lightning, directed the bolt at his adversary, but the man had
moved himself in time, leaving Evan in a present that
ticked by slowly. A second passed, two, three, while Evan
stood at the center of the attic room, his nerves strung
taut, and Franklin Simpson whimpered and beat on a
door that would not open. When time converged,
DaCosta reappeared close behind him. The guardian

threw an arm around Evan's neck and twisted with his other hand.

Evan transferred through the second sphere and emerged across the room. DaCosta moved through time again, but Evan ignored him, focused on the surge of power he gathered at his feet. The house rocked. Cracks webbed the ceiling, scarring the figures there.

DaCosta appeared at his side, one hand gripping Evan's chin, the other pressing the hypo against the vein throbbing in his neck. One part of Evan's mind seemed to detach then, wondering how long DaCosta's poison would take to do its work. He reached for the hand, tried to drag it away, and felt the strain as DaCosta forced his head around, stretching his neck beneath the needle. He felt the sharp prick of it, and let go of the energy he had compressed underfoot, using all of his strength now to push DaCosta's hand away.

For a moment the universe seemed to wink out around them, and DaCosta wavered. Then the house wobbled like a drunken dancer, cracks wide enough to stuff a fist in splitting the walls, the floor. Marble arches tumbled from where they held up the ceiling, and the pentagram began to crack. Evan felt the walls begin to disintegrate, heard the keening scream of Marnie Simpson cut off abruptly beneath the unsmiling face of Thot as he transferred out.

Chapter Thirty-one

The Pentagram, a star with five points within a circle, is a shape of power. If a man summon a daemon and call that daemon to appear within the circle, that daemon is held within the circle until his master bids him be away upon his task. But if the master bids not the daemon to return to the circle after the task is done, the daemon may return and slay his master, winning freedom an' the master will it not.

The palazzo Ca' DaCosta lay in irregular heaps of broken stone, with here and there the glint of marble reflecting the afternoon sunlight. Evan stood in the tiny piazza, watching the police and fire brigades crawl like beetles over the wreckage. An ambulance bobbed in the canal, too late to help Marnie and Frank Simpson.

Seemed like he'd been doing a lot of that lately, watching the destruction and the mounting body count. Too many had died, and for what? A promise of riches that didn't exist? Fear of death so fierce that the Simpsons would risk the vengeance of the daemons they bound to escape it? They'd lost that one, dead under a pile of rock. His fault, and their deaths had changed him. Evan felt it all from a distance, filtered through shock and exhaustion.

Tomorrow, he knew, he'd count his losses—friends, enemies, and the part of himself that could not kill another human being—and figure out how to live with it.

Across the crowded square, a somber Alfredo DaCosta leaned against a wall, watching him. Evan made his way through the crowd to face his enemy.

"A partial success," the man greeted him. "You're still alive, but you finally did eliminate our friends, the Simpsons."

Evan gave DaCosta the point. He'd done it, would carry the mark of their deaths, like the mark of their stone, on his soul forever. Was his life worth two of his enemies?

Hell, yes, the survivor in him answered. He didn't much like himself at that moment, but he finally accepted what he was. Not like his father, not quite human either, but enough of both to want to go on living and let his conscience deal with the cost later.

A figure in a tan raincoat picked his way through the rubble, and Evan groaned. He waited until the man reached them, and gave him a brief nod of recognition. "Inspector James."

"Mr. Davis. I came down to identify your remains. Happy to see that is unnecessary." James turned to briefly inspect the damage. "They're calling it a gas explosion," he commented. "Fire department figures a pocket of natural gas under the house ignited—maybe a spark from foundation stones settling."

"That must be it, then," Evan agreed. "Are you here to take me back, Inspector?"

"That was my original intention. Mr. Davis. Since then, I have had a long chat with your Ms. Laurence. She explained that you were both kidnapped by the couple who admitted in her presence to murdering her brother. A brave girl. Escaped the kidnappers from that very building. With a bit of help from your agency, we have determined that you are not the first rich young man to come to the Simpsons' attention. I don't suppose they were fortunate enough to escape the explosion."

"No, Inspector, I don't believe they were."

"Well, then. Just a matter of identifying the bodies, and we can close this case." Inspector James reached into his breast pocket and pulled out a passport. "I believe you lost this." He handed the document to Evan. "Your bag was impounded—very nice dinner suit, by the way—the department will return it to your legal address once the paperwork is cleaned up. You will be going home, Mr. Davis?"

"As soon as legally possible, Inspector." Evan looked beyond the man to where stretcher carriers made their way through the destruction.

"I believe you are free to go any time. And I am certain that the local caribinieri agree with my hope that you will do so with all haste. And stay there for a while, Mr. Davis. Please."

James gave a short parting nod and walked purposefully toward the stretcher bearers, leaving Evan alone again with the count.

"Are you still planning to kill me?" Evan asked, too tired to feel more than inconvenienced by the idea.

"Would it do me any good?" the guardian asked, the piercing eyes measuring Evan, summing him up, breaking him down.

Evan shook his head. "Not really. Could get messy, though. Brad never covered this kind of stuff," he nodded at the ruins, "so I don't really know what I'm doing. Maybe I'll get tired, slow down enough for you to get me.

Maybe I'll just get stronger with the practice. One thing I'm sure of, though: The fight would bring this city to the ground, maybe more. I don't want to do that. I just want to go home."

"So do I." The guardian stared off into the ruins, the centuries etched in the fine lines of his face, and a moment when, perhaps, the universes they called home had almost ceased to exist. "Get that training," DaCosta advised, "I'll sleep easier nights when you know what you're doing."

Evan nodded, watched the man—the guardian—walk away. "Home." A memory drifted out of long ago childhood—*click your heels three times*. He smiled. "There's no place like home."

Someone had scrubbed the pentacle from the bricks in the garden and set the patio furniture back in place. Fortunately, they'd also replaced the sliding glass doors; beads of rain clung to his jeans when he brushed past the tall spears of tulip leaves.

He'd slept for only a couple of hours, but waking up in his own bed did more for him than a full night's sleep in a Venetian hotel. Flipping a vinyl chair cushion to the dry side, he sat under the big fringed umbrella, his elbow on the table and his hands wrapped around a thick pottery coffee mug, considering his next move.

Claudia was going home to St. Louis, didn't want to see Evan again, didn't want to be reminded of what he had done, however unintentionally, to her brother. Jack was dead, and the memory punched him in the gut, forcing the air out of his lungs. If he had stayed away, Jack would still be alive, and Claudia would have lived out her life weaving rugs and weeding the roses, selling books for the bent little man they'd carried, burned beyond recognition, out of his shop. He knew down deep that Claudia was the real victim, had been from the start all those years ago in the Village. She'd never understood the stakes the rest of them were playing for.

Jack. The thought lingered in spite of his efforts to expel it. Jack had been waiting to die since that night in the Black Masque when he'd made the first blood sacrifice to a monster deity Omage created out of the frightened mongrel of two universes. Evan sipped the hot coffee, wondering if he would ever understand the urge to martyrdom, and trying to forget his own aborted plunge into the sun.

One more thing to do. With a last swallow of the bitter dregs, he set the coffee mug aside and stood up, shook himself down to the fingers to loosen up the tension that was tying him in knots at the thought of what he had to do. When he was as calm as he figured he was going to get, he painstakingly retraced the pentagram on the bricks, and stood at its center. Then he began the incantation:

"With a tranquil heart, and trusting in the Living and Only God, omnipotent and all-powerful, all-seeing and all-knowing, I conjure you, Badad, daemon of darkness, and you, Lirion, daemon of darkness, to appear before me. You are summoned by the Honor and Glory of God, by my Honor that I shall cause you to do no harm or injury to others, and for the greater glory of all creation both in the physical sphere and in the second sphere."

At first nothing happened, and Evan frowned, wondering if he'd gotten it wrong. Then the itch at his skin became a low rumble and the ground beneath his feet began to shake. He'd had enough of falling buildings to last a lifetime, and he cut the pyrotechnics short with an abrupt, "Cut the shit and get back here before I lose my temper."

The flickering blue figure appeared before him in a shock wave that blew breaking glass from the sliding doors into the living room beyond, and Evan sighed. They'd lose their insurance if they put in a claim for the same glass doors twice in one week, but he'd be damned if the replacement cost was coming out of his pocket.

"Who dares interfere in the affairs of Princes?"

Evan glared at the creature, naked, sexless, and twice as tall as the brick wall surrounding the garden. It didn't look much like the pictures of the devil in his books at school, but he figured he might be damned at that.

"Who the hell are you?" he snapped. "And get down here before somebody calls the police. I have to live in this neighborhood."

The blue figure glared back. "I could kill you where you stand, human."

"I'm not human," Evan pointed out, growing weary of the conversation. "My father is a lord of the host of Ariton and my mother is a human who didn't know any better. A monster, you might call me, and don't fool yourself. I don't suffer from the limitations of humans or the loyalties of your kind.

"As for killing me, if you could have, you would have done it already, so cut the crap."

"You have no dominion over me," the Prince of daemons thundered, but he contracted himself until only the top of his three horns could be glimpsed over the garden wall.

Evan dragged the hair off his forehead, raking his fingers deep and grabbing hold, thinking.

"Ariton, I presume," he concluded. "Since I called my personal daemons by name, I also presume they are in there somewhere. I want them back. Now." He didn't expect the Prince of daemons to understand the acid commentary loaded into the statement, nor was he disappointed.

"You take risks, monster," Ariton warned. "Those you call are at war, a war of your making."

"Not my making," he contradicted, and added, "the masters of the lords of Azmod are dead, the wand that bound them is shattered, and their jewel has been destroyed. By my reckoning, the war is over."

"There are slights still to be answered," the Prince objected, expanding in the small space of the garden again, until he loomed like a dark and lightning-charged storm cloud above the treetops.

"You will have to handle them with two less lords in your host, because I have a prior claim." He remembered then how literal daemons were—worse than lawyers—and he tried the summons again: "I conjure you Badad and you Lirion of the hosts of Ariton to appear before me alone of all your kind, and in the human forms by which I have known you."

Ariton laughed then, deep and rich and dangerous, like thunder rolling before a tornado. The Prince of daemons grew and filled the sky. Winds raged, tore the branches from the trees and threw them at the housetops.

Exasperated, Evan raised a hand, gathered his fingers together and the winds with them. The storm dwindled, faded, vanished. When he looked down again, Brad and Lily were stretched out on lawn chairs, glaring at the shattered doors.

"You've got to learn to curb your destructive impulses," Lily admonished.

"That's what DaCosta said." Evan examined the broken glass with a frown. "I thought you did that, or your Prince."

Her arms around his waist warned him that she'd moved, so the words whispered in his ear did not surprise him. "It was all you, little monster."

"I think I'm starting to understand that," Evan admitted.

"What happened?" Brad asked. His father wouldn't say it, but the daemon lord didn't seem too unhappy that Evan was still alive. "By my reckoning, you should have been dead two or three times today—yesterday—whenever."

Evan shook his head, not yet ready to discuss the empty place where Omage's stone had wrapped its tentacles in his mind.

"Closer than I'd have liked," he allowed. "But I survived. Our client and her husband didn't; they were dead when the police pulled them out of the wreckage of Ca' DaCosta."

Dead, along with Paul Carter, Jack Laurence, a shopkeeper off Charing Cross Road, and for what? So that he, Evan Davis, could go on living? For the first time in almost a year he thought of the gun hidden away in the safe. Pointless, he realized. Nothing would bring back his dead.

"I haven't cost Ariton the war up there?" He rolled his eyes heavenward, though he knew that direction did not define the sphere.

Brad shook his head. "Doesn't matter anyway. We'll win the next one, or the next. It's something to do."

Evan nodded, not really comprehending the politics of immortality and distracted by Lily's ministrations. Her fingers found the track of Marnie Simpson's cigarette, traced it a breath away from the reddened pucker of the damaged skin, and Evan remembered that he hadn't changed his shirt. Claudia had worn this shirt. He closed his eyes, seeing Omage pluck the buttons while the woman gripped his hand. Claudia was still alive—he hadn't destroyed everything.

"DaCosta sent you a message," he remembered. "He said I needed training."

"I noticed," Brad muttered. "But I think Lily will keep you out of trouble for the present."

It sounded like a good idea to Evan, and then Lily was touching him, finding unmarked skin, and adding the demanding tracks of her fingertips, sweet pain next to bitter.

"Upstairs?" he suggested.

She smiled.

Tanya Huff

ROSEMARY EDGHILL

☐ **THE SWORD OF MAIDEN'S TEARS**   UE2622—$4.99
It was Beltane Eve when Ruth Marlowe stumbled across the
elf Melior Rohannan of Elphame. Melior knew that he must
reclaim the magical Sword that muggers had stolen from him,
for any mortal who wielded the blade would be transformed
into a monster. But in a city with as many hiding places as
New York, what hope was there for finding the unstoppable
evil that had stolen Melior's treasure?

☐ **THE CUP OF MORNING SHADOWS**   UE2671—$5.99
When Ruth Marlowe found a Wild Gate in a library basement,
she ventured into Elphame in search of her lost love, Rohannan the elf. What she found was a land beset by human-
caused trouble. Knowing that what humans have caused, humans must fix, Ruth had no choice but to take up the challenge
of halting a rebellion that could forever overturn the natural
order of Elphame.

Fantasy at Its Best

Jane S. Fancher
☐ **RING OF LIGHTNING**   UE2653—$5.50

In the city of Rhomatum, three brothers, heirs to the ruling family, fight to wrest control of their city from a tyrant—their aged yet powerful great-aunt.

Ellen Foxxe
☐ **SEASON OF SHADOWS**   UE2620—$4.99

Was the greater peril from spies within their ranks or from the "magical" winged creatures which strove to drive the colonists from this new land?

Michelle West
☐ **HUNTER'S OATH**   UE2681—$5.50

In reparation to the gods, once a year the Sacred Hunt was called, the fulfillment of which was the kind of destiny from which legends were made.

Buy them at your local bookstore or use this convenient coupon for ordering.

PENGUIN USA P.O. Box 999—Dep. #17109, Bergenfield, New Jersey 07621

Please send me the DAW BOOKS I have checked above, for which I am enclosing
$_____ (please add $2.00 to cover postage and handling). Send check or money order (no cash or C.O.D.'s) or charge by Mastercard or VISA (with a $15.00 minimum). Prices and numbers are subject to change without notice.

Card #_____ Exp. Date _____
Signature_____
Name_____
Address_____
City _____ State _____ Zip Code _____

For faster service when ordering by credit card call **1-800-253-6476**

Allow a minimum of 4-6 weeks for delivery. This offer is subject to change without notice.

Mickey Zucker Reichert